Catch Me: The Life Ruiner Serial Killer

Catch Me: The Life Ruiner Serial Killer

Laj Posey

Copyright © 2022 by Laj Posey.

Library of Congress Control Number:		2022909155
ISBN:	Hardcover	978-1-6698-1863-2
	Softcover	978-1-6698-1862-5
	eBook	978-1-6698-1861-8

All rights reserved. No part of this book may be reproduced or transmitted in any form or by any means, electronic or mechanical, including photocopying, recording, or by any information storage and retrieval system, without permission in writing from the copyright owner.

This is a work of fiction. Names, characters, places and incidents either are the product of the author's imagination or are used fictitiously, and any resemblance to any actual persons, living or dead, events, or locales is entirely coincidental.

Any people depicted in stock imagery provided by Getty Images are models, and such images are being used for illustrative purposes only.
Certain stock imagery © Getty Images.

Print information available on the last page.

Rev. date: 05/18/2022

To order additional copies of this book, contact:
Xlibris
844-714-8691
www.Xlibris.com
Orders@Xlibris.com

841425

This book is dedicated to my inspiration, my sons Anthony and Justis I love you both with all my heart! To my wife Ife, you made me a stronger and better man, and I love you forever! To all my family and friends thank you for believing and supporting me!

Prologue

Jamal "Roc" Stone, April 4, 2020

My first kill I could remember like it was yesterday. I was scared to death thinking about everything that could go wrong, things like what if someone sees me with her or what if someone has a video camera catching me abducting her or what if someone sees me bring her to the place I planned on killing her and finally what if I leave evidence behind. Even though I learned all I could about forensic science, what if the cop discovered it was me. No matter what though, I had my mind made up and I was killing her ass.

She ruined my life by snitching on me. She set me up on a drug deal that put me away for ten years. The fucked-up thing was I loved her like a sister. I would have done anything for her, for heaven's sake. I was her daughter Emily's godfather. I was doing what I had to take care of my family and look out for hers. People have a choice if they choose to get high, why not give their money to me.

She got caught and testified against me. That was how this all started. Tanya had to die! You know the old saying snitches get stitches!

I'd been home for a year and a half living as a model citizen, working as a supervisor at Amazon. My now best friend Ethan Daniels got me the job and gave me the promotion. He was my boss.

I'd been hanging with my kids and my now six-and-a-half-month pregnant wife Kimberly Wade, now Kimberly Stone.

Kim was very beautiful. I'd known her for years, and she had heard I was locked up. Three years left in my bid, she found me and has been there for me ever since. Kim was a white woman that stood five feet seven inches and weighed one hundred and thirty-five pounds. She has long dirty-blonde hair that almost looks dark. She is a licensed practitioner nurse at Saint Mary's Cancer Hospital.

Lying in my bed thinking, I remember how I've been watching and planning to kill Tanya. She still lives in the same town Greenwich, New York.

I would drive the forty-five minutes after I got out of work at five-thirty, watch from six-fifteen until eight at night, and then drive home. Those were the days I would go over to Kim's house, and on the nights I didn't go to Kim's, I would stay in Greenwich until midnight.

Some nights I would see Tanya coming out of her house walking to the store, and most of the time, it was late. Tanya now had a man and two children. I thought about what was about to happen to their mother, and I felt sorry for her kids because their mother's days were numbered.

She and her boyfriend were drug addicts, so I thought maybe the kids would be better off without them. The sorrow I felt passed when I remembered that she didn't care about taking me from my family, so my heart went cold, and I focused on my plan.

I was a nervous wreck because I kept thinking about how I would feel after the fact, and that was what had been taking me so long. I kept thinking to myself, *Damn can I really kill someone*. Even though my mind kept going back and forth, I knew she had to die.

I had just come home from prison, so I had to take my time. I'd been home for over a year, and I had to build an airtight order about my life to my family, coworkers, and most of all my parole officer. I still had two more years I owed the State of New York even though I lived in Massachusetts.

I finally decided that this week it was going down, but at that time, I couldn't pinpoint the day. However, it happened on April 4, 2020, on a Tuesday around ten at night, and I couldn't believe how easy it went down.

I watched Tanya walk out of her house, and the street was unbelievably still and quiet. It felt like we were the only two people on earth, and my heart was pounding. I willed myself to relax and told myself that it had to be done. I took ten deep breaths and I was ready.

There was a small stretch of woods that had no houses. It would take two minutes of walking before you could see the Cumberland Farms, which would still take you five minutes to get to. I always parked at the end of her block because with my binoculars, I could see her house perfectly.

As I saw her leave her house, I turned off all interior lights and climbed out of the passenger side of the car. I was dressed in all black and had a mask that covered the lower half of my face and the hooded sweatshirt I wore over my head, so all that could be seen were my eyes. I also had on a pair of all-black Nike gloves and a pair of high-tech boots. I chose those boots because I always wore Timberlands, so if they had found footprints on the ground, well, I didn't wear those types of boots, and my shoe size was eleven but that was an average size. I wore those clothes because if she struggled, she couldn't get any type of DNA from me, but I hoped it didn't come to a struggle. I planned on knocking her ass out cold.

I hid in the woods on the same side she walked on. I hid there because I'd been watching her walk on the same side every time she went to the store. She always walked close enough to the woods that I knew she wouldn't have time to react.

As she was coming, I could see her, but she couldn't see me. She was on the phone talking to someone, and I could hear her saying, "I know bitch that was some crazy shit! Mike should've never showed up with Selena knowing Sasha was going to be there with her crazy ass! As soon as she saw Mike's arm around Selena, Sasha jumped and beat the shit out of her! Selena didn't even see it coming!"

Tanya listened for a second then said, "Wait, hold on, girl, I got another call!"

This event could not have gone any better, I thought.

Tanya clicked over and said, "Hello, hello!" but there was no response. So when she pulled the phone down to click back over, I was on her.

The shock of this all-black figure launching out at her had her freeze like a deer in headlights. She didn't scream or react. I just whacked her on the head with my black nightstick, and she went down and out cold.

I picked her up and brought her into the woods and got the duct tape out, then I wrapped her wrists and ankles and finally put tape over her mouth. I left her by a tree and went to retrieve my car.

I put her in the trunk then hopped in the car and drove off. I couldn't believe how smooth the kidnapping went, I mean not a soul around. It was like that nine times out of ten, but you always have in the back of your mind that someone might catch you!

Chapter 2

I had staked out this abandoned house in the middle of nowhere in New Lebanon, New York, three months ago, and I was lucky to find this place. The place sat off the road about a quarter of a mile deep in the woods.

The structure wasn't that stable, but it would be a good piece of land if you tore down the house and built a new foundation and everything. Shiit, I would if I had the money.

Over the time I've been planning this, I would drive down side roads hoping to find something. Some of the places looked like teenagers went to hang out and had bonfires, some had houses at the end, and others you could go up into the mountains.

For a month and a half since I found this place, I'd been staking it out until I finally decided to venture in. I tried the front door, and it had a padlock on it, but the door was dry rotted. The framed structure was not sturdy, and with what I knew about framing, I knew I would be able to get in. The house seemed to belong to nobody, so I broke the padlock and went in.

The floor was rotted and it felt like you would fall through, but with every step I took, it held. I didn't do a full tour because I wasn't planning on going upstairs. I did, however, locate the basement door, and that was where I planned on bringing Tanya.

It was waiting for me. I could tell because the steps were sturdy, and when I walked down the steps into the basement, I knew it would be the place. It had a concrete floor and walls. I didn't know how safe the foundation was, but I knew it would do for what I needed.

For the next month, I brought a metal chair, generator, razor, metal bucket, gallons of water, towels, car battery, jumper cables, hammer, spikes, and a light. I didn't know what I was going to truly do to her, but I did know I was going to torture her.

I wanted her pain greater than mine, and when I was in prison, I thought of so many ways I wanted to kill her, so maybe I got a little crazy with it but shit she did take ten years of my life. To me that was a lot of time to think about killing someone.

I was almost to the house when I heard Tanya start to stir in the trunk, but I didn't care because I would be there in one minute.

I pulled the car to the side of the house, so it wasn't visible unless you drove all the way up. I put my mask back on because I didn't want her to know it was me until I was ready. I had a thing for the dramatic. I planned on knocking her out again, so there was no struggle while I prepared her.

I opened the trunk and our eyes met, and hers grew large with fear. She began to cry and beg, but I couldn't understand her because of the tape. I stared at her for ten seconds, but I bet it felt like forever to her. Then I hit her over the head again, and she was out cold.

I carried her to the back door that I left unlocked the last time I was here. I carried her on my shoulders straight to the basement. I stripped her naked, so she could know what it felt like all the times I had to strip naked to be searched through my time in prison.

I cut the tape, sat her in the metal chair, then taped her wrists and ankles to the chair. The chair looked like an electric chair by design but smaller, and I anchored it to the ground.

When everything was set, I slapped her awake. I then stood back from the light as she regained consciousness.

Her head rocked side to side as her eyes adjusted to the light. When she came fully alert, she realized her dire situation. Her eyes got big with horror as she'd struggled to free herself from the bondage. She tried to talk through the tape but couldn't form words.

I stood back in the dark watching as she was processing her environment. She saw the tools laid out and then noticed she was naked. She started shaking her head in panic while her cries were muffled. She had realized that there was no escape, and she pleaded with her eyes and muffled cries. I removed my hood and my mask and slowly stepped into the light.

As she saw this dark figure emerge from the darkness, my face came into view. Her muffled cries slowed, and her eyes widened more than I believed was ever possible. I stared at her for what felt like forever but was only a minute.

I didn't un-tape her mouth because I wanted her to listen. I felt power rising in me because she never thought this could happen.

She looked at me in shock, probably thinking that I wouldn't be the person standing here. I said, "Eleven years and you probably thought you would never see me again, or maybe I got over it, and you were safe! Let me tell you, I've been thinking about you and this moment every day I spent away from my family because of your snitch ass!"

She tried pleading, but it was all muffled. I yelled, "Shut the fuck up!"

She quieted herself. "All you had to do was keep your fucking mouth closed. I told you time and time again if you're going to be involved in this lifestyle, then you have to man up to what you do!"

Stepping closer to look deeply into her eyes, she could see the sadness mixed with a crazed look in my eyes, "I told you many nights that if anyone took me away from my kids, I was going to end their life.

"But not for a million years I would've thought it would be you." I stood tall with a grunt, "But here we are!"

I paused and stared at her for a moment to let what I just said sink in.

Then I continued, "Look I'm going to remove the tape from your mouth. If you scream, I'm going to skip the chat and get straight to business. And for the record, no one can hear you scream anyway. We're in the middle of nowhere . . . Do I make myself clear? Nod if we're clear!"

She nodded and I stepped forward and removed the tape from her mouth. "I'm sorry, Roc!" was the first thing out of her mouth. "I was pregnant with Tyler and they said they were going to take him and Emily away, and that I would never get them back!"

I tilted my head to the side, and I stared at her with hate in my eyes and replied with maliciousness, "So you're telling me that your family and your freedom were more important than mine! Is that what you're saying?"

"No, Roc, that's not what I'm saying. I got scared and I panicked! I didn't know what to do! Please forgive me!"

"Forgiveness comes from God, not me! And I don't believe in God anyway! If there was a God, why do people suffer?" I asked, thinking about my kids growing up without me.

I reached for the towel because the first thing I wanted to try was waterboarding. Water-boarding was when you cover someone's face with some type of cloth and dumped water on their face. It gave the illusion of drowning without all the real consequences of drowning.

I grabbed a gallon of water and sat it on the table next to me as I said, "This is going to be long and painful! I'm going to get all my ten years back from your snitch ass!"

"No no no, please, Roc! I will do anything you want!" Tanya pleaded as she started to cry.

"Anything?"

"Yes, Roc, anything!"

I tilted my head, and I knew she could see the evil in my eyes. Her eyes got big, and she began to cry harder. I gave her an evil grin because I was enjoying the fear she was giving off.

I snapped the towel around her face as she tried to cry out, "Nooooo!"

Her sound was muffled under the towel as I yanked her head back and started pouring water on her face. She drank a lot of water because her mouth was open from her cries and panic.

She was trying to take in air, but there was no air to grab. She was choking and gasping, and because I didn't want her to die right away, I removed the towel.

She started choking up water, coughing, trying to gasp for air and words she couldn't find. When she did find her words, she begged as she cried, "Please, Roc! Don't do this!" She was coughing as she spoke!

"No begging," I replied angrily, "this is happening, so if you want to make it through the first phase, then you might not want to try to breathe while the towel's over your face and water's coming!"

"No—"

Before she could even get out the words, I snapped the towel back over her face and began pouring water. This time I almost emptied the jug.

When I stopped and removed the towel, she was barely breathing. I slapped her to get her to cough up the water, and when she did, she couldn't find words to speak, just panting.

It was crazy watching her suffer because I realized at that moment that I was having so much fun. I put the towel away and gave her a few minutes to come around.

At this time, she realized that she was going to die, but she wanted to live, so as I readied the razor for phase 2, she pleaded, "Please, Roc, don't kill me!"

She sobbed and begged, "I have children at home, please don't take me from them! Please don't!"

I heard her but I wasn't listening. I just shook my head as I removed the caps off the rubbing alcohol.

As she watched me, she said, "Hey, Roc, remember when you told me once that you would never let anybody hurt me? You said you cared about me!"

She screamed, "You're Emily's godfather for Christ's sake! Please I beg you, don't do this!"

As I finished preparing, I thought to myself for a second and then turned toward her and said, "Yeah, it sucks this has to happen, and I do feel some type of way because of Emily, but you should've thought of the consequences of your actions.

"And, I do remember those words! I also remember you saying those words in return! You didn't stick to them, so why should I?"

I walked up to her with the razor in my hand and started slicing deep cuts. She screamed. You could see her flesh beneath the skin. I started at the ankles to her thighs, then her arms, and stomach. I then cut over her pubic hairs near her clit, her tits, and shoulders.

Screaming during every cut, she begged, "Please . . . Don't, Roc!"

I stepped back and looked at my work. She was crying and begging, but I was so far gone that I barely even heard her.

I started dumping the rubbing alcohol on the cuts, and she screamed as I had never heard before in my life! I didn't even know the human voice could even get so loud or go so high, but I just kept pouring bottle after bottle until all six were empty.

I watched as she cried loudly. There was no more pleading or begging. She was angry and screaming, "Fuck you, Roc!" over and over.

I looked at my watch, and it was three in the morning. It was time to end this. She was no longer begging, and it was late so I started cleaning up because I didn't want to leave a trace of evidence.

She watched me cleaning up. I washed the blood off the razor in the metal bucket of water; put it in a plastic bag. I then picked up the empty bottles and put them into the bag along with the razor. I plan on throwing everything in the river on my way home.

All that was left after I cleaned up was the metal bucket, two metal spikes, car battery, hammer, and jumper cables. I doubled up the plastic bag, took them out to the car, and returned. I was so proud of myself because I didn't make a big mess like I thought I would.

I was standing in front of her again, and she looked up still crying, meeting my eyes. She pleaded while sobbing, "Roc, you don't have to kill me! If you let me go, I will never tell anyone what happened! Just let me go home to my kids! Please, Roc, I'm begging you!"

"That's funny because I was saying that for ten years! Please just let me go home to my kids! But I couldn't because your snitch-bitch ass put me in there!"

I leaned closer to her face. "So now you expect me to believe you're not going to snitch! Get the fuck outta here, bitch! Once a snitch always a snitch! Sorry, bitch, you died tonight!"

I grabbed the hammer and spike off the table and drove it into her thigh, and she screamed, nearly passing out. I then drove the second in the other thigh, snapping her back to reality.

After, I untapped her ankles and put her feet in the bucket of water as she cried. Satisfied, I then hooked the jumper cables to the car battery and sparked the other ends together, making sure juice was flowing.

I began to hook the black cable to the right spike as I said, "You know, Tanya, I am a man of my word, and I told you I would kill anyone who took me away from my family!"

Then I giggled, shaking my head. "But there was another plus side to this, and that is I'm having crazy fun!"

"Go fuck yourself you sick fuck!" she screamed through her sobs. "You're going to burn in he—"

I placed the red cable on the left leg, not letting her finish her last words, and I watched as the electricity flowed through her body.

She was jerking while she cooked from the inside out. I would never forget the smell of burning flesh. It stank to all hell! Her body stopped moving when there was no more life.

I left a note for someone to find that read, "She's a Life Ruiner, so she deserves to die!" I left the final phase of Tanya's torture on display for someone to find.

The next day I destroyed all evidence. I burned the clothes and boots I wore, and then I threw them in the river. I wanted to throw the clothes away on my way home, but I changed my mind because what if the clothes were found, and by chance, some type of evidence was found, so I burned everything and then threw it in the river.

The cops found Tanya a month later, and it was all over the news, getting national coverage. Her family had been looking for her all this time, and they only found her because some teenagers went back there to party. They found her in the basement and called the cops.

That kill was a high, so much so I knew I had to do it again, and that was how this all started. To the date, I've killed five more people since Tanya, three guys and two girls.

In my defense they all deserved it. Two of them were snitches, one raped five women, one raped and killed seven little boys and girls, and one shot a little boy during a shootout over territory. They all died differently, but there was always one constant, and that was the notes I left behind. The notes all said something different besides the ending.

The cops now believe that they have a serial killer on their hands, and they labeled it "The Life-Ruiner Serial Killer." Hey, they could call it what they wanted, but those people deserved to die! And guess what, I'm already planning the next one! So to the cops, "CATCH ME if you can! HA HA HA!"

Chapter 1

FBI—Albany, New York, Monday, February 4, 2022

Dir. Mike Wall

I got out of bed this morning feeling good about my life. My wife Kathy and I just got back from vacation in Hawaii, and our relationship had that glow like when we first fell in love, and that was twenty-five years ago.

Work was also going great. At FBI headquarters, we haven't had any major cases, and before I left we closed some of our cold cases. My plan was to go to work today and put up the new pictures Kathy and I took while in Hawaii. I also had some new pictures of my daughter and grandson. They came over for dinner last night, and we had a great night.

I got dressed then ate and was out the door by quarter after seven heading to the office. When I got there, all the agents that worked under me were glad I was back. They liked me because I was hard but a fair boss and very approachable.

I entered my office and put my briefcase on the side of my desk. I then went into my bag that held the pictures I wanted around my office, put them where I wanted, and then sat down at my desk. I fired up my computer and checked my email.

The first email I read had a transfer agent named Lori Reid from the Boston office. I picked up the phone and rang my secretary Julie Waters, "Hey, Julie, can you have Agt. Lori Reid come into my office. She's a transfer from Boston."

"That's funny you should mention her because she's standing here in front of me."

"Good, tell her to have a seat, and I'll be ready for her in a minute." I listened to Julie relay the message and hung up.

The next email I opened was marked urgent from Capt. Calvin Lewis of the Columbia County Sheriff Department, it read, **Director Wall, we have just received confirmation that in the tristate area we have multi-homicide in New York, Connecticut, and Massachusetts dating back to April 4, 2020. The body count as of now is six. We have reason to believe that we have a serial killer on our hands. As of now, we don't have any evidence other than the victims, and the notes left behind at the crime scene. The only reason we knew the murders were connected was because a cop in homicide from Greenwich, New York, and a homicide cop from Bridgeport, Connecticut, has a cousin that plays basketball at the University of Connecticut. They were at his game and happened to discuss their cases. They both brought a murder up that was so clean, but the only thing that was left behind was the notes. They reported it to their commanding officers and did some research. Other than those two murders, there were murders in Elmira, New York; Queens, New York; New Bedford, Massachusetts; and Springfield, Massachusetts. There are motives that are similar. And there's torture and notes. We have compiled a list of all the victims and all the forensics we have. I already FedExed all the documents. Please contact me with verification. #(518) 555-2378.**

Damn, I thought, *this is not how I wanted to return from my vacation*! I got up from my desk and went to get Agent Reid.

I opened the door and said, "Julie, I'm waiting for a package from FedEx to bring it in right away please."

"Sure thing, sir!"

I turned my attention to Reid and said, "Hello, Agent Reid, please come this way."

Agent Reid got up, followed me into my office and I shut the door. We shook hands and I said, "Please have a seat, Agent."

I looked over her file for about three minutes before I spoke. "So, Agent Reid, tired of the Bean City, huh? Here to join our fine establishment here in Albany, New York." I leaned back in my chair, "Why the change?"

"Well, sir, I put in a transfer over six months ago because Albany is closer to home, and I wanted a change of scenery. Plus, I heard this is the place for advancement."

"Well, you're right about that, and judging by your record, I believe you will have no problem with advancing. Matter of fact, you came at the right time. I just got handed a big case, and my top agent Terry Carter needs a partner." I picked up my phone and put up one finger. "One second, Reid."

"Hey, Julie, can you tell Agent Carter to come to my office."

"Sure thing, sir, and your FedEx package is here. I'm going to bring it in then get Agent Carter."

Julie brought me the package and left. I said to Agent Reid, "Just relax, this is all coming together. This is the new case Carter and you are going to be working on." I looked over the case while we waited for Agent Carter.

Chapter 2

Terry Carter

I had a great weekend with my daughter Neveah. I can't believe she's thirteen and acting like a little lady. It was seven thirty in the morning when we left for Neveah to school, where her mother Naomi would pick her up afterward.

During the drive, we were talking about our weekend when she changed the subject and said, "Hey, Dad, now that I think about it, why don't you have a girlfriend? It would be nice if you were dating or something."

I laughed because she caught me off guard. "Since when do you talk about dating, young lady?"

"Well, Mom has Vincent now, and I never see you with anybody. Are you keeping them away from me or something." She put her little hand on my lap. "Or if you're gay, then that's cool too!"

I looked at her in shock, almost driving off the road as I replied, "No, I'm not gay! As a matter a fact, Ms. Thing, I do keep them away from you. That's because you have to be special to me to meet my princess, and only a queen can meet you! Is that cool with you?"

She smiled. "That's right, Daddy! You always make me feel special!"

I pulled over to the curb in front of the school and parked. I kissed my princess on the top of her head and said, "That's because you are special, princess . . . You mean more to me than anybody! I love you more than life itself."

She kissed me on the cheek. "Thanks, Dad, have a good day at work!"

She got out of the car, and before she closed the door, I said, "Baby, I love you, and have a good day at school." I watched as she went into the building and then drove off.

I stopped at Dunkin' Donuts, got a cup of French vanilla coffee, my favorite, and I was at work five minutes to eight.

I went to my desk, checked my email, and then listened to my messages. I made some calls, and at about eight thirty, Director Wall's secretary Julie Waters called me on my phone.

"Good morning, Agent Carter. Director Wall wants to see you in his office right away."

"Okay, Julie, I'm on my way, and good morning to you too!"

I grabbed my coffee and left for Director Wall's office. I was glad he was back from his vacation. Mike and I were friends. We would go to each other's functions from time to time.

I walked into the reception area of the director's office and Julie said, "Go right in."

I went in and said, "What's up, sir?" I was being formal in front of the woman sitting in the chair in front of Mike's desk. I normally would just say, "What's up, Mike," but I didn't know who this woman was.

Director Wall was talking on the phone, saying, "Yes, Captain Lewis, I received all the files and took a look at them. I will put my top guys on this case."

While he was talking, the lady in the chair turned and looked at me with a smile. *She is absolutely beautiful,* I thought. I couldn't see her body, but her face was to die for. I wouldn't let my composure falter though. She was a white woman with long red hair, hazel eyes, a cute face with full, perfect lips, and the dimples to her smile made me melt.

I didn't notice Mike hung up the phone until he went up an octave when he said, "Hello, Agent Carter!"

I turned my attention to him and said, "What's up, sir?" snapping out of my haze.

Mike turned to the woman and pointed and said, "Agt. Terry Carter, this is Agt. Lori Reid, a transfer from the Boston office and now your new partner."

Lori stood up and I noticed she was five feet seven inches with an athletic, slim build. Her body was perfect to me. She put her hand out, and I shook it. I could tell she was taking in all this sexiness, six feet two, two hundred and ten pounds with an athletic build, caramel complexion with smooth skin, my deep brown eyes, low haircut with waves blended on the side, and a beard that was close and lined up sharply.

"Nice to meet you, Agent Carter!" She replied, loving the warmth and masculinity of his hand.

"The pleasure is all mine, Agent Reid," I replied, taking in her beauty.

We both turned back to the director and he said, "Now that the introduction is over with, let's get down to business!"

"Damn, sir," I said, "you just got back from vacation at work for maybe half an hour, and already you got business! By the way, how were yours and Kathy vacationing?"

"It was great and a breath of fresh air. It did me and Kathy some good. And believe me, if this wasn't urgent, then I would be taking a few hours to get myself back into work mode."

Mike shuffles through the file on his desk gathering them together. He continued to say, "This sucks to have such a serious case waiting for us on my first day back in the office, but this one is all kinds of crazy."

Mike handed me the file, and I looked at it quickly. The photo of the murders themselves was enough to turn my stomach. I said, "These are a lot of victims for such a small file. Are we expecting more on this case?"

"Nope, that's it because the detective in each one of these cases had little to no evidence left behind. The only reason they figured out that it was a serial killer was a stroke of luck. There were two homicide detectives that have the same cousin playing basketball for the University of Connecticut, and during a game, they brought up their unsolved cases."

"Well damn, sir, that was lucky," Lori said, trying to insert herself into the briefing.

"Lucky or not, it's our case now, and the two of you are in charge of solving it. Use whatever resources and manpower you need to get this done as fast as possible."

Agent Reid and I said at the same time, "You can count on me, sir!" We both looked at each other and smiled. *Damn . . . she's beautiful,* I thought. I turned back to Mike and said, "Is there anything else, sir?"

"No, just keep me updated on your progress because I know this may get worse before it gets better. This person already had a two-year head start on us, so you know he probably perfected his craft, and judging by what he has already done, leaving no evidence behind, I don't believe he's going to slip up any time soon."

"Alright, sir!" I said as I turned to leave the office, and Agent Reid followed.

In the hallway on our way back to my desk, I said, "I got the perfect team to help us with this case. I will gather them and meet you in conference room C. While I'm doing this, you can look at the files and break them down into states if you don't mind."

"Sounds like a plan to me. It was really nice meeting you, Agent Carter." She smiled as her eyes said more and then turned to go to the conference room with the file I just handed her.

She stopped and turned back. "Oh, by the way, Agent Carter, where is conference room C?"

I smiled at her dramatic spin back and replied, "One floor down on the elevator, make a right three rooms on the left."

"Thank you, kind sir," she replied with a bow and left.

That made me laugh a little. I shook my head and thought, *Beautiful with a sense of humor. Damn, I have to try to keep this professional.*

Agt. Susan Steals and Mark Dunn were at their desk that sat across from one another talking when I walked up. They both turned to look at me and said at the same time, "What's up, Terry!"

Mark said, "Yea, Terry, what brings you to our neck of the woods?"

"You know, taking a little stroll trying to stay attached to the slums!" I replied with an amused grin on my face, thinking my joke was funny.

"Ha ha ha, Terry, very funny," Susan said with her middle finger high and mighty.

"But no, for real though, I just got a big serial killer case, and I want you two on my team. Are you down for that?"

"Hell . . . yeah, Terry!" Susan replied. "It's been quiet around here. It's about time we get some action!"

"Well, I guess you have your answer then," Mark exclaimed, knowing Susan led and he followed.

"Cool then! I am going to get Gordon and Kevin to join us. Like I said this is a big case, and now that I think about it I'm bringing in Noel and Jason. Meet me down in conference room C at one o'clock, my new partner—"

"Wait, wait . . . did you just say new partner? Not Mr. Long Wolf, big bad Agt. Terry 'Take 'Em Down' Carter!" Mark said with a shit-eating grin on his face, and Susan laughed at Mark's comment.

"Very funny, Mark! You got jokes, huh!" I replied, laughing with them.

"Anyway jokester, she's in the conference room C, and her NAME is Lori Reid and she's a transfer from Boston."

"Oh, I can't wait to meet her. I have to meet who's going to be dealing with Terry's planet-sized ego!" Susan exclaimed, chuckling.

Mark said, "It's been a while since we worked together, Terry, so let's get this shit done!"

"Sounds like a plan to me!" I replied then turned away to go gather the rest of the team. I thought, *This case may be the biggest case of my career! It may make me or break me, but damn I love a challenge.*

Chapter 3

I contacted everyone I wanted on my team and told them to meet me in conference room C at one o'clock. I also told them to eat a good lunch and be ready for a long briefing.

Agent Reid and I took the time to put together a portfolio on the Life-Ruiner Serial Killer case. We had everything that the three states had on the victims that Mike gave us such as pictures, DNA testing, rap sheets, their victims, all interviews, family, friends, jobs, forensic analysis on the cause of death, and lastly, the killer's notes left behind. I knew this case wasn't going to be a walk in the park.

Reid and I brought everything to the conference room with folders that were labeled Life-Ruiner 1–6 and the respected states of the victims. After we organized their folders, we made two additional copies of each. We started at nine thirty and finished by eleven forty-five right before lunch.

I figured we arrived at a point where food was necessary, so Reid and I went to Panera Bread. It took us a little over five minutes to get there.

During the ride, I said, "So communication in the navy. I hope you don't mind. I took a quick look at your file when I had a few minutes."

"No, it's cool. I grew up in Pittsfield, Massachusetts, with my older brother and younger sister. My mother was a single parent. We didn't have much money, but Mom made due.

"She was an assistant manager at Walmart. My older brother went to prison for vehicular manslaughter. He's now at home after doing six years and living with Mom working at an auto body shop. My sister Samantha just passed the Massachusetts bar.

"I did a little running around with my friends getting into trouble, so I decided to join the navy when I was seventeen after graduating high school. I figured if I didn't, I was most likely heading down the wrong road.

"After my training as a seventy-two Zulu, which is a communication specialist, I was stationed in Norfolk, Virginia. During that time, I attended Virginia Tech and graduated with my communication degree.

"After serving ten years in the military, I took the FBI exam and was accepted to Quantico, and the rest is history."

Lori finished her story as we pulled into Panera Bread, we parked and went in. In Panera Bread, you had to go through a line to order and then get your food. Lori ordered a chicken Caesar salad and a cranberry juice. I ordered a turkey club with a chef salad and Fiji water. We took our food to our table and ate a little before we continued talking.

Lori looked at me and said, "So, Carter, how about you, why did you join the FBI?"

I finished chewing my food and answered, "I lost a bet!"

Lori was drinking her cranberry juice and started laughing, which caused her to struggle to keep her drink down. She spat a little out but managed to keep most of it down.

When she got a hold of herself, she said, "Boy that better be a joke, you have me dying over here!"

I was laughing as I shook my head and I replied, "Yea, that was a joke. I had to see how you would react. And just like I thought, I can dress you up but can't take you out!"

She laughed while I continue saying, "And I will remember you spitting as I tell this story for years to come! It's going to go a little something like this, remember our first luncheon and you spitted your cranberry juice all over your food, and I knew I could dress you up but couldn't take you out!"

"Oh, so we have a comedian in our midst! Okay, Mr. Funny Man!" she proclaimed while laughing.

I smiled. "Yea, I'm here all night!"

Lori shook her head with a big smile, and I continued saying, "Nah, but seriously, I knew I wanted to join the FBI from the time I was ten years old.

"My favorite little cousin Sandra was kidnapped by this serial killer who was driving state to state. My little cousin was only nine, and she was the seventh little girl kidnapped."

I took a sip of my juice. "She was missing for two weeks when the guy left to go to the store, and she escaped. She got to the road. Luckily someone saw her and stopped to help.

"It just happens to be the FBI who were responding to a tip that someone called in. And by the grace of God, she was right there walking along the road.

"The Feds set up a sting out of sight while they watch the guy return to the house. The killer didn't have a clue that Sandra escaped, and when they arrested him, they found his trophy collection of all the little girls. In the end, he confessed and showed them where the bodies of the missing girls were buried.

"When I graduated from high school I went right into the army fifty-seven Bravo, a field specialist. Then I went to Fort Bragg, North Carolina, and got my wings.

"Then I signed up for ranger school, ran a lot of special ops, did two tours, and then went to Quantico, and now here I am."

"Wow, that's deep!" Lori exclaimed as she finished her last bit.

"Well, you know everyone has a story. That just happens to be mine." I looked at my watch and saw that it was quarter to one. "Let's get out of here and go finish this briefing."

When Lori and I entered conference room C, everybody was in attendance. I said to the room, "I'm glad that all of you are here. First let me introduce my new partner Agt. Lori Reid, Lori,"

I started pointing at each agent, "This is Agt. Susan Steals, Mark Dunn, Kevin Williams, Gordon Yin, Noel Simms, and Jason Wise." Everyone raised their hands as I called their names.

We got down to business. I said, "First I would like to thank everyone for joining my task force. Lori's my second in charge, so anything you have for me, you can also bring them to her.

"Second, I'm going to lay the case out just as Director Wall laid it out to us. When I'm done, I will assign states and responsibilities. You will spend the rest of this week revisiting the victim's family, friends, and any witnesses interviewed by the homicide detectives.

"You will also meet with the detectives to get anything else they can tell you, something that would lead us in the right direction. We have full use of our agency and full cooperation of the locals.

"Agent Reid will fill you in on the rest." I turned it over to Lori, she stood, and I took my seat.

Chapter 4

Lori Reid

I listen to Terry opening the briefing. I couldn't help but drift off thinking, *Damn this man is sexy as hell. The way he had me laughing at lunch, that scored some points for him. Wait, what the hell am I doing? I need to focus on this briefing. But still though this man is fine!* I snapped back as Terry was handing the floor over to me.

I stood while Terry took his seat. I was passing out everyone's file while I said, "It's a pleasure to meet everyone, and I am very happy to be a part of the Albany branch."

I sat back in my seat. "What I have just given you are the files of the victims and their respective states. Agent Steals and Dunn, you will have Massachusetts. Agent Williams and Yin, you will be in Connecticut, and Agent Simms and Wise, you two are the computer and forensic team. Every team will be doing the analytical part until something else happens."

I took a sip of water then continued explaining, "This case will be known as the Life-Ruiner Serial Killer case. I can tell you now that it's not going to be an easy one as you can tell by the size of your files that there isn't a lot of evidence to go on.

"This killer we believe is averse in forensics, and he left little to next to nothing for us to get a lead. In all of your files, you will see that every last victim was left behind in their final phase of death—"

"Wait, what do you mean final phase of death?" Agt. Gordon Yin asked.

"The killer as it seems is torturing his victims in three phases. The first phase varies, but the second phase, however, is cutting and then using a burning liquid.

"As of now we know little but what's in these files. Take a minute to look at your files, and then I will try to answer any questions you may have."

They all opened their files and took a few minutes to look. As I looked around the room, I could see their disgust just like mine when I viewed the files.

After a few minutes, I said, "Do anybody have any questions?"

"So, Agent Reid, does this killer only kill snitches, rapists, and child killers?" Agent Williams asked. "And do we know if this is a man or a woman? Finally, do you believe that the killer thinks he is a vigilante?"

"What we know now is that this killer leaves a note behind at each murder, referring to the victims as Life Ruiners, so it's safe to say that the killer feels maybe he's getting justice for those people who were victimized.

"Secondly, I will not say he or she has limited themselves to those three categories. I believe that anyone that has ruined someone's life could be a victim."

"How do you think he or she is picking their victims?" Susan asked.

"We're not completely sure, but the killer could be getting their information from the news or the internet.

"Like I said, the murders were in different states, and the killer already has a two years head start. So we need to get him before his range gets bigger."

I looked around the table and asked, "Are there any more questions?" No one else said a word, so I handed the meeting back over to Terry.

I took my seat as Terry stood and said, "Okay, I've assigned everyone what state they will begin with and a file of the victims. Agent Reid and I will take New York. You have until Friday to review your file and gather anything more you can bring to the table. Now if there are no more questions, let's get to work."

Everyone got up and left. Terry and I remained behind. He said, "So would you like to have dinner while we work on our case?"

I smiled, thinking, *Dinner is not all I want from you!* But what I said was "Sounds good to me."

Chapter 5

Friday, February 8, 2022

Jamal

I got up this morning, feeling good. The boys came home for an early weekend on Wednesday, and on Thursday we had a cookout at their mom Jennifer's house. Everybody that was there took the day off from work, Kim, my sons Jamal Jr. and Jermaine along with their best friend Preston Turner.

Preston was Tracy Turner's son. Tracy was Jennifer, my ex-wife's best friend. Jennifer was also present. We all got along like one big happy family.

Jamal Jr. whom we called JJ for short looked a lot like me but taller. He was six feet four inches and weighed two hundred and twenty pounds with an athletic build. He had a very light complexion and a low curly-top fade haircut. JJ attended the Massachusetts Institute of Technology (MIT). He was a senior and was looking to graduate top of his class.

Jermaine, whom we called Main, was the same height as me, six feet two inches, and weighed two fifteen of solid muscles. He also had a light complexion but had long straight hair that he kept in differently designed cornrows. He had some of my features but resembled his mother more. He played football for Boston College. He was one of the top receivers in the college's division 1 football, and he was only a sophomore. The NFL had him coming out in the top five.

Preston, whom my boys called P-Dot, was six feet even and weighed one hundred and ninety-five pounds. He too was mixed and had a light complexion, had a curly baby afro that was blended on the sides and back. He played football with Jermaine at Boston College, also a sophomore, and played on the opposite side of Jermaine.

Jennifer was a petite white woman with long dirty-blonde hair down to the center of her back and had a very beautiful face. She was the CEO of World Corp. Technologies.

Tracy was a black woman with a thick curvy frame, long silky hair to her shoulders, and had an onion-shaped face. She was the co-owner of Jacobs & Turner Law Firm.

As I was saying, we had a great day. The boys and I played basketball in the driveway and then played catch with the football in the backyard. I played football in high school and college before I got hurt.

Kim, Jen, and Tracy were getting along like they were sisters. The best thing about the cookout was that the next night, I was ready to kill my next victim, Ofcr. Patrick Dawson, and I couldn't be happier.

Officer Dawson killed Ronald Strong, a black guy during a traffic stop with his white girlfriend Mary Thomas in the car. Mary was six months pregnant.

Strong and his girlfriend Mary were coming home from his little cousin's seventh birthday party around nine o'clock at night from North Adams, Massachusetts.

He was pulled over by Officer Dawson for rolling through a stop sign in Burlington Vermont. Officer Dawson asked for his license and registration. The report stated that Strong's movement was too fast, and Dawson pulled out his gun and told Strong to freeze.

However, what actually happened was Strong's phone fell in between the seat. He looked, moved his hands, and Officer Dawson shot him in the chest. Strong died on the way to the hospital. Officer Dawson was only suspended with pay until the investigation was completed.

Mary, during her interview, said, "Ron was doing nothing wrong! He didn't even roll through a stop sign because we stopped and kissed. I believe that he was pulled over because he was black and I was white! That racist cop killed my boyfriend and baby's father." She was sobbing. "Now what are we going to do!"

I thought, *This type of shit happens all the time, and it's time these people pay for it!*

Jamal Jr. taught me a lot about computers and technology. I now knew how to read people's emails and crack Facebook, Instagram, and Twitter accounts. I could also hack into video feeds through people's computers and phones. Finally, I could tap people's phones and text messages. This new-age technology made surveillance so much easier and my job so much fun. This asshole had to die, and I was going to have a great time doing it.

I realized a long time ago that no one was above punishment if they had ruined someone's life. I would get justice for these people whose lives were ruined when the system did little or nothing about it or just let them beat the system.

People that ruined other people's lives should hope that the law punished them because if I get my hands on them, then their lives were over as they knew it.

I couldn't stand law enforcement or city officials who were sworn to uphold the law and used their position to deal out justice the way they saw fit. So I was happy that I was going to kill Officer Dawson, and the great thing about it was I didn't even have to leave his house.

I thought, *This kill will be amazing, a fucked-up cop, my first one! This feels like popping my cherry all over again!*

Today we had to do inventory. Our shipment came in last night. I wanted to get this done efficiently and quickly. We started the inventory at eleven and usually finished by four thirty.

I ordered pizza and soda so everyone could eat and work. Everyone liked the free lunch idea, and they got paid for that hour.

It was ten fifteen when I was sitting in my office preparing for the inventory when my best employee Rebecca Soto came in and asked, "Mr. Stone, can I leave early today? I have to pick up Lamar and Christina from school because my mom can't. She has a doctor's appointment at two that she can't reschedule."

"Damn, Beck, you should've said something at the beginning of your shift. We've been here since seven. In a half an hour before inventory, you tell me you can't stay!" I replied, frustrated.

"I know, Mr. Stone, and I am so sorry! I came in here as soon as I remembered. I even tried my sister first, but she can't miss class! Please, Mr. Stone, I'll make it up to you I promise!"

I leaned back in my chair and replied, "Alright, Beck, only because Jamal loves the kids!"

She chuckled at that. "Look normally I wouldn't even give you a hard time, but you're my best employee and its inventory.

"With that being said, look on the three thirty to eleven thirty workers' list, and call someone to replace you. They can come in now if they want, but tell them that they have to be here before you leave."

"Thank you, Mr. Stone, for loving the kids!" We both laughed and then she left.

Rebecca Soto, I liked her. She was smart and dependable. She was working her way through Smith College majoring in project management, and she would graduate this year.

She had two kids with her fiancé that had been locked up for three years. She made sure he was good at all times, brought the kids to see him, and kept money on his books.

Lamar, her fiancé, had only two years left. He was locked up for selling drugs to take care of his family and was helping Beck financially through school.

I thought, *Damn, I don't need any holdups. This fucking cop has to die tonight. I've been watching this cop for six months, and this was the weekend that his wife was going out of town to see her mother. I'm killing his ass tonight!*

The rest of my day went through without a hitch. We finished inventory by four thirty and picked up Kim for the Chinese buffet. We ate and were done by six thirty.

On our way home, Kim was kissing all over my neck with her eggroll breath. I started laughing as I tilted my head to the right because she was tickling me. I said, "Get your greasy egg-foo-yung lips off me!"

She leaned back giggling as she replied, "You wouldn't be saying that if my lips were on your egg-foo-yung!"

We both were laughing hard as I replied, "Oh, now it's an egg-foo-yung. You weren't saying that last night!"

She reached for my manhood and said in a sexy voice, "You right about that, Daddy! Can Mommy ride that stallion tonight?"

My manhood was already standing from her kissing on my neck, and the way she was stroking it while in my pants, I was already ready to go. If I didn't have a business to attend to, we probably would have never left the bedroom after our shower.

"Baby, that sounds good as hell, but you know I have some business to take care of tonight."

But as I thought about it, I continued, "What you can do is lie in bed waiting for me butt-naked, and Daddy can give you some midnight loving!"

She unzipped my pants and grabbed her stallion while looking at me licking her lips as she replied, "But Mommy wants it now!"

Damn, that shit felt good, but I had to stick to my schedule because I couldn't let anything mess with my timetable. Once I let things like that happen, shit would fall off course, and that was when mistakes happened.

It was Friday and I had to cross my Ts and dot my Is. Dawson's wife was supposed to leave tonight, and I had supplies I needed to pick up. "Sorry, baby, I have something that needs to be done tonight, but I'll be home at midnight!"

"Okay, baby . . ." She looked slightly disappointed, "Can you please bring home some cookies and cream ice cream?"

"Yes, for you, anything!"

That was one of the things I loved about Kim. She never asked or questioned what I was doing or where I was going. It made it so much easier to move around without having to lie, and if she ever got questions, she would have plausible deniability.

We pulled up to the house and got out. I waited for Kim to come around the car, so we could go in together. As I always did, I put my arms around her, and then slapped her on the butt, but this time she beat me to it and then ran big belly and all into the house.

"Hey!" I said, shocked. "Get your ass back here, you stole my move!"

I chased her into the house as we were laughing. I caught her and she fought to break my grasp as I gave her raspberries on the back of her neck. I spun her around looking into her eyes causing her to slow her giggling to a sexy smile. When she did, I kissed her passionately.

When we came up for air, I said, "I'll see you when I get back, beautiful. I love you so much!"

"Okay, baby, and I love you more than life itself!"

As I released her, I slapped her on her ass and said, "Gott-cha!"

She was laughing as she went upstairs. I grabbed her car keys and left for Jen's house.

Chapter 6

Jen only lived one town over in East Hampton, Massachusetts. I built a man cave underneath her garage a year ago, and it had all the state-of-the-art computers and electronics equipment thanks to Amazon.

Jen's another one that did not ask a lot of questions, but she sure as hell wanted to know why I wanted to build a man cave at her house.

I'd told her that she had the space, and her neighbors were far enough apart. I also told her that I need a place to go when Kim had her friends over when I wanted to watch my football and basketball games in peace, finally. The boys and I could hang out when they were home and not be in the house bothering her.

She liked that last statement because we were always running through her house and taking over her living room. When our boys were home, she barely got one second of peace and she usually left.

Jen let me renovate the garage, and the boys and I hung out down there, but they knew it was our spot and I didn't want anybody knowing about it, not even Kim. No one was allowed down there. The boys had their own computers and games with a studio in the basement. Jen rarely parked in the garage. She kept her Mercedes-Benz Coupé in the driveway covered when she knew I was coming. This had been happening for the last six months.

To be able to enter my cave, you have to have my keypad. It was the only thing that could open the mechanical slide latch. If you were looking for the irregularity super hard and only if you knew it was there, you wouldn't be able to see or find it.

I pulled up to Jen's and nobody was home. She must either be working late or visiting her friend. She usually went over to Tracy's house and had a few glasses of wine after work.

I went into the garage and hit the button on my keypad that opened the trap door. When that happened, the lights automatically came on in the cave, leading to an eight-by-ten-feet room that was a little bigger than the garage.

The steps led down at a forty-five-degree angle, and at the bottom of the steps was a switch that turned on the power to everything. As you look into the room, on the left mounted on the wall was a fifty-five-inch LCD Sony Smart TV.

I built shelves into the wall where the Xbox One and a Sony PlayStation 4 sat with their own wireless modem. On the floor laid a six-by-seven-foot 49ers rug that Jen and the boys bought me for Christmas.

Sitting in front of the television was a nice wooden futon with cream cushions, and next to it was a round wooden chair also with a cream cushion. It was all laid out nicely around the television.

Behind the futon was a long computer desk, which had two computer screens with two towers, and to the right at the end of the desk sat my laptop. Next to that was a large cabinet where my tech gear rested. I had all types of sizes of digital cameras, camcorders to charger outlet camcorders. I also had bugging equipment and different types of binoculars.

I went over to my computer and fired it up. I typed in a few commands and presto I was looking into Detective Dawson's home.

About three months ago, I was sitting down the road from his house around eight thirty. He and his wife got in their car and left. I waited five minutes then drove up to their block and parked right in front of the entrance to a park next to their house.

It was quiet on the block, but I moved like a ninja gaining access to the wooden gate on the side of the house. The gate wasn't locked. I went in and around to the back of the house. I was about to jimmy the window, but I decided to just check the back door first. As the back door came open I thought, *What the hell! This is going to be easy.*

I went in and started putting cameras in hidden places like vents and smoke detectors. I then plugged in my USB computer scanner to hack his computer information and then tapped their landline. After that, I was out the way I came in.

When I went out the back door and got to the gate, I heard voices at the house across the street. Their kid was getting dropped off by someone. They were saying thank you and see you later. I waited until the people were inside the house, and the porch light went out, then I got the hell out of there.

I said to myself as I drove off, "I should've been an assassin for the CIA."

At my computer desk, I sat monitoring the cameras I set up in Dawson's house. I took in the surroundings of the living room, and I saw good-old-boy Pat sitting alone, throwing back some Jack Daniels. I watched for about five minutes before his phone rang, and I listened in on his conversation.

"Hey, Pat, how you been, buddy? Did Heather leave yet?"

"Yea, she's gone, Ted, left around five for her mother's."

"So what are you doing tonight then? Shit, I still can't believe you're still suspended!"

"I know! But that's one less fucking black guy dating our white girls! Cap said it won't be long before this blows over, and I'll be back to work."

"Awesome! So what are you doing right now?"

"I'm drunk as hell! Heather's not here to nag me about drinking. I can get pissy drunk and not hear her fucking mouth about it!

"Oh, I'm watching *Die Hard 3* on AMC." Patrick slurs.

"Well, I'll get with you tomorrow, and maybe we can go bowling!"

"Sounds good to me. Call me tomorrow."

"Cool!" Ted said, finishing and then hanging up the phone.

After hanging up the phone, Dawson threw back another gulp and continued to watch television.

I thought, *Tonight might be the best time to kill this racist motherfucker*!

I clicked on Word on my computer and started typing out the kill note for this dead cop asshole then I printed it out.

I retrieved my black duffle bag that had the clothes I used to commit justice. In it was my all-black-everything, jeans, T-shirt, hooded sweatshirt, high-tech boots, tight sport Nike gloves with the black logo, and my mask that only covered from my nose down, so the victim could only see the eyes of their reaper.

I put the note in the bag and headed out to Home Depot to pick up my supplies. It was just before nine when I hit Home Depot, so I figured I could go home, take a shower; then climb in the bed with Kim sooner than expected, and be out by midnight. I should be at Dawson's before one thirty.

At Home Depot, I bought duct tape, rope, a nail gun, liquid Drano, and bleach. I then thought about it, and what I had planned for Dawson didn't involve rope, so I still bought it because I could use it for another time. I almost forgot the nails, so I went back and grabbed two boxes. I cashed out, then headed home.

I was thinking during my drive, *It would probably take no more than three hours to kill this guy, but I want this to be fun!*

I took a shower then climbed in the bed with Kim, and just like I asked her, she was waiting asleep butt naked. I cuddled up next to her. She snuggled close to me in a spooning position, and said, "Umm, honey, you're home so soon?"

I whispered into her ear, "I just couldn't stop thinking about you lying here waiting for me naked, I had to get here!"

My manhood was ready, so I inched down and slid right into her. She felt like heaven. I was so excited not because I was with her but because I knew I was killing someone tonight.

The thought of it made me stroke harder and deeper. I rolled her on her stomach still in her; got behind her, and grabbed her waist pulling her ass up to me as I thrust deeply in and out harder and faster. I then slid her one leg forward so I could go deeper.

I was hitting her G-spot, and she went crazy moaning, "Oooohhh, baby, you're so deep! That's it right there, Daddy. Oh, oh, oh, I'm . . . I'm cumming!"

As her body shook from the orgasm, I continued to hit her G-spot. She moaned loudly with pleasure as her body shook with another orgasm.

I still wasn't done, but I could feel that I was about to explode, so I kept stroking, still hitting her G-spot as she continued to moan, "Damn, baby, again!"

This time we both came together, and I collapsed on top of her.

We moved to a spooning position and lay there panting, saying nothing, as Kim drifted off to a comalike sleep. She slept like that the house could be burning down, and I couldn't wake her up.

At eleven thirty, I slid from behind her to get up. I put on my all-black-everything heading out the door ten minutes before midnight. I was on my way to kill another life ruiner, and this time it was a good old boy.

I was so excited! I put my supplies in the back seat and turned on 2Pac's "Machiavelli" because that song got my murder mind focused. I pulled out of the driveway and was heading up the block just as 2Pac said, "I ain't no killer but don't push me, revenge is the sweetest joy next to getting pussy!"

Chapter 7

February 8, 2022

Terry Carter

I arrived at the office early because I wanted to assign someone else the other case I was looking into and wanted to get the okay from Mike. It was a cold case that I had some leads on, and I didn't want the leads to go cold. The case was a sex trade case, but someone must have tipped them off and we never made a bust.

I gathered the case file and went to ask Agt. Tony Riley if he would take over. "What's up, Tony? What are you working on?" I said.

"Hey, Terry," Tony replied, looking up from his computer, "I'm finishing up this probate thing that I have with Shelly. She's trying to get full custody of Racheal. She's trying to say that my job is dangerous, and I'm never around."

He leaned back in his chair. "The damn woman is so stubborn, and I am just asking for joint custody but she's difficult!"

"That's messed up, Tony. You're a good father, and I hope everything works out for you."

"I'm sure it would, but what's up though, you need something?" Tony asked to change the subject.

"Yea, I'm on my way to Director Wall's office to hand over this sex trade case, and I thought you would be perfect to head it up. I have a case with multiple homicides, which we believe is a serial killer.

"I got some new leads on this sex trade case, so I came to you first to see if you would like to take it over."

"Sure, Terry, I could use some real fieldwork to keep my mind off this probate shit. I'll come with you to Mike's office." Tony replied, getting up from his chair.

We both were shown in by Julie, and Mike looked up from his papers on his desk and said, "What's up?"

"I have this sex trade cold case that I've made some progress on but because of this new case, I won't have the time. I do not want my new leads going cold, so I ask Tony to take over. Is that cool with you?" I explained, knowing Mike wouldn't have a problem with this.

"I have no problems with it, just as long as Tony is not working on anything that needs his immediate attention."

"I'm good, Mike, I can take over. I wasn't really working on anything important. I just finished a case on Tuesday, and you probably already read the report," Tony replied.

"Yea, I read it. Job well done, Agent, go ahead and take the case from Terry. Anything else?"

"Nope, just wanted to clear that up. I have a meeting to get to," I replied then Tony and I left.

I handed the file to Tony and thanked him as I headed for conference room C where my task force should be waiting.

I walked into the room, and everyone was in attendance. Lori was passing around coffees to everyone that she bought from Dunkin' Donuts. Susan said, "See, I like this chick already! Thanks, Lori!"

"No problem, Susan, I know we have a long morning, so I figured we could use a little sugar and caffeine." Lori turned to me. "French vanilla, Terry?"

I was shocked that she even noticed. "Yes, thank you, Lori! That happens to be my favorite!" I took the coffee and continued to say, "Everyone, take five more minutes before we get down to business."

When everyone was settled, I said, "Lori and I will go first since the first three murders were in New York. As you know, we have labeled this case the Life-Ruiner Serial Killer, and his first victim to our knowledge was Tanya Spencer."

I clicked the button on the overhead projector of a picture of Tanya. "Tanya was thirty-four years old and was born September 15, 1985. Mother

Sandy Spencer and father Thomas Spencer. They are still together living in Greenwich, New York.

"Tanya rented the apartment that was on the side of their home. Tanya has one sister named Racheal Spencer who's twenty-eight years old Racheal and her boyfriend Tobi Miller lived in Albany, New York.

"Tanya's kids are Emily Spencer whose fifteen, and Tyler Spencer whose thirteen, they both live with their grandparents. Tanya had a number of friends, Tara Smith, Megan Starback, Quincy Hamilton, Michael Bennett, and Stacy Simpson. Tanya was on the phone with Tara Smith the night she was abducted."

I clicked on Tara Smith's picture and then continued, "Tara said that Tanya was walking to the store when she put her on hold to answer her call. Tara held on for a few minutes, and Tanya never clicked back over.

"Tara never thought anything of it because Tanya did that sometimes. That was around nine in the evening and the phone record shows that.

"Next picture was of Tanya's boyfriend. Jason Stewart, Tanya's boyfriend, was at the house with the kids. He stated that he just got home from working a long day from six in the morning to seven at night doing construction. He was dog-tired and didn't want to walk to the store. He said she wanted some fresh air and a break from the kids.

"Tanya was collecting unemployment. She dropped out of high school at seventeen when she was pregnant with Emily. In 2002 she was arrested for shoplifting. She received probation in 2004. She was arrested for seventh-degree possession and received a drug program.

"In 2008 she made numerous sales to an undercover cop, and when they raided her house, they found forty-five grams of crack cocaine, twenty bundles of heroin, seventy-five hundred dollars, and scales.

"She struck a deal with the DA, and she flipped on her supplier Jamal Stone a.k.a. Roc. She set Jamal up, and Jamal was convicted and received twelve years, doing only ten. She got six months and five years' probation."

I put Jamal Stone's picture up on the overhead. "Let's talk about Jamal Stone a.k.a. Roc for a minute. Jamal Stone from New Castle, Delaware, graduated from Dover High School.

"Jamal landed a scholarship to play football for Delaware University, graduated and then enlisted in the United States Army and served six years then left.

"Met his first wife Jennifer Wilson now Stone at twenty-two while in college their senior year. They had their first son Jamal Stone Jr. that first year, and two years later had Jermaine Stone. You might know Jer—"

Mark cut in, "Wait! Not the same Jermaine Stone that plays receiver for Boston College! The same kid that's about to enter the NFL draft after only two years in college!"

"The one and the same!"

"Damn, that boy is good! You know he runs the forty-yard dash in 4.25 seconds! That's blazing speed, and he can catch the hell out of a football!" Mark proclaimed, giving praise.

"Well, I see that you're a fan, Mark, but let's get back to business! Now his oldest son Jamal Jr. is a tech wiz at Massachusetts Institute of Technology in Boston."

Now it was Gordon who chimed in, "Damn, Terry, this Jamal breeds some studs. Brains in one, and bronze in the other!"

"Well, they both are smart as hell. Jermaine carries a 3.8 grade point average in music engineering and business as a minor.

"Jamal was an all-American football and basketball player in high school but wanted to go to MIT where he currently holds a 4.0. But with that being said, let's get back to business."

"I'm sorry, Terry, but damn that's impressive!" Noel proclaimed, taking in a breath and shaking her head.

I continued to explain, "Jamal is now married to Kimberly Wade, now Stone, and yes, the first wife kept the Stone name.

"In Jennifer Stone's interview as a person who knew Tanya, she said that her kids will always be Stones, and so would she. The new wife is cool with it, and they even get along."

I paused to see if there was something from the peanut gallery then continued, "Kimberly is now six months pregnant, and she works at Saint Mary Cancer Hospital as an LPN.

"Jamal has been working at Amazon for the last three years and now is the warehouse manager. Lori and I watched his interview after Tanya was found, and to his knowledge, he didn't know she was missing until it came out on the news.

"Jamal now lives in North Hampton, Massachusetts, and has been living there since his release. He has a solid alibi, and in his interview showed no sign of panic.

"He even said that he's forgiven her and was sorry that something happened to her. I looked into his incarceration record, and he was a model inmate, no history of aggression or mental instability, and has turned his life around since his release. As of now, he isn't even a suspect.

"Tanya was the first victim, and we need to know everyone she'd victimized. These killings all started with her. On April 4, 2020, between the hours of nine and ten, Tanya was brought to an abandoned house in New Lebanon, New York, tied up in the basement and tortured." I clicked on the overhead of the gruesome pictures of her death.

"Damn," Kevin said, "that's messed up to do that to someone!"

I looked around the room, and I could tell they all felt the same way. "The autopsy suggests that she was waterboarded because water was found in her lungs.

"And as you can see, she was sliced from head to toe with a razor. She had rubbing alcohol poured all over her body, and the cause of death was electrocution."

The pictures showed Tanya taped to a chair and two spikes impaled in both thighs with jumper cables attached to the spikes and car battery.

I continued, "The killer wanted her to be found this way. The only things left behind were the method of death and a note that read, *not all snitches deserve to die, but the snitch that put someone away that was taking care of their family is a 'LIFE RUINER' AND DESERVES TO DIE.*

"There was no other evidence left behind. The place was clean as a whistle, except what he wanted to be found. I now turned it over to Lori."

Chapter 8

Lori Reid

It was my turn to give the overview of the second victim in New York, so I clicked on the overhead and a picture of Derek Thomas a.k.a. Little Man came up. "This is Derek Thomas a.k.a. Little Man, age twenty-seven, mother's name is Annette Thomas, father unknown. He has two brothers Shamel Thomas aged twenty-four and Tarik Thomas aged twenty.

"Little Man lived in Queens, New York. He had some small arrests for fifth-degree possession in 2011, contempt of court in 2014, and resisting arrest in 2016. His last arrest was in the same year February 12, 2016, for possession of ten bundles of heroin, and he turned state for a lesser sentence."

I put a picture of Kareem Hunt up. "He set up Kareem Hunt, and Mr. Hunt was given six years. Mr. Thomas was given a county year and five years' probation. Mr. Hunt only had a few misdemeanors prior to this arrest.

"He was twenty-four years old and paying his way through community college. He was set to have his associate degree in hotel management that year. Mr. Hunt also has twins, one girl Tasha Hunt and a boy Terrell Hunt both two years of age. Mr. Hunt's girlfriend and the mother of his kids was named Tamara Crane.

"Mr. Hunt is still in prison at Mohawk Correction due to be released in July of this year. Tamara posted on Kareem's Facebook that Little Man snitched, and that's why her man was in jail.

"Little Man was released in February of 2020 and was killed on September 23, 2020. That's five months after Tanya Spencer's death. He was found on Liberty Street off 147th in an abandoned house in the basement."

I clicked the button on the projector and the pictures of Derek Thomas popped up one by one. "He was found hung upside down butt-naked with a bag over his head. In the bag were three city-size sewer rats.

"His mouth was sewn shut and his eyelids taped to his forehead, both eardrums busted, and a knife cut under his chin. If the rats didn't kill him, then he would have bled out anyway.

"The killer wanted him to suffer, and believe me, he suffered. Derek also had slices all up and down his body just like Tanya Spencer, but the liquid poured on him was ammonia."

I then clicked more photos of Little Man during the autopsy and photos from the crime scene. His whole head was eaten by the rats to the bone, and his eyes were eaten out. "He was found three days later by Jackie Finns who closed on the house a week ago. It was a fixer-upper in a decent part of Queens." I put the note on the projector and it read,

See no evil, speak no evil,

this man was a "LIFE RUINER" AND DESERVED TO DIE!

I cleared the projector and said, "At this crime scene, the killer left no evidence. The place was clean just like Tanya's murder.

"Again, the only thing left behind was the method of the murder and the note. This killer is very creative with his torturing methods.

"Next, we have Simon Tully from Elmira, New York, a rapist, and Terry will brief you on that."

Chapter 9

Terry Carter

I took over again from Lori and put up Simon Tully on the project. "Simon Tully is a child rapist from Elmira, New York. He was charged and not convicted of raping his girlfriend Renee Baker's daughters Mary Baker age eleven and Kristen Baker age nine.

"Tully worked for PSE&G Gas Company, no family and no criminal record other than traffic tickets. Renee Baker worked the second shift at Applebee's on June 7, 2020.

"Approximately eight thirty in the evening, she came home and alleged that Simon was screwing her eleven-year-old daughter Mary, and Kristen was in her bed naked, crying. Renee attacked Tully. She was overpowered by him, and he beat her.

"Tully tries to apologize to Renee, saying he needed help, and it would never happen again. However, Renee was not hearing that and called the cops.

"Simon Tully was arrested and given bail that he posted, but the court put an order of protection against Tully. Renee found out the rapes were happening to Mary since she was nine, and it's been going on with Kristen since she turned nine, and that was four months ago."

"That's fucked-up! If that were my kids, I would be fighting for a temporary insanity plea right now!" Noel said, feeling heartbroken for Renee, Mary, and Kristen.

"Yea!" Susan agreed. "That's something I feel that the system is to light on, and the fact that he got bail. Shit's fucked-up!"

I thought, *I couldn't agree more especially if that happened to Neveah.*

I continued after the girls made their statement, "Both girls are physically okay, but emotionally, it's a different story. They're seeing a child psychologist. Ms. Baker though is destroyed because she's blaming herself. She is also seeing a psychologist."

"I hate to say this, but Tully got what he deserved in this one even though I know no one should take the law into their own hands! That guy took something from those girls that they could never get back!" Noel said, thinking, *Good riddance!*

"I couldn't agree more, but it is not up to this killer to dish out punishment," I replied then got back to business. "Simon Tully was killed on December 15, 2020, at three in the morning. Just like the others, he was tortured.

"Tully was taken to an abandoned house in a neighborhood in Elmira where the homes are far apart, no one seen or heard anything."

I clicked the button so the picture of Tully's death came up. "Tully was found in the basement of this nice house that was on the market to be sold.

"He was tied feet and hands up in the air to a bean spread eagle. His private parts were superglued to his stomach, and when I say superglued, I mean he would never be able to peel it away if he was alive without ripping it off.

"Just like the others, he was sliced up and down his body, and he was covered in paint thinner. All his fingers were cut off, and get this, a pool stick was jammed so far up his ass that it should've come out his mouth."

I flipped through the pictures, letting everyone take them in, then continued, "There was no evidence at this crime scene either. As you can start to tell, our killer has knowledge of forensic pathology. The method of death was left behind with a note."

I put the note on the overhead.

Rapists are the scum of the earth,
this man destroyed the innocence that gives birth!
He's a "LIFE RUINER" AND DESERVES TO DIE!

I finished the briefing on Simon Tully and asked, "What consistencies have you noticed with the MO of the killer?"

Kevin spoke first, "He likes abandoned homes with basements."

"It seems like he tortures in three phases," Jason explained. "The first one is different from one another. Second is consistent slicing and a liquid that burns. When it hits the cuts, it's like being set on fire. I believe it's to bring the victims back to consciousness."

Susan chimed in, "The killer seems like he's OCD. The way he cleans up the crime scenes, I wish he can come clean my house."

Everyone laughed and I asked, "Is there anything else?"

No one had any more to add, so I said, "Alright, we'll take a break for lunch and pick up at one thirty." Everyone got up and left for lunch.

Little did they know a coworker of Jamal's was the sister of Renee Baker. Her name was Melanie Cooper. Melanie came to work one day upset and was too sad to work. She went to Jamal and told him about her nieces, told him the whole story, and that was how Simon Tully became victim number 3.

Chapter 10

Susan Steals

Susan Steals was a pretty woman with a curvy shape and hit the gym hard. She was a health nut. Her brunette hair was cut short to her chin in a really nice style, and you could tell that she was half Asian and white because her eyes were slanted with a really beautiful tanned complexion.

It was one thirty on the dot when Mark and I walked into the conference room. Mark and I had been partners for the last five years, and he was my best friend. My kids loved him—and Zack, my husband, hung out with him from time to time. They were friends too.

My victim was Bruce Matthews, a child rapist and murderer from Bedford, Massachusetts. I picked up the clicker for the projector and put his picture up then started. "I'm sure we all remember the case where seven bodies were found.

"It was four little girls, three little boys who were raped and murdered. The jury couldn't convict because of a lack of evidence, but we and all the world knew he did it.

"Bruce Matthews, age thirty-eight, white male, grew up in Tulsa, Oklahoma, only child of Liz and Brett Matthews. Parents are very religious people. Bruce left home at the age of eighteen and has been in Bedford, Massachusetts, ever since.

"Bruce worked at Walmart for six years, and all his victims' family shopped at Walmart. Bruce's abduction was kind of weird unless our killer was Houdini because someone should have seen something.

"It's not like nobody didn't know who Bruce was. I mean he worked at the town Walmart, and he was on the news. My guess is someone saw something and just didn't care! They probably thought he deserved what he had coming.

"Anyway, Bruce left Walmart from shopping around midnight technically March 7, 2018. His car was found in the parking lot with the doors open and bags still in the shopping cart. He was later found in a basement of an abandoned house on the outskirts of New Bedford, 118 Summit Ave."

I clicked the photos from the crime scene on the projector. "Bruce was found naked on the floor with his hand tied to the pole that supported the structure, and his legs were spread-eagled with his butt slightly elevated off the ground. Bruce, just like the others, had slices all over his body and smelled like acetone.

"Get this, his private parts were burned all to hell—and he had a hot poker jammed up his ass, you know—the poker from the fireplace. Like Tanya, he had spikes coming out of his thighs and jumper cables hooked to him and the car battery. Bruce was cooked to death."

After I showed the rest of the crime scene photos, I put up the note that the killer left behind up. Before I read it, I said, "This crime scene was as clean as the rest and like the others the method of death, and note was all that was left behind." It read,

> *He was a rapist and a killer,*
> *so, I got him ready for a thriller!*
> *Those kids will never know life,*
> *so, I hooked him up to my device!*
> *He's a "LIFE RUINER" AND DESERVES TO DIE!*

I was finished, and I thought, *This killer is crazy, but the last two victims, I kind of agreed. Those two motherfuckers deserved to die, but I would never say that out loud.* I said, "Mark, you're up."

Chapter 11

Mark Dunn

Mark Dunn was a stocky and well-built white guy with dark hair, blue eyes, and always had a five o'clock shadow. He had an angular jaw but was fairly handsome.

I received the clicker from Susan, and I put on the projector a photo of Carmela Lopez from Springfield, Massachusetts, then started. "Damn, this killer is a creative madman! Carmela Lopez from Springfield, Massachusetts, age thirty-one, Latina with two kids. Diego Lopez age ten and Selena Lopez age seven.

"Carmela was arrested in November of 2015 for assault with the intent to cause bodily harm. She did a county year. Other than that, she had some traffic tickets. On June 17, 2018, her home was raided, and the cops arrested her and her boyfriend Rico Sanchez."

I put two pictures up, one of Rico and the other a black guy and continued, "Rico was doomed anyway. He was going to prison no matter what. The detectives knew that Rico had a partner named Lenny Burns a.k.a. Money.

"Lenny has three kids with Tamika Burns, his wife. Money did three years back in 2008 for distribution of cocaine and conspiracy to violate drug laws. Lenny and Rico have been running together since 2004."

I moved back to Carmela and continued, "Carmela knew where they kept their product, and she struck a deal with the detectives.

"She could have walked away with just probation because Rico took full responsibility, but the detective scared her into setting up Lenny.

"Lenny went to the house where the product was, and they had Carmela ID Lenny. They then got a warrant from her statement, and when Lenny went into the house, they raided it.

"When they kicked in the door, Lenny attempted to escape and caught a bullet in his back that hit his spine, and now he's paralyzed from the waist down.

"Lenny was sentenced to seven years. The DA took it light on him because of the shooting. Lenny was looking at fifteen years easily."

I took a sip of my coffee and then continued, "Carmela's kids were taken by the Department of Child Services, and she had to take parenting classes to get them back.

"Rico received ten years. After five months of doing what she had to do, she goes missing. The last person she talked to was her best friend Stephanie Wright, but nobody has seen her since.

"Ms. Wright said she was talking about this new guy she met two weeks before she went missing, and his name was Sync. That was the only name Carmela gave her. She also said that Sync was from Chicago.

"Stephanie asked Carmela when she would get the chance to meet him, and Carmela told her soon. She never met the guy, and the night she went missing, she had a date with Sync. That was a Saturday night. They were supposed to go to dinner and a movie."

I took another sip of coffee because my throat was getting dry, and then I continued, "The report stated that the cops didn't know the race of Sync.

"Stephanie assumed he was black or Spanish because she never knew Carmela to mess with a white boy, so she never asked.

"The call between Stephanie and Carmela was June 25, 2018, around five o'clock. We checked Carmela's phone record, and she had multiple calls from a 413-775-8252 number. We checked the phone, and it was a burner, which was only used for three weeks. All calls from that burner were only made to and from Carmela."

I clicked on photos of the crime scene. "Carmela Lopez was found dead on September 1, 2018, in West Springfield on Fuller Street by some little kids who were playing hide and seek. She was in an unfinished basement."

I clicked to more pictures of the murder scene. "Now here comes the creative madman part, and believe me when I tell you, she suffered. I mean this girl really suffered.

"She was bent backward over a hurdle! Yes, a track hurdle, which was set at the one-ten setting. The hurdle was mounted to the floor, and her legs were duct-taped to the hurdle all the way to her knees.

"Her wrists were tied with the rope, then duct-taped from the wrist to the shoulders on this metal bar, which immobilized her.

"The rope was long, pulled between her legs and the hurdle. The ropes were hooked up to a motorized pulley.

"She had slices all over her body, and she was covered in mint green rubbing alcohol. Her body was bent back into a U shape, snapping her pelvis and spine. She also had a bag over her head with a boa constrictor snake which strangled her. Her mouth was duct-taped."

I could see the disgust on the faces of my fellow agents, and I knew they all wanted to catch this killer.

Terry said, "Let's take a fifteen-minute break and come back to finish up."

We came back from our break, and I was ready to finish. I clicked the button on the projector and the note popped up and it read,

> *This snitch crippled a man from the waist down,*
> *so, I did some investigating and it is true what I found!*
> *Away from his family for the next seven years,*
> *so, before she dies all she's going to know is fear!*
> *She's a "LIFE RUINER" AND DESERVES TO DIE!"*

I turned to everyone and said, "Also like every other victim, there was no other evidence left behind." I took my seat, and I turned it over to Kevin and Gordon.

Lenny Burns was Jamal's cousin, and Lenny's mom told Jamal what happened, that it was Rico's girlfriend Carmela who set him up because she was the only other person that got in trouble and knew where the stash house was. Jamal did some investigation and found out that it was in fact Rico's girl who had a hand in what happened to his little cousin. Jamal planned on making her torture as painful as his imagination could come up with. Jamal set out as Sync, a hustler from Chicago, and Carmela fell right into his trap.

Chapter 12

Gordon Yin and Kevin Williams

Gordon Yin was a first-generation Asian-American from Korea who looks like Bruce Lee. If you saw him from a distance, you would swear that he was Bruce Lee who came back to life.

Kevin Williams was an all-American white male, all muscle. Kevin looked more like a movie star than an FBI agent.

Yin took the lead.

"Last we have Demarcus Way," I clicked the button and his picture popped up. "Twenty-five years old, black male from Bridgeport, Connecticut. His street name is Guns, and he is a part of a gang named BMB, Black Mafia Boys. Known associates are Mike Swiss a.k.a. Hammer, age nineteen, Carmon Peterson a.k.a. Cannon, age twenty-four, Rahim Miner a.k.a. Shooter, age twenty-two, John Green a.k.a. Kaps, age twenty-six, and Martin Lane a.k.a. Pistol, age twenty-five. The older members all met in Berkshire Farm's detention home for boys, and Mr. Swiss is a new member.

"The BMB is larger than these boys, but they all hang together. Mr. Way's mother's name is Kelly Way, but they don't talk. She has six other kids, and she said she doesn't want him influencing them, so she doesn't let him come around. She told the detective during her interview that she knew he was going to be just like his father, in and out of prison or dead.

"Demarcus's father's name was Benny Miles. Benny died in July of 2012 during a robbery, he was shot and killed.

"Demarcus has no girlfriend and lives with Peterson and his girlfriend Shawna Lewis. When the crew was interviewed, they all gave the detective nothing. They all said, and I mean at different times as if they were one and the same, and I quote, 'Fuck the Po-Po we don't talk to you, motherfuckas!' We have no leads on this case." I finished and pass the rest over to Kevin.

I flipped through the file for a second and then said, "Demarcus Way was in a shootout over some territory with another gang called the five hundred. During the shootout, a five years old named Kane Rogers was hit with a stray bullet in the head and died instantly. The neighbors observed the shooting, and they told the detective that it was Way's bullet that hit Rogers.

"This was around four o'clock on August 31, 2018. Way went into hiding but was found in an abandoned building by Tyson Curry who's fifteen years old and his girlfriend Carrie Styles who's sixteen years old.

"They said they went to hang out at the house that Way was found, and when they got there they had a look around and then went into the basement and found Way's body displayed like this." I brought up the photo of Way's final stage. "It was the scariest thing they had ever seen."

I clicked through the photos of the crime scene of Way's on the overhead. "The kids found Way on Second Street in Bridgeport at around five fifteen on December 5, 2018.

"He was found sitting on the floor of the basement, and he was duct-taped from the waist to his chest and attached to a support beam. Both his legs and arms were pulled back facing the opposite direction as if his back was his front.

This time the cable was wire, and they were attached to his shins and forearms, and the duct tape held them in place. The wire was attached to a motorized crane and he was naked."

The picture showed the unnatural state of his body. The only thing that was facing forward was his penis.

I continued, "Just like the others, Way's body had cuts all over and smelled like nail polish remover. He had an extended three-by-four drill bit left in the middle of his forehead, and the note attached to it." It read,

There's no excuse for a five-year-old to get hit with a stray, so, this man will learn his lesson today!

*This is a gang-related battle over turf nonetheless,
so his soul will be sent to hell while his body remains here in a mess!
He's a "LIFE RUINER" AND DESERVES TO DIE!"*

I shook my head and before I handed the briefing back over to Terry, I said, "This killer should be called the punisher because he's going ape shit on his victims!"

Terry looked at his watch. It was now three thirty, and I knew he wanted to end the briefing before six.

He said, "Do y'all wanna push on, and let Noel and Jason finish this up by brainstorming a workable profile with little to no evidence of who or what our killer looks like or break?"

Everyone agreed to push on, and Noel gathered her notes that she took during the briefing.

Jamal knew about this incident because the mother of Kane Rogers's mother's sister Mellissa Cook was another friend of Jen's. Jamal contacted Melissa and told her to keep him posted on Demarcus's whereabouts. Mellissa's ears were always on the street, and when she found out, she told Jamal, and Jamal went to work.

Chapter 13

Noel Simms

Noel Simms was a beautiful African-American woman. She hid her eyes behind her glasses, and she always kept her long black silky hair in a long ponytail. She was married with a four-year-old daughter.

I was about to pull a rabbit out of a hat, and I didn't know anything about magic, but that was exactly what I'm about to do with this profile.

I took a deep breath and said, "The time I had to look over these files and the notes I just took, I must say that this killer is very good at planning the way he intends to kill his victims.

"First, I believe he does reconnaissance on his victims, learning their patterns and best time to attack. Given the time frame between his kills, I would say anywhere between three to six months before he strikes. We know that the killer likes abandoned homes with basements.

"He also likes to torture his victims in three phases; doing this usually between midnight and five in the morning, torturing and murder his victims. The killer does this when most people are sleeping.

"He is done and gone before they awake. That's why no one sees him or anything. If the murders are done in a neighborhood where the victim could be heard, then he tapes their mouths shut but in an excluded area then he doesn't."

I looked at some notes for a sec then continued, "During Susan's briefing, she mentioned that our killer may be OCD. This could be true, but what I believe is he has knowledge of forensics. The killer leaves no evidence whatsoever behind other than the method of death and a note.

"The killer knows we would have a hard time tracking him. The killer is creative and poetic. He believes this is art, and as you can see his notes are beginning to be more poetic. He is aware of social media or a personal connection."

This was a far-fetched analysis, but hey, it was what I believed.

"I believe our killer is a white male between the ages of thirty-five and forty, stands between five foot eleven inches to six foot two inches and weighs from one hundred and eighty-five to two hundred and twenty pounds and is very fit. I say white male because serial killers usually are, but I am not completely ruling out other ethnicities."

I paused for a moment to let it sink in and for them to finish writing their notes. When it seemed like everyone was done, I asked, "Any question or input on the workable profile?"

Kevin asked, "Should we assume that all the people that were victimized by the victims have some common denominator. I mean there has to be some kind of connection between the killer and the people who were victimized by the victims."

I looked at Terry to help me out on this one and he did. Terry answered, "Kevin, when we enter the field to start reinterviewing family, friends, and witnesses, our hope is to build a workable lead, and hopefully we head in the right direction. Everything right now is an assumption but is food for thought."

Terry left it at that, and I continued, "Last I will try to psychoanalyze our killer from his notes left behind. As you can tell, the notes have morphed into a more poetic tone and structure. This means the killer is getting more comfortable and confident in his cause.

"This tells me that the life of the killer is in order, everything is going well, and he's at peace in his surroundings. In each of the letters, the killer states that he or she is a Life Ruiner and deserves to die, which means at some point in time his life has been ruined and that it was ruined badly enough to punish and kill."

I wrapped it up by saying, "Our killer is a psychopath with sociopath tendencies with forensic knowledge, very smart, and his life is in order and has nothing to worry about, so he's just going to keep at it. Now Jason will give us the forensic analysis."

I leaned back in my chair, took a deep breath, and Jason started.

Chapter 14

Jason Wise

Agent Jason Wise was a thirty-seven years old white male with a swimmer's build, dark hair and wore glasses.

I took over from Noel and started with "Every piece of evidence found at the crime scene belongs to the victims. All the locals of each state looked at each death as a single murder.

"So I believe if they knew that this was a serial killer, they would've combed the crime scene differently. Now that we know that we're dealing with a serial killer, we will make sure every crime scene will be checked thoroughly."

"So what do we have so far?" I asked rhetorically.

"This killer is there until the very end of his victim's death. He leaves them in a manner like sculpting art. Afterward, he cleans up using his knowledge of forensics and leaves behind the items of the final stage of death.

"The killer must wear some protective gear, but we know he wears gloves because there are never any fingerprints at the crime scene.

"One thing I know the pictures don't show is that every victim was struck with a blunt object to the cerebral cortex, which would easily knock them unconscious. This would explain how the killer moves the body with no struggle, ease, and quickness.

"The tools he uses for the method he plans on killing his victims are purchased beforehand and then set up at the place he plans on killing. This explains how he's able to keep his killings in a time frame, and no one sees any funny business."

I flipped my notes over and took a deep breath then continued, "Now let's look at the similarity of each victim. They all have multiple cuts. I believe that this is somehow significant and that it carries two meanings.

"The first meaning is a metaphorical message that symbolizes the victim cutting the people whose lives were ruined by their act.

"Second, which leads me to the liquid substance used on his victims, all these liquids burn like hell and would bring anyone back to consciousness with an ear-wrenching scream.

"Finally, the autopsy shows that each victim has been tortured in three different ways. The last phase is death for the victims, and then he leaves a note behind that poetically tells why and how the victims died.

"Just like Noel said, he's a psychopath with sociopath tendencies, and I believe he likes being a vigilante who's having fun with his murders. It's like it's a part of him, and it brings balance into his life."

I was finished with my briefing and handed it over to Terry.

Terry looked at his watch and said, "Okay, it's four thirty-five. Does anyone have any questions or input to add to the briefing?"

Everyone had taken plenty of notes throughout the briefing and didn't have anything to add.

Terry stood and continued. "Here's what we are going to do, make copies of your notes and give them to everyone else. I want everyone to review everything and then get out there and start your investigation.

"Take a day and enjoy your families because we are going all out, and you will be in your respective states."

We all shared a few minutes of conversation then we left.

Chapter 15

Terry

After the meeting, I asked Lori to have dinner with me tonight and tomorrow. I wanted us to get to know more about each other and go over our notes for the case. She said dinner sounded great, and I asked her where she would like to go, and when she told me Buffalo Wild Wings because her Celtics were playing, I was blown away. I couldn't believe that this beautiful woman loved sports too.

Naomi, my ex-wife, hated sports and was always bothering me when a game was on or always had a task for me. I hated that. For basketball, Lori was a Celtics fan and for football a Patriots fan.

It was five fifteen when we arrived at Buffalo Wild Wings. We took our own cars. We sat at a two-person table in front of the big screen TV, and a waiter came right away and said, "My name is John, and I will be your waiter for this evening. What would you like to drink?"

I turned to Lori and said, "Since you're a Pats fan, you're no lady, so I'll order first! Can I have a Corona with lime?"

Lori laughed as she replied, "Another sour face because my Pats won the Super Bowl, and we have the best quarterback to ever play the game, but that's okay, I'll let you get that one! Men! Freaking poor sports!" The waiter laughed while taking her order. "John, can I have the same please."

"Coming right up!" John replied then left to get our beers.

"Let me guess you're a Giants fan?" Lori said sarcastically with a smirk on her face.

"Till the day I die!"

"Well, you just might be before they win another Super Bowl!" she exclaimed, laughing her head off!

"Oh, you got jokes, huh?" I replied laughing with her.

"Of course, I do. You must think you're the only funny person here! I got jokes for days. Don't let me get started."

"Alright, but let me say this all we need is a quarterback because Manning is washed up! If we get Dwayne Haskins from Ohio State, we would make the playoffs and be Super Bowl contenders in the next four years. So sorry to say I will still be here, alive and kicking, and Tom Brady will be in a retirement home!"

The waiter walked up right at the end of my last statement with our Coronas. After he placed our beers on the table, he asked, "Do you guys need a minute?"

I looked at Lori and said, "I know what I want, do you?"

"I just want wings and fries! So I'll have ten sweet and sour and a basket of fries."

I thought, *Damn I wish all women this beautiful were this cool!* "I'll have ten barbecues and a basket of fries."

The waiter wrote down our order and left. It was fifteen minutes before the game started, so Lori struck up a conversation. "So, Terry, no wife or kids?" she asked then drank some of her Corona.

I sipped my Corona and then replied, "I was married when I was in the army at twenty-two to my high school sweetheart Naomi, and we have a daughter together. Her name is Neveah. She's thirteen, and her mother and I divorced before I went to Quantico.

"Naomi believed that I would be home more after the army, but she said I was trading the military for another and that I was choosing my career over our family. I told her I was choosing this career for our family.

"She then said I would always be gone and that she would be wondering if she was going to get that call, out there chasing bad guys. She went through that while I was in the army, and she wasn't doing it again, so we divorced.

"Naomi is now married to this guy named Vincent Stewart who's an international banker, and they have two more kids."

I took another sip of my beer then continued, "Naomi and I still get along, and I get Neveah anytime I want and she spends most of her summer with me."

I showed Lori some pictures of Neveah and me, and she said, "She's so beautiful!"

"Yea, that's my princess! So how about you, kids, husband?"

"I was in a relationship for four years, and I thought he was the one until one day I came home early from work, and I thought he was at work.

"I heard noises coming from our bedroom, so I went to check it out with my gun drawn because I didn't know, but I was hoping that it was a burglar."

She took a deep breath before she continued, "So I kicked the door open, and there was Lewis tied up with my best friend . . .

"Well, I thought Holly was my friend, but she was riding him cowgirl style. I knew they were friendly, and because I care for them both, I was cool with it but not with them fucking."

Lori finished the rest of her beer, and so did I as the waiter brought our food to the table.

I ordered two more Coronas, then she continued her story before we ate.

"So I moved out of our home, and he was begging me to stay saying he was sorry, but I wasn't hearing that shit! I put my transfer in because I wanted to move out of Boston, so here I am seven months later!"

I thought, *Damn, this might be a lucky situation because we're both single. But I should try to keep this professional because we're working on a big case, but damn she's pretty!*

The game had started, the Celtics versus Raptors, and the waiter dropped off the Coronas. We ate, drank, and watched the game. Two-thirds of the way through the wings and fries, Lori broke the silence.

"So this case is puzzling, and it's all over the place. It looks like we're missing a lot of pieces. The killer himself is all over the place too. Judging by his method and planning, it's going to be hard as hell to pinpoint this guy!"

"One thing about killers like him, they get cocky and comfortable, so they're bound to make a mistake or slip up, and someone will see him. Anyway, he doesn't know that we are now on his trail, and if I was to bet money, it would be on us!"

"I couldn't agree more!"

We finished our food and had a couple more drinks. Lori was going crazy throughout the game because Kyrie Irvin was on fire. I just watched Lori in complete awe, thinking, *Damn, my new partner is beautiful, cool as hell, and loves sports. When this case is over, I have to make her mine. I usually don't break my rules, no office romances, but for her, I'm breaking it!*

The game ended at eight forty-five, and I walked Lori to her car. Lori was getting in her car as I asked, "How about dinner tomorrow night after work, let's say seven thirty, I'll cook, and we can review the case?"

"Oh, I don't like burned hotdogs!" she replied, laughing at her own joke!

"See now you're trying to play me! After I cook for you, don't ask to marry me because we just met!"

"Oh, that good, huh! Well, we'll see if it's the kind of cooking that's 'til death do us part!"

"Yes, you will see! Good night and have a safe drive home!" I said then went to my car to go home. I thought as I drove home, *She's going to be my wife!*

Chapter 16

February 9, 2022

Jamal

It's twelve thirty in the morning, and I just hit route fifty-seven, which would take me into Vermont. I synced my phone with my computer, so I could now see everything that was moving in Detective Dawson's house. He was passed out in his recliner and hadn't moved. Everything was all planned, but watching him made everything that much easier.

During the time I was watching his house, it would have been much more delightful if his wife was attractive and sexier. They barely had sex, and when they did, it was usually over before it started. I couldn't imagine being in a relationship like that. When she was home alone, she had toys to masturbate with, but that was gross.

It was quarter to one when he got up stumbling to go take a piss from being pissy drunk. When he was done, he went to the bedroom and just fell out on the bed, back to sleep in seconds.

I thought, *Why did he take his ass upstairs? I wanted to drag his ass into the basement. Shit, I guess his bedroom would have to do. They have dark drapes in the bedroom anyway.*

It was one fifteen, and I just hit Burlington, Vermont, five minutes ago. I pulled onto Crane Avenue where Dawson lived, and it looked like a ghost town.

This is a well-designed area for what I had to do because the houses were not so close, so you couldn't eavesdrop on your neighbors but close enough to be on your lawn and say howdy.

I drove down Dawson's street, and his house was two-thirds down on the left. To the right side of his house was his garage and driveway and next to that was a playground. His garage was not connected to the house. He had a fence with a gate that went from the side of the house to the side of the garage that led into his backyard.

I pulled up like I was a visitor and parked close to the playground, but it was only a hop-skip and I jumped to Dawson's gate. I was glad his car was in the driveway because that added a little more stealth.

I turned off the car lights, waited another ten minutes, observing the street, and checked my phone to see if there was any movement. The block was sound asleep, so I got out of my car, crouching low with my bag of supplies, and closed the car door lightly.

I stayed low as I moved to the gate dressed in all black, so when I got to his dark-blue car, I knew it was hard to see me. I tried the gate. It was locked, but the good thing was it was a slip lock, so it was easily opened.

I grabbed the bucket that was on the side of the house, put it in front of the fence, and then before I stood on it, I checked over my shoulder to make sure the coast was clear. I then pulled out my tool to lift the latch.

I picked up my supply bag after I moved the bucket back to the side of the house and then went into his backyard. I got to the back door prepared to jimmy it, but for shits and giggles, I checked the door, not thinking it would be unlocked, but sure enough, it was.

I thought, *Shit, this is the second time that people don't lock doors around here, oh well, good for me!*

Before I moved fully into the house, I checked my phone to make sure he hadn't moved. After everything was good, I turned off my phone and proceeded to creep through the kitchen down the hall.

On the right was the living room and the stairs were to my left, so I headed up. I took light steps even though I knew Dawson was in a drunken coma. You still couldn't be too careful. Shit, I was going to commit murder. The steps creaked but not loud.

When I got to the top of the stairs, the master bedroom where Dawson was passed out was on the left. I knew the layout of the house, so it was easy to be where I needed to be.

I opened the door, crept in, and set my bag down. I retrieved the duct tape out of my front-hood sweatshirt compartment and took out of the bag my black nightstick.

Through all this Dawson didn't budge a bit. I moved in closer and shook him. When he stirred and tried to adjust his eyes to what he was seeing in his drunken state, I whacked him over the head and knocked him out cold.

I moved the chair where I wanted it and pushed Dawson to the floor. I was hoping he woke up, so I could knock his ass out again, but he didn't. I guess the booze or getting hit hard over the head kept him out cold, maybe both.

The fact that he was still breathing was all that mattered, and plus I didn't want him to die before I had my fun.

Anyway, I put him in the computer desk chair then duct-taped his ankles and wrists to it. I also duct-taped his torso to the chair.

I checked my watch. It was two o' five, and I wanted to be gone before four. I put duct tape on his mouth and then slapped his ass awake. I always loved this part when they came to, and their eyes would get real big realizing they were in a fucked-up situation.

He looked around the room until his eyes became fixed on me, and through the tape, I understood his muffled words, "What the fuck!"

I stepped closer, taking off my hood and my mask. I then replied, "Patrick Dawson, you are a Life Ruiner, that's what the fuck!"

I gave him a second to try to digest why I was here, and he was there. He said something, but this time I couldn't understand him.

I continued, "Now here are the rules. I'm going to say what I need to say and tell you your crimes, and then I'm going to remove the tape to say your piece."

I went into my bag, pulled out my electric nail gun, and then plugged it into the wall.

I then said, "See this here"—holding up the nail gun—"this is a very powerful tool, so as I was saying, I will remove the tape and let you say your peace, but if you scream or yell, I will shoot you in the mouth and throat! Nod if you understand?"

Dawson nodded slowly and I began, "Det. Patrick Dawson of the Burlington County Sheriff Department, you are here tonight because you are a racist and a life ruiner.

"You killed Ronald Strong during a traffic stop in front of his pregnant girlfriend Mary Thomas. Do not lie about being a racist because I've been watching and listening to you for the last three months, and I know what was said between you and Ted Connors tonight."

Dawson's eyes got big when I said Ted's name. I smiled. "Yes, that's right Ted Connors. I bet you wish right now you went bowling."

After giving time for a dramatic pause, I continued, "Anyway, you are the worst kind of cop and to think the chief was going to allow you to come back. Detective Dawson, you have abused your power when you are supposed to protect and serve. Now Ronald's girlfriend has to raise her child alone with no father, so for that justice will be served!"

"Are you ready for your piece?" I asked.

He nodded and I removed the tape. He fixed his mouth from me, ripping off the tape and then said, "So you know I am a cop, so I guess you know how much shit you're in!" Dawson proclaimed, hoping I would fear the idea of him being a cop. Little did he know that was the fun of it!

I spoke calmly to his question because I knew he wanted me to answer. So since it was his turn, and it was part of my rules for my victims to have their peace even if I have to answer questions.

"It looks to me like you're the one that's into some shit. Say what you will because your time is limited, and you do not want to waste it on trivial shit."

"Okay then, for what it's worth, I really didn't mean to shoot that kid. When he reached for his phone, I thought it was a gun or some type of weapon, so I got scared and panicked.

"I can't take back what has already happened. I told the family I was very sorry." He then laughed like shit was funny, and I knew then that he was not sincere.

"What so fucking funny?" I was pissed at the audacity of this motherfucking racist dick.

He calmed down a little. "You come in here like you're the fucking dark knight trying to avenge for the people who can't!"

He went off hysterically, which made me slam the tape back on his mouth.

I laughed as I said, "You know what, that is kind of a funny analogy, but the difference between Batman and me"—I looked dead straight into his eyes, brought my face closer—"is that he locks people up. Me, it's always a death sentence, and, motherfucker, you're going to die!" Now it was my turn with the hysterics.

I laughed while I shot nails all over his body. First, I shot his feet then both shoulders. His muffled screams were music to my ears. Then I moved to his thighs, kneecaps, forearms, his hands, and last his dick. That last one, he lost consciousness but was still breathing.

I opened up the two bottles of bleach and poured them on him. That snapped his ass back to consciousness, screaming through his tape.

I said, "How's this for a dark knight? Not so fucking funny now, asshole!"

He pleaded with his eyes for me to stop. They all pleaded for me to stop, but little did they know I was always having so much fun!

"Yes, Detective, you're going to die tonight because you are not above the law!"

I grabbed the liquid Drano and the plastic hose then got behind him with my nightstick, whacking him over the head. I wanted him out cold so I could hook him up to my device.

I removed the tape and put the hose in his mouth as far down as I could without causing him to gag and then taped it to his mouth.

I grabbed the other end of the hose and poured Drano in. As the Drano sat in the hose, I put the bottle down and picked up the bleach to pour it over him again.

He snapped back to consciousness, but this time he was gagging as he tried to stop the liquid from going into his stomach. I put my hand over the tube so the Drano wouldn't come out, and then I ripped a nail out, which caused pain so his throat could open by the scream, and the Drano went down.

I picked back up the Drano and continued to pour as his eyes got big. He started convoluting, and then his eyes rolled to the back of his head.

I finished the bottle, but by that time, his body had already given up to the poison, and he was dead.

I grabbed the nail gun and shot his body a few more times, then lastly twice in the chest. The second nail to the chest had the note attached.

I cleaned up everything like I always did, using my forensic knowledge, and I left the victim sculpted artistically in the last phase of his death.

I crept out the same way I came in. It was three fifty-three when I looked at my watch as I drove down the street. When I got to the highway, I turned up my music, and Ice Cube was singing. "Today was a good day" was pumping on my speaker.

I thought, *Yup, today is going to be a good day!*

Chapter 17

February 10, 2022

Heather Dawson

I spent the weekend with my mother and sister Katy. We had been having a great time since my sister and I got there. On Saturday we were about to go to the movies, but before we left, I tried to call Patrick, but he didn't answer, so I figured he was out with Ted and would call when he got a chance. I just left a message and went to the movies.

We returned from the movies around eight thirty in the evening, had some wine, and talked about the old days when Katy and I used to sneak out while Mom and Dad were asleep. We were laughing our asses off because Mom didn't have a clue. I was having such a great time that I forgot to check my phone before I went to bed.

Sunday when I woke up, I had a slight hangover, but I checked my phone before taking something for my headache. There were no missed calls from Patrick, and now that I thought about it, I hadn't heard from him all weekend. I tried to call numerous times but kept getting his voicemail. I was starting to get worried, but I had plans with my mother and sister.

During lunch, I kept trying to reach Pat, and it was still going to voicemail. I said to my mom and sister, "I'm leaving early because I have some papers to grade, and I have to finish my lesson plans for Monday."

I lied because I didn't want them to share in my worry for Pat, and if they thought something was wrong, then they would've come with me home because they loved him too.

They bought my excuse, and Mom said, "Do you mind if we stop by the grocery store on our way back to the house?"

"No problem, Mom," I exclaimed, knowing I wanted to get back home because it wasn't like Pat to go this long without talking to me.

We stopped at the ShopRite supermarket then we went to my mom's house and dropped off the groceries. I kissed them goodbye and left.

It was one thirty in the afternoon when I left Concord, New Hampshire, and it was an hour and a half drive to my house.

On my way home, I kept trying to reach Pat but still straight to voicemail. I gave up trying and decided to call Ted.

Ted answered the phone on the third ring, and I didn't even wait for him to say hello! "Hey, Ted, are you with Pat?"

"No, I haven't seen or talked to him since Friday. We were supposed to go bowling, but he never called me or answered my calls. I just chalked it up as a hangover because he was hammered Friday night when we talked."

"So he was drinking! Goddamnit! Okay, Ted, thanks, it's probably nothing. I'm on my way home now, so I'll call you when I get there."

"Okay, Heather, do you want me to check on him?"

"Nah, it's okay. I'll be home in less than an hour. I'll call you later!" I said then hung up.

"I couldn't believe his ass! I'm going to kill him when I get home! He knows he's not supposed to be drinking!" I said out loud to myself.

I was just glad that that was all, but I was mad as hell because he had me worried, and I left early from spending time with my mother and sister.

It was three o'clock in the afternoon when I pulled up to the house, and his car was in the driveway. I parked on the side of his car and got out to go into the house.

I went into the living room, and a bottle of Jack Daniels was on the end table almost empty next to his recliner. I said to myself, "I'm going to kill him." I walked up the stairs, yelling, "Pat, are you up there? Patrick, Patrick!" I yelled louder!

When I got into our bedroom, I couldn't believe my eyes!

Patrick was sitting in our computer chair taped to it with cuts all over his body, a plastic hose coming out of his mouth, and nails coming out of his body like a pincushion!

As it finally registered in my head that Pat was dead, I screamed, "Oh, Patrick, no no no, Pat!" I walked closer to the body, shaking my head, sobbing, "Oh, my god, Patrick!"

Then I noticed the note attached to him, and I read it.

> *Ronald Strong should've never been shot at a traffic stop,*
> *so I poured Drano in this racist cop's stomach so it can go pop.*
> *No one is above the law,*
> *so this racist cop motherfucker had to fall!*
> *He's a* LIFE RUINER AND DESERVES TO DIE*!*

I left everything the way it was and called Ted.

When Ted picked up, I was sobbing as I said, "He's dead, he's dead, oh, my god, Ted, Pat is dead!"

"Wait, wait, just hold on a minute, Heather! What you mean Pat's dead?"

"I just got home, and he's dead!"

"Listen to me very carefully, Heather, did you touch anything?"

"No!" I replied, sobbing!

"Good! What I need you to do is call 911. Heather, wait for me, okay, I'm on my way!"

I called 911 as Ted told me, and then I called my mother to tell her what happened because she would want to know right away.

Ted arrived in ten minutes, and then the police and homicide detectives were there five minutes later. Ted went to see Pat, but he knew not to touch anything because he was a cop.

Det. Keith Paris, Erin Cave, and the forensics team were the ones who showed up, and by four fifteen, it was a media frenzy. The detectives took in the scene of my dead husband, who was one of their own while the forensics team combed the area for evidence.

Detective Cave said to Paris, "See the note left on Officer Dawson? I've read it, and I believe this is the work of that serial killer that we just got that memo on, the Life Ruiner." Detective Cave pointed to the note, "See it even says it!"

Detective Paris read it and then replied, "Sure is, Erin." Keith got the attention of the forensic team. "Look, guys, don't move nothing after you do your thing. I have to contact the FBI. This is the work of that life-ruiner serial killer."

Detective Paris took out his phone and called the chief at home.

The chief picked up the phone on the fifth ring, "Chief Bullock!"

"Hey, Chief, this is Keith, you're not going to believe this, but we have one of those Life-Ruiner serial killer cases, and you're not going to believe who the victim is!"

"Shit, not in my fucking backyard! Who's the victim?"

"It's one of our own, Patrick Dawson!"

"Jesus fucking Christ! I was just about to bring him back to duty." He sighed. "Okay, I'll call the FBI, and remember to leave everything the way it is!" He hung up.

Detective Paris turned to Detective Cave and said, "The chief is going to contact the FBI, so I expect them here in the next several hours!"

Chapter 18

Terry

I was just saying bye to my daughter Neveah when Director Wall called me. I answered, "What's up, Mike?"

"Terry, we have another killing in your case. This one is in Burlington, Vermont. It's a cop this time, named Patrick Dawson. He's the cop that shot that black kid during a traffic stop."

"Oh yea, I remember that!"

"Well, get up there and catch this killer. Now he's knocking off cops, which means no one is safe. He's killing scumbags and city officials alike. This is already getting out of control, Terry! Put the fire out!"

"Gotcha, Mike," I replied before hanging up.

"Shit," I said as I dialed Lori's number. She picked up on the third ring, "What's up, Terry?"

"Sorry to tell you, but we have to change our plans!"

"Wow, Agent Carter, not a good start in this love affair," Lori proclaimed jokingly.

"It's not like that," I said, laughing. "I figure we could take a trip to Vermont"

"Oh really, now we're talking! I love road trips," she replied in a sexy voice.

"I figure we'll go check out some artwork."

"Oh shit, don't tell me our boy struck again. And here I thought you were trying to be romantic!" *Damn, she's sharp*, I thought.

"Boy, Lori, don't tell me I open a can of worms I can't close." I was referring to the joke I made at our first luncheon.

"Well, at least you know I'm not boring!"

"I know that's right! Anyway, do you want to ride together?"

"Sounds good. I'm at 123 Baker—"

"I know where you live. I'm already on my way. Be there in fifteen."

I hung up the phone, called Noel and Jason, and filled them in on what happened. I gave them the address and told them to bring the forensic equipment. I wanted them to comb the crime scene and compare notes with the forensic team that was already there.

I already had everything I needed in my car like my Glock 9 pistol, and my FBI bag was in my trunk. I pulled up to Lori's house and blew my horn. She came out and hopped in.

"So much for a day off, huh?" she said as she put her bag in the back seat.

"I know right! I already contacted Noel and Jason and told them to meet us there. I guess we got an early start."

We sat quietly for a few while Lori tried to find something on the radio. She stopped at Post Malone's "Better Now" and said, "This is my song!" She turned the radio to a level where we could talk and not yell.

She asked, "How was your day with Neveah?"

"Oh man, you would think she's already in high school the way she shops. I think her mother was giving her ideas about what to buy when she goes shopping with me!

"We also went to a matinee after shopping, then we got something to eat, ate at the fountain while we talked. My little girl is getting older, and today she even talked me into upgrading her iPhone to an iPhone 10.

"But all and all, just like Ice Cube said, 'Today was a good day!'

"Well, that's until I got the call from Director Wall! So enough about me, how was your day?"

"I talked to my mom this morning. She wants to have a day with my sister and me on Saturday, but I told her I couldn't because I had to work.

"She then goes on about how I need a man in my life, that I'm getting older, and if I wait too long, I'll be old and nobody will want me. Oh, and before I forget the best part that she'll be dead before I give her grandkids.

"She goes on talking about between Sam and her job and Tommy and his homebody, her family going to end with us."

We arrived in Vermont and we were still twenty minutes out. Lori continued, "And I talked to Sam this morning too. We're getting together when this case is over. She also talked about this guy she just met."

"Oh, then I took a bath and walked around naked until I felt like getting dressed. That's pretty much it!" She smirked.

I cut my eyes at her, smiling. "Oh, is that what we're doing now Lori?"

"Whatever do you mean, Terry?" she replied sarcastically, putting her hand on her chest and batting her eyes.

"Oh, as if you didn't know, trying to put a picture in my mind by ending your today's to-do list with 'I walked around naked'!"

"Did it work?" she said, laughing!

"Yes yes, it did!" I replied as we both laughed!

We listened to some music for about five minutes then I broke the silence, "Hey, Lori, you know the cat is out of the bag now because our killer killed a cop, and the media will be all over this one. I think it's time to address the media and get the word out there so that people can be on the lookout for strange people and activity."

"That's a good idea because we truly have nothing to go on, and I'm almost certain that he didn't leave us much to go on at this crime scene either."

"I couldn't agree more!" I replied as we pulled up.

I pulled up to the yellow tape, Lori and I exited the car, and the media was thick. I looked around, and I spotted her, Ms. Brenda Mendez. I knew she would be there.

I turned to Lori and said, "See that woman over there"—I pointed at Brenda—"that's Brenda Mendez from CNN. We're national now!"

Brenda saw me and busted through the crowd of reporters. All I thought was *Here we go!*

Brenda Mendez was CNN's number one field reporter, she reported on a couple of cases I worked on. She's a Latina woman with a beautiful face, dark long hair, and tan skin.

As she walked up to Lori and me, I thought about the *first case she covered and how we got hot and heavy, dated for about six months until she wanted more, and I didn't.*

Remaining professional, she said, "Agent Carter, can you tell us anything about this murder?"

"No comment until we know more!" I replied as I push through the crowd of reporters surrounding the Dawsons' house with Lori in tow.

Brenda was relentless and yelled over all the other reporters, asking, "This house is a cop's, isn't it, Agent Carter?"

I turned to Brenda and replied frustrated, "We just got here, Ms. Mendez! We will be holding a press conference after we get more information! Now if you'll excuse us, we need to do our job!"

We finally made it into the house and were greeted by two detectives. The detective said, "Hello, Agents, I'm Detective Paris and this is Detective Cave!"

"Hello, Detectives," I replied, "this is Special Agent Reid, and I'm Special Agent Carter!"

We all shook hands and Detective Cave said, "This way, Agents, two of your people are already here combing the crime scene."

I looked at Lori and wondered, *How the hell did Noel and Jason beat us here!*

"I've never seen anything like this before, and the place smells like bleach. It's like the killer cleaned the body, and room before he left," Detective Paris said as we followed the detectives upstairs.

"Don't get me started," I said. "This is the seventh victim, and believe me the others are pretty bad!"

"No shit!" Paris fired back!

We entered the bedroom, and Officer Dawson was still sitting in the same position his wife had found him in. Jason was combing the floor with a black light that showed fluorescent marks that the normal eye couldn't see, and Noel was doing the same to the body.

I said, "What's up, guys, did you find anything we can use?"

Neither of them responded to my question because they were busy analyzing what they were looking at.

Attached to the black light was a trigger that took pictures of anything the agents wanted. They both snapped a few pictures, then Jason turned to Noel and said, "I'm good. How about you?"

Noel snapped two more pictures and replied, "All set!"

Jason turned to me and answered my question, "Actually, we have more than any other crime scene but not much more. We've been here for the last forty-five minutes, and we focused on things that the first forensic team did not."

I was stoked how they got there before us, so I asked, "Not to jump off subject, but how did you get here before us and for forty-five minutes?"

Noel answered, "We were already together when you called us. We were working on the case at Jason's house, and the van was there so we jumped in and came right here!"

"Oh!"

Jason continued. "The first team did a thorough job, but I brought in the black lights and combed the room and body. What we found was some hiking boots prints about size eleven or twelve.

"The killer came in through the back door, down the hallway, up the steps, into and all over the bedroom, and right back out the same way he came in.

"We have finger marks on the hose, but I don't believe their fingerprints. We have the point of entrance and exit. He knew exactly where to go when he came in because there were no other prints anywhere. So I asked Agent Simms to do an electronic sweep of the house."

Noel took over and said, "I swept the whole house, and sure enough, there were cameras all over the house. They were in smoke detectors, vents, and in every room."

She went into the evidence bag, pulled out some of the cameras, and continued, "These were found. The killer was watching them."

I asked, "Is there anything else we can go on?"

"That's it," Noel replied. "Other than what the first team found, which is the same as usual, the place is clean, and this time with bleach."

"Alright, get the coroner in here and get the body to the morgue for an autopsy. Where's the note?"

Jason reached into the evidence bag and pulled it out and handed it to me. Lori looked over my shoulder and read the note with me.

After we finished reading it, I gave it back to Jason and said, "Good job," then turned my head toward Noel. "Get this packed up and get the autopsy as soon as possible even though we already know the cause of death by the letter."

I turned to Lori and said, "Let's go question the wife and see if they had any maintenance men out here in the last several months. You can do the honors!"

We followed the body out of the house. Reporters were all over the place taking pictures like this was the red carpet. There were questions being shouted coming from every direction, so I beckoned everyone to be quiet so I could answer their questions.

I waved my hands in a downward motion as I said, "Can I have everyone's attention! I would like to make a statement!"

The reporters went quiet. "As of now we are following leads on an unknown serial killer, and that's why we, the FBI, have stepped in.

"We will do all we can to catch this killer. We will be holding a press conference tomorrow at 10:00 a.m. where you can ask your questions, and we will try to answer them to the best of our ability. Thank you and good evening!"

Cameras started flashing, and reporters started shouting more questions. I pushed through to my car while Lori followed. We hopped in and drove off for the Burlington County Police Station. Heather Dawson was there, and we had some questions.

Chapter 19

Lori Reid

It took Terry five minutes to get to the station. I looked at the clock when we entered the station, and it was already six o'clock. Mrs. Dawson was waiting in the conference room drinking coffee. She had already been interviewed by Detective Cave and Paris, and they told her that the FBI had some questions also.

Terry and I entered the conference room sitting on the opposite side of Mrs. Dawson. I said, "Hello, Mrs. Dawson, I'm Special Agent Reid, and this is my partner Special Agent Carter."

Mrs. Dawson, we could tell, was still suffering from the shock of her husband's death, but she did manage, "Hello, Agents."

"We are both sorry for your loss, Mrs. Dawson. I know you've been questioned already by the detectives, but we have some questions of our own."

I gave her a few seconds before I continued. "Are you okay to answer my questions, Mrs. Dawson?"

She nodded while saying, "Sure, go ahead, ask away."

Terry took out his pad and pen while I started. "Mrs. Dawson, when was the last time you saw your husband alive?"

She took a drag from her cigarette, shaking with red eyes, then replied, "It was Friday. I had plans to go to my mother's house for the weekend. Every so often my sister and I go and pal around with her.

"Since my dad died, we try to spend as much time as we can, and we leave our husbands home. So the last time I saw him was around quarter to five in the evening."

"When was the last time you spoke with him?"

"It was when I got to my mother's house. I called him to let him know I made it safely, so he wouldn't worry. He's always worried when I drive long distances alone.

"Patrick is always talking about car accidents, and people getting kidnapped at gas stations. That phone call was around seven."

"Did you try to contact him any time before you came home?"

"I called him around four in the evening on Saturday, but he didn't answer. When he doesn't have to work, he usually stays up late and sleeps in, so when I called again and he didn't answer, I thought he was doing something with Ted or sleeping."

"Ofcr. Ted Connors?"

"Yea, Ted and Pat are friends. They're usually together bowling, fishing, or watching a game or something."

I looked over for a quick second and saw that Terry was taking notes, so I decided to keep going. "So is that the only time you tried to contact your husband?"

"Well no, I mean I didn't try to call him back that night. My mom, Katie, and I went to a matinee movie around four, and when we got back, we had a couple of glasses of wine and talked. After a while, I was tipsy because I don't usually drink, and when I do, it's usually with my mom and sister, but after that I went to bed.

"I did check my phone when we got back, and I thought it was strange that Pat didn't call me back, but like I said, I thought he was with Ted or sleeping, and I needed to lie down.

"So when I woke up this morning, I checked my phone and had no missed calls from Pat. I kept on trying and trying, but it kept going to voicemail so that's when I got really worried.

"I had plans with my mom and sister for a brunch before we went our separate ways, but I was so worried I cut our brunch short, took my mom to the grocery store then came home.

"On my way home, I called Pat a few more times then I called Ted. Ted told me he talked to Pat on Friday, and he was drinking. When I got home, I saw the bottle on the end table.

"Anyway, Ted said that they were supposed to go bowling, but Pat never called or answered, and because he was drinking the night before, Ted assumed the same story."

Mrs. Dawson started to cry. "I told that big lug no more drinking, but he didn't listen! Now look what happened!" She broke down.

Terry and I gave her a moment. Terry got up to get her some tissue while I patted her hand, and said, "It's okay, Mrs. Dawson. Let it out!"

Heather cried for a few more minutes then gathered herself and said, "Sorry, I'm so sorry!"

"No no, don't worry about it. You just went through something very tragic. If you like, we could finish this another time?" I didn't really want to come back to finish when I said that, but I wanted her to feel like she had an option.

"No no, I can finish. I need to get clothes. I'm going back to my mother's for a few days. I've already called the principal of the school I teach at and took the week off."

She blew her nose. "Ted asked if I wanted him to check on Patrick, but I said no I'll be home shortly, and when I got home, that's when I found him. I called Ted back and then 911."

"Mrs. Dawson, did you or your husband have a maintenance or a tech guy come to your home over the last several months?"

I could tell Mrs. Dawson thought that was an odd question from the look on her face. It was probably a question that differed from the detectives. "No." She thought a little harder. "Anything that goes wrong, Pat usually can fix it. Why you ask?"

I looked at Terry to see if it was cool to answer her question, and he gave a small nod. I answered, "Well, apparently someone went into your home and installed cameras all over your house. We found them in all your rooms."

Heather gasped, "What! But how? We're home every night, and Patrick has been home since that incident with that kid in the car." She leaned back with her hand covering her mouth, now realizing, "Oh, my god! That's what the note was talking about!"

"Okay, Mrs. Dawson, I need you to think! When was the last time you and your husband left home together?" I didn't know she read the note or knew about it.

Heather thought hard but couldn't remember. She started. "I can't rem—oh! I do remember! About a month or so after the incident with the kid, Sabrina Connors, Ted's wife, invited us over for dinner. They wanted to do something to get Patrick's mind off the incident, but that was in September."

I was finally done with the questions and said, "Thank you, Mrs. Dawson. You helped a lot, and again sorry for your loss."

I turned to Terry and said, "Agent Carter, do you have any questions for her?"

Terry reviewed his notes for a brief second and then replied, "No, all set. Mrs. Dawson, I'm also sorry for your loss."

We interviewed Ted Connors, and he confirmed everything Mrs. Dawson had said. We had a press conference tomorrow at ten in the morning. It was seven thirty in the evening, and we decided to get something to eat and go back to Terry's to review everything. Terry ordered Chinese takeout, and we were back at his house quarter after nine.

We got back to Terry's house and I was starving, and I assumed he was too. Terry had a nice house. It was a three-bedroom, two-bathroom, kitchen, dining room, and living room duplex.

He had pictures of his daughter Neveah growing up, pictures of him and Neveah, of him in the military, and pictures of some other people that look to be family members.

Terry was setting us up to eat in the living room when I asked, "Hey, who are these lovely ladies?" I picked up one of the pictures on the end table.

He looked over my shoulder and replied, "The one on the left is my aunt Doris. The one next to her is my aunt Jackie. My grandmother is in the middle. The one next to her is my mom Annette and lastly my aunt Keisha."

I sat that one down and picked up the other one, "And these guys?"

"My dad Lawrence is to the left and my uncles Mickey, Isiah, and Darrell. I have tons of photos if one day you would want to go through them with me. After the case, we can make it a date."

I set the photo down, sat on the couch, and said, "A date, huh?" with a smirk on my face.

I wasn't going to deny the attraction between Terry and me, but solving this case was very important. I didn't want my attraction to interfere with the task.

Terry took a seat next to me on the couch and said, "Look, Lori, I'm going to keep it real with you. I am very interested in getting to know you on a personal level, and I was planning on waiting this out until after the case, but hey, I can stay professional and work with someone I am interested in."

I was tearing my food up hoping he didn't mind while he was talking. After he finished, I paused with my cheek stuffed like a squirrel and looked at Terry, shocked because I was just thinking that.

I chewed, swallowed my food, and because I wanted to respond, I took a gulp of my Mountain Dew to wash it down.

I then replied, "I couldn't agree more. But I don't want to rush into anything. But just for the record though, I share the same interest in you."

"Now that's out in the open, we can get back to our regularly scheduled program!"

I chuckled as I continued to eat my Chinese food, and Terry dug into his.

We both were quiet eating for a little while. I guess he was just as hungry as I was.

Terry broke the silence and asked, "Lori, you chose Albany, so does that mean you have family and friends here?"

"I do have friends here that I went to college with at UMASS. My girl Debbie is a corporate banker here at First National Bank. Jessica works for the Hall of Justice, and Natia is a lawyer for Jacobs and Turner Law firm. We used to get together regularly before I went to Quantico.

"I was placed in Boston, so when the opportunity presented itself, I moved here. They are the ones who helped me find my duplex. Before I started working, we hit the town a few nights, and sometimes we had lunch."

"That's cool, so you know your way around Albany?"

"I grew up in Pittsfield, Massachusetts, my mom and brother still live there. So yes, I am very familiar with this region among others."

We finished our food and talked for another fifteen minutes, but it was getting late and we had a long day tomorrow.

Terry got up and said, "Let me get our files, so we could plan our strategy for the press conference."

I cleaned up while Terry went to retrieve the files, and when he got back, he saw me in the kitchen washing a few dishes. He smiled and said, "You are my guest. You don't have to clean up. I would've done it."

I turned around from the sink after I folded the cloth I washed the dishes with and replied jokingly, "A guest? And here I thought I was moving in, honey buns!"

Terry laughed and said, "Honeybuns? I didn't know you were checking out my butt!"

I walked toward him, giving my sexiest smile, and I replied, "Not just the buns, but the whole package!" Terry laughed harder at my comeback and followed me into the living room.

We sat back at the coffee table and started reviewing the files. It was amazing how naturally we switched back to work mode. We reviewed the notes from Heather Dawson's interview.

I said, "We have some new evidence to go on even though it isn't much. We definitely know that it's a man wearing a size eleven or twelve shoes unless it's a really big woman."

We laughed as I continued. "Whoever this person is has some knowledge of tech gear. Also, his last kill before this one was in September, so we know he took at least three to four months surveying Officer Dawson before killing him. That's about as much time the killer takes between kills. I believe that we have that much time until he strikes again."

I could see that Terry was thinking about what I just said. He replied, "Yea, but I notice he did something different this time. The killer didn't use a basement!"

"So do you think he's evolving?"

"I'm not quite sure. Let's think about this for a minute. He set up cameras to watch the Dawson's, so he knew the layout and what they were doing."

Terry was silent for a moment then continued. "The killer must have tapped their phones. I bet their home line is tapped and their cell phones too.

"This is how we're going to play it. Noel and Jason will check Dawson's phones and conduct the interviews of this murder. When they get everything back from the lab, they can build a case file.

"The reason why we took New York is because this is where it all began, and it would be easier if we took it from the beginning. Plus, the other guys will get what we need to pull all this together."

I couldn't agree more with Terry. I took a deep breath and said, "We have a big puzzle, and all the pieces are in different boxes."

We reviewed Tanya Spencer's and Derek Thomas's files because they were the first, and both were snitches. We spent an hour coming up with a plan. It was a quarter to midnight, and we had a press conference at ten in the morning, but after that, we were heading to Greenwich, New York.

Terry took me home and suggested that we should ride together. I agreed so he'd pick me up at nine for the press conference. I had no problem with that. I got home and didn't remember hitting the bed.

Chapter 20

February 11, 2022

Terry

I arrived at Lori's house at eight thirty with coffee and everything bagels. She left the door unlocked because when I called her and said I was on my way she said she was still getting ready.

I let myself in and shouted, "Honey, I'm home! And I brought you breakfast!"

Lori was in the bathroom putting her hair up in a ponytail. She shouted back, "Be right there!"

I looked around Lori's home and thought, *Our houses are very similar, but it looks like she is still settling in.*

Khalid's "Location" was playing on the stereo as I went into the kitchen. I sat the bag of bagels on the counter as Lori came into the kitchen. She said, "Do I smell everything bagels?"

She opened the bag then looked at me with a smile and said, "How did you know? I love these, and you brought cream cheese."

I smiled back as I replied, "Don't forget the coffee. I brought you hazelnut, and I took a guess on the bagels!"

"Well, you guessed right. Thank you, Mr. Carter! I love hazelnuts, but I guess you already knew that!"

I finished chewing the bite of the bagel I took and chased it down with my coffee, then said, "I've already briefed the director this morning, and I've already called the team to fill them in.

"I called Jason and Noel and told them what we discussed last night, so all we have is the press conference and Greenwich."

Lori grabbed her coat and gloves, and we were off to the state-building.

When we arrived, all the networks were in attendance. Usually something like this would be held in front of the state-building, but it was a cold rainy day, so they set us up in one of the big conference rooms.

We met Mike in the adjoined room, and he shook both of our hands as he said, "What a mess this is turning into. A cop from Vermont, this guy has to be caught ASAP. Are you guys ready for this media frenzy?"

I replied, "Everything is in motion like I said earlier when I talked to you. Susan, Mark, Gordon, and Kevin are already on their way to conduct interviews, so we can put the pieces together. I've assigned Noel and Jason to Vermont. We're still waiting for labs from Vermont. Lori and I are heading to Greenwich after this."

"Very good! And what do you have planned for the press conference?"

"Well, we planned on letting the cat outta the bag. We need civilians on the lookout for anything suspicious going on in their neighborhoods."

Mike looked at his watch then said, "Three minutes to showtime. Okay, Carter, it's your show. Let's get ahead of this thing."

I went to the door, looking out at the crowd we were about to face, and among them, I spotted CNN's very own Brenda Mendez. I turned to Lori and said, "Let's get this show on the road."

I opened the door to the conference room, walked straight to the podium, and Lori followed, standing next to me. I adjusted the microphones while the media quieted down and I began. "Ladies and gentlemen, thank you for coming.

"Yesterday Ofcr. Patrick Dawson of the Burlington County Sheriff's Department was found dead in his home in Burlington, Vermont, around three o'clock. Officer Dawson is the seventh murder victim in the case we are calling the Life-Ruiner Serial Killer."

I could see the shock on their faces, and some were mumbling. I continued. "The killer's first victim dates back to April 4, 2020, in Greenwich, New York. The victim's name was Tanya Spencer.

"The other Victims are Derek Thomas of Queens, New York, Simon Tally of Elmira, New York, Bruce Matthews of New Bedford, Massachusetts, Carmela Lopez of Springfield, Massachusetts, and Damarcus Way of Bridgeport, Connecticut."

I took a drink of water that Lori poured for me and then continued.

"They'd all been murdered by this serial killer. As of now, we are going to be interviewing people who may know the victims, family, friends, coworkers, and anyone who may have ties.

"We are asking the public if they witness any suspicious activity going on in their neighborhoods, or if there's someone that looks like they don't belong, please contact the police.

"The killer is targeting anyone that he feels has ruined someone's life. Now, the floor is open for any questions."

All the reporters were shouting, trying to get my attention to pick them. I chose first Al Jameson from the *New York Times*.

He asked as the rest quieted down, "Agent Carter, is it true that he's torturing his victims?"

"The victims are undergoing strange methods that the killer sees fit to execute, so yes, he's torturing them."

Next was Tom Swartz from channel 7 news in Vermont.

He said, "My source told me that Officer Dawson was killed because he killed that kid Ronald Strong and that the killer left a poetic note behind on why and how he killed him."

I was shocked because that information was not privileged. I replied, "Wow, Mr. Swartz, you have some source there! But to answer your question, yes, it was because of Mr. Strong, and yes, he did leave a note behind."

I had to let Brenda ask a question or she would cause more trouble than it was worth. "Ms. Mendez, go ahead."

"My question is a two-part question."

"Why am I not surprised, Ms. Mendez!"

The crowd chuckled and she smirked at me with a cold stare as she continued. "Why are the FBIs just now getting involved after seven murders? And do you believe he is acting vigilantly?"

"The reason we just got involved in this case is because the killer was committing murders in different states and towns. In the beginning there was no connection. Every police department was treating it as a single homicide.

"It wasn't until the last two kills before this one and a stroke of luck of circumstances. We were able to put two and two together, realizing we were dealing with a serial killer.

"And to answer your second part, the killer may believe that he's acting on the behalf of others, but answer me this, why isn't he just killing them? He's torturing them before killing them.

"That is not an act of vigilance. He's enjoying killing them, and to me that makes him a sociopath. No matter what happens no one should take justice in their own hands."

I took a couple more questions and then said, "I would like to thank everyone for coming, but now my partner Agent Reid and I have a killer to catch."

We exited the room at the same door we came in, and Mike was waiting. He said, "Good job, Carter, that was a very informative press conference."

"Thanks, Director. We're on our way to Greenwich. I'll keep you informed."

Lori and I left and headed to my car. As we approached, we saw Brenda Mendez was waiting, eyeing Lori and me. I thought as we walked up, *This woman has some nerve, and this is going to be interesting!*

I didn't say anything when we got to the car because I didn't want her to think I was interested in the conversation. However, Brenda broke the ice, "I see you got a new partner, Terry?"

"I did," then introduced them, "Agent Reid, this is Brenda Mendez from CNN."

The ladies were not interested at all in one another, and the tension was noticeable. Brenda's presence was annoying the hell out of me, so I got right to it.

"So, Brenda, what's up?"

"Nice to see you too!" she replied with an attitude!

"Come on, Brenda, not right now. You know I got things to do! So what's up?"

I could tell that Lori was sensing that something had gone on between me and Brenda as she watched the body language.

"Well, I won't keep you," Brenda said. "I was just wondering if I can get a personal interview on the case?"

Brenda cut her eyes at Lori then came back to me walking closer as she continued in her sexy voice. "You know, like we used to!"

She was close enough that if either of us leaned in, we would kiss. I knew she was doing this to spite Lori.

I put my arm out to give Brenda and me an arm's length of separation and said, "No, Brenda, and there is no more like we used to be neither."

"But I miss you, Terry," Brenda exclaimed with a pout.

I saw Lori out of the corner of my eyes. She was frustrated and I didn't have time to deal with this. Lori and I have a long day ahead of us.

Brenda continued. "You know how I am, Terry. I'm on the case now, and you know I will be everywhere you are until you catch this guy."

Beyond frustrated now, I sighed then replied, "Well, Brenda, that's your job! Just don't get in our way, and as for the case, I will update you with the rest of the media. Now, if you don't mind, please step aside."

Brenda moved and Lori and I got in the car. I looked at Lori and said, "Sorry about that."

"Nah, it's cool. She's a little obsessed, don't you think?"

"Nah, not really, she did that for your benefit because trust me that woman is only about self, believe that!" I replied as I started the car and drove off to Greenwich.

Chapter 21

February 11, 2022

Jamal

I woke up feeling like a million bucks. I had a great weekend. Kim and I did some baby shopping. I finished painting the baby's room and put up the border.

When I came in Friday night, which was truly Saturday morning, I showered, climbed in bed, put my face between my wife's legs, and had amazing sex, and it was like that all weekend. I'm saying we didn't make it through a whole movie all weekend. We were hot and heavy, and to top off my weekend, I felt my little girl kicking.

I talked to Jamal and Jermaine this weekend. Jamal told me that he was working on his final project for his computer engineering final.

Jermaine asked my opinion on entering the NFL draft after his sophomore year. I told him that he would have to go with what was in his heart, and I asked him if he spoke with his mother. She had said pretty much the same thing but added, "Doing what you love is better than any kind of money you can make doing something you hate or taking a chance at having a short sports career."

Jermaine loved music, and he was at Boston University majoring in music engineering and a minor in business because he wanted to produce and own his own label. He told me that he wanted to finish school and then go pro and save his money to start his own label. I thought that was such a grown man's decision. I was so proud of both of my boys.

Finally, that life-ruiner cop I killed couldn't have gone any smoother. So I was having a great morning, and work was moving without a hitch.

I went to Benny's pizzeria for his famous stuffed peppers, and while I was waiting, I watched his TV that was tuned to CNN. I thought that Brenda Mendez was hot as hell as I watched her report. I was so focused on her until I heard her say "Life-Ruiner serial killer," and that caught my attention.

I focused on what she was saying, "During a ten o'clock press conference with the FBI, they are now on the case after the Life-Ruiner serial killer has already killed seven people. The FBI lead agent is SA Terry Carter and his partner SA Lori Reid. The FBI held a press conference today after Ofcr. Patrick Dawson of the Vermont, Burlington County Sheriff Department was found dead by his wife Heather Dawson Sunday afternoon. We now tune in to the press conference."

I stood there mesmerized as this Agent Carter was talking about the victims, the notes left behind, and how he wanted people to be on the lookout.

I thought my notes were poetic. *That's good! I want people to know if they ruin someone's life they could be next. Shoot, if the system wasn't going to make them pay, then I would.*

I turned back in and I heard Brenda ask why they took so long to get involved and did they believe I was a vigilante. I smiled at the answer Agent Carter gave on why they took so long, but when he started talking about me being a sociopath and not a vigilante, I was pissed off.

I thought, *What the fuck does he know about being tortured! Did he even consider the pain these motherfuckers caused! When they put a person in jail for trying to take care of their family or the mental destruction of the kids that were raped by a monster or a life taken from a family before their time! What does this motherfucker understand about torture! These people have years and some have a lifetime of torture because they will never see or recover from what has been taken from them!*

I stared, looking at the two agents, and then I realized something that the woman Lori Reid standing next to Agent Carter looked familiar, but I couldn't place it, but I thought I knew her.

My food was ready, so I turned back to Benny and paid for it, but I wasn't even hungry now. I got back to my car thinking about Agent Reid, and as I was driving, I was still thinking about where I knew her from.

I got back to my office and ate half of my stuffed peppers, not being able to remember where I knew her from was driving me crazy.

I put the rest of my food in the refrigerator, and I spent the rest of the afternoon in bliss. I was mad as hell about what that bastard Agent Carter said about me being a sociopath and that I tortured people for my amusement. I then thought about it, and I really did enjoy torturing them, but that was not the only reason I tortured them. I had a method to my madness, but that didn't make me insane or a sociopath.

Or did it?

Wendy Sanders came into my office talking about something about the forklift. I was so deep in thought I didn't really hear her until she got a little louder and said, "Mr. Stone! Hello, Earth to Mr. Stone!" She was waving her hands in front of my face, which caused me to snap out of my thoughts.

"I'm sorry, Wendy, what were you saying?"

"The forklift, Mr. Stone, the forks won't rise all the way up."

"It's okay. I'll get maintenance to look at it. Just park it and get Ramirez to use his forklift to get down what you need."

As Wendy started walking away, she turned back around and said, "Oh yea, Mr. Stone, I got accepted to UMASS this fall. So I was wondering if I can work on the weekends and school breaks?"

"Sure, Wendy, that's great, congratulations! Just call during the week when you know that you're coming home, and I'll put you on the schedule for that weekend."

"Thanks, Mr. Stone!" And she was off.

I leaned back in my chair, and that was when it hit me! It was something that Wendy said then I thought, *UMASS!* I said out loud to myself, "That's where I remember Agent Reid from!"

Chapter 22

April 2008

Jamal

I was leaning back in my chair, and I put my hands behind my head and thought back to when I met Agt. Lori Reid!

I was twenty-nine years old, and Lori was twenty-two. Jennifer, now my ex-wife, and I had been together for eight and a half years. Jamal Jr. was eight years old, and Jermaine was six.

I was hustling drugs, and Jennifer and I kept fighting about me getting out of the game. She would say, "Jamal we both have our degrees now, and plenty of money to start our lives. Why do you have to keep hustling?"

She was right and I was ready to get out, but I was addicted to the lifestyle and easy money. I replied, "One more year then I'm out, I promise! I have a few more things to take care of then I will step down."

I would say that, but there were never a few more things. I enjoyed "the life" and that was that!

Jen kept nagging and I would leave the house sometimes not coming back for a few days. One day I came home late, the kids were in bed, and she was sitting at the dining room table. I thought she was going to yell, threaten to leave, and take the kids with her.

However, she calmly asked me to take a seat at the table because she needed to talk. I was nervous because Jennifer was never this calm especially after we fight, and I disappear for a couple of days.

I sat down at the table, and she reached for my hand and began saying,

"Jamal, you know I love you with all my heart, and I will always stand by you no matter what!"

I was really nervous now because I thought she was going to leave for real this time, so I said, "Baby, I love you so much too! I'm sorry, and I'm ready to change! I promise I'm done at the end of this year."

She looked me straight in the eyes, and I could see the sadness in her heart. She took a deep breath and replied, "Look, Roc, I know you can quit now. We have enough money, and I know there isn't a few more things.

"You're addicted to running the streets, selling your drugs, and doing God knows what! You can quit right now, and we can go on with our lives. I don't plan on leaving you even if you stay in until the end of the year, but if you get caught and I've been trying to tell you to get out, I'm not going to wait for you when you get out."

I was kind of mad at what she was saying, but I figured I would never get caught. I'd been doing this before I went to college and while I was in the army. Shit, I put both of us through college, but here she was saying this shit, and that cleared my consciousness of any wrongdoing with other women. After that conversation, we both were cool.

I was still going out with my right-hand man Kyle Winter a.k.a. Cash who was a little younger than me, twenty-six to be exact. Cash was messing around with this girl Natia who lived in Albany but went to UMASS. We met some of Natia's friends at a place called the Monkey Bar in Amherst, Massachusetts. I met her friends Jessica, Debbie, and this beautiful blonde, Lori.

Lori was sexy, fun to talk to, and knew a lot about sports like she was an analyst herself, so we hit it off. I was married with two kids, so I didn't think about what if, but what I did think about was fucking the shit out of her.

We were drinking and having a good time. Cash and I were paying for the whole night, but Lori kept saying, "I don't need you to pay for me. I got my own money!"

I touched her hand when she went for her wallet and said, "That's one thing I admire about you, but don't look at it like we're paying for you, but like it's the gentleman thing to do."

She smiled, removing her hand from her wallet. She leaned closer as she put her other hand on top of mine and replied, "Thank you very much, and yes, you are a gentleman!"

She stood. "Would this gentleman like to dance?"

"Yes yes, I would," I exclaimed, taking her hand and guiding her to the dance floor.

They were playing Usher's "U Got It Bad," and then they followed it up with TLC's "Red Light Special." It was like the music was trying to tell us something.

Cash was calling me Roc all night, so Lori whispered in my ear while we were dancing and asked, "What's your real name, Roc?"

She grabbed my ass, pulled me flat up against her pelvis, and my manhood was already at full attention. She continued. "Oh, I see why they call you Roc, but if you're going back with me, I'm going to need your real name."

I wasn't with giving people I'd just met my real name even if I was turned on by her, so I replied, "If I tell you, then it has to stay between you and me."

"Agreed!"

"Anthony," I whispered in her ear.

She looked me in my face to see if I was telling her the truth, but I gave no indication that I wasn't and she said, "You look like an Anthony." Then she kissed me, and we made out until "Red Light Special" ended.

We went back to our table and did a few more shots. Jessica and Debbie were with some guys from their school that they introduced, but I didn't remember their names.

It was close to two o'clock in the morning, and it was the last call for alcohol, so we all did another round of Buttery Nipples. Jessica and Debbie tried to get us to go back to their friend's frat house, but both Natia and Lori said they were good. The great thing about that each one of them was the other's roommate, so I would have Lori all to myself.

The four of us stumbled back to the dorms laughing and holding each other up. Their dorm rooms were right across from each other. Both Cash and I were making out with the girls as they tried to put the key in the door. Lori and I fell inside still kissing as I kicked the door close behind me.

We both started removing our clothes at the same time. She took off her pants and had on no panties. I pulled off my pants along with my boxers, and she jumped on me, wrapping her legs around me, and her arms wrapped tightly around my neck, all the while we were still kissing.

I palmed her ass with one hand, and with the other, I unsnapped her bra. I then grabbed my manhood and guided it inside her while we were still standing, and she was so tight and wet. I had to lift her up and down, so I could get all of me in her.

She moaned, "Oh, my god you're so big!"

She held tightly with her face in the crook of my neck as I lifted her up and down. I was digging so deep in her that she squirted on me while her body shook from an orgasm.

She was going crazy, telling me, "Please wait, pleas—oooohhh no, I'm coming again!"

She squeezed my neck so tightly I thought she was going to break it. I walked her over to the bed and dropped her on it. She sat up, grabbed my manhood at the base, squeezed, and took me into her mouth.

I removed my shirt, and she ran her hand up and down my six-pack. I put my hands on my head while she continued to do her thing. I was turned on so much when she looked up at me. I had to take over. She thought her head game was fiery. Well, I knew mine would blow her mind.

I pushed her back on the bed, and her legs were still at the end. I dropped to my knees, then threw her legs over my shoulders, and I started going to town sucking all over her clit and taking all of her into my mouth. I sucked up her juices and then tongue-fucked her.

After the tongue fucking, I locked on her clit, taking the tip of my tongue and wiggling it back and forth slowly at first and then faster. I then inserted my two fingers and started finger-fucking her. Then I pushed my two fingers as deep as they could go and started rubbing the roof of her cave.

That made her go crazy. She squirted in my mouth as I pulled back, and it was like a water fountain.

She held her blanket tight in her grip as her body shook while saying, "Oooohhh!"

I licked up her body to her breast and then made circles around her nipples and then sucked on them before I went face-to-face with her. Her body was still shaking from the orgasm. She shook her head no and couldn't form words.

She extended her arms to my chest and finally said, "Give me a minute, I didn't know my body could do that!"

I smiled devilishly and replied, "Do what?"

"You know what I'm talking about. I never squirted before. I thought I was pissing myself!"

I laughed hard and she slapped me, saying, "That shit ain't funny!"

Instead of replying, I grabbed my manhood and slid it inside her, and she gasped with big eyes and said, "My god!"

I slowly went deep inside her and slowly pulled out to the head, letting her feel every inch of me. I repeated that a few times before I sped up.

I was hitting her G-spot as she started to dig her nails into my back, but I grabbed her hands and pinned them above her head.

After she dropped another orgasm, I flipped her over and started hitting it from the back. After about five minutes from that position, that was when I felt

I was about to climax so I grabbed her by the hips and started slamming her butt into my pelvis.

She moaned, grunting, "Oh, my god not again!"

This time as her body shook with an orgasm, so did I. We both collapsed beside each other, breathing as we had just run a marathon.

We took a few minutes to gather ourselves. Then she broke the ice, "Damn, Anthony, I think that's the best sex I've ever had. My body has never done any of those things before."

I looked at her lying there sexy as hell and replied, "You're not so bad yourself!"

"Oh, that's all! Not so bad!" she said, slapping me with her pillow!

"I put my hand up laughing and proclaimed, "I'm just joking! That shit was the bomb, and you're sexy as hell too!"

"That's better!" she said as she dropped the pillow, snuggling up next to me and kissing me on my neck to my lips.

I got up to go to the bathroom after lying there for fifteen minutes, and I checked my watch, and it was four in the morning.

I cleaned myself up and looked in the mirror with a wicked smile and said, "I have to stop this shit!" I shook my head and walked back into the bedroom.

As I reached for my boxer, she said, "Hey there, sexy, you're not leaving, are you? I want some more of that Roc between your legs!"

She crawled over on all four sexily, and just the sight of her made my manhood stand at attention. I said, "What the hell," and jumped back in bed for round two.

It was quarter to six when I slid from under her, waking her up. I whispered, "I had a great night, and maybe we should see each other again."

She stretched and replied, "I would love to see you again. We have each other's numbers, so call me." She kissed me passionately and lay back down, "Can you lock the door on your way out?"

I locked the door and knocked on the room across the hall where Cash was. He came out already dressed and we were out.

That was the last time I saw Lori. Three months later I was doing ten years in Comstock prison behind Tanya snitching on me.

I came out of the reverie, and I thought about how Lori looked exactly the same, sexy as hell, and now she was the FBI. Boy, my life just got really interesting!

Chapter 23

February 11, 2022

After my reverie, I got back to work with some clarity, and the rest of the day flew by. I was driving home thinking about my day, but most of all, I was thinking about that night with Lori. I thought, *This is going to be a freaky situation because I know they are coming to interview me again.*

I got home and Kim looked exhausted. I put my keys in the basket, and I went to sit next to her on the couch. I kissed her on the cheek, then asked, "How was your day, honey?"

She took a deep breath and replied, "I got heartburn, my feet are swollen, and I'm tired as hell!"

I sat at the other end of the couch and grabbed her feet, so I could rub them. I said, "My mom always said if a woman is having heartburn while she's pregnant, it means that the baby has a lot of hair."

She laughed and exclaimed, "Well, her hair must be down to her butt because I've been having heartburn since the fifth month. She's due in April, and I cannot wait for this to be over!"

I start cracking up, then I said, "Down to her butt!" I chuckled a little more then asked, "How was the doctor's appointment today? Sorry, I should've been there."

"No worries, baby, the heartbeat is strong. She's growing just fine, and Sarah came with me."

"Oh good, how is Sarah doing anyway? I haven't seen her in a while."

"She was going through that divorce with Freddie. She said she's glad it's over."

I turned the TV to CNN to see if there was anything more on my killings. As I watched, they were doing the same segment from earlier.

Kim said to me, "Did you see that, Jamal? Someone is out there killing people that ruin other people's lives. And get this, the girl Tanya that snitched on you was the first one to be killed by this serial killer. How crazy is that?"

I listened to my wife but kept looking at the news. I wonder what Kim would think if she knew it was me and what she thought about why the killer was killing.

She continued. "This has been on the news all day, I mean on every news channel. Jamal, he killed three snitches, two rapists, and one of the rapists was killing kids.

"The killer killed a guy that shot a five-year-old baby, and that cop that killed that black kid with his pregnant girlfriend in the car on their way home from a birthday party. Shit, I think all those people deserved what they got! What do you think, baby?"

And there it was, I thought, the answer to one of my questions. I replied, "I couldn't agree with you more, babe. Those people got exactly what they deserved!"

We sat quietly for a few minutes and watched the rest of the segment. Kim broke the silence, "Oh yea, babe, remember when the cops came in and asked you questions about Tanya?"

"Yea, Kim, I remember."

"As if you would have anything to do with that," she exclaimed as she turned her body around to lay her head on my lap.

Kim gave me an alibi that day I was interviewed. She told the cops that it was no way possible I could've had anything to do with that because I was with her the whole night Tanya died.

Little did she remember that my nights with her were so sporadic. I was coming and going so much during our engagement that she assumed I had to be with her.

Like I said before, Kim never asked where I was going or what I was doing. All she cared about was that I loved and cared about her, and she trusted me.

We left things at that and found a movie to watch. The whole time I was sitting there, I kept thinking about Lori, not the fact that we had an amazing one-night stand but that she was the one trying to arrest me.

I got kind of excited that the Feds were on the case. *Now it's more like a game,* I thought. *The chase is on and I'm not going to stop. People are going to pay for ruining lives, so let's see if they can CATCH ME!*

Chapter 24

Terry

The hour ride with Lori went better than I expected after the encounter with Brenda. I could tell it was on Lori's mind, but the fact that she didn't let it interfere with our day made me like her even more.

When we got to Greenwich, none of the interviews was resourceful. Tanya's parents and kids didn't know much. The only thing her parents said was Tanya kept her life from them, and she always told them everything was okay. It was as far as they could tell.

We asked them about Jamal Stone. All they said was that they knew Tanya testified against him and that Emily was his goddaughter. They met him on a few occasions and he was always polite, and Tanya loved him like a brother. Emily used to go to his house a lot before the incident.

They didn't know before Tanya died if Jamal came around, but after Tanya's death, he would come around to see Emily and still did take her from time to time.

We asked why Tanya testified against Jamal? Mrs. Spencer said that "the police were going to take Emily and Tyler after he was born. Tanya was still pregnant with Tyler at the time, so she did what she felt she had to do."

I finished with a question about Jason, her boyfriend. Mrs. Spencer answered, "They were together for six years. He was good to her but had a little drug problem, so they heard." They brought it to Tanya's attention, and Tanya reassured them all he did was smoke weed.

We interviewed Tanya's friends Ms. Smith, Starback, and Simpson. Mr. Hamilton and Mr. Bennett all said pretty much the same thing. They partied with her mostly, but she spent most of her time home with her kids, and Jason worked a lot.

When I asked them about Jamal Stone, they said that he was cool, and Tanya would always talk about her brother Jamal this and Jamal that, but Jamal never partied with them. But Tara and Stacey had slept with Jamal, and they were very detailed.

Lori asked Tara about the night Tanya was abducted, and Tara said she couldn't tell us much other than she was on the phone with Tanya and that she clicked over, and Tanya never came back. Tanya always did that, so she thought nothing of it.

We interviewed Jason, the boyfriend, and there was absolutely nothing he could help us with other than he came home from work. Tanya left for the store, leaving him with the kids. He took a shower and waited, an hour went by and then two. He then walked to the store while the kids were sleeping and asked the clerk if he saw Tanya that night, and the clerk said no, so he came back, called Tanya's mom, and then the cops.

The last person we had to interview was Jamal Stone, but he lived in Massachusetts, so I talked to Lori and we decided to go see Jamal after the trip to Queens. After interviewing everyone there, no one had anything new to add, so Lori and I went to our hotel room at the Residential Inn.

We went over all our notes again, but so far, we had nothing new. It was ten o'clock when we decided to give it a rest for the night.

My phone had been going off all night, and I didn't answer it 90 percent of the time. I only answered the calls when the other teammates called, once for Naomi and once for Neveah. Lori was being a good sport because she didn't say anything even though she knew it was Brenda I was ignoring.

Lori went to the bathroom with her bag and took a shower. She came out in yoga pants and a T-shirt. I couldn't take my eyes off of her.

She said while jumping under the covers, "This Jamal Stone guy, everyone seems to like him. They say nothing but good things about him, especially Tara and Stacy." She laughed. "It seems like he ruined them girls for real! They're going to compare every lover to Jamal!"

I got up and grabbed my bag to go shower and replied, "Lucky for him, well, he seems to be perfect after doing ten years! I can't wait to meet him." I left Lori lying with her hands behind her head and went to take a shower.

I got out of the shower and left the water running, so I could call Brenda back. She answered on the first ring, "Hello, sexy!"

"Brenda, why are you calling my phone like that? You know I'm working a case." I replied with my voice low and annoyed.

"Well, I wouldn't call like that if you answered!" she spat back!

"What, now all of a sudden, you're blowing up my phone! We haven't spoken in months, and don't say it's about the case because you would have just left a message for me to call you back."

Brenda took a deep breath and said, "Okay, you're right! I was just happy to see you, and I was thinking that maybe we can get together sometime soon?"

"Well, it's not the best time, and last time it didn't end so well between us. I think we should just leave it at that."

Brenda was not used to being put to the side, and her jealousy came out. "Well, I wanted more, and you acted like I wasn't good enough to be in a relationship with, but I was good enough to fuck! Look at me, Terry, I can have any guy I want!"

"And that's the problem with you, Brenda. You're so full of yourself, how can there be room for anybody else?" I replied angrily, getting frustrated by the second!

She picked up on my tone and yelled, "That's bullshit, Terry, and you know it! I wanted to give you me, but I get it now Terry, why so low? And what's that in the background, is that the shower running?"

Sighing with an attitude, she said, "Huh what, in the bathroom, so your new partner doesn't hear you! Is she your new thing of the month, Terry?"

I was done with this conversation and replied, "See it's not like that, Brenda, and if it was, what's it to you! You haven't changed, still jealous, Brenda! I'm done with this conversation!"

I was about to hang up when she said, "I'm sorry, Terry. You know how I am and how I feel about you. Can you please forgive me?"

"Look I got to go!"

"Can you call me when you get time please, Terry?"

"Maybe, I got to go!" I replied then hung up before she could say anything else.

When I came out of the bathroom, Lori was watching CNN. They'd been repeating the conference all day trying to get citizens to be on the lookout. It was just Brenda's questions when I flopped on the bed and sighed as I saw her.

Lori noticed my frustration and said, "That was a long shower."

I knew she wanted to see how I would reply, and by her asking, I already knew she knew.

I replied, "I wasn't in the shower the whole time. I returned Brenda's calls. She was the one calling all day. It's funny because we haven't talked for months, and now she won't stop calling."

"You would think that you guys just stop talking this week the way she was acting by your car."

"She can get very jealous when she sees someone she wants walking with someone else.

"That's why I stopped messing with her almost six months ago. She's self-centered and self-involved." I had to tell Lori the truth if I was going to have a chance with her.

I climbed into my bed and said, "The TV is all yours. I'm going to sleep. We have a long day tomorrow. Plus I want to get to Massachusetts as early as possible to interview Mr. Perfect!"

Lori smiled, turned off the TV, and replied, "Terry, you're beginning to be one of my favorite people."

"You too!"

Chapter 25

February 12, 2022

Lori

This morning I felt great. Terry kept it real with me about Brenda, and I could tell only a good man with some good sex could make a woman act the way Brenda did yesterday. I went to sleep with Terry on my mind.

I woke up at six, got dressed, and then woke Terry up. He looked like he was already up because there was no stretching or morning voice, and he popped right up.

He said, "You're finally dressed."

"Oh what, you were watching me or something?" I replied with my hand on my hip and with a little sass and smirk!

"Or something!" he replied with a smile!

"Well, if that's the case then, I'm going to watch you get dressed, Mr. Sneak Peek!"

"Be my guest!" Terry replied as he got up and broke into a little dance.

"Boy, hurry up if you want to get to mass and interview Jamal!" I said, laughing at his corny butt!

Terry got dressed fast, and we were out the door by six thirty. We went to Dunkin' Donuts, got our usual, and decided to take fifteen minutes to eat.

Terry said, "Kareem's in Marcy Correction, so I think we should start with Anita Thomas, Derek's mother. Then Kerry Hunt, Kareem's mother, Tamara Crane, Kareem's girl, and lastly, we can talk to known acquaintances and get the hell up out of there hopefully before lunch."

I took a sip of my coffee to wash down my bagel and then replied, "Sounds like a plan. Oh, and, Terry, thanks for keeping it real last night. I just don't want anything to do with a deceiving man anymore."

"No problem, Lori. I will always be forthcoming because I'm not trying to play any games. I'm too old for that." We finished up and were on the road a little after seven.

We arrived at Derek's mother's house around nine o'clock. We knocked on the door a few times before Anita answered. I spoke first because when we interviewed women, Terry seemed to think it would make them comfortable faster.

"Hello, Ms. Thomas, I'm Agent Reid, and this is my partner Agent Carter. If you have a few, we would like to ask you some questions about your son Derek."

Anita was dressed in hospital scrubs. She replied, "I just got called in to cover someone's shift. It's my day off, so I can only give you fifteen minutes."

"Perfect, Ms. Thomas."

She led us to the living room, she sat in a chair, and we sat on the couch. I started asking, "Ms. Thomas, before your son died, when was the last time you've seen him?"

"Derek was here the day he went missing. I kept trying to tell him he needed to go back to school and he told me that he wanted to leave the streets alone, so he could be a better role model for his brothers and sister. I was so glad to hear that."

She pulled out a letter. "Look I got this in the mail a week later after he died."

I took the letter and Terry and I looked at it. It was an acceptance letter to Stratford Community College. I asked, "Did you know he wrote a statement and planned to testify against Mr. Kareem Hunt?"

"I knew Derek was dealing drugs, but he was a good boy. He wanted to be down with his so-called friends. When he got arrested, he was locked up for six months, and the detectives came to him with an offer of time served, and if he didn't get into any more trouble, he could have his slate wiped clean under the Second Chance Act.

"They wanted Kareem in exchange for the deal. At first, he wasn't going to do it because he didn't want to be labeled as a snitch. It's hard out here if you're labeled that.

"The detectives assured him that no one would ever know who told them. Derek only knew Kareem from school. They were not friends or anything, but they knew each other."

"Ms. Thomas, who are the other friends that Derek hung around?"

She thought for a moment then replied, "There's Chris Carson, Little Mikey. I don't know his real name, and his cousin Peewee, Kevin Porter."

Terry wrote down the names, and I asked, "Do you have any idea who might want to harm your son?"

"Huh, Agent Reid, we live in New York City. There are all types of gangs, and young people robbing and killing each other, take your pick! I don't know everything Derek was involved with, only God knows. I just hope you catch the person that did this.

"I've seen you two on the news. You believe it's that serial killer? Well, I hope you catch the bastard because my son didn't deserve to die like that."

Anita was a strong woman I could tell, but remembering her son brought tears to her eyes. I said, "I'm sorry for your loss, Ms. Thomas, and thank you for your time. We'll do our best to put your son's killer behind bars."

"Yes, Ms. Thomas, sorry for your loss!" Terry followed up, and we got up and left.

Chapter 26

Terry

We headed to Kerry Hunt's house. She also lived in Queens, and it took us ten minutes. Kerry Hunt was a widower. Her husband Marcus Hunt was a fireman and died in the line of duty four years ago. She used to work at the hospital until her husband's death, and now she sat at home living off his pension and life insurance.

We knocked on the door, and Tamara Crane answered it. She said, "How can I help you?"

"Hi, Ms. Crane. I'm Agent Carter, and this is Agent Reid, is Kerry Home?" I spoke first.

"Yea, she's here. She's upstairs giving the twins a bath. Is there something I can help you with?"

"Matter a fact you can. We're here to talk to Ms. Hunt, and we wanted to talk to you too. Is it alright if we come in, it won't take long?"

We could hear Kerry in the background. She yelled, "Who's at the door Tee-Tee!"

Tamara turned around and yelled back, "It's the FBI. They want to ask us questions about Kareem!"

Lori and I could hear the kids coming, and Tamara still hadn't let us in the house. Kerry said, "Well, let them in."

Tamara let us through, and she led us to the living room where Kerry was. Tamara said to the kids, "You two go to your rooms so Mommy and Nana can talk to these nice people."

Tasha Hunt Kareem's daughter ran over to Lori and said, "We're going to see my daddy today!"

"That's awesome!" she replied, smiling at the little girl, "I bet your daddy will be so happy to see you guys."

Terrell came up, grabbed his sister Tasha's hand as he said, "Come on, Ta, you heard what Mommy said."

"Okay, Rell," she replied and they were off.

I took a seat next to Lori who was already sitting on the love seat. Kerry Hunt was giving me the once over, so I felt that I should take the lead on this one. Kerry said, "What's this about my son?"

"It's not really about your son per se, it's about Derek Thom—"

Before I could finish, Tamara jumped in. "That piece of shit snitch motherfucker! Why would we care anything about him? He's the reason my kid's father is in prison. Did you know Kareem was just finishing college ready to get out the life before Little Man ruined everything?"

Lori and I let her vent because people usually give information in a fit of rage.

I could tell Kerry was undressing me with her eyes. She said, "I know who you guys are! I saw you on CNN about that life-ruiner serial killer. Remember, Tee-Tee."

Tamara thought for a second, "Oh yea, I remember now that you said something. Look I don't think Little Man should have been killed, tortured maybe but not killed! This is New York City tho, and sometimes snitches get stitches if you know what I mean!"

I asked, "Do you know anyone who would retaliate for Kareem and cause harm to Derek?"

Tamara answered, "Kareem did what he did in those streets for school and his family. He didn't want this life for us, so he never hung out with gang members even though he knew them.

"Kareem never chilled with people whose life was on the streets. He had a plan and socialized with people that were going to school with him and his family."

"How did the word get out that Derek was a snitch?"

Tamara answered again, "When Kareem got his discovery, it had a written statement by Derek attached to it. Kareem sent it home to me, and

I posted it all over the internet, like Facebook, Instagram, and this snitch site called 'Can't Trust Them.'"

I looked at Lori to make sure she wrote that website down, which I knew she did. I asked, "Do you know Chris Carson, a Little Mikey, and Kevin Porter nicknamed Peewee?"

"No, should I?"

"Well, do you think Kareem may know them?"

"I wouldn't know, like I said Kareem doesn't hang in the streets."

I could see Lori looking at Kerry staring at me. I called out to Kerry, "Ms. Hunt, excuse me, Ms. Hunt!"

When I finally got her attention, she said, "I'm sorry, what were you saying?"

"Is there anything you can add?"

"Not really, Kareem was going to school and taking care of his twins. I always wanted the twins to come over, but he was always busy and Tamara was working. Now that he's doing time, Tee-Tee and the twins live here with me.

"I hate the fact someone took Kareem away from his babies, but I can't imagine who would kill Derek, but like Tee-Tee said, this is New York City, and snitches get stitches. I do, however, feel sorry for Anita. I used to work with her down at the hospital before my husband died four years ago."

I was done questioning them, so I stood and Lori followed suit and I said, "Thank you, ladies, for your time, and I hope your kids enjoy their visit with their dad."

Lori said, "Nice to meet both of you," and shook both their hands.

I shook both their hands, and Kerry held on a little longer so that I had to snatch my hand back.

We got in the car and Lori was laughing. I said, "Oh, something funny! I felt like she wanted me to get up and start Magic Miking her!"

Lori burst out laughing even harder, and I joined in with her as we drove off to see if we could catch up with the guys Derek hung out with.

We got the chance to see each one of them. They were home asleep. They couldn't tell us anything other than they couldn't believe Little Man was a snitch. When they found out, Derek was already not coming around.

Derek's cousin Peewee said he went to his aunt Anita's house to talk to Derek a week before his death, but he didn't see him after that.

Lori and I had lunch at Wendy's, and we were on the road to North Hampton, Massachusetts. It was a five-hour trip, and it was fifteen minutes 'til one when we left.

Chapter 27

February 12, 2022

Jamal

Sleep didn't come easily last night. I laid awake thinking about Lori and the fact that the Feds were now on the case. I wasn't too worried about them finding evidence left behind because I'd studied and read a lot of forensic books when I was locked up and when I got out. But still it was the FBI, and I knew that they had a few tricks up their sleeves that I may not be familiar with, hence the uneasy night. I fell asleep around three thirty in the morning and had to be up at six thirty if I wanted to make it to work on time.

I got up, took a shower, and got ready for work. Kim was already making my breakfast, a Western-style omelet, sausage, toast, and coffee. I had a feeling that I was going to need a lot of coffee today, and I also considered drinking a five-hour energy drink.

I got to the kitchen and Kim was putting my food on my plate. I walked up behind her and wrapped my arms around her waist and kissed her cheek. I said, "Morning, babe, thanks for breakfast!"

She leaned back and kissed me then replied, "Morning to you too, and you're welcome! A good breakfast makes a strong day!"

I released her and sat at the table while she put my plate in front of me. She made my coffee just the way I like it and said, "Baby, I'm so bored being at home. I can't wait to get back to the hospital."

Kim turned from the stove in haste from making her plate and said,

"Oh, I forgot to tell you what Sarah told me! Dr. Ann Rawlings, the head doctor who does the cancer testing, was discovered trying her own treatments on some of her patients.

"She also diagnosed people with cancer when they didn't have it, then eventually injected them with cancer so she could experiment with her treatment! How fucked up is that? Talking about ruining someone's life, and God what about their family. You have to be a wicked person to do some shit like that!"

I perked up when I heard what she said and replied, "Dr. Ann Rawlings, didn't you introduce me to her at your Christmas party last year?"

"Yup, the one and only Dr. Rawlings. She was arrested yesterday. I was so tired when you came home, and then you were rubbing my feet, thanks very much for that by the way. Then we turned off CNN and watched *Get Out* and then I fell asleep."

I didn't notice anything after the press conference. I totally missed it, I thought. *Wait, I do remember seeing something like that, but I didn't pay it much attention.*

I asked, "Is she still in jail?"

"No, the crazy bitch made bail. I'm glad she didn't do anything to the kids, but still that's messed up!"

"Sure is," I replied, happy that I had my next victim.

It was time for me to leave for work, and I was no longer tired. I gave Kim a kiss and slapped her on her ass. She turned trying to hit me back.

I dipped out of the way, saying, "Too slow, gotta go!" I took off running to the door.

I was energized, and it wasn't the coffee even though that might be part of it. I couldn't help but jump in my car and turn on 2Pac's "Machiavelli". After that, I played 2Pac's "All Eyes on Me" and then "Tunnel Vision" by Kodak Black. I was so alive that it felt like I just came out of a coma.

Work was a breeze. Everyone was on point, and there were no complaints. I was so uninterrupted that I came up with the method of death for Ann Rawlings. I already knew she didn't have a husband.

Kim was always talking about how she needed a man and that she lives up the mountain off Williams Street. Kim would point it out every time we drove up to Jen's house. Jennifer lived twenty minutes away from her. That was what I liked about Jen's. All her neighbors were so far apart, and someone was always building a home out there, so the hunt began.

I was thinking about killing her in her house, but what I had planned needed to be set up. I would start looking for a place this weekend. I would also go to Jen's house a few times this week. I also thought about the note I was going to leave behind for this cancer-giving, life-ruiner bitch.

Work flew by. I got home around five, and the house smelled good as hell. Kim was making her baked chicken with steamed broccoli and rice. She greeted me, "Hey, babe, how was work?"

"It was a smooth day," I replied, giving her a kiss. "Got some paperwork and some planning done."

"Dinner will be ready in twenty minutes. I laid some sweatpants and a T-shirt out on the bed. You have twenty minutes if you want to take a shower."

I smiled. "Damn, baby, you spoil me! But don't you think it's ironic how I left you in the kitchen this morning, and when I come home, you're still in the same place? What, you didn't move all day or something?"

She turned to face me while laughing as she replied, "Don't be silly!"

We kissed again, and I turned to walk away, and she slapped me on my ass, then turned back to what she was doing.

I was laughing as I walked away to go take a shower and said, "You got me on that one, but this ain't over by a long shot!" I could hear her laughing as I climbed the steps.

I finished my shower and dinner was ready. Kim and I were enjoying a quiet dinner when a third of the way through someone was knocking on our door. I asked, "Are you expecting someone?"

"No, babe, you?"

The second set of knocking came as I reached the door, and I wasn't surprised by who it was when I answered! I said, "Hello, Agent Carter and Agent Reid."

They both looked at each other, and Carter replied, "Well hello, Mr. Stone, have we met?"

I smiled and said, "Come in," as I moved and they walked past, "No no not met, but both of you guys are all over the news."

I spoke aloud so Kim could hear me, "Honey, the two FBI agents Carter and Reid are here! You know from that Life-Ruiner Serial Killer case!"

Kim struggled out of her chair and came to meet them. "Welcome, we were just finishing dinner, would you like to join us?"

I spoke before they replied, "I don't know what my wife's talking about, but I'm far from done eating! Her chicken is slamming!"

Agent Reid started laughing while Carter chuckled as he said, "No, we can't. We didn't mean to impose!"

"You're here now, and we won't take no for an answer. We have plenty to go around, and plus you don't want to come between a black man in his chicken!" I replied.

We all laughed at that, and they decided to join us.

Kim set their plates, and we all dug in. I said after a moment, "It looks like you're glad you took us up on our offer."

"Sure am, you were right, this chicken is slamming!" Carter replied.

Reid responded in kind, "Yes, this is wonderful, Mrs. Stone!"

"Thank y'all very much," my wife replied.

I looked at Carter and said, "Who said white girls can't cook chicken, so good make you wanna slap your momma!" everyone laughed.

During dinner, I kept cutting my eyes at Lori as I thought, *Still sexy as hell!* I caught her looking at me a few times with a puzzled look on her face. I thought, *Yea, it's me, Anthony!* But I knew she couldn't place me.

Back then I had a Caesar cut with waves flowing like crazy and a clean-shaved face then, and now I have cornrows and a full beard.

I would not let her look into my eyes too long. I liked knowing she didn't remember, and I did. Shit, it took me a while to remember her.

Dinner was done and Agent Reid assisted in helping Kim clean up. Carter and I went into the living room, and I turned on ESPN. *NFL Live* was on, and they were talking about the draft. Carter and I talked about Dwayne Haskins possibly going to the Giants, and Odell Beckham Jr. being traded to the Browns when Kim and Reid walked in the room.

Reid jumped right in. "That pickup for the Browns is why they're going to the playoff this year. Baker Mayfield is great, and now he has sure hands to throw too."

Kim then said, "Yea well, all that's great, but my Pats can't be beat!"

"Here you go with that shit again!" I replied, waving her off!

Kim and Reid high-fived each other, and they both at the same time said, "Brady all the way!"

They laughed at their timing, and Carter said, "Please don't get her started! Agent Reid is a freak of nature when it comes to sports. She should've been an analyst!"

I laughed. "So is Kim! Why do you think I married her? She's beautiful, laid back, cool, and a sports junkie just like me. Can't find too many like that!"

It was ironic how Kim always reminded me of Lori even though we had a one-night stand. That night though we talked about so much, and sports was what pushed her over the top because Jennifer wasn't a sports fan. She tolerated it.

I thought, *Damn, instead of sleeping with the enemy, I was eating with the enemy, how poetic!*

Carter cut through my thoughts and got down to business. He said, "Thank you for dinner, and your hospitality. Dinner was great, Mrs. Stone. Now, for the reason why we are here if you don't mind me getting to that?"

"Not at all," I replied.

"We came today to ask you some questions about Tanya Spencer."

"I figured as much. You do know that the homicide detectives already pulled me in for questioning?"

"Yea, we know but we are doing our own investigation, and we need to reinterview everyone to try and put the pieces together, so we can catch this guy. So we had to start at the beginning."

Agent Reid kept looking at me, so I kept obverting my eyes. I knew she couldn't figure it out by face alone, but the eyes were a dead giveaway if you looked long enough.

I replied, "Sure, Agent Carter, ask away!"

I noticed Agent Carter looked down at my feet, but I didn't care because I had my slippers on, and it would be hard to judge my foot size.

He looked up and asked, "So, Mr. Stone, how long have you known Tanya Spencer?"

"I met her right before she got pregnant with Emily, my goddaughter, so she was seventeen."

"Can you describe your relationship with her from beginning to end?"

"I met Tanya through an associate of mine. Back then I was dealing drugs. I'm sure y'all know that, and she was doing coke.

"So one night after we met, she came up to me in a bar asking if I remembered her. I told her yea, and then she asked if I would sell to her. So I said maybe, but you'll have to hang out with me tonight, so she did.

"She started making sales for me and made me fifteen hundred that night. I told her that she was an earner, and I would mess with her. We hooked up that night, but since she was going to be working for me, I told her we were better off as friends. I would give her free coke and money, and she kept making me money.

"When she got pregnant with Emily, I made her quit doing drugs. I started treating her like a little sister, and she treated me like her brother. She and Jennifer became good friends, and Emily was always with us. I met Tanya's parents and her friends. I didn't really like her friends too much, but I did spend some time with Tara and Stacy. Everything was great until 2008. She was pregnant with Tyler and she got herself into a jam and used me as a bailout. I received ten years, and she got six months and five years' probation."

Reid was taking notes and still trying to catch my eyes, but I wouldn't let her. Carter's next question was "How did you feel when she testified against you?"

"I was heartbroken," I replied, agitated. "How would you feel if a person you loved, cared about, and called sister set you up and put you away for ten years. I have a family. I was ready to leave the game. I lost my family behind those ten years.

"Thanks to the divine that I still have them and my new family. Kim has been a blessing. Jennifer and I have a good relationship, my boys are excelling, but yea, I was hurt, who wouldn't be. I'm still Emily's godfather.

Kim and I pick her up from time to time, and so does Jen. Jen, Kim, and I help her grandparents."

"Have you seen Tanya since you've been home?"

"No, I haven't. She wanted to see me. Jen and her parents tried to convince me to talk to her, but I couldn't. Emily will always be my goddaughter, and I don't blame her for her mother's actions, but I couldn't see Tanya."

"Mr. Stone, did you have Tanya killed?"

I was shocked that Carter just came right out asking some shit like that. I looked at him appalled and replied, "Hell no! Why would I do that? That would be crazy, and then I would have to look into Emily's face knowing I took her mother from her.

"Of course, I wished death on her for the first three years I was locked up, but I forgave her, so I could have peace with myself. But with that being said, I would never deal with her again."

"I'm sorry if that was a little harsh, Mr. Stone, but there was no other way to ask it."

"Nah, I understand!"

Kim jumped in and said, "That was a little rude, Agent Carter, if you don't mind me saying, but I can assure you that Jamal was with me the night she was murdered, and my husband would never do something like that."

"Like I said, sorry for the harsh question." Carter cleared his throat. "And I guess that answers my last question about your whereabouts on the night Tanya was killed."

I said, "Agent Carter, I don't live in New York anymore and haven't since I came home. I have a good life, good job, great family, and great hobbies."

"Well, thank you for your time and dinner. It was a pleasure to meet both of you," Carter said as he stood up, and Lori followed.

Kim and I stood up also, and we all shook hands. I said, "The pleasure was all ours, and I hope you catch the guy that's doing this because the last thing we need on the street is a sociopath."

I led them to the door and they left.

In the car Lori was beating herself up because she never forgot a face, and Jamal Stone looked familiar. As they pulled off, Terry broke her train of thought and said, "I guess he is Mr. Perfect!"

Chapter 28

February 13, 2022

Terry

I contacted everyone that was on my task force after I dropped Lori off. Everyone was done conducting their interviews. It was eleven in the evening when I hit the bed. Sleep didn't come easy because all mine and Lori's interviews turned up nothing, and I couldn't get the visit with Jamal Stone off my mind.

Jamal's life seems like a happily-ever-after movie. Jamal Stone was the perfect person. Lori was even impressed by him especially after doing ten years in prison. I thought there was something so Medford about him and his wife. After replaying everything in my mind over and over again, I finally fell to sleep around three in the morning.

Lori

I had a restless night. When I got home, I called my sister and then took a shower. As I lay in bed, I thought about the interviews, and I kind of expected them to go that way. Those murders happened years ago. My restlessness came from our last interview with Jamal Stone. I knew other than the case I didn't know Jamal's name, but I had excellent facial recognition. Jamal looked familiar to me, but I couldn't figure out why. It ate at me until I fell asleep around two in the morning.

Terry

I drove to work that morning, and I could tell that when I saw Lori that she didn't sleep much either. I ask Lori, "You alright? You look like I feel. I didn't get enough sleep last night, and to top it off, I didn't have time to stop for coffee."

"I didn't get much sleep either, and I was running late this morning, so no coffee for me either."

We both entered the briefing looking like zombies. To our surprise, Susan brought DDs for everyone. Lori grabs a cup out of the tray as she said, "There is a God! Thank you so much, Susan!"

Susan put her hand on her chest bashfully and replied jokingly, "I never been looked at as someone's god! You're welcome, my daughter! You and Terry looked like y'all was burning the midnight oil!" She eyed us suspiciously.

"Yea well, we got back late, and I had a few things to do before I went to bed." Lori proclaimed as she sipped her coffee.

I didn't reply to Susan. I just let Lori do it because if I would have said something too then they would've thought we were hiding a love affair. So I said, "Let's begin."

Lori and I covered all three murders that happened in New York. Well, almost all three, Renee Baker moved, and we hadn't been able to locate her as of yet. So we just stuck with the files on Simon Tully. But with that being said, no one we'd interviewed could provide us with anything useful, and those were cold cases. So I said, "Let's see what everyone else has."

Susan led the way. She began. "The victim in Bedford, Massachusetts, Mr. Bruce Matthews was a dead end. No one saw anything, and no one cared. They all felt that he got what he deserved. The killer probably picked this one from the media."

Susan flipped to a page in her file and continued. "Next we have Carmela Lopez. We interviewed Rico Sanchez's little brother Corey who was three years younger. Get this, I took a shot into the dark and started asking him about Tanya Spencer and Jamal Stone. At first the names didn't register to him, but then he said that Money used to talk about his cousin Roc and sometimes he would say Jamal.

"He didn't know if I was referring to the same guy, but when he was twelve, he remembered that Rico and Money used to get their coke from Roc, but that was over ten years ago or something like that.

"So I got to thinking that there might be a connection. You know two victims. There might be something there."

Lori replied, "That's good and we won't overlook the possibility. Let's add that to the suspicion of Jamal category. But as of now, that could just be a coincidence." *Damn, it sounds like I'm defending Jamal!*

I chimed in, "We met Mr. Stone, and now we have to keep all avenues open. Jamal landed on his feet after doing ten years. Not saying he's not capable because we're all capable, but I have no indication that he's our guy."

Susan said, "We have nothing so far, so we have to start somewhere, and a connection is somewhere!"

She was right, so I said, "Okay, Susan, we won't rule it out." I turned to Kevin and Gordon, "So what do you have?"

Kevin said, "Pretty much the same. No one has seen or heard anything. Nettie Rogers is glad Way is dead. She wouldn't tell us anything if she knew something, her exact words."

Kevin and Gordon did their interviews on the first day. Kevin thought, *Damn, I wish we did what Susan did, and see if there was some type of connection to the first murder.*

Last was Noel and Jason. They had the most recent case, and they did the forensic, and the questioning of the witnesses. They also were waiting for the autopsy report.

Jason took the lead. "We got the lab and autopsy reports back. The finger marks are as we expected. He wore gloves. These gloves left fibers behind, so we know they are cloth and not latex.

"The indentations on the ground are from a boot, size eleven and a half, and the killer weigh approximately one hundred and ninety to two hundred and five pounds and stand over six feet.

"Other than that, the crime scene is clean, so we know that the killer has forensic knowledge. The cause of death is as the note suggested liquid Drano. The two nails in the chest would have killed him if the Drano didn't. Officer Dawson suffered."

Jason passed the rest of the briefing over to Noel. She began. "We interviewed the neighbors, and on the night of the murder, the neighbor Lucy Strain who live across the street said that she seen a dark-colored car parked in front of the playground, but close enough to Officer Dawson's house. She didn't know exactly what color the car was, but it was dark.

"She knew Mrs. Dawson left for her mother's because they're friends and they talked. She assumed it was someone visiting. When she got up to go to the bathroom around one, she looked out the window, and the car was still there. The next morning it was gone."

It was a little after eleven, so I said, "Alright, we have to come up with something, so if you want to miss lunch, dinner, and sleep, then we need to come up with something to track this sociopath."

We all sat for a few minutes thinking of ways to approach the situation to get out in front of it. The truth of it was we had nothing to go on or any idea on how to go about it. We all shot ideas out there, but none of them would seem to get us on the right track.

At a quarter 'til two Noel came up with something we could work with. She said, "Maybe we're looking at this all wrong on how to catch this guy."

She had all our attention, and Lori asked, "What do you mean the wrong way?"

"This killer is targeting people who he believes have ruined someone's life. So he's doing research and looking for victims.

"Right now, he's only killing in surrounding states, so let's see, we have three kills in New York, two in Mass., one in Connecticut, and one in Vermont. The only place in our geographic circumference left is New Hampshire. So what we should do is conduct our own search using social media, and the news in all these states."

I thought about that for a second then said, "Noel, you're definitely on to something. Lori and I just got this website called Can'ttrustthem.com. It's a snitch list. This is a great idea, Noel!"

I took a few minutes to write some things down then continued. "Okay, people, this is how we're going to do this. Everybody does the search in their states. Noel and Jason do Vermont and New Hampshire. Oh, and Kevin and Gordon do New Jersey too.

"Do a list and compile notes, and we'll have a meeting every Monday at nine sharp, any questions?"

There wasn't any and I said, "Good shit, Noel! Everyone, get to work and see you on Monday. And if you guys come up with anything, I want to be the first to know about it.

"Meeting was over, and everyone left. Lori stopped me and said, "I'm tired as hell. Do you mind if we start fresh tomorrow?"

"That's cool because Neveah has a piano recital at six. I'll go and then crash. You down with breakfast in the morning?"

"Sounds good to me. Enjoy the recital!"

Chapter 29

February 16, 2022

Jamal

The rest of the week flew by, and I'd been to Jen's three times. Every time I passed Dr. Rawlings's house, there were news reporters all around. The East Hampton police were there to make sure nothing went wrong. I was surprised Dr. Rawlings didn't put up a gate to seal off anyone from being permitted on her property, but hey, good for me.

On Thursday I slow down to watch the commotion. Ofcr. Frank Mason was there to keep an eye on the situation and keep traffic moving. I stopped to ask Frank what all the commotion was about, and he replied, "Did I live in a cave?" I told him that I didn't know this was Dr. Rawlings's house.

Frank was a big fan of my son Jermaine, and he asked, "Is Jermaine going to enter the NFL draft?" I told him, "I didn't really know, but the last I talked to my son. He told me he wanted to finish school and enter later." Frank was surprised but said, "Good for him." I guess Frank thought all black kids wanted to go to the pros if they had the chance.

The police in this neck of the woods knew me very well. When I first started coming up here, they pulled me over regularly. I would sometimes leave Jen's late because I was always there with my boys when they came home, but now it didn't matter what time I would drive through, I was never bothered.

Today both my boys were coming home for their mother's birthday, and Jen invited Kim and me over. My boys and I used to throw Jen surprise birthday parties, but she always hated them. Since we've been separated she hasn't had one. Now she just has a small gathering with us and her friend Tracy.

We arrived at noon, and the boys and Tracy were already there. We walked into the house into the living room, and Jen and Tracy were chatting away. I said loudly, "Happy birthday, old woman!"

"Oh, go to hell, Jamal, like you're not older than me!" she replied with her middle finger!

"Happy birthday, Jen!" Kim said.

Jen got up, went over to Kim, put her hand on her stomach, and said, "Damn, girl, you're about to pop." She hugged Kim, "Thanks for the b-day wishes, but who cares!" She released her. "I'll be twenty-nine until the day I die! I'm just glad that I will never have to go through being pregnant again. You can have that! Shittttt, I remember those days."

After Jen said what she had to, Kim turned to Tracy and said, "Hello, Tracy, how have you been?"

"I'm good. When are you due again because you look like you're due any day now."

"April 20 and it can't come fast enough!" Kim exclaimed, and the ladies laughed as she took a seat on the couch.

I broke in and said, "What's up, Tracy. Did Preston come home with Jermaine?"

"Yea, all the boys are in the basement studio. They were there all morning. Preston slept over last night, so I didn't see him until I got here."

"Shit, they were there in the studio all night too!" Jen chimed in.

"Well, boys will be boys." I gave Kim a kiss on the cheek, "I'll leave you ladies to your girl talk, and before I forget, what time is the food getting here? I know Jen catered!"

"Damn right I did! My boys are grown, and my cooking days are over, and if I get a new man, his ass better know how to cook or his ass is out the door." The girls started laughing, "There's finger food in the kitchen if you're hungry now, but you'll be lucky if there are any wings left! You know your sons and Preston, they can eat you out of house and home if you let them, and that includes you too! Anyway, the food will be here at four o'clock."

"Cool!" I replied as I headed to the studio.

When I entered the studio, Jamal and Preston were at the mixing board, and Jermaine was in the booth rapping. They both turned quickly when I entered the room, and Jamal said, "What up, Dad?"

"I'm good. I see y'all doing your thing?"

Preston said, "What's popping, Mr. Stone! Maine's doing his thing. I go next!"

I'd been listening from the time I came in, and after Preston said that, I focused on what Jermaine was saying. Then I replied, "Yea, Jermaine sounds good, and that beat's fire!"

Jamal said, "It better be fire! We been up all night mixing it!"

Jermaine finished with his bars and took the headphones off to come out of the booth. He said, "What's popping, Dad?"

"Yo, those bars are fire!" I said, slapping hands and then hugging.

"Thanks, Dad! The beat we just mixed had been in my head all week, and Jamal and Preston put the final touches it needed, and I already had the bars."

Jermaine sat at the mixing board with Jamal and Preston, and I waited until Jamal did a few more things. I knew enough about what they were doing to put the song together. Back in my day when I was in the streets, I messed around with some trying to be artists, and my boy Cash used to produce them.

After Jamal was done, Jermaine took the headphones and listened to what they put together so far. Jermaine was bopping his head, saying, "Yeah, boy, that's it. This shit's fire!" He took the headphones off and handed them to me, "Dad, listen to this!"

I put them on and he hit playback, and the song came to life with Jermaine speaking, *"I'm no street nigga, but I'ma nigga with game! I know y'all see me, but y'all don't know what it's like to be me."*

Then this fire beat dropped then Jermaine spat the chorus, *"My game is tight /when I'm on the field everything feels right, / but the fame ain't free, / y'all don't know what it's like to be me!" /*

Then a few seconds of the beat, then his verse dropped, *"I never been in the streets so I don't know what it feels like, / but the words come easy every time I pick up the mic / when I'm on the field everything is in slow motion. / I'm cutting in dipping flying by, / and when I catch a touchdown, it's like a crackhead getting that first high, / but I love this music shit /. Laying bar is better than fucking the baddest chick, / but y'all don't know what it's like to be me. / People are chasing me for an NFL deal, / y'all hear me on this mic you*

108

can tell I got mad skillz, / so my decision is made, / college I will stay because the tuition is paid!" Then the chorus came back.

Preston said, "Yo, that shit is hot" as he took off the other set of headphones!

"Jermaine, you did your thing, my boy! Y'all did a great job on that beat too!" I said happily, glad my boys were working together on this project.

Jermaine poked me and said, "Dad, I'm finishing school. I already told Mom!"

I knew he was referring to the decision he made about the NFL draft. I replied, "Jermaine, it's your future, but I am proud of the decision you made. It shows what type of man you are, and what type of man you will become." I hugged him.

"Thanks, Dad!" We released then he said, "Oh yea, Dad, we're shooting a video for this song using some of mine and Preston's touchdown highlights, but we have to wait until Jamal finishes his final. We're gonna shoot it after the semester is over."

Preston was in the booth, and Jamal just finished prepping. He clicked on the intercom and said, "We're ready, Preston, but give me a few so I can talk to my dad!"

Preston gave him a nod, and Jamal turned to me. "So, Dad, I got this concept for the video in my head, but this final is kicking my ass. I got the bugs almost figured out, so I should be ready to test it."

I had no idea what he was working on, so I said, "I know you thought you probably told me what you're working on, but I don't have the slightest idea."

"Oh," Jamal replied while chuckling, "that's right I haven't told you. It's a 3D X-ray video camera that can see through solid objects like through walls into someone's room.

"You can adjust it, so you can get a clear shot of what a person is doing behind that wall, shooting a feed to my monitor, but I'm also trying to make it go to my phone. My problem for the phone is creating an app that would receive the feed."

I couldn't believe what I was hearing. I thought, *This boy is a fucking genius, especially if he's saying what I think he's saying, and not for nothing, but he could solve one of my problems.*

I said, "Let me get this right! If I was standing outside your mom's house and pointing your camera at it, I could see what's going on inside?"

"Exactly, it would start out as an X-ray. You could see the structure of the house and the skeleton of the people moving around inside.

"But when you adjust it, you'll be able to see as if you were standing in the house recording clear as day. I'm calling it an Optimal Visual Display, OVD for short."

I was blown away by his invention. I was so excited that I gave him a dap and held on to his hand, pulling him into a hug while saying, "Son, you're a fucking genius!" I let him go. "I'm going to come up to the school next weekend, and take a look at it. If you don't mind? You know I'm always interested in what you and Jermaine are up to."

"Nah, Dad, I don't mind at all. I'm trying to get it to have a range up to fifty yards. Right now it's at twenty-five, so come on up!"

I grabbed both of my boys and said, "I'm so proud of both of you! What role models your baby sister gonna have." I let them go. "I'll let y'all finish up, and remember dinner is at four, and then we have to cut the cake."

I told them both again how proud of them I was and left to go back upstairs.

When I got upstairs, all three ladies were laughing and drinking wine. I hated coming in at the tail end of a joke, so I said to Kim, "Your one glass so early?"

"Yea, but I'll have a half a glass at dinner. It's Jen's birthday, so I don't think Evelyn will mind."

Jen turned to Kim. "You didn't tell me you already named her!"

"Yea, girl, Jamal and I came up with it Monday night, so I figured I'll tell you at your birthday dinner."

"Well, that's a beautiful name!"

I took a seat and said, "So what's the joke I missed?"

They started laughing again, and that gave me the feeling that the joke could've been about me. Tracy was the first to regain her composure and said, "Lady talk remember, Jamal! If you were here, then you would know!"

"If I was here, then the joke probably wouldn't be told!"

They all start laughing at me, and Kim touched my face and said, "Oh, baby, the joke is not on you!"

There was a slight pause, and Jen said, "No, Jamal, it's not on you. It's about you!" The girls all burst out laughing again.

Now, not believing anything they were saying, my nostril started flaring because I hated being the butt end of someone's joke. Kim and Jen knew that meant I was getting mad.

Jen said, "Calm down, boy! I was just telling them about the time when we had our cats before the boys, and you were running through our little apartment, and you went to turn the corner into our bedroom, flew in the air, landing half on the bed, falling off into my vanity mirror, and you laid there checking to see if you were still alive."

I smiled, chuckling remembering that incident and said, "I didn't think those damn wooden floors would be so slippery!"

They started cracking up and I joined in as I said, "Plus, how did I get into the bedroom flying at that angle anyway?"

We all burst out laughing harder. I was in stitches, and I knew they were too.

After some small conversations, Jen broke in, "You guys see the commotion at Dr. Rawlings's house? What a crazy bitch to do that to those people! Hey, Kim, that's the hospital you work at, right?"

"Sure is! I was just telling Jamal about that this morning."

Tracy jumped in, "The system ain't shit! They even gave her a reachable bail! I'm a criminal lawyer, and I'm surprised! See, someone like that, you couldn't pay me enough to represent."

"You guys heard about that life-ruiner serial killer?" Kim asked.

Jen and Tracy replied at the same time, "Sure did!"

Tracy continued. "Now, I would represent a guy like that. The system really is letting people get away with some bullshit or setting a bail that some rich crazy motherfucker can make. Shoot, if you ask me, those people are getting exactly what they deserve.

"I mean I don't think snitches truly deserve that kind of fate but rapists, people killing kids, and that cop!

"Now come on, that kid Strong wasn't doing anything wrong, and that cop killed him in front of his pregnant girlfriend! Like for real y'all what is this world coming to?"

Jen said, "I wouldn't be surprised if she's on that killer's hit list. If I was him, that's who I would go after next!

"And about snitches, I'm not going to lie, when Jamal went to prison I wished nothing but death for Tanya in the beginning. It even took me longer than Jamal to get over it."

She looked at me. "What, Jamal, it took you like three years or something like that?"

"Yea, three years!" I replied, trying to keep my mouth shut and listen to how the women in my life felt, and I was pleased with the feedback.

Jen continued. "It took me five years. Tanya kept using Emily, trying to make peace. Jamal and I kept telling each other that we couldn't blame Emily for her stupid-ass mother, so eventually I started picking Emily up again. I love that little girl as if she was my own."

Jen sipped her wine then continued, "One time I went to get Emily, and she begged me to let her explain. Even though I didn't give a rat's ass what she had to say, I let her.

"From a mother's perspective, I understood, but I said to her, 'Jamal looked at you like a sister, and you took him from his family.' I told her that Jamal knew the consequences of his actions, and you knew too. But out of all the people Jamal dealt with, not in a million years he thought it would be you to get him locked up.

"As I was about to walk out the door, I said to her, 'You took the best man anyone of us would probably ever know out of our lives with betrayal,' then I left."

Jen took another sip of her wine. "But I didn't want her to die. But these snitches are ruining people's lives, and they don't even think about the other people affected by it."

I thought, *It's too late for Tanya now and all the rest! Thanks to my son's invention, Dr. Rawlings will be victim number eight. And now I have a great lawyer I could use if anything happens.*

I kept money in my safe inside my bunker game room below Jen's garage just in case of an emergency. I saved almost one hundred thousand dollars from online betting and poker.

It was four o'clock, and Patty's catering service was on time at the door. I was hungry as hell, and Jen ordered all the soul food a man could ask for. I said to no one in particular, "I'm going to bust all that down, and I don't think I'm going to have room for cake."

Jen replied still, "You can just take the cake home."

I open the basement to the studio and yelled, "Dinner is here, and if you don't want me to take it home with me before y'all get some, then you better bring your asses!"

I heard some moving around, and then I saw the first face. Jamal had the lead and here came the stampede. Jamal could have been a basketball or football star, but he chose games and electronics. Cool, whatever floats his boat.

I said as they passed me, "Whoa, whoa, boys, don't kill me trying to get to the food!"

Jermaine stopped hard in front of me and handed me a CD they burned of the song and said, "Dad, you got the first official copy of 'Be Me'!"

I took it as I replied, "I'll bang this hotness every day, all day! Consider this my new anthem!"

We all sat down and tore into the food. Kim had her one-third glass of wine and ate as much as us men. We also shared with the family that we were naming the baby Evelyn, and everybody loved the name.

It was a great feeling to have the people around me that I love the most laughing and talking. After the meal, we sang happy birthday to Jen, and she cut the cake, then opened her presents. It was a great day indeed!

Chapter 30

February 16, 2022

Terry

I've been spending a lot of time this week with Lori, and even though that time had been focusing on work, compiling a list of targets consisting of snitches, rapists, or anyone we could find that ruined someone's life, it had been great working next to her.

As far as work, no one was off-limits to the search, government officials, cops, regular Joes, and even agents of the FBI. Lori and I shared breakfast, lunch, and dinner all week. She slept over a few nights, and I slept over at her house once.

I could tell that she was feeling me, and I knew I was feeling her. We focused on getting what we needed to be done for work, so we could do a day-to-day check on the targets we compiled. By Friday night, we had everything in order.

One pile was of snitches, and there were over four hundred names throughout the State of New York. Another pile was of sex offenders. There were fifteen hundred with priests and city officials among them. We even compiled a list of freed felonies with shootings, gang members with victims that were tragically injured, and so on. There were so many possibilities that the list felt endless.

We narrowed it down to three years prior to February 15, 2022, and the list was still long. We still got it all done, and I was glad too because I have plans with Neveah Saturday and Sunday.

I slept in until nine in the morning and got up to take a shower. While I was taking a shower, I thought, *I'm glad Lori agreed to spend the weekend with Neveah and me. Damn, this is a big step for me. I've dated women in the past but never had them interact with my daughter, not even Brenda. Brenda would've been the one if she wasn't so full of herself! And the fact that she really wasn't about kids and just her career ruled her out. Not being about kids is a no-go for me. Lori on the other hand always asks about Neveah and wants to meet her. Lori's future plan was to have kids in a family. She even said, she wants a girl and a boy and be married. Now that's what I'm talking about.*

I finished showering and got out. I had lunch plans with Neveah. I was taking her to the new Dave and Buster's, and this was going to be Neveah's and Lori's first meeting. I wanted a cool place to break the ice and what better place than Dave and Buster's. I got dressed and left to go pick up Neveah at her mother's.

I pulled up at eleven o'clock and then knocked on Naomi's door. Vincent, Naomi's new husband, answered, "What's up, Terry, how's it going?"

"Everything is fine, Vincent. How are you?"

He let me pass. "Good. I saw you on the news. You're working on that serial killer case," he said, snooping for information.

"Yea, I'm covering the case but not at liberty to discuss it."

Vincent yelled up at the steps, "Neveah! Your dad's here!"

Naomi yelled back, "I'm almost done with her hair!"

I hated waiting around. Vincent always wanted small talk, and just like I was afraid of, he said, "My mother is taking Racheal and Derrell, so you're still going to be available for April 25 to take Nevaeh for Naomi and my trip to Jamaica? You know, with everything going on with your case."

I was annoyed by that statement as I thought, *Nothing short of death would come between me and my daughter, and he knew that!* So I replied, "Vincent, you know for a fact that I don't break plans with my little girl, so you can count on me always being there for her."

"My bad, Terry, I didn't mean to imply anything."

"It's cool!" I said. I wanted this guy to just go away.

Just then my angel came down with a big smile on her face with Naomi in tow. Neveah said, "Hey, Daddy" she hugs me, "So what's the surprise? Where are you taking me?"

I smiled when she leaned back with her hand on her hip and the look of a grown woman. I replied, "If I told you, then it wouldn't be a surprise, now would it?"

"I guess not, Daddy!" She took the keys out of my hand and kissed her mom, "Bye, Mom, bye, Vincent! I'll be in the car, Daddy!" and left for my car.

Naomi looked at me and shook her head. I said with a raised, sarcastic tone, "What?"

"You know what, Terry! You're spoiling her to death! And when she comes home and can't get what she wants, she always says Daddy would let me! You only have her a few days out of the week."

I was taken aback by what Naomi just said because I didn't have the slightest idea what she wanted. So I asked, "What do you want me to do about it?"

"Just talk to her, Terry, about the differences, explain to her about appreciating all parts of her life!"

"Will do and I will try to make her next recital on Wednesday the twenty-sixth." I turned and left.

When I got in the car, I asked Neveah, "You wanna drive?"

Her eyes lit up and replied, "Can I, please, Daddy?"

"You sure can, baby, in about another three or four years!" I answered while laughing!

She slapped me on the arm playfully as she said, "See, Daddy, you play too much!"

As I was pulling out of the driveway, she turned the radio on and Alissa Cara's "Scars To Your Beautiful" played out of the speakers. She was singing it word for word. I thought, *Damn, my baby sounds like she could do this professionally!*

After the song was done, I turned down the radio and said, "Baby girl, you sound good!"

"Thanks, Daddy!" she replied, bobbing her head.

Changing the subject, I said, "Hey, pumpkin, I want to introduce you to one of my friends today. Her name is Lori Reid, and she's going to join us."

She never met any of my friends, so she was used to always being the only girl in my life. She always told me I needed to meet somebody. She replied, "It's about time, Daddy! Is she your girlfriend?"

"You know I always keep it real with you, so I would say this. I would never put any woman before you, baby, and you know that, right?"

"Of course, Dad, but you need a woman!"

I started laughing, shaking my head as I replied, "Ha ha ha very funny!" I settled with a smile. "But anyway, funny pants, I'm very interested in her, and I believe she likes me just as much. She's also my new partner at the FBI, so with all that being said, are you cool with meeting her?"

She crossed her arms and started tapping her chin as if she was in deep thought, then snaking her neck, she replied, "Huh, let me think about it, Dad, yea! I want to meet her! If you like her, and you want us to meet then she must be cool. Oh, and let me guess, she likes sports too like us?"

"Wow, I got a feeling that I may be left out!" I answered jokingly!

We both start laughing as I pulled into Lori's driveway.

Chapter 31

Lori

I watched Terry, and his daughter Neveah pull into my driveway. I was standing in my doorway because Terry called to tell me he would be there in twenty minutes, and as I grew to know him, he was always on time. However, he was five minutes late, but I knew he was picking up his daughter.

This was a big step for me to meet his daughter, but I liked Terry a lot so I wanted to take this step forward. When he first asked me, I wasn't so sure. I'd spent a lot of time with him in these last two weeks. I started catching feelings for him, and I knew he was feeling me too. I started getting turned on around him the more time we spent together.

He was a fine-ass brother, and I wanted to fuck the hell out of him, but I had to maintain my composure. I could see a life with Terry, and meeting Neveah meant more, so here we were.

I shut my door, and as I approached the car, I could see the lust in his eyes. I mean I wasn't wearing anything sexy. I had on a pair of Jordan 3s, dark-blue curve-fitting, boot-cut women's Levi jeans, and a black waist-length leather jacket with a pea collar and a leather strap belt tied in front. Now that I think about it, Terry never saw me with my hair done. I had it in a wrap style in my hair hung to the lower part of my shoulder blades.

When I got to the car, Neveah got out of the front seat and said, "Hi, Ms. Reid, it's very nice to meet you!" Neveah put her hand out.

I thought, *What a beautiful and nice little girl*. I shook her hand and replied, "It's very nice to meet you too, Neveah. I heard so much about you from your dad. You're so beautiful. I've seen pictures, but they don't even compare."

"Thank you, Ms. Reid, and you're beautiful too," she replied then climbed in the back seat.

I sat in the front seat and closed the door. I turned around and said to Neveah, "You can just call me Lori. Ms. Reid is my mother."

"Okay, Lori."

I turned my attention to Terry and said, "You're late, so you owe me fifty push-ups!"

Terry laughed as he replied, "What! That's not my fault! That's miss cutie pie in the back, she had to get her hair done! She owes you fifty push-ups!"

"What!" Neveah snapped with sass. "No way, Dad! Don't blame me for your clock being off!"

"She's right, Terry," Lori defended her. "You can't blame her for your poor calculation, so I will be cashing in later!"

Neveah and I laughed at Terry, watching him shake his head. He said, "What have I done! You two gonna be ganging up on me now? Pumpkin, you're supposed to be on my side!"

"Dad, this is 2022! Woman power all the way!"

I start cracking up, thinking, *I like this little girl already!* I turned to Neveah, giving her a high five and said, "That's right, girl! I think I just found my new bestie!"

I turned to Terry sticking my tongue out, and Terry started laughing.

Halsey's "Without Me" came on the radio, so I turned it up and said, "This is my song!"

Neveah said with excitement, "Mine too" and started singing!

We were singing together, and I noticed that this little girl could really sing.

I noticed Terry looking from me to Neveah while we were dancing and singing together. I could tell he was happy that Neveah and I were hitting it off. A couple more songs played then we pulled into Dave and Buster's.

Neveah was looking out the window as she said excitedly, "Daddy, no way! I can't believe we're going to Dave and Buster's! My friends and I were just talking about coming here. They opened last week.

"Tasha, Liz, and Becky were talking about coming here this weekend. Maybe we'll see them here?"

"Maybe!" Terry proclaimed.

We got out of the car and went inside. Everyone could tell that this place had a family atmosphere. Neveah asked me, "Lori, could you take a picture of me and my dad in front of the Dave and Buster's sign?"

"No problem." I took her phone, which was an iPhone 10, "Dang, Neveah, your phone's better than mine!"

"It's nice, isn't it? My dad got it for me last weekend! I'm the only one in my school that has it."

I took the picture and showed Neveah. "Nice," she said, "now you and my dad!"

I thought, *This little girl has won my heart* as I snuggled next to Terry in a tight hug, and we faced the camera. The top of my head came to his bottom lip.

Neveah stepped back a little and said, "Cute," then snapped the picture.

She looked at the picture and said, "Dang y'all look good together, Daddy!"

She brought the phone to show us, and I thought, *Damn, Terry is sexy as hell* as I replied, "It is a good-looking picture!"

"Hey, Dad, now take one of me and Lori!"

Terry took the phone while Neveah and I posed, and Terry snapped the picture. He looked at the picture and said, "Y'all both are so beautiful! I'm so lucky!"

He handed the phone to Neveah, and we both looked at it. I thought, *This little girl is so beautiful, and if Terry and I had a baby, I wonder what he or she would look like.*

Neveah said, "Lori, we look good!"

"We sure do!"

Waiting to be seated just like us was a lady and her two children, whom I believed were her kids. Neveah went over to her and said, "Excuse me, ma'am, can you please take a picture of the three of us?"

"Sure, young lady," the lady replied, then Neveah handed her the phone.

Neveah got between her dad and me, and we posed for the picture. The lady took the picture, looked at it, and handed it back to Neveah. Neveah said, "Thank you so much, ma'am!"

"No problem, sweetie, you guys are such a beautiful family!" she replied and then went back to her kids.

It was another five minutes before we were brought to our table. On our way to be seated, Neveah started uploading her pictures to her social media. I looked around and the place was huge.

I turned and leaned toward Terry and said in a low voice, "She is such a sweetheart and so well mannered. Good job, Mr. Carter."

"Thank you, but I can't take all the credit."

"Well nevertheless, she's a sweetheart!"

When we got to our booth table, I sat next to Neveah and said, "Can you send me those three pictures?"

"Sure can! What's your phone number?"

I gave Neveah my number and said, "Save it and call my phone, so I can save your number if that's cool with you!"

"Most definitely!"

We saved each other's numbers, and she sent the pictures. She finally looked around and said, "Dad, this place looks great. I'm so glad we came here!"

There were so many games to play all over, and so many prizes were hanging up behind the ticket counter. The waiter came to our table, we ordered drinks, and the waiter went to get those before we ordered.

I could see that Neveah was ready to bolt out of her chair and go run around. She asked, "Dad, can I go play some games?"

"Tell me what you want first!"

"Dad, like you don't already know! I want grilled chicken with no bread or toppings, french fries, and a strawberry milkshake!"

After Neveah told her dad what she wanted, I asked her, "Do you mind if I join you? I want to play Whac-A-Mole, and Dance Revolution!"

"That's cool, Lori, I love Dance Revolution! Come on!"

I turned to Terry and said, "Can you please order me the grilled salmon and french fries!"

"For you two lovely ladies, anything, but what about me? I want to play some games too!"

"Dad, just find us when you're done ordering!" Neveah replied and we were off.

Chapter 32

Terry

When Lori came out of the house with her hair done, she was breathtaking. She was beautiful, but at that moment, she had my heart skip a beat. The way she and Neveah clicked right from the start, I knew she would be the one for me. They were singing and dancing and talking to each other like Lori had known her since she was born.

The way she held me during the picture Neveah took of us, it felt like a perfect fit, and we looked as if we belonged in a happy-ever-after movie.

Everything was going great. When we got to the table, Neveah couldn't wait to run off and do her thing. But when Lori asked her to go play games with her, I could tell that Neveah liked her very much because they didn't hesitate to leave me with the ordering duties.

When the waiter came back to take our food order, he chuckled and said, "Oh, I see the ladies couldn't wait and stuck you with the ordering detail!"

I chuckle with him while replying, "I know right! That must happen all the time here!"

"Yea, it kind of does, but it's usually the other way around, and it's sons and fathers!"

I gave the waiter our orders, and he left. I got up and went looking for my two ladies. I found them at the Dance Revolution game. Lori and

Neveah were on their third game, and people were watching. I thought, *Damn, they're killing it! I just might've hit the jackpot with Lori!*

The looks on both of their faces as they danced together, money couldn't buy. I watched for another five minutes before they were done.

When they got off, I said, "You two looked like y'all been playing that game together forever!"

"I know," Lori replied. "After we passed the first game, we were in sync, and that game is a workout!"

Lori turned to Neveah and said, "Girl, you got energy for days! You don't even seem tired or even winded for that matter!"

"I'm not tired! Shoot, I'm just getting started! After I eat, I'm going for the rest of the time I'm here! I'm going to try to play all the games even the stupid ones!"

We got back to our table and the food was being set up. We sat down at the table and Neveah said, "Lori, that was fun! My dad has two left feet and is always trying to do the backpack dance!"

Lori laughed. "No, he doesn't." Lori looked at me. "Please tell me you don't be trying that little kid's dance!"

I started laughing as I got up, replying, "What you mean! I look good doing the backpack!"

I busted out and started swinging both of my arms in front of me, moving my hips side to side, and after three or four swings, I moved one arm to the back and kept one in the front, swinging them and rotating my arms from back to front while my hips were still moving. It was a sight and I knew it wasn't right, but I was being funny. Neveah and Lori burst out laughing!

Lori was trying to catch her breath as Neveah said, "See what I mean, Lori! One time he dropped me off at school, and I was meeting my girls in the front of the school, and he yelled, 'Neveah,' so me and my girls turned around, right. Then he yelled, 'Love you, honey,' and started doing that thing he calls the backpack.

"My friends were cracking up while I was embarrassed. My friends talked about that all week, and they still bring it up!"

Lori and I were cracking up. I laughed even harder because I remembered that. Lori said to me as she caught her breath, "Why you embarrass her like that!"

"I'm her dad! I'm supposed to embarrass her," and I got up again and started doing the dance!

Other families were looking at me, and the kids were laughing. Neveah and Lori looked around and Neveah said, "See! He's so embarrassing!"

Lori grabbed my arm and said, "Cut that out, Terry. You're embarrassing both of us now!"

I was cracking up thinking that was what I wanted as she pulled on my arm, sitting me down. But I kept getting back up doing my dance.

I said, "I'll stop if you take back your fifty push-ups!"

I still had all the kids laughing all over the restaurant, and Neveah was trying to hide her face. Lori exclaimed, "Okay, okay, you win! Now sit down!"

I took a bow to the other tables and then sat down. Then Neveah and Lori hid their embarrassment by eating their food.

As we were eating, I saw Tasha, Liz, and Becky walking up to our table. When they arrived there, Neveah picked up her head and they all freaked out!

All the little girls said in unison, "Hi, Mr. Carter!"

"Well hello, ladies!"

Neveah cut in, "Lori, I want you to meet Tasha, Liz, and Becky! These are the friends I was just talking about! Girls, this is Ms. Lori, my dad's new girlfriend!"

I saw Lori blush at the new girlfriend comment as they said, "Hi, Ms. Lori, it's nice to meet you!"

Lori shook their hands one by one, saying their names, "Hello, it's nice to meet you too!"

After the introduction, Becky turned to Neveah and said, "We called your phone an hour ago to see if your mom would let you come here with us."

Neveah picked up her phone and looked at it, and then replied, "Yea, I see that I have two missed calls from you and Tasha and a text from Liz. I'm sorry I didn't get it, girl, but I was on Dance Revolution with Ms. Lori!"

Tasha chimed in, "Anyway we saw your dad doing that dumb dance, and we knew you were here!"

The three girls laughed, and Neveah cut her eyes at me and then turned to Lori and said, "See, Lori, what I'm talking about, EM-BAR-RAS-SING!" Lori laughed!

Liz asked Neveah, "You want to come with us?"

"Dad—"

Before she could ask me, I said, "Go ahead, we'll come find you when we're ready to go!" She hugged me then Lori and left with her friends.

After the girls took off, I turned to Lori and said, "I see that you and Neveah are hitting it off!"

"What's there not to like? I mean she's well mannered, fun, and very sociable. Second, she didn't give me that who's-this-with-my-daddy crap, so all in all I like her very much."

I heard my phone ping, and I thought it was about work, but when I checked it, it was a text from Brenda. I read it to myself, *"What you doing sexy, wanna have dinner tonight, and have me for dessert!"*

I couldn't believe the nerve of this woman, and to make matters worse, she texted me a few more times, but I didn't answer. Neither did I tell Lori who it was.

I could tell that she saw that I was annoyed by the text. She asked, "What's up, Terry, is it work?"

I didn't want to lie, but I also didn't want to put a sour taste in her mouth. Brenda's timing sucked, not that I would be interested in talking to her anyway, but today was such a great day with Lori.

I replied, "No, not work." and left it at that because I didn't want to spoil the day.

I changed the subject and said, "Are you okay with going to the mall? Neveah wants to see the movie, *Alita: Battle Angel*."

"I plan on spending the whole day with both of you, so I'm down for whatever!"

I was glad she didn't question me about changing the subject, and we continued to have a great day. We talked for a little while longer, then I paid the bill, and then we went to find Neveah.

Neveah was at the prize counter cashing in her tickets. She had enough to get a black light. Her friends were standing with her when Lori and I walked up.

I said, "Neveah, cool prize! It's three fifteen, and *Battle Angel* starts at three fifty, we should get going if we want good seats."

"Okay, Dad!"

Tasha said, "Dang, Neveah, I want to see that movie too!"

"Yea, me too!" Liz and Becky said at the same time sourly.

"Well, I'll see if my mom will take us tomorrow!" Becky said to the girls.

Neveah gave her friends hugs and said, "I'll call you tomorrow, and if the movie is good, maybe I'll come with y'all if my dad doesn't have plans for us."

"Okay," the girls said and we left.

We got to Crossgates Mall, and the ticket line was long for *Battle Angel*. I was so glad I paid for them online. I bought three tickets knowing Lori would join us. We had good seats because the online ticket line was short, and there were only like twenty people that went in ahead of us. We watched the movie, and it was great. It was over at six fifteen.

We got home from Crossgates Mall quarter to seven. On the way home Lori and Neveah had a great time talking about where Lori was from, her sister and brother, and friends. They also talked about Neveah's grades, her friends, and what she wanted to be when she grew up. They were best friends when we got to the house.

We all went into the house and kicked off our shoes at the door. After kicking off our shoes, Neveah said, "I'm going to my room, Dad. I texted Tasha and them, and they want to Facetime. Oh, and I'm going to print out the pictures we took so I can put them in a frame."

She turned to Lori. "I had so much fun today, and I'm glad my dad likes you! I never met any of my dad's other girlfriends, so you must be special!"

"I had a great time too, and it was really nice meeting you!" Lori replied.

Neveah took off upstairs, and Lori turned to me, "So I'm special, huh?"

"Maybe!" I replied as I started walking away.

Lori followed me into the kitchen and said, "Neveah just said she never met anyone else, how come?"

I grabbed a Corona and asked, "Would you like one?"

"Sure."

"You want a lime too?"

"That's the only way to drink a Corona, and don't ignore my question, Terry!"

"I'm not!" I replied as I pulled the Grey Goose out of the freezer. "I want you to try something first!"

"What?"

I pointed at the bottle just above the Corona label and said, "Drink this to here."

As she drank the beer, I cut the lime, poured two shots, and then I did the same. I poured the two shots into the Coronas and handed one to Lori.

"Plug it with your finger and turn the bottle upside down," I said.

We both did it and watched the bubble rise to the bottom of the bottle, then we flipped it right side up, and put the limes in. Lori said, "What is this going to do?"

I gave her a devilish grin as I replied, "Drink it then ask me later!"

We moved to the living room, and I said, "To answer your question, I don't just bring anybody around my daughter.

"She has to learn that everyone isn't always welcome to the things or people you hold close to your heart, and I hope when she starts dating at the age of thirty—"

Lori broke out laughing and said, "Thirty, yea right!"

"Well, a man can dream, can't he?" I replied, laughing.

"That's right, buddy, dreaming! You see how pretty Neveah is. I wouldn't be so surprised if she didn't have a little boyfriend already!"

"Lori, don't make me go to her school and shoot a kid!" Lori burst out laughing!

"Like I was saying, when she is thirty—"

Lori burst out laughing again, and I smiled as I said, "Stop, Lori, I'm serious!"

She laughed even harder as she said, "I'm so sorry, Terry. I guess it's the alcohol!"

"Anyway," I said with playful sarcasm, "I hope she doesn't just bring home any Tom, Dick, or Harry to meet me or her mother!"

Lori was still laughing, and I pulled her by her legs close to me and started tickling her, saying, "Something funny?"

She shifted, trying to get out of my grasp as she replied, barely able to form words, "Stop-p-p! I can't breathe-e-e. I'm extremely ticklish!"

I stopped and as her laughing slowed down. We gazed into each other's eyes, and at that moment, time stood still.

She adjusted her body and met me halfway with a passionate kiss. As I kissed her, I thought, *What a perfect moment! Our day was incredible, and her lips are so soft!* During that kiss, I felt like time didn't exist until we heard someone clearing their throat.

We looked up and Neveah was standing at the entrance to the living room. She was smiling with one of her little hands on her hip and said, "I'm not interrupting, am I?"

We both sat up on the couch as if we were teenagers and just got caught by our parents. I replied, "Nah, baby girl, it's all good! What's up?"

"Well, I just got off Facetime with Becky and them, and they want to know if I could go to the mall with them tomorrow at one? Becky and Tasha's moms are going to be with us, and Becky's mom will drop me off at Mom's when we are done."

"I don't see a problem with that. I'll call your mother!"

"Thanks, Dad! Can I have some money to go?"

"I'm only giving you fifty dollars."

"That's cool, Dad. I'm out, so y'all can get back to y'all . . ." She made kissing sounds and then ran off.

Lori shook her head while laughing and said, "She is something else!"

"That's my baby!"

Lori looked at her Corona, and it was half gone. She looked back at me and said, "What the hell, Terry! You slipped me a Mickie or something!"

I laughed knowing she was loaded and replied, "Nope, it's the mixture! One gets you tipsy, and two is what happens in Vegas stays in Vegas!"

"You must be right because I'm only halfway through the first, and I'm already in Vegas!"

She smiled devilishly, "Oh, I see you're trying to take advantage of me, aren't you?"

I started to reply but before I could say anything, she jumped on top of me and started kissing me again.

When she pulled back, she answered her own statement, "Not if I beat you to it," and she was kissing me again!

Chapter 33

Lori

Damn, I had a great day with Terry and Neveah. That little girl has won me over, and her mannerism was a direct reflection of her dad, which made me like him even more.

We got back to the house after the movie, and Neveah left us and went upstairs. I asked Terry a question, but I thought he was trying to avoid it. I followed him into the kitchen, and he pulled out two Coronas and some Grey Goose.

He handed me a Corona and asked me to drink a little. After I drank it to the top of the label, he poured the Grey Goose into my Corona. I was confused, wondering what the hell was he doing.

However, after I drank half of it, I was tipsy as hell. I'd never been tipsy after one drink, let alone a half a drink. All I knew was that it was some good shit.

We were kissing on the couch, and Neveah walked in and caught us. We felt like teenagers getting caught by our parents. After she left, I couldn't wait to jump on him again, and I did!

We kissed for a while and then we separated. It was getting late, and I was tipsy as hell. I could tell Terry was buzzing too.

He said, "If you want me to take you home, then now would be the time!"

I thought, *There is no way I'm leaving tonight!* I bit my lower lip and replied, "Do you want me to go home?"

Terry just shook his head no, came in for a kiss, and I thought, *Damn this brother is fine and this man can kiss, and he tastes good as hell too!* He was kissing me, running his hands all over my body. I was horny as hell.

Terry stopped and said, "Let's go upstairs. Neveah's bedroom is down the hall from mine and on the other side."

I hopped up, downed the rest of my drink, and so did Terry. I led the way and Terry followed, grabbing my ass on the way up.

We were giggling, and shushing each other as I said in a low voice, "I have to go to the bathroom."

"Okay, I'll go check on Neveah."

I went to the bathroom because that drink had my bladder hurting, plus I wanted to freshen up a little. I thought, *The things women go through!*

When I was done, I went to the room. The lights were dim and Terry was already there naked waiting for me, and it was cool because I had a towel on but nothing else.

He said, "Neveah is out like a light!"

Terry thought as Lori dropped her towel, standing naked in all her beauty, *Damn she's sexy as a motherfucker! I love how her hair cascades over her shoulders toward the front caressing her breast!*

Terry was standing there looking at me with lust in his eyes. I couldn't help but take him in too. He was amazingly fit for thirty-six, caramel complexioned, chiseled chest, six-pack, muscular legs, tight ass, and his manhood was above average probably eight inches. I thought, *I could love this man!*

I walked slowly toward Terry and when I reached him, he took me into his arms, and we started kissing passionately. He grabbed my ass with both hands with a force of control but pleasant and lifted me up with such power he had me filled with ecstasy, I just wanted him inside me.

I wrapped my legs around him, sliding down into position while we continued to kiss. Terry turned me toward the bed and laid me down gently while he stayed on top kissing me.

He started kissing down my neck, sending chills down my spine. Then he moved to my breast, taking one hand and cupping each breast as he took them into his mouth.

My nipples were hard as he sucked on them. He then took his hand off my breast, supporting himself on his elbow while continuing to suck on my nipples, moving his other hand down to my wetness and moving his fingers expertly. This had my body going crazy, and I could feel my first orgasm coming on, but then he stopped. I thought, *No, keep going!* But I didn't say that.

He kissed down to my belly button and continued south. He was an expert as I felt an orgasm rising, then he stopped again, changing what he was doing.

When he went back to where I was about to climax, I moaned, "Right there, Terry! Right there!"

He maintained his rhythm, causing me to release. It wasn't the orgasm that was building up, but it was still good.

He kissed back up to my lips and kissed me passionately. He entered me and started making love to me.

We forgot about protection, and at that point, I didn't care because he felt so good. I moaned, "Oh, that feels so good!" His rhythm was so good that it brought me to an orgasm.

I was a little more than tipsy that I was still ready, so I took over. I climbed on top and said, "My turn, baby!"

I never liked leaving my lover unsatisfied so I took control until he moaned, "Damn, girl, I'm about to cum!"

When he climaxed, we did it together, and our bodies shook as we lay there hugging up enjoying the orgasm.

After a minute of breathing heavily, he said, "Damn, Lori, that was good as hell!"

"I couldn't agree more!" I replied with labored breathing!

We lay there as I thought, *It was good but we could've done so much more. Maybe he was holding back because it was our first time!*

Then I thought about Anthony when I was in college. *He was the only one that made my body do the things it did. I hated comparing every lover to him, but Terry is a good lover, and as he gets to know what I like, he'll be the perfect man for me!*

That was the last thought I had as we both drift off to sleep.

Chapter 34

February 18, 2022

Terry

It was a great morning for me. After the amazing sex with Lori on Saturday night, we woke up Sunday morning having breakfast with Neveah and hung out for a couple of hours. Lori and I decided after Neveah left we would do some work and then spend the rest of the day together, so at ten o'clock, Lori used my car to go home to get some stuff.

Neveah and Lori hugged each other, letting each other know that they had a fun time hanging, and they were looking forward to spending more time together. I hung out with Neveah a little while longer. She told me Lori was cool, how much she really liked her, and she hoped I'd marry her one day.

Before she left with her friends, I gave her a hundred dollars instead of fifty and told her not to tell her mother. I contacted Naomi and told her that Neveah was going with her friends to the mall, and Becky's mom would drop her off after they were done.

When Lori came back, we did some work putting a list together of likely and unlikely victims. Then we had dinner and spent the rest of the evening together watching movies and making out. Later on, we went to bed, and the sex was even better than the first night. After she fell asleep, I watched her a little, thinking, *Damn she's beautiful! I'm so lucky!* Then I fell asleep.

On the way to work this morning, we stopped at DDs and got our usual and were in the office by eight thirty. Lori was glowing as we walked into the building, laughing.

When we entered the briefing room at a quarter to nine, everyone was already waiting. I said, "Good morning, everyone! I hoped everyone had an eventful and good weekend?"

Everyone looked back and forth from Lori and me, and Mark replied with a smirk, "It looks like you had an eventful weekend!"

I saw Lori looking bashful, and I cut my eyes at Mark. I said, "Mark, what are you implying?"

"Everyone at the same time said, "Umm-huh!"

"Whatever!" I replied, "Let's get down to business!"

Susan couldn't help herself and said, "Looks like y'all already got down to business!"

Everyone laughed, including Lori and me. I smiled as I said, "Anyway, Susan, I'll let you get that one, but on a serious note, did everyone receive my texts about the most likely victim's scenario?"

They all nodded yes, and I continued. "Lori will cover our most likely."

Lori started to say, "When we compiled our list of possible victims using the MO from the previous victims, along with other reasons he would think someone has ruined someone else's life, the numbers were large.

"So we narrowed it down, removing people that were already convicted, people in jail waiting to be prosecuted, and people outside the five-year mark. Then we narrowed it down to within three years prior to February 15, 2022, and then took the most likely targets. I know we've texted everyone throughout the weekend on how we isolated our targets."

Lori turned on the overhead projector and posted our top 10: three snitches, (1) Mike Tomlin Lake George, NY, (2) Tamika Sneer Bronx, NY, (3) Lorenzo Rodriguez Yonkers, NY; three rapists, (4) Monty Walker Hudson, NY, (5) Keith Keller Albany, NY, (6) Dennis Sharper Amsterdam, NY; one man for vehicular manslaughter who killed a seventeen-year-old while drunk driving, (7) Baxter Sawyer Catskill, NY; wrongfully convicted a man who was murdered in prison, (8) Jdg. Martin Richard Salem, NY; officers who killed three people on a drug raid where no drugs were found, (9 and 10) Ofcrs. Mark Fuller and Britney Brick Newburgh, NY.

Lori said after giving them a few to look over the list, "These are our top 10, and we will be giving everyone a copy of these names to be on the lookout. We're also contacting all local police in each area to keep a close eye on these individuals. Go ahead, Susan and Mark, you're up."

Susan took the lead and said, "We compiled a list of only five because Massachusetts holds on to their highly regarded suspects, and if they deem a crime is severe enough, then making bail is next to impossible. Commonwealth, got love 'em!"

As Susan was talking, Mark put the list of their five targets up on the projector: two snitches, (1) Bobby Trainer Pittsfield, MA, (2) Kevin Curry Lawrence, MA; a mad doctor giving her patient cancer, (3) Dr. Ann Rawlings East Hampton, MA; a rapist, (4) Phil Carson Concord, MA; a man suspected of killing his wife and son, (5) Mitchell Planter North Adams, MA.

Susan gave everyone a few and said, "That's all we got for now, and we already contacted the locals to put surveillance on these targets."

Everyone else did the same thing for their targets, and in the end they had a list of forty-two most likely targets.

It was twelve thirty-five in the afternoon when I said, "Good, everyone already contacted the locals. As you do more research on possible targets, add them to your list and contact the locals. This just might work if we can guess the target before he selects them. Alright, people, good work, same time next week."

Everyone was gathering their things when I remembered and said, "Oh, one more thing if you come across anything that you believe we should have an emergency meeting about, contact me and we'll go from there."

The meeting was finished, and Lori and I left back to business as usual. As we were walking, Lori stopped and said, "Terry, do you think we covered every possible angle. I just feel like we're missing something."

I took a deep breath and replied, "I'm not going to lie. Our direction has more holes than the Grand Canyon! This killer leaves us nothing or any clues to point us to him. I mean all the clues are so spread out that we don't know our asses from our faces!"

We got to our desks and got to work.

Chapter 35

February 23, 2022

Jamal

My week was great. It always seems that way when I had a target. Everything just felt in tune. Other than Justin Prior crashing the forklift into the stock shelves, work went by smoothly. Kim and I had been relaxing, having a lot of sex, and I even took off Wednesday to go to the doctor's appointment with her.

Jen was so busy at work that she was never home when I went over. Every time I drove to Jen's, I checked for the reporters at Dr. Rawlings's house. They were dying down, and by Friday they were nowhere to be found, even the news on TV moved on to other stories.

I started buying supplies for Dr. Rawlings: duct tape, three knives that I sharpened so they could cut through raw meat with ease, five jars of hair perms from five different stores, and last twenty ultraviolet (UV) floodlights and metal stands I could clamp them to. I already had a generator, so the power wouldn't be a problem.

I didn't worry about the place for her demise. I figured I would pick the place closer to that time, plus there were a few homes being built up that way maybe ten minutes from Jen's house so it was only a matter of time.

The newspaper said she wasn't scheduled for court for four more months, so I had until June, and by then Evelyn would be born.

I hit the gym all week. All five days I was up and ready to hit the gym by quarter to six in the morning, there by six and done by seven fifteen. I then came home showered, dressed, and at work by eight.

I also spoke with Jermaine and Jamal all week. Jamal and I made plans for me to come up on Saturday at one, which was today. Damn, I loved it when everything was aligned. I'm an hour away from Jamal's school MIT in Boston to spend the day with him and looking at his invention the OVD.

I pulled up to the house Jamal shared with his two roommates. They both go to MIT with him, but they studied different things. I parked behind Jamal's Lexus and got out. I walked up to the front porch and rang the doorbell. Jamal's roommate Justin Pratt answered the door.

Justin was a white kid from Freehold, New Jersey. He said, "Mr. Stone, how have you been? Jamal told us you were coming today."

I shook his hand then replied as I walked by, "Yea, he told me about his OVD, and I wanted to see it. It sounds like pure genius!"

Justin yelled from up the steps, "Jamal, your dad is here!" He turned back to reply, "Jamal is a very smart guy. He figures everything out if you give him time. Shoot, sometimes I have to ask him to help me look at some of the projects I am working on."

Jamal came downstairs with his camera, thirteen-inch monitor in hand, and Corey Tran, Jamal's other roommate was behind him. Corey Tran is an Asian kid from New York City.

Jamal said, "What's up, ad, see you made it on time? I was just upstairs on my computer working on the algorithm for the app to transfer the video feed to my Galaxy X Samsung phone. I know I will have it worked out by the end of this week.

"I did, however, got the camera to see over fifty yards away, but that includes the length of the house."

Before I had a chance to respond, Corey said, "What's up, Mr. Stone? Jamal's camera is dope! Last night we tried it on the Alpha Delta Sigma sorority, and this thing is the best invention ever! Those sorority girls be wearing next to nothing around their house!"

"Is that so Corey!" I replied with a smile.

Jamal's roommates knew I was cool as shit, so they never hid anything from me. I turned to Jamal and said, "What do you think Shelby would think about you doing that, huh?"

Shelby Lane was Jamal's girlfriend from London. They had been together since his sophomore year, and she was a hottie! She was here on a scholarship, and she was also an electrical engineer in her junior year. She was five feet eight inches with mocha skin and naturally curly hair that came to her shoulder blades. She had a curvy, slim-fit frame.

Jamal and Jermaine had great taste in women just like me. Jamal replied, "Go ahead and tell her. She was with us when we did it!"

I put my hand up for a high five as I said, "That's what I'm talking about, son!" Jamal slapped it. "It's amazing when your girl wants to join in the fun and games! That means she's a keeper!"

Just as I was finishing, Shelby came down the steps and said with her British accent, "What fun and games, love? And how come I wasn't invited?"

Shelby saw me standing in the living room when she came completely around the corner and continued, "Hello, Mr. Stone, I didn't know you were here yet! Sorry I missed Jamal's mum's birthday party.

"I just had so much work to do on my final project. It's not easy like one, two, three like it is for Jamal," she said, looking into Jamal's direction jokingly with a sarcastic smirk and tilt of her head.

Jamal caught the sarcasm and replied, "Don't do that, babe! You're more brains than beauty, and that's a hell of a lot because you're more beautiful than a motherfucker!" He kissed her.

She pulled back from his kiss and replied, "Quite the charmer, aren't you? That's why I love you!" She pecked him on the lips.

I asked Shelby, "Are you coming with us, so I can see the camera work?"

"No no, Mr. Stone, I had enough of spying on naked girls last night. I have to get back to my flat to get ready to meet the girls at the mall."

She turns to Jamal and kissed him once more and then said, "I'll see you later, babe!"

She turned to me and continued, "Always a pleasure, Mr. Stone! I'm always glad to see what Jamal's going to look like when he gets older! Such a hottie!" She grabbed her bag and said, "Bye, guys," and left.

We loaded up my new 2022 Chevy TrailBlazer and headed to the dean's house on campus. The dean's house had a lengthy front yard probably a little over an acre. Jamal knocked on the dean's door, and he came right out and walked with Jamal toward my truck.

Dean Stan Riley was in his sixties and heavy in the belly area with thick cheeks but handsome in that graceful kind of way. He loves Jamal because he's been on the dean's list since his freshman year.

Stan arrived at my car, and I rolled down my window. He said, "Well hello, Jamal, it's really nice to see you again. It sure is cold out here, but at least it's clear."

"Good to see you again too, Stan. How's the wife?"

"She's good!"

"You're right though, it sure is cold, but we're not going to be out here too long. I have a pregnant wife at home, so I gotta get back soon."

"Oh, that's right, Jamal, here is about to have a little sister soon. When is Kim due?"

"April 25 and we named her Evelyn."

I turned to Jamal and said, "Why don't you go set up, and I'll be there shortly."

Jamal, Corey, and Justin left to go set up the camera forty yards away from Stan's house. I hopped out of the truck, and we continued our conversation.

Stan said, "That's a beautiful name. I bet she's going to be just as smart as your other two."

"Well, that's kind of you to say, Stan, thank you. Oh, and thanks for letting us use your home." I replied, wanting the interaction with him to be over.

"Anything for Jamal. He's going to be graduating from MIT at the top of his class, and he's probably going to win first place for his Optimal Video Display . . . Well, I'll let you get to it. Again, it was nice seeing you."

"You too, Stan!" I replied and he walked to his house and me toward the boys.

When I got to Jamal and them, everything was ready to go. Jamal started hitting some buttons on his control panel, and a few seconds later, Stan's house was in a skeleton view.

I could see everything Stan and his wife were doing and going. It was like looking at an X-ray in motion. It was amazing. Jamal then hit a few more buttons, and the view on the monitor came in as clear as day as if I was watching them on TV. I said, "Damn, Jamal, that camera is the shit!"

"I know, right!" Corey proclaimed, shaking his head with a silly smirk on his face. "Jamal, show your dad the heat-signature mode."

Jamal hit a couple more buttons, and sure enough, the heat signature popped up and we could see Stan and his wife's body heat signature walking around on the monitor.

Jamal said, "It even has night vision!"

I was happy as hell with what my son just invented. I said, "Show me how this works?"

This was how I learned all the tech-savvy stuff I knew because Jamal always showed me the ins and outs of all the technology I came across.

Jamal handed me the controller and started pointing to a button that would maneuver the camera. As I was working it, Jamal said, "I can apply the technology to any size camera."

I turned with big eyes and asked, "So if I had a minicamera, you can program it to feed into my computer at home?"

"Sure can, and as soon as I finish writing the app for the phone, it will be able to feed to your phone!"

I was blown away by what Jamal created. I thought, *My boy is smart as hell!* Ask Jamal about English, history, or art, and he would look at you like you have five heads, but math, physics, electronics, or anything about any type of science, he would know all of it.

We were done so we packed up the equipment and loaded the truck. I had a long drive back, and it was almost three when we got to the pub in Boston. We ordered wings, fries, and a few beers. We talked and laughed then we left.

I dropped them off at five fifteen, and when they got out to unload the truck, I told Jamal to hold tight and said to Justin and Corey, "Can y'all please unload while I talk to Jamal?"

"Sure thing, Mr. Stone, and it was cool hanging with you!" Justin proclaimed.

"Yea, Mr. Stone, it's always cool chilling!" Corey followed up, and they both got out to unload.

I focused back on Jamal and said, "Look, son, I want to use your OVD. Can you hook it up to my computer in my bunker? I want to be the first to use your invention, and I also want you to know how proud of you I am!"

"Thanks, Dad, and that will not be a problem. Shelby and I are going to Mom's in two weeks. We're going to this technology convention in Springfield, and I'll set it up then.

"I should have everything working to full specs way ahead of my final schedule. I'll call you that Sunday so you can come over. I still have the extra pod key, so if it's okay, I'll just go in and do it."

"That's cool," I replied then I changed the subject, "You know that CD you and Jermaine made? I've been bumping it since I got it last week!"

"That shit fire! I got people asking me who that is, and when I tell them it's Jermaine and Preston, they all want copies. So I been selling them for five dollars."

"That's my boy, make that money!" I replied, rubbing his head!

Jamal was about to get out of the car but then turned back and said, "Oh, before I forget again, I'm going to London after the semester for two months with Shelby. Her parents said I'm welcome. They want to spend time with their daughter."

I exhaled then replied, "That's great, just don't end up in one of those hostile movies! You know how those Europeans get down!"

We both were laughing as Jamal said, "Dad, you're crazy as hell! Don't worry I'll push Shelby into their arms and run like hell! Shit, she's from there!"

We both started cracking up even harder as we both dap-hugged and said "peace" at the same time! I thought, *Damn, that boy's funny as hell, like father like son!*

I wasn't too keen on him going so far away, especially overseas, but I wanted him to know the world as I did. He also knew that I knew he would lay his life on the line for Shelby, and that was for damn sure because he was a Stone. We ride for ours. I took off hoping I could make it home before eight thirty.

Chapter 36

March 1, 2022

Lori

Two weeks flew by for me. Terry and I had been spending a lot of time together personally and professionally. I loved the beginning, you know getting to know him on both levels, and he was such a great father.

But I knew after this case if we were going to keep seeing each other, we couldn't be partners or vice versa. I had to let it go for now because we were no closer to catching this killer than we were when assigned this case.

I knew we had workable profiles on the targets, so getting ahead of this guy was very possible with a stroke of luck. I also knew we had nothing on a possible ID or even a suspect.

Terry and I were working a regular nine to five, Monday through Friday a week until something would happen. That was the shitty part of this case because we had no other choice but to wait until then because we had nothing.

I had thought a lot about Jamal Stone since I met him. I kept trying to place his face but nothing. Maybe I was mistaken about the possibility of knowing him, and he just had one of those faces.

I went to visit my family last Saturday, and I told them about Terry and Neveah. They were very happy for me and wanted to meet them. I told them that they could meet after the case was done because we were so busy, and there wasn't time. Well, that was the excuse I gave them, so they wouldn't keep asking.

Early this week I talked to Jessica, and she suggested that we get together with the girls and had a night out because we hadn't seen each other in a while. Jessica Gonzalez was my sexy crazy Latina friend, who couldn't keep a man to save her life. She worked at Locke and Martin as a financial advisor.

Jess said that our other friend Debbie was down too. Deborah Canyon was thicker with curves. She worked for National Bank as a corporate manager.

After I agreed to the outing, I remembered that I made plans with Terry, so I asked if it was alright if I brought him with me. She was cool with it but then brought up a memory from college about when Natia brought her friend Cash and Roc to the Monkey Bar.

I thought about Anthony as soon as she said it, then out of nowhere, I remembered that in Jamal's file, his alias was Roc. Then I thought that Roc was a common nickname in the streets, so I left it at that.

I asked Jess if she talked to Natia about the night out. She told me that she hadn't called her yet. I told her that I would call Natia and told Jess that we should meet at O'Riley's Bar and Grill. They had pool tables.

Natia, our other friend, was the tallest of us all. She had hour-glass curves and long silky black hair. She was a black beauty queen that could have been a model but went into law and now worked for Jacobs & Turner Law Firm.

Wednesday night after Terry and I had sex, we were lying in bed talking. I asked him if he wanted to go out Friday night to O'Riley's and meet my friends. He was cool with it because he didn't get Neveah until Saturday at eleven, which was perfect because we could sleep in.

Friday was here and we were finished with work. Walking to the parking lot, I said, "Terry, can you pick me up at nine from my house? I want to pack a bag for the weekend if that's okay with you?"

"What do you mean okay with me," he replied with a smile, "your stuff is already mixed in my laundry. You practically live there!"

I put my hand on my hip, sassing my head as I replied, "Oh, is that a problem!"

"Hell no, that's not a problem! Shit, you can move all your stuff in if you want!" he proclaimed as he grabbed and kissed me! Then we got in our cars and left.

As I was driving home, I couldn't help but keep thinking about Jamal. It was still eating at me, so I made a mental note to look up Jamal's mugshot and rap sheet from 2008. Now that I thought about it, that was around the same time I met Anthony and Cash.

I got home around six and took a bubble bath. As I shut my eyes, relaxing and thinking about how long it had been since I saw my girls. I reminisced about when I met Anthony.

I watched as Natia's friends Cash and Roc came into the Monkey Bar. I knew Cash was Natia's man because he was light-skinned and fit the description she had explained. Roc on the other hand was fine as hell, a mocha-complexioned brother dressed in a pair of black Levi's, an all-white button-down Shawn Jon shirt, all-white air force ones, and an all-black Yankee fitted hat.

His jewelry was shining but not loud. He had on a black Movado watch, a black diamond chain with a black cross, and black diamond earrings. I thought they were fake until he told me that the chain and earring cost eighty-five grand.

He was so sure of himself, cool, and such a gentleman. There wasn't a dull moment, either we talked about sports or our aspirations.

I remember dancing to Usher, TLC, and the sex, oh my god! I still couldn't find anyone that ever made my body do and feel the way he did, I mean my vagina squirting like that, and I thought I was pissing myself. It was the first and only time that has ever happened.

Terry was a damn good lover, but Anthony was everything you would want in a man. I thought for sure he was going to call, but then he disappeared. When Natia asked Cash about Roc, Cash just said that he was going to be gone for a while and left it at that. I never saw him again.

I snapped back to my bubble bath, checked the clock, and realized I'd been soaking for half an hour. I pulled the plug and turned on the shower.

After washing up, I put on my bathrobe and wrapped my hair in a towel. I then turned on some music, allowing Jhené Aiko's "B.S." to set the mood, while I laid out my casual wear for the evening, and packed my bag for Terry's.

I got dressed then blow-dried my hair and styled it in a wrap because that was the way Terry liked it. I was all set as I stepped in front of the mirror. I wore my camel and brown Louie Vinton sneaker, black-fitted boot-cut women's Levi's jeans, and a camel-colored sweater knitted to let air circulate. It was a perfect look for a night out with the girls.

It was eight thirty when Terry called telling me that he was ten minutes out. I hung up and put my bag next to the door then checked my phone. Earlier I tried to call Natia, but she didn't answer so I left her a text.

Natia texted back: **yea girl I need a night out! Shawn wants to come, is that cool?**

Me: **yea it's cool. Terry is coming, and who's Shawn?**

Natia: **a guy I've been seeing for the last three months I think it's getting serious.**

Me: **Cool, can't wait to meet him.**

I heard Terry pull up, and ten seconds later, he was knocking on my door. I shouted, "The door is open!" I was upstairs checking on my finishing touches.

I came down the steps, and Terry was standing in my living room. I couldn't help but notice how fine this man was. He wore quarter-length black and gray Polo canvas shoes, Black Dave Hollister jeans, and a gray V-neck thin sweater. All you could see was the top of the V-neck because he had a black pea coat on. He must have just gotten a haircut because his waves were flowing, his lineup was sharp, and his beard was trimmed to perfection.

Terry held up a bottle of CÎROC Red Berry and said, "The last time I was here, I saw a bottle of Sprite in your icebox, so I figured a drink before we left?"

I grabbed the bottle as I replied, "Very observant, what are you FBI or something?"

He grabbed and kissed me and then said, "Yea, but I'm also CBU!"

I looked at him like what the fuck does that mean. I asked, "What in the world is CBU?"

He smiled and answered, "Crazy 'bout you!"

I kissed him while laughing because that was some corny but cute shit. "What, did you just make that up?" I asked as I walk to the kitchen with Terry in tow.

"Sure did, beautiful!"

We took a shot and then left for O'Riley's.

Terry and I walked into O'Riley's, and I spotted Jess and Deb already at a table next to the pool table. I walked up to them, and we all hugged each other screaming in excitement. Deb picked up her head, and right on cue, Natia was there to share in the hugging and excitement while Terry and Shawn watched.

Shawn was a very slim-fit black guy with a light fade. Shawn leaned over and said, "Girlfriends." He turned completely toward Terry and reached out his hand. "Shawn Casey."

"Terry Carter," Terry replied, shaking Shawn's outreached hand.

I turned from my girls and put my arm around Terry and said, "Girls, this is Terry." Then I pointed to each one of my girls. "Terry, this is Natia, Jess, and Deb!"

Natia also introduced her date as she put her arms around him, "Everyone, this is Shawn. Shawn, the girls and this one is Lori." She was pointing at me!

My girls were about to order drinks when I said, "Wait, wait, I want everyone to try this new thing Terry just taught me with the drinks. Trust me it's going to be easier on our pockets."

I looked at Terry, and he was smiling as he said, "Giving away trade secrets, are we?"

I started laughing as I replied, "Trade secrets, you should trademark this shit!"

Terry was laughing as Jess jumped in, "Now I have to try it! What is it?"

"It's better if I just show you," I proclaimed. "But before you order any more drinks, you have to finish this one!"

The girls looked at each other, and Deb replied, "Deal!"

All the girls agreed then I turned to Shawn and asked, "Are you in?"

"I'm game!"

I ordered six Coronas, six shots of Grey Goose, and a plate of limes. While waiting for the drinks, Natia said, "Let's go pick some songs on the jukebox!"

"Cool," Jess replied, "I hope they got some decent songs to choose from!"

I turned to Terry, giving him a kiss then said, "I'll be right back, babe. Don't you boys get into trouble while we're gone!"

"You're all the trouble I need," he replied, and as I started to walk away, he slapped me on my butt!

As we were picking the songs, I looked back over to our table and saw Terry and Shawn getting along, and it made me smile. I turned to Natia and said, "Look at our guys getting alone over there!"

She looked over her shoulder, smiling as she replied jokingly, "Yea, it looks like love at first sight!"

Deb was picking Maroon 5's "Sugar" from the jukebox when Jess said, "Damn, y'all have some cuties over there! How come Deb and I always wind up without guys!"

Jess turned, leaning her arm on the jukebox facing Natia and me,

"Okay, like remember back in college when Natia brought Cash and Roc to the Monkey Bar. It's like history repeating itself!"

"Oh, my god, Jess, you're right!" Deb proclaimed.

"Yea, I remember," Natia replied, "but I didn't bring Terry this time. And shittttt, Lori and I had a great night!" She turned to me and we high-fived!

"Anyway," Deb chimed in, "so, Natia, how long have you and Shawn been seeing each other?"

Natia smiled and moved closer, and we all huddled as a reflex. She answered, "It's been three months, and I think we're getting serious. He's in corporate law here in Albany at one of the big firms."

I didn't have to tell my girls what Terry did for a living because they all saw him on TV with me, and they all called that day. Plus, I told them that Terry and I were becoming romantically involved. I said, "He sure is fine Natia, but is he good in bed?"

Jess and Deb perk up because they wanted to know the answer to that question too. Natia smiled brightly as she replied, "And you know it!"

We were high-fiving and laughing as Jess said, "I need something like y'all have!"

Deb started laughing harder then tried to catch her breath as she replied, "Jess, you always have a fine-ass man, but your crazy ass keeps kicking them to the curb!"

We all started cracking up because Jess knew we knew she was tough to deal with. She exclaimed with a smirk, "I wouldn't have to if they were half the man they should be! Shit, I get a little sassy when I get an attitude! That shouldn't mean my dick's bigger than his.

"Shit, he should man up. I have more respect for a man that can put me in my place, of course without being physical! What do you expect, I'm a Latina. How else should I be!"

We were laughing at the response Jess had made as we walked back over to Terry and Shawn. Terry looked up from the pool table and with some attitude said, "What took y'all so long! The drinks been here for five minutes!" He took his shot and leaned the stick against the pool table.

Jess leaned over to me and whispered, "See, attitude!"

I laughed and then changed the subject. I said, "Gather around, people! Take your Corona and drink it down to this part of the label." I pointed to the top of the label on the bottle and then drank mine to that point.

They all followed suit, and I continued. "Now take the shot and pour it into your Corona."

Everyone did. "Now plug your finger over the bottle and turn it upside down until the bubbles rise to the bottom of the bottle and after that put your lime in."

Everyone completed the task. "Now you can drink!"

Bruno Mars's "24K Magic" filled the air while the girls and I talked, and Terry and Shawn even joined in the conversation.

As soon as Halsey's "Without Me" came on, the girls and I went wild! "This is my song!" We said collectively.

Deb was halfway through her drink when she looked at the bottle, then at me, and said, "Damn, Lori, it feels like I had five drinks, and two shots already!"

"I know right!" Natia confirmed.

"Yea, Lori, what the fuck!" Jess chimed in. "I wish you had this recipe when we were in college! Shitttt, going out would've been a lot cheaper!"

We all started laughing as I replied, "Yea well, you can thank Terry! He got me out of my panties with this one!"

They started cracking up at that response, and Deb said, "Girl, you nasty!"

I high-fived Deb as replied, "And you know it!"

Everyone was having a great time. The girls and I excused ourselves for the bathroom, and since our drinks were gone, Natia said to Shawn, "Babe, can you order us another round of The Terry's?"

Terry laughed and said, "Oh, that's the name you're given!"

I kissed Terry and replied, "Trademark, babe, trademark!" Then the girls and I went to the bathroom!

<u>Terry</u>

Shawn and I were talking at the table after ordering more drinks, and the girls were gone for only two minutes when I felt a tap on my arm.

I turned around and I couldn't believe my eyes. "Hello, Terry, fancy meeting you here!" Brenda said and stood there with one of her girlfriends.

I felt like this woman could not have had the worst timing. I replied with an annoyed tone, "Hello, Brenda, what are you doing here!"

"Having a night out with my girl Cindy. Cindy this is Terry Carter, Terry, Cindy Hernandez! And who's your friend?"

"Shawn Casey, this is Brenda Mendez!" I introduced them, wanting her to just walk away!

"Well, I guess this meeting was meant to be! You're here with your friend. I'm here with my friend. How lucky can a girl get? Do you mind if we join you?"

Lori

We were in the bathroom for ten minutes before we came out. As I exited the bathroom laughing with my girls, I looked up at our table. I saw that bitch Brenda and some other chick talking to Terry and Shawn.

I looked at Natia and she sassed her neck. Us girls all hurried over to our table. We popped up at the table like a reappearing act, and Natia draped her arms over Shawn.

I walked to go between Terry's legs, bumping past Brenda while saying snottily, "Excuse me," then laid a fat kiss on his lips!

The drinks were already at the table, so I said, "Hey, babe, let's mix these drinks! The girls love The Terry's!"

I turned and sat on Terry's lap then grabbed my bottle. As fakely as I could, I said, "Oh hi, Brenda, what are you doing here?"

I could tell that Brenda was in shock at what I just did, but fuck that bitch, Terry was mine now. Brenda must have thought, *Oh no, this bitch didn't just try to play me in front of everybody! I got this bitch!*

I watched Brenda put her hand on Terry's shoulder, and I was ready to punch this bitch in her face. She said, "I'll call you later, Terry!"

I was so mad that I replied, "Yeah right, bitch, and I'll be the one answering!" as they walked away!

I turned to Terry and asked, "What did she want?"

"I don't have a clue! She just walked up to me. I didn't even know she was here until she touched me on my arm from behind!" Terry replied, stunned by Lori's actions, which turned him on.

"When that bitch calls again, give me the phone. I bet she won't call ever again!"

The girls started laughing, shaking their heads, and so did Terry and Shawn. Jess said, "Oh, and I'm the crazy one!"

We start cracking up as I replied, "And if you don't know now you know, b-a-by, b-a-by!" We all laughed harder.

We didn't let that ruin our night because a girl's night out with mine and Natia's man was a perfect night. We didn't need too many drinks, which were cheap in our pockets thanks to The Terry's.

It was around three in the morning when we all said our goodbyes with promises to make this a regular thing. It was such a good night that when Terry and I got home, we had freaky sex until dawn then went to sleep.

Chapter 37

March 2, 2022

Jamal

Every day this week was fine except for Thursday. Kim must've had the sick-of-being-pregnant woes because as soon as I got home from work, she started flipping out.

She screamed, "Why have you been coming home late at night, Jamal! And when you do come home after work you're right back out the door!

"What, you have a side piece or something and don't want me no more because I'm fat!"

"Come on, babe, you know that's not the case at all! You're my queen, and nothing will ever change that! You know I've been going over to Ethan's house, sometimes drinking a few beers and watching the game."

Ethan Daniel was another friend of mine since I came home from prison. He was my boss and the reason I had the position I had now at Amazon as a warehouse manager.

She exclaimed, "Well, Jamal, you never tell me anything, so how do I know where you are or what you are doing? I just feel lonely sometimes!"

I grabbed her, hugging her real tight. I pulled back and looked into her eyes with the deepest sincerity and said, "You are my beauty queen. You are all I will ever need and want, and, babe, you can always trust me."

I kissed her lips and then continued. "I'm sorry if you feel I've been taking you for granted, but you have never asked questions before about where or what I'm doing, so I didn't think anything of it. What I will do is let you know if that'll make you feel better?"

She kissed me then held me real tight as I replied, "No, baby, I trust you, so you don't have to change. I just needed some reassurance at times, and to know you are still with and love me!"

"Oh, babe, I love you with all my heart! And I will always ride for you!" I proclaimed, leaning my forehead against hers.

"I know, Jamal. I guess it's my hormones, and I'm just ready for Evelyn to come so I can get my body back!"

That night I stayed home rubbing her feet, watching movies while I stroked her hair, and before we went to sleep, we made love. The next day everything was back to normal.

There were days I drove to Jen's house to look in on Dr. Rawlings even though the reporters were gone the cops still stayed posted up outside her house. One day on my way, I saw Frank posted outside her house and I stopped.

I said, "What's up, Frank? I see that you're still posted outside Dr. Rawlings's. Do y'all think she's going to pack it up and run for it!"

Frank Mason was a member of the East Hampton Sheriff's Department. A tall slim white guy, he kind of reminded me of Shawn Bradley that used to play for the Philadelphia 76ers.

I knew Frank wasn't supposed to tell me anything, but after he stopped me one late night coming from Jen's and found out I was Jen's ex-husband and Jermaine's father, we became drinking buddies metaphorically. I always gave him and his sons tickets for Jermaine's games at Boston College.

Frank replied, "Well, Jamal, I shouldn't tell you this but because Jen lives up this way, I want her to be safe too.

"The FBI thinks Dr. Rawlings might be a target for this serial killer guy, and we've been watching her house for weeks now and ain't shit happening.

"So now we just ride through every other hour and sit for fifteen minutes. We are the police for Christ's sake, not fucking babysitters!"

We talked for a few more minutes than I was on my way.

I thought about what Frank said, so I began to watch the cop's pattern. It was like Frank said. Sure enough every two hours someone was sitting out there for fifteen to twenty minutes.

I knew I had to plan this murder to the T. I had to get the cameras in and out along with her. I knew this new technology could be traced, so there was no way I could leave it behind.

Tonight, after I rocked Kim's world, she fell asleep, and I couldn't sleep. I got up to go on my computer and searched the web for possible targets. I came across a few snitches on this website "Can't Trust Them" where people post snitches and what they lost because of them. I didn't really come across anything that stuck out. I mean I hate snitches, but I was always looking for mothers or fathers that were taken away from their children, young hustlers that were trying to get ahead like going to college, paying bills, or helping their families, but nothing was posted.

I read about some rapists, and I thought all rapists of minors, or forced, deserved to die unless the girl was lying, then she deserved to die.

I came across one story that stuck out to me. It was two cops in Newburgh, New York, Ofcrs. Mark Fuller and Britney Brick who raided a house they suspected to be a trap house, and it wasn't. Three kids were killed, and their mothers and family members were demanding justice for their sons. I thought, *Now that's a pair of cops that needs to pay.* I would keep a close eye on this case.

Next, I came across thirty-seven years old Dennis Hawkins. Dennis was a black guy who was wrongfully convicted of murdering an old couple during a robbery. They finally found the guy responsible for the criminal act, and before Dennis was released back to his family, he was murdered in prison. It was found out that the judge knew the old couple, and because of that Jdg. Martin Richards convicted the first suspect.

The judge was being investigated for judicial misconduct by the US Supreme Court. Dennis was a husband and a father of three. The neighbors saw the robber flee from the scene, and when the cops saw Dennis walking home not too far from the upscale neighborhood, fitting the description, they arrested and charged him.

I thought, *Now this judge ruined the lives of a wife and three children that would never know their father.*

I located Fulton County where the judge held court. I found his address in Salem, New York, which wasn't easy if my son Jamal didn't teach me the things I knew. I knew this judge would probably walk and only be asked to step down maybe!

I knew he wouldn't pay fully for his negligence, for taking his job personally, and that was why this asshole was mine. He was going to know how personal things could get. I didn't have much time if I wanted to get to the judge, so Dr. Rawlings had to be done soon. I finished and went to sleep.

Chapter 38

March 3, 2022

Jamal called me this morning around eight o'clock and said, "Dad, it's all set, but I need you to come and let me add the monitor app for the OVD to your Galaxy phone.

"Mom wants to have lunch with me and Shelby around noon, so by two we would like to be on our way back to school. I told Shelby that I will help her with her final since mine is done."

"I can be there in an hour, is that cool? How much time do you need?"

"Well, only fifteen minutes for your phone. I already programmed all your cameras, so all you would need to do is select which model you want to use, and it would pop up on your monitoring device, so come on I'll be waiting for you."

"Alright, I'll leave shortly, and, son, thank you, I'm so proud of you!"

"Thanks, Dad!" Then we hung up.

I got up and noticed Kim wasn't next to me. Then I took a sniff of the air, smelling bacon, and I knew she was in the kitchen cooking breakfast. I took a quick shower, got dressed, and headed downstairs.

"Good morning, beautiful, it smells good in here!" I said as I walked up behind her wrapping my arms around her waist and kissed her on the cheek as she leaned back into it.

"Morning to you too, babe! Who was on the phone?"

"That was Jamal. He and Shelby are at Jen's, and he wants me to come up, so he could show me something. Would you like to come with me?" I answered as I went to the table to sit down.

She sat my plate in front of me with my coffee as she replied, "Yea, I'll come. I need all the exercise I can get. Plus, I love talking to Shelby, listening to her British accent." She sat down with her plate to eat with me.

We pulled up at Jen's and parked behind Jamal's Lexus. I got out and went around to help Kim get out of the car. She was in her last month, but even though she'd been working out and could get herself out of the car on her own, I wanted her to feel I was there to help no matter how big or small the task.

We walked up to the door, and it was locked, so I knocked. Jen answered the door and said, "Look at you, Kim, you're even bigger than the last time I saw you!"

Kim wobbled past Jen as she replied, "Tell me about it! And next month this will all be over, and the real shit begins. Plus, I'm peeing every ten minutes!"

Jen laughed. "I remember those days! Well, at least you got Jamal. He'll be there to let you sleep and help you with everything."

Kim and Jen walked into the living room and sat down on the couch. I asked, "Where's Jamal?"

Like I summoned him, Shelby and Jamal popped into the living room. I turned and gave him a hand slap-hug as he said, "What's up, Dad! Least I know you're always on time!"

"That's because procrastination is the key to all fuck ups!" I turned to Shelby. "Nice to see you again, young lady, and so soon too!"

"Well, the pleasure is all mine, Mr. Stone!"

Shelby walked over to Kim and said, "It's so nice to see you, Kim. I heard the name of the baby is going to be Evelyn. Can I touch your stomach?"

"Nice to see you too, Shelby, and yes, you can!" Kim replied, allowing Shelby's hand to rest on her stomach.

As Shelby touched Kim's stomach, she said, "Hello, Jamal's little sister, I can't wait to meet you!"

Jen said, "The baby shower is next week, Shelby, you do remember?"

"Yea, I'll be here!"

Jamal and I left the ladies to do their thing, and we took off to my bunker. On the way, Jamal said, "Dad, guess why Mom wanted to take me to lunch?"

He answered his own question, "Her company World Corp. Technology wants to offer me a developer position. They are offering me seventy thousand a year with full health benefits, 401(k), and stock options. What do you think about that?"

I thought about it for a minute as we entered my bunker, then I replied, "Well, knowing your mother, she probably got you the best starting offer she could get, especially coming out of MIT! That's a damn good start, to be honest. But—"

"How did I know there's going to be a *but*?" Jamal proclaimed with a smirk, knowing me so well.

"The but is just another view, Jamal. I'm not saying don't take it, what I'm saying is, look at all your options.

"For one, your OVD is worth billions, especially to the government, and with that kind of money, you can start your own tech company. Your mom can come work with you."

Jamal sat behind my computer, and I gave him my phone. I said, remembering, "Now that I think about it, I have a friend that works for the government.

"You remember Craig Matthews, the guy I went to school with at Delaware University?"

"Yea, kind of!"

"Well, he works in DC. I can set up a meeting with him, and you can take it from there."

"You know what, Dad, I never thought of starting my own tech company, but I'm definitely interested in doing that if I could. I rather like being my own boss.

"See, that's why I always bring stuff to you. When can you set it up?" he replied as he typed on the keyboard.

"I'll contact him tomorrow, but because he works for the government, it may take a few days for him to get back to me. But you know I got you, son!" I proclaimed as I rested my hand on his shoulder, "I must say if you do this, then it might ruin your trip to London!"

Jamal gave me that crazy look that we would give to people that said something stupid and replied, "For a billion dollars, her parents can Skype me!"

"Shit, Shelby will probably say screw London herself!"

I started laughing my ass off because this boy was funny as hell.

He continued. "I'm going to talk to Shelby on the way back to school and keep Mom's offer on the back burner."

"Now you're thinking!"

We turned our focus on the project at hand, and Jamal started showing me what he had set up so far. After he finished, he said, "Now all I have to do is program the app to your phone."

I turned my phone on and went to work. He asked, "Hey, Dad, grab your Sony minicam out of your cabinet and let me show you?"

I got the camera out, handed it to him, and watched as he did his thing over his shoulder.

He said, "I built you the exact same control panel but smaller than the one you use at my school, so it's familiar to you.

"Now all you have to do is select what model camera you're going to use while the camera and monitoring device is connected to the USB port on the control panel.

"Once you have selected it one time, it'll save onto the control panel, and you can always select it without ever hooking up again."

Jamal showed me what to do and then the feed from the camera popped up on the monitor of my computer first, and then we hooked up my phone and then downloaded the app.

After the OVD app was finished downloading, we selected it, and the feed popped up and the room came into view on my phone.

Jamal handed the phone to me, and I spun the camera around, watching in amazement. "Son, this is extraordinary! I mean, a billion-dollar extraordinary!" I slapped him on the back. "Let's try this on your mom's house!"

We grabbed the control panel and went outside. I pointed it at Jen's house, and it popped up on my phone clear as day.

I sat the camera down on the picnic table, and Jamal handed me the controls. I started maneuvering the buttons, and it started working as it did at MIT.

I yelled, "Hey, Jennnnn! Check this shit out! Our son is a fucking genius!"

We left the camera outside and went into the house, and they could see Jamal and I enter the room with the girls on my phone.

Jen replied, "Why the hell are you yelling? I already know Jamal's a genius! Check what shit?"

Jen was sitting on the couch next to Kim when I handed her my phone. She looked at it and said, "So what, it's a video camera looking at us!"

I looked at Jamal and smiled. I looked back at Jen with a smirk, and with a sarcastic tone, I replied "Yea, but the camera is outside looking through the wall!"

"No, it's not, the camera is on you!" she proclaimed herself.

I asked Jamal, "You didn't tell your mother about your senior project?"

"She knew I was working on a project, but I didn't get into specifics!"

"Jamal, you and Shelby stay here. Kim and Jen come with me!" They got up and followed me outside to where I placed the camera.

I picked up the camera, and Jen still had my phone, I said, "Keep your eyes on the phone."

Kim stood beside Jen, looking as I moved the camera around. The picture was blurred because of the settings of the OVD.

I moved the camera back to Jamal and Shelby, and the view came in clear as day. Kim said, "That's fucking cool as hell! Jamal made this?"

"He sure did, and that's why I went to his school two weeks ago!"

I could tell by the look on Jen's face that she was amazed by what her son had created.

She said, "I work for a tech company, and I've never seen or heard of anybody trying to create something like this!"

Jen was the chief financial officer at World Corp. Technologies, so she would know everything that was going on there.

We went back inside and Jen said to Jamal, "I undersold you to my company! This—I mean you are worth so much more!"

"I know! I told Dad about the offer, and he suggested that my device alone is worth billions. He has a friend Craig Matthews who works for the government in DC who possibly could get me a better offer for my OVD."

Jen cut her eyes at me evilly. She said to Jamal, "I could get you a better offer from my company!"

"Well, Mom, let the games begin. I mean if I could sell it and get a shit load of money like Dad suggested, then I can start my own tech company.

"Instead of me working for someone, someone could be working for me. I could become the next Steve Jobs or Bill Gates!"

I cut in, "And Jen that's not all it can do!"

I showed them the X-ray, heat vision, and night vision. They were in awe as I switched between modes. Jen turned to Jamal and said, "Son, you're a fucking genius!"

Jamal and I started laughing as he replied, "Those were Dad's exact words!"

After the shock of Jamal's invention was over, we all talked a little while longer.

Jen said, "Well, since the lunch was to talk about my company's offer and now we know they are on the back burner, we should all go have lunch because I have a reservation for Mikey's Bistro."

"Sounds good to me! I can eat a house right now!" Kim proclaimed, causing us to laugh.

I thought, *It's funny how every time we come to Jen's and I walk off, Kim never asks where I go. What's funnier is that Jen has never told her about the bunker. Maybe Jen assumes she knows. Now that I got my OVD, I'm going to kill this bitch before my angel is born!*

We all got our stuff and went to Mikey's and had a great lunch. We went back to Jen's to say our goodbyes to Jamal and Shelby, and everyone went their separate ways.

Chapter 39

March 7, 2022

It had been four days since I got my OVD from Jamal, and tonight I was ready to put it to work. On Monday around midnight in between the cop's posts, I set up a Sony minicam in a tree five yards down from Dr. Rawlings's house, surveillance enough of Williams Street to where I could see the cops posted up.

I watched the cops over the next few days, and they posted up every two hours, and only watched no longer than a half an hour. I figured I would park on Carol Street in the neighborhood, it was the street before you turn on Williams Street, and there were a lot of cars parked on the curb and in driveways.

Williams Street ran all the way up through the mountains. It was known as Money Lane, only people making six figures or better could afford to live up that way. Behind Carol Street was the woods that run up the mountains.

When I went through the woods, I would have to cut through two other properties before getting to Dr. Rawlings's. Since the pattern was consistent with what Frank told me, I figured tonight when Kim was asleep, I would go set up my OVD.

I already picked the system up from Jen's on Wednesday when I stopped to plow her driveway and salt her steps. We had a snowstorm on Tuesday, and we were supposed to get another one tomorrow.

One thing I loved about Massachusetts was when it snowed, the plow trucks did their job right away. However, I was annoyed at work today because three people used that excuse about being snowed in, so I was short-staffed today so I had to work the floor. I was no stranger to work because I always helped out when need be, but to have three people call out on a shipment day when the weather was bad, well, not for nothing, that shit sucked!

I was tired as hell when I got home. Kim looked beat sitting on the couch when I entered the living room. She said, "Damn, babe, you look worn out!"

I flopped down on the couch next to her as I replied, "Yea, I am! Three people called out today, and I had to receive the spring shipment, so you know it was a full trailer."

"Well, that sucks!" she exclaimed as she snuggled up against me. "I would rub your back if I didn't feel like a house.

"I've been drained all day, and Evelyn's been trying to kick her way out! I didn't even make dinner. I ordered Chinese food, but when I ate some of it, it gave me heartburn. It's in the kitchen if you're hungry!"

I stood up, leaned over, and kissed her then replied, "Thanks, sweetheart. I think I'll eat a little, then take a shower, and lie in bed. We can watch a movie if you want?"

"Sounds good to me. I'll lay some clothes out for you while you're in the shower," she replied as I helped her up.

I ate then took a shower and crawled into bed next to Kim. She put her hand on my chest and started rubbing me as we watched the movie *Game Night*. I looked at the clock, and it was seven thirty, and with Kim rubbing me, I was out in the first ten minutes of the movie.

When I woke up, Kim was passed out. I rolled over and looked at the clock, and it was twelve thirty in the morning. I thought, *Oh, shit!* I eased myself out of the bed and threw on my all-black-everything and headed down the steps.

When Kim was out, it was usually over, but lately, she'd been getting up to pee. I thought, *I'll cross that bridge when I have to.*

I got in my car and picked up my phone and checked the view of Williams Street. I thought, *Damn, Jamal's advanced camera made everything else look primitive!*

The cops were parked outside at their post, so I started my car and left for Carol Street.

When I got to Carol Street, most of the cars were in their driveways, and not too many were parked on the street but enough.

I pulled down to the second to last house and parked my car. The street was quiet as I checked my surroundings. I checked my phone, noticing the police were still sitting there. I figured. It took me twenty minutes to get here, so they should be leaving soon.

As I sat there, I noticed the car was cooling down, and it would soon be cold in here. It was snowing lightly, but one could tell that it was going to pick up soon. The storm was on its way.

I thought, *After this kill, I'm getting rid of this car. I just bought the 2022 TrailBlazer. Kim has a car, and both my boys have a car, so why am I holding on to this 2012 Camry? I don't want it on my insurance, but hey, I could see if Shelby wants it. I wonder if she has a license. She's always driving Jamal's car, so I know she knows how to drive.*

I wonder if Lori figured out who I am by now. Shit, she is an FBI agent. I laughed! *Damn, I had them sitting in my living room, eating dinner with me—the guy they're looking for and Lori not being able to put two and two together!* I shook my head as I checked my phone again, and the cops were gone.

I checked my surroundings again, put my backpack on, and then exited my car. It was one o'clock. I wanted to get this done and get back home before Kim woke up.

I got to the woods without incident. I was traveling about a hundred yards deep into the woods, and the snow from Wednesday was deep and a pain in the ass. I saw now that I didn't think this all the way through.

I loved hiking, so I thought how difficult could it be, but let me tell you, it sucked! I'd never been in these woods before, and by the time I made it to the first house, I was ready to turn around. I must have moved deeper into the woods because I was almost twenty yards from the house.

I kept going because I was a third of the way there. As I moved along, I tried to stay on a straight path.

I spoke out loud to myself, "What the fuck was I thinking! Crappy day at work, crappy weather, and now, these crappy-ass woods! This shit sucks!"

I kept moving and ten minutes later, I was at the second house. I heard the wilderness moving about, which scared me a little. I didn't know what was in these woods truthfully, but I did, however, know that black bears roam Massachusetts. *Damn, I hope I don't run into one of them!*

I finally made it. I was twenty yards away from Dr. Rawlings's house. I went a little deeper into the woods and found a tree with a clear shot of her house.

I checked my watch and it was ten minutes past two. There was a light on in one of her rooms. I didn't know which one was hers, but soon enough, I would have the layout and view of the whole house.

I was able to climb the tree to pick a spot and sit comfortably. I said to myself out loud, "Finally something going my way."

I turned my backpack to the front of me and pulled out a thin spike that was four and a half inches and my rubber mallet. Hammering in the spike barely made a sound. I left enough space so my Sony minicam could fit between it.

I then grabbed my Velcro straps and secured them. This camera was slightly bigger than the one Jamal and I used at his mom's, but this camera had a wider view range, and the battery could run up to two weeks. I adjusted slightly to make sure it pointed directly to the house.

I already programmed this minicam for the controller and my phone, so I selected the OVD on my phone. The screen was still black, and I said in a low voice, "What the hell?"

I checked the camera and realized I didn't turn it on. I sighed, turned it on, and hit the view button on the controller, and the house came into view. I then adjusted the camera again so the whole house was able to be seen on my phone, and then I hit a few more buttons on the controller, and the X-ray came up. I then pushed the up-arrow button, and the camera came into full view of the inside of her house.

I could see everything, the living room, kitchen, den, another living room, dining room, and the downstairs full bathroom. I looked into the basement and then upstairs.

She had five bedrooms and a full bathroom, and in the master bedroom, she had another full bathroom with a Jacuzzi tub. *Damn, this house is nice as hell! I can't believe this woman has all this space just for herself!*

I checked my watch and it was two twenty-seven, so I looked at my phone to see what Dr. Rawlings was doing.

I froze as I focused on her, and I couldn't believe what I was seeing. It was just after two-thirty in the morning, and she was still up. She had an almost empty bottle of wine on her nightstand.

She was slightly laid back in her bathrobe with the front of it wide open, and she was butt naked. She had her vibrator, pleasing herself. Dr. Rawlings's body was hot.

She had a long slim-fit body with curves, a four-pack, and long blonde hair. Her womanhood was shaved, and I couldn't believe that this beautiful woman was alone in the world and did that crazy shit to those people.

I sat there for a while watching as she brought herself to an orgasm. I was so turned on by this woman. I thought, *Wow, I wish I didn't have to kill this bitch*!

I had enough and I got going because I had a long walk ahead of me. It only took me twenty minutes to get back to my car.

I got in my car and thought, *That was fast as hell coming back!* I checked my watch and it was three.

I got home, went upstairs to change into my PJs, and climbed into bed next to Kim. She snuggled up against me in a spooning position as she said tiredly, "Baby, you're cold. Did you just come from outside or something?"

"I woke up and couldn't get back to sleep, so I went downstairs and watched some ESPN, and then took out the garbage."

Kim had on her nightgown, which was slightly up, and even though she was pregnant, she was still sexy as hell. We spooned and as terrible as it sounded, I started thinking about Dr. Rawlings and got aroused.

We made love spooning and afterward we just lay there with her in my arms as we fell asleep.

Chapter 40

March 8, 2022

I got up this morning and Kim was still out. I was still tired from last night's events, and I needed a shower to wake up, but first, I had to start the coffee. The hot shower rid me of my chills I was having when I woke up.

I made my coffee and decided to make Kim breakfast. I wasn't going to the gym today because I didn't have that kind of energy. I cooked some buttermilk pancakes, bacon, and Western-style omelets. I would usually bring her breakfast in bed, but since her third trimester, she hadn't been comfortable eating in bed. As I was cooking, I heard Kim get up and go to take a shower.

Just as I was putting breakfast on the table, she walked into the kitchen. I put her plate on the table and then gave her a hug and kiss. I said, "Good morning, beautiful mommy!"

She smiled as I pulled her chair out so she could sit down. She replied, "Morning, baby, I don't feel beautiful, but thanks, that's so sweet. Breakfast smells good. I see you made your famous Western omelet."

"See, babe, true beauty, no matter how you slice it, is being able to carry and bring life into this world! My bonus is my baby mom is hot!"

She laughed as she replies, "Boy you must be talking about Jen because I look like a blimp!"

"A beautiful sexy blimp and yea, both of my baby moms are hot!" I said as I stood slightly bent over and put my finger to my ass, making a sizzling sound.

"Boy, let me find out," she proclaimed while laughing.

"You already found out. Jamal and Jermaine are grown. They ain't babies anymore, so you're my only baby momma. Jen was just my kids' mother now, and one day so will you!" I said as I was laughing, trying to get her going.

Her fork hit the plate and she looked at me crazily with a cut of her eyes, a smirk, and replied, "Oh, so just your kids' mother like Jen! So what are you planning, huh, replacing me?"

I continued to laugh at her attitude as I answered, "Well yea, when you get old, I'ma have to trade you in for a younger model!"

"Oh yea buddy, well not if I trade you in first! Now!" she answered as she stuck her tongue out at me, and we both laughed.

I loved joking with Kim like this because we both knew that we were secure in our relationship, and when our morning started off like this, then the day was always great. We finished breakfast, and I had to get to work.

All morning I was looking at Dr. Rawlings's house on my phone except during breakfast with Kim. Now on my way to work, I was checking my phone, and this woman walked around her house butt naked, which I thought was strange, but I guessed if it were your house and no one lived with you, then you could walk around in whatever you want.

I got to work and looked at my planner for the day, remembering I set a meeting with my staff at three this afternoon. I wanted all of the second shift present for this meeting. Everyone was here today, and the day flew by fast and without incident.

At three o'clock once everyone was present in the back where my office was located, I started. "First I would like to think everyone that made it in yesterday to handle the spring shipment. For those who called out knew that this shipment was coming in."

I looked around the room, spotting faces who knew I was talking about them. I continued, "Y'all left the ones that did make it in with a rough day. So from here on out, if you plan on calling out on the day you're supposed to be working, I want a doctor's note or something that justifies your absence.

"I believe we pay a great wage for people to be responsible for their attendance and actions. Now, if you know that you're not going to be here on a certain day or even if you need the next day off, you need to find your own replacement or do a shift swap.

"I know before we didn't do shift swaps, but I'm trying to find a way that we are not short staff, and people don't get screwed doing twice the work. So please notify me if or when you need to have a day, so I could verify the switch.

"Everyone here knows that the spring and summer are high-volume times. If the rules for absences are not followed, then you may be suspended without pay or even fired. I will post the new policy on the information board."

I had to come up with this new policy because yesterday sucked. I used to be lenient when it came to missing days because sometimes you just need a day, but shit, I'll be damned if I was going to suffer from it.

I continued. "Second, this is a high-volume season from March to September, so overtime will be available. No one can work more than sixty hours a week unless it is approved by me and then Ethan.

"If you try to do more hours without approval, then you will be fired, and I will find a replacement. I will not be paying for your extra hours out of my pocket, and that is exactly where it would come from. I know no one wants to give someone else their money they make here, and neither do I."

I looked around the room at everyone's faces, and I could see them shaking their head to my last statement. I ended the meeting and either people left for the day or went to work.

I left at four thirty and I drove toward Jen's, but that wasn't my destination. I passed her house further up the mountain. I stopped by three homes that were almost finished being built. The second one I liked the best.

The basement was unfinished, the ceiling had exposed beams, and there were two columns in the middle of the basement. I thought, *Why those column supports are still there.* But the house still had quite a bit of work left. I knew that they weren't going to be done by Friday, so this was the place.

I made a mental note that I would need rope. I checked one more thing and that was power. I checked the breaker box in the basement and switched it on, and it had power. I figured the power would be still on because of how far along the project was.

It was dark outside when I walked out to go home. When I pulled up to my house, I checked my watch, and it was seven thirty. When I got to the door, I heard laughing inside.

I went in and in the living room, Kim and Sarah were there talking away. Sarah Cane was a fourth-generation Asian. She was thirty-six years old with long jet-black hair, caramel complexion, slanted eyes, and slim curves. She was cute as hell.

Kim spotted me and said, "Hey, babe, how was your day?"

I walked over, gave her a kiss, and replied, "Work was smooth as a baby's butt! But I did have a meeting about calling in and overtime. I'll be damned if I'm going to get stuck like that again."

I turned to Sarah. "What's up, Sarah, long time no see?"

"It's only been a long time because I was kicking Freddie's ass to the curb. It's finally done, and I don't have to worry about his cheating ass no more!"

"I'm glad for you because Freddie was a dick, and he was no good for you. You deserve so much better.

"That's why I never chilled with him unless you brought him here. I knew he was a slime ball, plus he wasn't good-looking either."

I sat down and put my arm around Kim as they both were laughing. I continued. "I mean, look at you. All you Asian women go for those white boys even if they're ugly as long as they have money.

"Sometimes, I think you Asian women don't even know what good looks look like. I mean it's not like you need him to get in America for Christ's sakes. You were born here."

They both started laughing again as Sarah replied, "Well, it's not just about looks, Jamal! He was nice in the beginning, and besides his money was fine as hell!" Kim hmm-hmmed while laughing with Sarah.

"So, Kim, what's your excuse then? I was broke and fresh out of prison!"

"First of all, Jamal, I knew you before you went to prison. I wrote and hooked up with you while you were there.

"And most of all, you're handsome as hell, baby! I wanted you before you went to prison, and I'm damn glad I got you now!

"Shit, and that ten inches between your legs is better than any man I've been with!" She high-fived Sarah.

Sarah said, "She's right, Jamal, you are handsome, but most importantly, you're good to her. I thought she was crazy when she told me she was talking to you, but I'm glad she has you. I would kill to have a man with your qualities."

Kim smiled at Sarah and then changed the subject. She said, "Babe, there is steak, rice, and asparagus in the oven for you!"

"Well thanks, Sarah, and you too, babe," I said.

I kissed Kim on the cheek and stood up, put one hand on my hip another behind my head, and started swaying side to side in a sexy dance while singing, "They think I'm handsome. They think I'm hot . . ."

I then popped my pelvic and started hopping out of the living room still singing, "They think I'm sexy . . ."

As I walked into the kitchen, I could still hear them cracking up. I thought, *Damn I have a good life! All the people I love are doing good. Maybe I should stop killing!* I let that ride around in my mind for a few minutes, and then to myself in a low tone, I said, "Nah . . . I'm having too much fun!"

Chapter 41

March 9, 2022

Lori

Today I was bringing Terry and Neveah to meet my family. I was still stunned by yesterday's discovery and couldn't get it off my mind. Two weeks ago, Terry and I had a great time out with my girls, and Jess got me thinking about our college days, that one night in particular.

It was the night I met Anthony a.k.a. Roc at the Monkey Bar. I was busy with Terry all week, so I didn't get around to looking up Jamal's mugshot from 2008 until yesterday.

When I looked up his mug shot, I couldn't believe my eyes, and my heart skipped a beat. I thought, *Jamal and Anthony are one and the same! Well, I'll be damned! I can't believe this shit, and I bet he knew who I was the night Terry and I had dinner with him and his wife. Son of a bitch!* Now since I figured it out, all I could do was think about Jamal.

Now today since I put two and two together, during the drive to my mother's, I couldn't help but think about Jamal. I drifted back to 2008. I thought about the sex and how cool and laid-back Jamal was. I snapped back when Terry called my name.

We arrived at the suburb where my mother now lived ten minutes outside of Boston. It was a nice neighborhood, and the houses were split-level homes.

We pulled up and before we got out, Terry asked, "Lori, are you alright? You've been kind of spacey!"

"No, I'm fine! I'm just nervous about introducing guys to my family. This is a big step, plus the last guy, well, you know what happened." I lied but I couldn't tell him what was really on my mind.

I perked up and continued, "Okay, guys, let's do this!" We all got out of the car.

When we got to the door, it was unlocked, and I led Terry and Neveah into the house, shouting, "Mom, I'm here!"

Janet came out of the kitchen, replying as she approached to hug me, "Hi, honey, it's so nice to see you!"

Janet Reid was the spitting image of me but shorter with gray hair. After we hugged, I said, "Mom, this is Terry and his daughter Neveah!"

My mom shook Terry's hand. "It's finally nice to meet you, Terry. I heard so many good things about you!"

"It's nice to finally meet you too, Ms. Reid"

"Oh please, Terry, call me Janet." Then she turned her attention to Neveah. "Well, aren't you beautiful, Ms. Neveah?"

"Hello, Ms. Reid, it's very nice to meet you."

"Welcome, mi casa, su casa!"

When we walked into the living room, my brother Charlie was sitting on the couch watching *Dragon Ball Z*. I got his attention by kicking the couch. "What up, Charlie, this is Terry and his daughter Neveah?"

As usual Charlie wasn't all that interested in life itself, but he was polite as he replied, "What's up, sis. And it's very nice to meet the both of you." He turned back to his show.

"Charlie, why don't you go upstairs and watch your show if you're going to be anti-social, and let Lori's guests have a seat!" Janet said, annoyed at Charlie.

Charlie got up with an annoyed sigh and left for his room. Charlie was a very tall blond with a thin face.

Terry and Neveah sat down when Charlie left, and Neveah pulled out her iPhone.

"Where's Sam, Mom? I thought she would be here by now!"

"You know your sister when she first starts seeing someone, she's always late for something.

"She did call though and said she will be here shortly! I had her stop and pick up the Alfredo sauce for the chicken Alfredo I'm making for dinner."

Neveah's head shot up, "Chicken Alfredo is one of my favorites, Ms. Reid!"

"I know, Lori called and told me, and I knew you had to try mine!"

Terry and I sat talking with my mom for a little while Neveah played on her phone, only answering questions when asked. It was five minutes to three when Sam walked into the house. My mom and I stood and went to meet her at the door.

My mom hugged, gave her a kiss on the cheek, and took the chicken, "Nice to see you, honey" and went into the kitchen.

I hugged my sister. "Hey, baby sis, come in and meet Terry and Neveah."

Sam followed me into the living room, "Terry, Neveah, this is my sister Samantha."

Sam's skin was light mocha, and she had beautiful dark curly hair. She's the same height as me but thicker, almost like Jessica Rabbit from *Who Framed Roger Rabbit*. She looked like a darker version of Lori and her mom.

Terry shook her hand. "Finally I get to meet Mr. FBI my sister told me so much about!"

"Well, it's very nice to meet you too, Sam, and I heard a lot about you too!"

"All good I hope!"

She turned to Neveah, "And it's nice to finally meet you too, Miss Neveah with the iPhone 10! My sister said that you are pretty, but wow, did she sell you short. You're gorgeous!"

"Why thank you, Miss—"

"No no, Neveah, call me Samantha or Sam!" Sam said, cutting her off, "Miss just makes me sound old like my mom or married!"

"I heard that, Sam!" Janet yelled from the kitchen, "I'm not old. I'm seasoned!"

We all laughed and Neveah replied, "Okay, Sam! Well, it's nice to meet you. Wow, and your hair is just like mine!"

"I guess Lori didn't tell y'all, my dad is black!"

Terry thought, *I can't believe Lori never mentioned her sister was half black, especially that she's been around Neveah so much. Wow, who would've guessed, everybody's white but her, go figure!*

"Well, Sam, how was I supposed to bring that up in a conversation! Yea uh, let's go to Wendy's, and oh yea, by the way, my sister's half black!"

"Anyway, Lori, guess what? I got approached by DA Faith Whittaker, and she asked me if I want to become an assistant DA under her!"

"Oh my god, Sam, that's great! So what are you going to do? I mean you always said that you want to defend people, not prosecute them!"

"Well, if I take this job, then I could see it from the prosecution side for a few years, and that could help make me a better defense attorney, hands down!"

"You know, Sam, that's a good idea. It would also give you a bullshit meter when you take on clients!" Terry said, joining the conversation.

"That's what I was thinking. That way I could just give it to my clients straight!"

We all sat talking for a while, and even Neveah joined in while my mom was in the kitchen finishing up dinner. Sam then said, "Terry, Neveah, do you mind if I steal Lori for a minute?"

"By all means, Sam, she's your sister, plus I want to watch the college basketball game!" Terry proclaimed.

"Yea cool, I want to see who's winning the North Carolina game!" Neveah grabbed the remote from her dad and turned to ESPN 2.

"Oh, my god, Lori, she's a sports junkie like you!" Sam said while laughing and getting up to lead me upstairs.

"I know, right!"

We got to our old room and sat on the bed. "So, Lori, what do you have to tell me that I had to wait until today.

"You know you can't keep me in suspense like that!

"Are you pregnant?"

"Girl, are you crazy!" I replied with shock. "Nothing like that! I would've told you and mom together.

"Anyway, remember when I was in college, and I met that guy Anthony I told you about!"

"Yea, the one you said was the best sex of your life and that you wouldn't mind having kids with him, but then he disappeared."

"Yes, that Anthony, and thanks for the recap!" I replied then shifted to look my sis dead in her eyes.

"Anyway, listen to this shit. So I'm working on this Life-Ruiner Serial Killer case, and before you ask, I can't give you any details.

"But anyway, we had to backtrack all the way to the beginning of this case. So we go back to the first victim Tanya Spencer, and Terry and I are in charge of combing New York's victims—"

"Oh, my god, Lori, is Anthony the killer!" she asked in shock!

"No no, just listen, damn!

"Anyway, we had to conduct new interviews surrounding the victims. So we go to this guy Jamal's house because Tanya is the one who sent him to prison for ten years, but he's doing fantastic now. I mean great for someone coming home after ten years.

"Anyway, so Jamal and his wife invited Terry and me to have dinner with them because we came in the middle of them eating. So we did and his wife could cook some chicken.

"But after a few minutes into dinner, I started thinking I knew Jamal from somewhere. You know I have great facial recognition, dead-on to be exact!

"So through dinner and the interview, I couldn't figure it out! You know how obsessive about shit I can get.

"So a few weeks flew by, and it was still on my mind. I get up with Jess and the girls for a night out, and Jess brings up the night in college when I met Anthony. But now Jamal kept popping up in my head.

"Now, Jamal has cornrows and a beard with gray in it, and Anthony was clean cut. But then Jess brought up Anthony a.k.a. Roc and so is Jamal's.

"Now, I said to myself that it's a common street name, but the coincidence was too much, so I made a mental note to look up Jamal's mugshot from 2008.

"The same year I met Anthony, and the same year Jamal went to prison.

"Girl, I almost fell out of my chair at work when I saw Jamal's mugshot. They are one and the fucking same Sam! I couldn't believe it!"

"Now that's a fucking oh my god if I ever knew one!" Sam proclaimed in shock with her mouth open to the floor. "Oooohhh shit, Lori, do you think he knew it was you? I mean you still look pretty much the same!"

"I asked myself the same question since I figured it out. And now that I think about it, the way he was acting, trying to avoid eye contact, the little grins at times like he had a secret that no one knew about. Oh yea, he knew who I was! I almost called him yesterday!"

"And say what, Lori! Hi, remember me Agt. Lori Reid. My partner and I were the ones who interviewed you to eliminate you as a suspect of a serial killer.

"Oh yea, by the way, I don't know if you remember me, but you made me squirt back in 2008 when we had sex, and oh, by the way, you gave me a fake name!" Sam joked sarcastically!

I started laughing because she was right. "Well now, at least I know what happened to Ant—I mean Jamal! I wasn't a one-night stand, or he thought I was some college hoe!"

"But you want to know what's crazy? Terry is a damn good lover, but sometimes when I want to get all the way there, I think of Anthony, who now is Jamal!

"What the hell am I going to do, Sam?" I said out of frustration.

"What do you mean do, Lori!" Sam replied looking at me like I was stupid.

"Jamal's a married man with a child on the way, an ex-con! You have Terry and Neveah, and you're FBI!

"Move on with your life, Lori, and don't do your obsession thing that you do!

"Now you know what happened to your Anthony and everyone else's Jamal, just leave it at that! Plus, you have a fine-ass man, and he breeds well. Look at that little girl downstairs, she's so beautiful!"

I left the conversation at that because Sam was right. I did have an obsessive personality. I let it go, and we went back downstairs.

We laughed and talked while watching the basketball game. When my mom called for dinner, we ate, and Neveah loved my mom's chicken Alfredo. We all had a great time!

Chapter 42

March 14, 2022

Jamal

The week went by pretty fast. I remembered the rope, and I checked on the murder house every day this week. I started to set up a camera at the murder house, but the home had a work crew. It would be possible for it to be discovered.

I thought it would be a good idea for the cops to see me coming and going from Jen's, so it would give them the idea that I was doing a project for her. Every time I passed them, I would honk my horn and wave, and whenever Frank was there, I stopped and talked with him.

I put all the supplies I was going to use in my bunker. Jen had been working late all week because she had quarterly financial statements due for her company.

I also got a call back from Craig, my friend in DC on Wednesday. I texted him a week ago. We caught up a little and then I told him about Jamal's Optimal Visual Display and the way I explained what it could do, he was blown away.

He told me to give him a little bit, and he would get back to me, especially if it could do what I said it could do; then the military would most definitely be interested. I called Jamal, giving him the news from Craig, and he was very happy about that.

The only stressful thing this week was how I was going to get Dr.

Rawlings out of her house. The logical thing to do was to carry her through the woods to my car, but that would suck.

I couldn't pull into the driveway or park in the street. I also couldn't pull halfway in because that meant I would have to carry her halfway from the house. Well, I couldn't expect all my kills to be easy, so through the woods, it would be. Other than the few things I mentioned, I did spend the week with Kim.

I checked my OVD on Dr. Rawlings a lot, and the camera that was watching the cops made sure the pattern stayed the same.

Thursday night while watching a movie, I told Kim that Jamal, Jermaine, Preston, Corey, Justin, and I were having a guys' night out on Friday, and I would only be stopping home for a little before I meet up with them. She was cool with that because Sarah was coming to hang out.

I already told both of my boys to cover for me with the going-out story because I was going to my bunker to drink a few beers, watch the game, and that I didn't want to drive home drunk. Even though I lied to both parties, all my angles were covered.

I came home early from work today, and Sarah was already there. "Hey, babe," I said as I went over to kiss my wife.

Then I slapped Sarah on the butt, I said, "What's up, Sarah!"

"I heard you're going to hang out with a bunch of college boys," Sarah said with sassiness, slapping me on my arm.

"Yes, I am Sa-rah! My sons invited me out, and this is their last time going out before they prepare for their finals," I replied.

While I moonwalked out of the living room, I said, "Plus I make the party pop!" Then ran upstairs.

I heard both of them laughing, and I heard Sarah say, "Your husband is so crazy!" I laughed.

I took a shower and prepared myself because I had to give the illusion that I was going out. I already had everything black at my bunker I brought up with the supplies.

It was six thirty when I jumped back down the steps. Kim said, "Damn, honey, you look good! If you didn't have all that gray hair in your beard, you would look like a college kid!"

"Well, not smoking, only social drinking, and staying in the gym keep me young, babe!" I replied, giving her a kiss.

I jumped on Sarah, bear-hugging her and lifting her little ass off the couch as I said, "Later, little bit." I dropped her back on the couch!

Kim was laughing and Sarah said, "You play too much, Jamal! See, Kim, I told you your man was crazy!"

I quickly went to the door, grabbing my jacket and the keys to the Camry. I whipped my head around in a cartoonish way as I replied, "Crazy as a fox!" I snapped my head forward and bolted out the door.

I drove to my bunker, and when I got there, I loaded all my supplies in the car. I recently bought a Taser, and if this baby hit someone's neck, they were going down in and out. If I hit them in the stomach, they were going to shit themselves. I had that in the bag with my all-black-everything.

After I got dressed, it was seven fifteen, and I didn't plan to go to the murder house until eight to set up. I had to type up the note for Dr. Rawlings, so I sat at my computer and went to work.

After the note was finished, I pulled up the camera that was watching the cops on my computer monitor, and on my phone, I watched Dr. Rawlings. *I could retrieve the OVD before I go into Dr. Rawlings's house. I have to get it before someone finds her body and before the media frenzy*, I thought.

While I was watching Dr. Rawlings, she was on her phone and cooking something to eat. She moved all through her kitchen until she had everything set, and the food was set to slow cook. She poured herself a glass of wine and drank it all in one shot and then poured another.

I said, "Damn that woman is an alcoholic!"

She hung up then called someone else. *Jamal should probably add a high-frequency sound detector to the OVD. I didn't have a clue what she was talking about. Oh damn, I almost forgot. I have her North Star security code for her alarm. That would've sucked if I forgot it!*

It was a little after eight, so I wrapped everything up, hopped in my car, and headed to the murder house. All the crew was gone for the day. I went to the back-glass slide door where I thought it would've had a bar in it, but it didn't, and it wasn't even locked.

I carried everything in to set it up. It was a laundry table down in the basement, so I set the five jars of perm, knives, and the bottles of bleach on it.

Then I set up the poles for the UV lights in a U-shape close to one another. I clamped the light to the poles, and in the middle was a chair. I then ran the power cord to the breaker box. I knew the breakers were all twenty amps, so I was confident the power would hold. I hit the switch, causing the UV lights to come on, and they were so bright that it was damn near blinding. I turned them off and I was all set.

I then went upstairs and turned off every light switch in the house. There was only one window in the basement, so I was good with that. It was only nine o'clock so I went back to Jen's.

Jen still wasn't home when I got back, so I called her. She answered on the second ring, "What's up, Jamal, is everything alright?"

"Yea, everything's fine. I'm at your house in my bunker, and you weren't here, so I was checking to see if you're alright?"

"I'm fine. I'm over Tracy's house having some drinks, and we might go out tonight to 614 North Street Bar, so I'm probably sleeping here tonight.

"Work was long this week, I finally finished the quarterly statements."

I heard Tracy ask something in the background, but I didn't quite get it. Jen replied, "It's Jamal checking up on me like he's my dad or something!"

Tracy said something then Jen continued, "Jamal, Tracy said hi!"

"Tell her I said what's up."

"Okay, I'll—"

"Wait, don't hang up! I just remembered I talked to Craig today about Jamal's OVD, and he sounded very interested. He even said that the military could use it and that he will get back to me soon."

"That's what's up. I mentioned it to the board at our meeting last week. They wanted to table it until after the quarterlies.

"But that's good about Craig though. We'll talk about this later. If you're in the house, make sure you lock up before you leave," she replied with a slight slur.

"Okay, will do, bye." I hung up.

I switched back over to check the cops, and they were there chilling. I checked back with Dr. Rawlings, and everything was all cleaned up.

It was nine thirty and she was in the living room sitting on the couch watching TV and drinking wine. Then after the show, she started moving through the house doing her evening ritual that I'd been observing since I put up the camera.

As usual she finished her night off by pleasing herself. I thought, *Damn, I'm about to watch her go through her late-night ritual, and not for nothing, this crazy-ass woman is sexy as hell! Too bad she has to die!*

She stripped butt naked, walked back to the bathroom in all her glory, and boy was it glorious! She stepped into the tub and slid down until the bubbles were at her neck. She grabbed her wine and started sipping it. I was shocked.

I checked for the cops and they were gone. I focused back on Dr. Rawlings, and she was just lying there relaxing.

At ten fifteen the cops pulled up and then left at ten thirty. I believe that was the last check before the shift changed. I thought, *This journey through the woods is going to suck!* I then remembered something that made me smile, *Last week it snowed. This week has been sunny and warm. I'm sure the snow melted by now.*

I came out of my thoughts when I noticed that Dr. Rawlings was standing to get out of the tub in all her naked beauty. She dried herself off and stood looking at herself in the long mirror she had on the back of the bathroom door.

She turned at different angles and then grabbed her breast, lifting and squeezing them together. I could tell she enjoyed the way her body looked, and so did I. I was not a pervert or anything like that, but I do get a pass on this.

Anyway, she finished admiring herself, slid into her silk robe, and left it open as she finished off her wine and headed to the bedroom.

She sat the glass on the nightstand next to the bottle and picked up her remote, turning on her TV. "Oh, my she's watching porn!" I said in shock!

She lay back with her robe open putting her two fingers in her mouth and then started rubbing her nipples. When they were nice and hard, she squeezed her breast and then brought them to her mouth, rotating her nipples as she sucked on them.

After she was done, she moved her hand down to her love muscle and started pleasing herself. I checked my watch. It was eleven fifteen and the cops hadn't pulled up yet, so I went back to watching Dr. Rawlings.

She was still pleasing herself, adding two fingers into the mix. I was so turned on that I started touching my manhood. Now, I thought I may be a little perverted, but hey, it was like watching porn.

She then pulled out her toy, letting it take over as she tilted back and I saw her body shake, and I knew she reached an orgasm. It was beautiful and I would always remember this moment.

It was eleven thirty when the cops pulled up, so when they left, it was showtime. I grabbed the few things I needed and the note then turned off everything, and as soon as I saw the cops pull off, I was out the door to Carol Street.

I turned onto Carol Street, and I wanted to be facing Williams Street, so I pulled into someone's driveway, turned around, and luckily, I was able to get the same parking spot I did the last time I was here.

I sat in the car for a few, checking on the cops and Dr. Rawlings. She was watching TV and the cops just pulled away. I figure I had about two hours to do what I needed to get in and get her out.

I checked my surroundings, and it was quiet. I set my watch to beep in one hour and forty-five minutes. I got out and took to the woods. Just as I thought, the snow had melted, but it was very muddy.

I moved quickly through the woods, and I made it to her house in twelve minutes.

I then checked to see what Dr. Rawlings was doing, and she had passed out with the TV still on.

I check for the North Star security code, 19855, and then pulled out my Taser. It was my first time using it, so I had my nightstick strapped to my side just in case.

As I approached her back door after I jumped over the fence, I pulled out my lock-picking kit. I decided to leave the camera up until I left. I was about to pick the lock then decided to try the door first.

The door was unlocked, and I thought, *What the hell, people don't lock their doors these days. Don't they know a killer is on the loose!* I smiled at that thought.

I move to the front door to check the alarm because the alarm could still be set even if the door was unlocked. I was right. The alarm was at fifteen seconds and counting down.

I entered the code and it asked for armed or unarmed. I unarmed the system and checked my phone to see if she stirred. I thought, *She's pissy, drunk, and relieved!* I headed upstairs, and as I moved up the steps, I could hear her TV still on.

I crept into her bedroom, and her back was toward me. Her blanket covered her knees, and her robe covered the rest of her. I crept behind her, pulled out my Taser, and shot her between the shoulder blades. Her body arced and fell still. I pushed her a couple of times and checked to see if she was still breathing, and she was.

I then duct-taped her ankles then rolled her on her back, and her robe fell open. Her body was even sexier up close. I admired her for a few seconds then I duct-taped her wrists and mouth and covered her up.

I wrapped her in the little blanket that was at the foot of her bed. I picked her up, slinging her over my shoulder, and she was light as a bag of feathers.

I carried her down the steps, and with her on my shoulder, I rearmed the alarm and went out the front door carrying her along the side of the fence, dipped in the woods, and went to the back of the house where I had to retrieve the OVD.

I sat her up against the tree and then climbed the tree, retrieved the camera, and climbed back down. I kissed the camera and put it into the front pocket of my hoodie with the duct tape. I already put the Taser in my right cargo pocket of my pants, and lock-picking kit in my left.

I checked my watch and I still had thirty-seven minutes left before the cops came back to their post. I picked up Dr. Rawlings, slinging her over my shoulder again, and I was out. I thought as I was walking, *The Taser must have worked really well, or she's just drunk as hell.*

It took me twenty minutes to get to the edge of the woods and about five yards away from my car. I looked down the street before I came fully out of the woods, and I saw a car running in someone's driveway, and someone was sitting in the car. *Damn,* I thought.

I waited with her on my shoulder for about five minutes when a girl came out of the house and jumped in the passenger seat. They pulled out of the driveway, heading in my direction and right past me. It felt like forever waiting for them to leave.

The street was finally clear. I had already taken out my keys while I was waiting, so I hit the button on the trunk and hurried over to put her in the trunk.

I hopped in my car and sat long enough to take a deep breath and checked my watch. With still ten minutes to spare, I started my car and headed up Williams Street.

As I drove by Dr. Rawlings's house, the cops were already posted up. I drove by this time not honking my horn, I wanted them to think it could be me or maybe someone else with the same car since this was a common car.

I pulled up to the murder house, and it was five minutes 'til two, and I wanted to be out before five just in case the work crew worked on Saturday. I know I did when I did framing work, but this house was almost complete.

I popped the trunk and she was still out, and I checked her pulse just to make sure she didn't die. I picked her up, carrying her around the back through the sliding door and into the basement.

I leaned her up against the wall next to the table. I then took everything out of my pockets and set them on the table and then grabbed the four pieces of rope.

I cut the tape off her wrists and ankles and slid her robe off, leaving her butt naked. I then sat her in the chair, tied each ankle and wrist with the rope, and then duct-taped the rope to hold it tighter. I then threw the other end of the rope on her wrist over the unfinished beam, and the ropes around her ankles, I put them around the columns.

I then stood her up and I was thankful that she was light. I secured the right wrist, tying it to the beam with her arm fully extended, and then I did her left the same way far enough apart for her to form a Y. She was now hanging from her arms, and the weight of it must have hurt because she started to stir.

As I was tying her left leg tightly to the column, she came to. She started looking around with her head swaying because she was still kind of out of it. I secured the right leg, and her body now formed an X.

Because her weight was supported by her arms, it brought her to full consciousness. She began to go hysterical, trying to scream, but her mouth was covered.

All Dr. Rawlings could see was a dark figure moving around with only the faint light of a sixty-watt light bulb as she tried to adjust her sight.

I then pulled the laundry table closer to me just outside the floodlights. I knew she was watching me while she tried to talk with muffled cries as I unscrewed the perm tops. However, I didn't say a word.

After everything was set, I turned to her, so she could see me in all black with the hoodie on my head and my black ski mask that covered the lower half of my face. I did this so she could see into my eyes, and I could see the fear in hers. As our eyes met, I stared for a few, and I watched her eyes get big, and tears streamed down her face.

I then removed my mask and stared at her nakedness. I thought, *For the first time since I've been killing, I felt sorry for my victim, but oh well, she's a monster.*

I said, "I will remove the tape from your mouth if you promise not to scream. I would like to talk to you. Shake your head if you understand and agree."

She nodded and I removed the tape. She said, "What's going on, what do you want from me?"

"First let me tell you how this is going to work, and if you're a good girl, then we can get this over quickly!"

"Please don't rape me, I can give you money!" she exclaimed in a panic!

"I must admit, Dr. Rawlings, you are a stunningly beautiful woman, but I'm not here to rape you or your money.

"So what do you want?"

"Well, we'll get to that!" I replied as I checked my watch, and it was quarter to three!

I thought, *I don't know how long it's going to take to cook her ass, so I need to get this moving along.*

"Ann, do you know who I am?" I ask, calling her by her first name for the very first time.

She looked at me as I removed the hoodie off my head and stepped closer to her. I could tell she was searching her mind and then a light came on.

She answered, "I do know you . . . You're Kim Stone's husband. I met you at the hospital Christmas party. Uhm . . . Jamal, right?"

"Good memory, Doc. Is that all you know? How about why you're here?"

She thought about it for a few seconds and then another light went off. "You're that life-ruiner serial killer!"

"Two for two, boy you are smart! Kim did say that about you! She thought you was a genius, but it was very fucked-up what you did, giving people cancer to conduct your own experiments.

"So let me ask, why would you do some crazy shit like that? Didn't you know you were ruining these people, and their families?"

"Please, Jamal, let me down. It really hurts being tied up like this!" she asked, pulling on her restraints.

"That's not how this works, Ann. Like I said, if you cooperate, this will be over soon."

"Okay, okay, ten years ago, I lost my eleven-year-old son Tommy to bone cancer." That had me frozen as she continued. "My husband Bill and I did everything we could to save our son.

"When he died, I fell apart, and Bill tried to help me through it. I was lost without my son, and I was so bitter that Bill couldn't stand to go on with me like that, so he left.

"I hated myself because not only was Tommy gone, but so was Bill, and he was a great husband."

I turned to face her and she stared me in the eyes as she continued,

"Bone cancer, Jamal, is a death sentence, and there are not a lot of cases of experiments to help find a cure.

"I started working on this cure, Jamal, so no one would have to go through what my Tommy went through. I needed patients to work on my treatment. I went to the board but they shot me down. So I did what I felt needed to be done.

"Jamal, you should know that bone cancer is the hardest cancer of them all and next to impossible to cure?"

"And the most painful, I heard!" I replied, feeling sympathy.

"Right, so the treatment I came up with was a highly radiated chemo laser treatment that radiates right to the bone.

"Mixed with this medicine, I created DXC42 injected right into the bone. It would break down the cancer and eliminate it.

"I developed this treatment, and no it hasn't been approved, but it was working with a few setbacks, but if I had time to tweet it I would've found a cure for bone cancer."

I listened to her story and I felt bad for her son, and I thought about my sons going through that. *Shit, I would burn down half the world to cure my boys.*

But the fact that her son was already gone, that was the issue.

"Ann, that is a very noble quest, but we all know that you could've waited, and through the right channels have people with bone cancer volunteer for your treatment.

"Trust me, I am sorry for your loss, but the fact of the matter is that your son is already gone.

"I love my kids to the fullest, and if your kid was still alive fighting for his life and you did this, then we would not be here.

"Those people you affected did not deserve this, and neither did their families. Now those people are going to die a painful death, and their families are going to be the ones who pay the price for your sorrows." I picked up a knife and her eyes got big!

"Please, Jamal, you don't have to do this. The courts will punish me!"

"If they were going to punish you, then how come they gave you a bail that was reachable?

"That's the thing about our system, Ann. It screws the people that are trying to do right and small stupid shit, but people like you get all the breaks!"

"Please if you let me go, I won't tell anyone who you are I promise! I'll do whatever you want just don't kill me!"

She started crying as she screamed, "Help me, please somebody help me!"

"See I was going to let you go, but now." I shook my head and faced her. "Here you are breaking our agreement, and you want me to believe you're not going to tell anyone!"

"I promise Jam—"

I sliced her across her breast, and she screamed at the top of her lungs! I then sliced her on her stomach, arms, legs, back, and pelvis.

I said, "You can scream all you want. No one can hear you!"

I watched while her body was dripping blood, and she came to a moaning cry. She said, "Just kill me, why torture me?"

"Because the people's lives you ruined will be tortured, and because radiation burns, so will you!"

I took a bottle of bleach and poured it all over her, and she screamed so loud that probably the whole county heard her! Because she drank, the alcohol thinned her blood, and mixed with the bleach, she was leaking blood all over.

"Please, Jamal it burns, just kill me already!"

I threw more bleach on her, and she wailed, "Please no more . . . Please!"

"I am going to kill you, Ann, but you will suffer first as you die." I pointed. "See these lights all around you. It's like the lights from a tanning salon but stronger!"

I took off my black gloves, put on some latex, and picked up a jar of perm.

I first put the perm in her hair, and then I spread it all over her body, enjoying touching every inch of her sexy ass.

As the perm touched her cut, she screamed, fighting against her ropes. When I finished with her legs, I put it all over her womanhood, and she screamed louder at the top of her lungs.

"Oh my god, it burns!"

"Yes, it burns, Ann. It's hair perm. Just sitting too long will burn your skin off, but that would take longer than I have, so I'm going to heat it up. But before I turn on the lights, I want to read you this note."

She was crying and fighting against her ropes, repeating, "Oh my god, it burns" as I took off the latex gloves, put them into one of the empty perm jars, and put back on my black gloves.

I retrieved the note and said, "Listen to this, Ann."

> *A mad doctor you are but giving people cancer you've gone too far.*
> *You use radiation in your personal experiment knowing it*
> *will burn*
> *so guess what, Doc, it's your turn!*
> SHE'S A "LIFE RUINER" AND DESERVES TO DIE!

I set the note down and asked, "How did that sound, Doc?"

"It burns so bad! Why are you doing this to me?" She sobbed.

I thought, *This woman must be delirious because I just told her why!*

I looked at my watch, and it was three minutes to four. "Oh shit! Damn, Doc, time sure does fly when you're having fun, but I'm cutting it too close, so let's see if we could speed this up!"

I went to the breaker box, plugged in the power cord, and when the lights came on, they blinded both of us. That shit was brighter than the sun!

When my eyes adjusted to the light Ann was begging as the perm heated up, "No no, please Jamal, just kill me!"

I believed that she knew just what would happen once I heated up the perm on her skin. I knew her ass was starting to cook because I could smell it, and she started screaming. That perm shit stunk something terrible. I watched as her skin blistered, and she was definitely cooking.

I started gathering all my things, and after my stuff was in my bag, I dumped bleach all over the table and the floor. I wiped down the breaker box and the whole time I was doing this, she was screaming.

By the time I finished cleaning and I turned to look at her, she was dead.

I left the lights on, watching as the blisters on her skin popped, her hair burned off, and her skin melted.

I couldn't believe how fast it all happened. Dr. Ann Rawlings was no more.

Her skin started to blacken and turn crisp, and I noticed that she pissed and shitted all over the floor. I went to the breaker box and killed the power. The smell in that basement would forever be with me!

I left everything as is other than the bag I packed and headed up the steps with a flashlight in hand. I came across her little blanket and was glad I threw it off her coming down the basement steps.

I probably had blood and bleach on me, so when I got to my car, I put the blanket on the driver's seat and then hopped in the car. I checked my watch. It was ten minutes to five, and I headed to Jen's.

When I got to Jen's, she wasn't home, so she must've stayed over Tracy's as she said. I stripped down to my boxers in the garage and then put my clothes in a black plastic bag.

I grabbed the paint thinner, poured it into the bag, and then put lye on top. I then put the plastic bag into the black gym bag with everything from the murder, along with five bricks and threw more lye into the bag.

I then put the gym bag into another plastic bag, tied it tightly, and then put it in my trunk.

After all that was done, I went into my bunker and put the lock pick, Taser, and camera into my cabinet. I then grabbed the clothes I had on early when I came to Jen's and then went to shower.

I could still smell Ann with that burned perm smell. It was something I would never forget. I bet that house was ruined. It was a murder house with a really bad smell.

I must have been in the shower for an hour because when I got out and looked out the window, it was daybreak. I got dressed, went downstairs, and fell asleep on Jen's couch.

I woke up to her shaking me. "Jamal, hey, Jamal," I opened my eyes, staring at her like she was crazy. "Jamal, what are you still doing here? Why didn't you go home?"

"I was watching the game and fell asleep," I lied. "What time is it?"

"It's ten fifty in the morning. Does Kim know you're here?"

"No, she thinks I went to Boston to hang out with Jamal and Jermaine. I told her that so I could come here and watch March madness in peace.

"When you told me you weren't coming home, I came in here."

"So I have to cover for you too? Damn, Jamal, do Kim still not know you have a bunker here?"

"Yes, please cover for me, and no, she still doesn't know, only you and the boys. That's one thing I want to keep for my first family.

"I love all y'all, and yes, I still love you. You may not be my wife, but you will always be my first love and family!" I replied, put my shoes on, then stood, and gave her a hug.

"I love you too, always! Now get your black ass home to your second wife!"

I kissed her on the cheek and then said, "Peace! I'll talk to you later!"

I hopped in my car and drove deep into the woods to the river. I got out of the car, retrieved my bag out of the trunk, carried it out to the cliff where the river ran, and tossed it off. I watched it sink, then went back to my car and drove home. I spent the rest of my day with my wife.

Chapter 43

March 17, 2022

Terry

    I woke up next to Lori and watched her as she slept. I thought about how distant she had been all weekend. I realized that since Friday when we went to visit her family, she'd been kind of spacey. I asked her all weekend if she was alright, and she always said she was, but I could tell that she was just going through the motions as if her body was on autopilot. She was usually very quick and witty with her responses, but I found myself repeating things over and over again to her.

    On Sunday after we brought Neveah home on the drive back, I asked, "Lori, you can tell me the truth, are you having second thoughts about us, do you think we're moving too fast?"

    "No, I am not having second thoughts, Terry, and we're moving just fine. I'm really enjoying spending time with you and Neveah."

    She sighed. "However, I've been thinking about us moving forward, and after this case, if we're going to do that, then we should find different partners."

    She rested her hand on my leg, "I mean, I do enjoy working with you, but I don't want to work side by side with someone I'm romantically involved with.

    "It's good right now, but what if we have an argument and then have to be under each other during that time? Not having the space to process, if you ask me, that's failure waiting to happen."

"I couldn't agree more, beautiful. Is that what's been bothering you?"

"Yea," she lied, "it's been on my mind for a while, especially since I developed strong feelings for you!"

When she said that, it made me feel like I was on top of the world. The fact that this woman was most likely in love with me, it validated my feelings for her.

She relaxed a little after that, and everything felt like it was back on track, but she was still a little spacey and I could tell that something still was bothering her. I didn't want to be one of those guys that harassed his girl so he could get what was wrong with her. So I figured in time she would either tell me or not but eventually get over it. As long as we were good, that was all that mattered.

It was six fifteen when I got up, and Lori was still sleeping, so I went to shower. We had a briefing at nine, and I wanted to have breakfast.

While I was in the shower, I thought, *Damn this case! It's going nowhere, ain't shit happen in weeks. The two good things about this are that no one has died, and Lori and I get to spend all this time together.*

I heard Lori come into the bathroom, which pulled me out of my thoughts. She sat on the toilet to piss and then hopped in the shower with me.

"Morning, babe, you're not done yet, are you?" She moved closer to me, rubbing her body against mine, and put her hand on my chest.

"Not now. I'm not!" I replied as my manhood stood at full attention!

"Good, now that both of your heads are focused!" I smiled as she kissed me.

She pulled back. "I'm sorry I've been so distant, and I'm glad we talked about our personal, and work relationship," she said, thinking, *Damn I got to get Jamal out of my system!*

She reached down grabbed my manhood and started stroking it while we were kissing. I picked her up, pressed her against the wall of the shower, and we were at it.

"Oh, Terry, right there!" she moaned in my ear!

When she moaned in my ear, that shit turned me all the way up, so I started pumping harder feeling her body jerk every time I hit deeply.

She squeezed me tightly as she was about to release, still moaning in my ear, and when she released, I released with her.

I put her down and she kissed me deeply. She pulled away from the kiss. "Thanks, babe, for the shower quickie. I needed that!"

"So did I!" I replied while washing myself. "I already washed up, so the shower is all yours!" I kissed her and got out!

I dried off and went into the bedroom to get ready. Thinking, *Damn, I needed that. It couldn't have been at a better moment!*

When I walked into the bedroom, my phone was ringing. I looked at it and it was Director Wall. I had three missed calls from him. I answered, "Sorry, Mike, I was in the shower. What's up?"

"Well, sorry to be the bearer of bad news, but we have another Life-Ruiner Serial Killer murder in East Hampton, Massachusetts, and guess who the victim is?"

I thought for a second. "Is it that doctor who gave those people cancer A-A-A-Ann Rawlings?"

"Bingo! Get out there and call the East Hampton Sheriff's Department. Terry, this lady was probably going to prison, but she doesn't have to worry about that now."

"Okay, Mike, we're on it!" I hung up!

I went back into the bathroom, and Lori was just getting out. "Hurry up, beautiful. We have to get to Massachusetts. We have a body in East Hampton, a Dr. Ann Rawlings."

Lori was drying off while she was listening and paused, "Wait, isn't she on our possible target list?"

I walked back toward the bedroom as she followed. I answered, "She sure is. I'll call Mark, Susan, Jason, Noel and tell them to meet us there.

"Susan and Mark are in charge of this jurisdiction, and they were the ones that dealt with the EHPD. They were supposed to keep eyes on her.

"You call Kevin and Gordon, tell them the briefing is canceled, and if they want, they could join us."

"Well, here we go! At least Noel was right about tracking the killer by using possible targets.

"Shit, we have seventy-five names and five different states, and all we ask is for the locals to keep an eye on these people!" Lori said while getting dressed.

I was dressed, so I called Mark. After he answered, I took a deep breath and then said, "What's up, Mark, get Susan and meet us in East Hampton, Massachusetts. Address, 1955 Williams Street. Dr. Ann Rawlings was killed!"

"No shit! We told the local boys to keep a very close eye on her because if I was the killer, she would be at the top of my list!"

"Well, they did a poor job babysitting her, and now the woman is dead! I'm calling Noel and Jason, so they can meet us there. Lori and I are leaving in ten, so give us two hours give or take fifteen."

"Ain't this some shit. Alright, Terry, we'll see you there!" We hung up.

Lori already called Kevin and Gordon and had just finished getting dressed. "Lori, can you call Noel, and I'll call Jason?" I turned on the TV to the news.

While she dialed Noel's number, she asked, "It's seven. Do you think it's already on the news?"

"The reporters are like flies on shit. If there's shit, then they're there!"

Lori laughed and then started talking to Noel. I was talking to Jason, but sure enough, there was a Fox news break and I turned it up.

The anchor reported, "Just in, Dr. Ann Rawlings was found murdered this morning by the crew that was contracted to build a house in East Hampton, Massachusetts.

"You may know Dr. Rawlings from Saint Mary Cancer Hospital. She was allegedly giving people bone cancer to work on her experimental cure.

"She was arrested and given bail and was due in court in two weeks to start her process for trial. At this time, we do not have any details of this crime."

I turned off the TV as I said, "I'm ready, and do you want to dry your hair a little?"

"Nah, I'm good. Ponytail it is for work you know that!"

She kissed me. "You can go warm the car though, and I'll be right there." She put her hair in a ponytail. "Thank goodness we had that quickie this morning, that was like a shot of espresso!"

I headed to the door, "Yea, that was good, but I'm still getting my French vanilla! She's not going to be any deader if we squeeze coffee and bagels in. We can eat on the way."

Lori started laughing as I headed down the steps and said, "You're right about that!"

Two hours later Lori and I pulled up to the crime scene, and as usual, the media was in full force and Brenda Mendez was also present.

As we walked through the reporters, they were shouting questions, and then Brenda jumped in our path, "Agent Carter, is it true that the FBI is no closer to catching this killer? Is it also true that he has outsmarted you every step along the way?"

I knew that Brenda's questions were because she was sour, and so did

Lori. I wasn't surprised when Lori answered, "No comment at this time" and pushed past Brenda as I followed!

I was chuckling as we approached the door, "Well done, Agent, you know those questions were a dig at us right?"

"I sure did. She's a sour bitch and doesn't know when she's lost!"

We followed the flow of cops to the basement, and when we went down the steps, the smell was indescribable! "What the hell is that smell? I've never smelled anything like it in my life!" Lori asked as she covered her nose, and so did I!

"Yeah, me neither! I was wondering what that smell was when we came into the house!"

We hit the basement floor, and I couldn't believe what I was seeing! The corpse that was hanging was unrecognizable. The body was charred damn near burned to the bone with no hair, and if I didn't already know it was Dr. Rawlings, it would've been a while before forensics would have been able to identify it. "Who's in charge here!" I asked.

"I am, well, until you get here! I'm Det. Kent Murphy," he answered, stepping forward and reaching out to shake my hand.

Kent was a stocky black man with a bald head. I shook his hand, "Nice to meet you, Detective Murphy. I'm Agent Carter and this is my partner Agent Reid!

"I have more agents on the way along with my forensic team. Even though we're here to take the lead, you and your team are more than welcome to assist us."

"Very well, Agent Carter!"

"So tell us what you got so far?"

"Dr. Ann Rawlings has been dead for two days, and so far, no evidence has been found, but our forensic team is still working on that.

"EHPD was keeping surveillance on Dr. Rawlings. She barely left her house, but on Fridays, she would go to the grocery store and come home, and that would be the last they would see of her. This was her routine since we'd been watching her. We had all our shifts doing a half an hour post every one to two hours.

"This morning we got a call from David Carr the contractor at six this morning. Ofcr. Kate White was the first to respond, and I'm sorry to say, but that's her vomit over there. She said when she got down the steps, the smell was so overwhelming it just happened."

"Well, I could understand that!" Lori exclaimed, feeling like throwing up herself!

Just then Mark, Susan, Noel, and Jason all came down the steps. "My god," Noel said, "that smell is ungodly! The bleach can't even hide it. It smells like perm that has been left in too long!"

"Not to mention burned flesh!" Mark chimed in!

"Damn, I think this may be the worst one yet! The sad thing is that she's been at the top of our list as a target!" Susan said, shaking her head!

I gathered my team around, inviting Detective Murphy to join us. After the introduction, I said, "Look, Agent Simms and Wise will do the forensics here while Agent Steals and Dunn comb the scene. Agent Reid and I will go to Dr. Rawlings's house to see what we can find."

I had Detective Murphy fill in all my agents on what he told Lori and me. After he finished, I said, "Detective, you can help my team with your team here. Do you already have people over Dr. Rawlings's?"

"I sure do, Agent. My partner Kristen Marks is on scene. I'll call her and let her know you're coming," he replied, taking his phone out!

Lori pulled me to the side, "Terry, why don't you let Noel come with us? She could get forensics done there. That will kill two birds with one stone."

It was a good idea. I turned to Jason, "Are you okay with handling this scene yourself, and if you need anything, you have Steals and Dunn, plus the detective's team."

"I'll be fine and if it's like the other scenes, then I won't find much anyway. I got the note. Do you want to read it before you go?"

I took the note and read it out loud so everyone could hear it. After I read it, they all turned to the body, and Mark said, "And burn she did!" We all shook the chill from our bodies!

Lori, Noel, and I left them there to do their job and headed out the door on our way to Dr. Rawlings's.

Noel grabbed a few things from the FBI forensics van then put them in the trunk of my car, and got in the back seat.

She said as she closed the door, "Thank you, Lori, for getting me out of there! I mean I would've done my job, but I've only seen shit like that in horror movies, and the smell, it took everything in me not to lose my breakfast!"

"I know, girl. I saw your face and I thought you were about to lose it! I would have saved Susan, but this is her assigned state, plus Terry already gave her orders. I just thought you could get a possible layout on what happened at Dr. Rawlings's."

I pulled into Dr. Rawlings's driveway, and there were reporters there too with the police keeping them at bay. I pulled to the side of the driveway kind of on the grass because it was full.

We walked to the barricade, showed our badges, and were let through. When we entered the house, Det. Kristen Marks was waiting for us.

Kristen Marks had long blonde hair and an athletic, slim build. Detective Mark said with her South African accent, "You must be, Agent Carter. Murphy said you were coming!" She stuck out her hand.

I thought, *Damn, she's fine with her accent. I wonder what she is!*

I snapped back when she finished talking, and I took her hand as I said, "Yes, I'm Agt. Terry Carter, and this is Agent Reid and Agent Simms. What do you have so far?" I got right down to business, so it wasn't noticeable how infatuated I was.

"Please follow me!"

She led us to the backyard and pointed to the fence as we walked toward it, saying, "The perp came over the fence, see the footprints leading to the house."

She showed us the prints as we followed her back to the house. "Come in the back door and go to the front door. He must've known the security code because we contacted North Star Security, and it was unarmed at one ten and rearmed at one thirty."

"Look here"—she pointed—"the footprints go up the stairs and back down but don't go back the same way he came in. They go out the front door."

She opened the front door and walked out with us in tow. She pointed to the prints on the ground, "See, the prints go alongside the house then into the woods."

We continued to follow her into the wood along the fence, keeping our eyes on the prints. She continued. "As you can see, the prints are deeper than the ones coming in through the back door. This tells me that he was carrying her, and the prints led to this tree."

She squatted and pointed. "See this indentation in the ground, this is where he leaned her up against the tree."

"What do you think he was doing right here? I mean, why not just keep going where he has to, but he stopped here maybe to retrieve something.

"Maybe he had a camera here like the Dawson's, but because of the alarm system and Dr. Rawlings constantly being home, he couldn't get into the house," Noel stated.

I took a deep breath and then said, "Get a team to look around the area other than where the footprints are and look up into this tree.

"I want to know why he stopped here too! Detective, could you get some people on that right away and have them report to Agent Simms?"

"No problem, Agent Carter," she replied, smiling and looking deeply into my eyes.

She turned. "He picked her back up, and as you can see, walked this way. We already followed the prints, and they led all the way to Carol Street."

We followed Detective Marks back into the house and up the stairs. "As you could see by the muddy footprints that he came right into her room like he already knew the layout like he's been here before."

We went into the room and on her nightstand was an empty bottle of wine along with a vibrator. "She must have been bombed and relieved. Look at this." Marks grabbed the remote to turn on the TV. "She was watching porn!"

I thought, *Now I must be bugging because the way Detective Marks was looking at me while talking about porn, and relief, it seemed like she was coming on to me!*

I looked at Lori and she didn't miss a beat. "Is that everything, Detective?" Lori asked with a sassy, annoyed tone.

Oh shit, I could see that Kristen picked up on Lori's cattiness, and I didn't want any part of that.

I turned to Noel, "Noel, collect everything you can find for evidence, and let's see if our guy left anything behind."

I headed down the steps as Lori and Kristen followed. In the living room, there were a few cops talking as we walked in. They froze and gave us their undivided attention.

I said, "Hello, Officers, I'm Agent Carter and this is Agent Reid. We are in charge of this investigation and would like to ask you a few questions."

Detective Marks cuts in, "Agent Carter, these are the men I'm going to use to search the area." She pointed from the right. "This is Ofcr. Kenny Buyer, Seth Moore, and Frank Mason."

"Nice to meet you, Officers. Now as I was saying, how often was Dr. Rawlings's house watched?"

"In the beginning when she was released on bail, we had someone posted every shift. Then after the media frenzy and a couple of weeks after that, we were posting up for half an hour once every two hours.

"We all took shifts but we had other responsibilities to handle as officers," Officer Buyers exclaimed.

"Well, I believe that y'all were contacted by us, and were told to keep eyes on her at all times because of our investigation.

"Now because those orders were not followed, we now have a body on our hands! Anyway, who's mostly familiar with this area?"

"I am." Officer Mason steps forward. "I patrol mostly in this area. I mean we all do, but I'm mostly familiar with the people. Williams Street is known as Money Lane, and all the homes after Carol Street are in the high six figures range."

"Officer Mason, can you name all the owners on Williams Street from Carol Street to this address?"

"Sure can!"

Officer Mason started naming all the homeowners, and when he got to Jennifer Stone, I said, "Wait, stop,"—I looked at Lori and back—"Jennifer Stone, is that any relationship to Jamal Stone?"

"Yea why? That's Jen's ex-husband. She lives fifteen minutes down the road from here. Jamal comes up all the time.

"His kids are in college, but they come home often, and he helps Jen around her house. Jamal's new wife Kim comes with him sometimes too.

"They have a very unusual but comfortable relationship. Jamal even gets my boys and me tickets to Jermaine football games," Frank replied, giving off too much information.

I looked back at Lori again but didn't say anything because she knew exactly what I was thinking.

"By the way," Officer Mason continued. "I think Jamal's wife Kim used to work with Dr. Rawlings. I believe she's an LPN at Saint Mary's Cancer Hospital."

"When was the last time you saw Jamal?"

"Seen him, well I see him all the time. Matter of fact, I talked to him this past Tuesday or Wednesday.

"We were talking about his son entering the NFL draft and getting tickets to the Boston College football game. My sons love Jermaine. They play football too!"

"Thank you, Officer Mason!" I turned to the ladies. "Can you start the search and have the rest of your team help Agent Simms?"

Kristen rested her hand on my arm. "No problem, Agent Carter!"

She turned and said to the officers, "Start searching the area around the tree in the back where we suspected Dr. Rawlings was leaning up against. Get someone to climb that tree and see if there is anything there that can tell us something." Then she went upstairs, looking back and smiling at me as she went!

Before the officers moved, they stared at me then shook their heads with smiles on their faces and went to do what she'd asked.

Lori put her hand on my shoulder, "No problem, Agent Sexy Carter!" she said with a joking and mocking tone.

"Ha ha, very funny! Let's go see if we can catch up with Ms. Jennifer Stone."

Chapter 44

Lori

I couldn't believe how unprofessional that detective was, all but made out with Terry at a dead woman's house. I could tell Terry thought she was attractive, and I couldn't blame him. She was hot. At least he remained professional and didn't give me the vibe that I had to worry about him being around beautiful women. That made me a little more secure in our relationship.

When I heard Officer Mason bring up Jamal's name, I thought there were just too many coincidences around this man, but I still couldn't see him being involved in any of this nonsense.

I still wanted to ask him about some shit, so I could clear my conscience. I knew now from the information given to us that I would be seeing Jamal again.

It was eleven thirty, and Terry and I were on our way to Jennifer's house. It had been a full day already, and the day just started. When we got to Jennifer's house, she wasn't there, so we got her work address in North Hampton, Massachusetts, a company called World Corp. Technologies.

On our way over, Terry told me to take the lead. He wanted me to feel like I was fully involved in the case, but to tell the truth, I didn't want to be the one questioning Jamal's ex-wife.

We pulled up to this ten-story building in downtown North Hampton, and Jennifer's office was on the third floor.

We arrived at the receptionist's desk, "Good morning, is Jennifer Stone in?"

"Do you have an appointment with Ms. Stone?"

We both pulled out our badges, and the receptionist's eyes got big. "Oh, one moment please!"

She picked up the phone and two seconds later, she said, "Ms. Stone, the FBI is out here to see you."

There was a pause. "I believe it's the FBI they showed me their badges." There was another pause. "Okay, Ms. Stone, will do." She hung up. "Ms. Stone will be right out. Y'all could have a seat if you like."

Before we had a chance to reply, Jennifer came out of her office to the receptionist's desk, "I'm Ms. Stone, how can I help you?"

I thought, *Damn Jamal has a type. This woman is beautiful!* I stuck out my hand. "Hello, Ms. Stone, I'm Agent Reid and this is my partner Agent Carter." She shook my hand and then Terry's.

"Ms. Stone, we would like to talk to you in private. I promise we won't take up much of your time."

"Follow me." She led us to her office.

When we got into her office, Jennifer sat behind her desk and pointed to the two chairs in front of her desk. "Please have a seat. What can I do for you, Agents?"

After Terry and I sat, I took a deep breath. "This past weekend there was a murder on your street not far from your house. Dr. Ann Rawlings was killed, do you know her?"

Jennifer gasped. "No way, are you sure? I kind of knew her, but I haven't seen her in months. I've been working a lot, but with all the commotion, I couldn't help but know what she did to those people."

"I understand that Jamal's wife Kim worked with her at Saint Mary's Cancer Hospital?"

"That's right but she's been out of work on maternity leave since February 15. What does she have to do with this?" Jen replied, feeling a bit suspicious!

"Nothing, this is just routine questioning. You live on the same street and Kim works with her, so it's natural we ask these questions, and anyone that may be connected." I made this statement to soften her up for my next question.

I really didn't want to start questioning her about Jamal, but that was the real reason we were here. "Ms. Stone, how often does your ex-husband Jamal come to your house?"

I could see the smoke clear in her eyes as she now realized the true reason why we were here. From a woman-to-woman aspect, she was ready to be defensive.

She leaned back in her chair. "Oh, now I see! All of those other questions have nothing really to do with why you're here!"

She sighed, shaking her head. "Ain't this some shit! If you must know, Jamal and I have an open family relationship. He can come to my home freely as he wants.

"Kim and I are very good friends. We even shop together sometimes. Jamal is the father of my kids and a damn good one. He also takes care of my house so I don't have to pay for it."

"I'm not implying anything, Ms. Stone. Again this is just routine questioning. Now, if you could tell me, do you know where Jamal was this past Friday night?"

"Jamal was in Boston with his sons having a guys' night out!"

Jen saw right through their questioning because this wasn't the first time she had to deal with this shit, and she wouldn't let them try to make him a suspect. She thought, *There's no way Jamal could be involved in this shit!*

"How do you know for sure that's where he was?"

"Okay, what the hell is this all about! Are y'all trying to pin this shit on Jamal? I mean what's all these questions about Jamal?

"I did just tell you that he was in Boston with our boys, and I know this because I talked to them on Friday night, and that's how I'm sure where he was!"

She thought, *Well, that's half the truth. I did talk to all three on Friday just not together!*

"We didn't mean to upset you, Ms. Stone!"

"Well, you know Jamal did ten years in prison! Since he's been home, he has been a great father, hard worker, great friend, good husband to Kim who's about to have their baby, and this is the happiest I've ever seen him. And I knew him for over twenty years.

"Now, here you are trying to catch a murderer in here asking questions about Jamal. In his past, he sold drugs but he never hurt anybody, so not for nothing, you're barking up the wrong tree! Jamal's a good man!"

"Thank you for your time, Ms. Stone, and if I upset you, I'm sorry that was not my intention."

Carter and I stood and so did she. I said, "Have a nice day, Ms. Stone!"

"Y'all do the same!" she exclaimed.

We left and didn't say a word until we got to the car. I know I was just processing what just happened. Terry said, "So that went better than expected!"

"I guess, I mean she has been through a lot with Jamal going to prison, and now Jamal has a baby on the way with his new wife."

"Well, it had to be done! Let's go pay Kim and Jamal another visit!" We headed to Jamal's house first.

Chapter 45

<u>Jen</u>

I was working on some account records when my receptionist called me and told me two FBI agents were here to see me. I thought it could be for audit reasons. Never in a million years did I think they would be here questioning me about Jamal for the death of Dr. Rawlings.

I was shocked but not surprised that the killer killed her. I was shocked because Kim, Tracy, Jamal, and I were just talking about that exact thing.

I couldn't believe that they were trying to pin this shit on Jamal. But they said once a criminal always a criminal, but Jamal was not a murderer. I mean if they were investigating some drug shit, then I wouldn't put it past Jamal, but what the fuck, murder! They had to be out of their goddamn mind! So when they left, I was pissed off, and I called Jamal.

As the phone rang at his job, I thought, *I know Jamal has a dark side. That's how he was able to make so much money in the streets. I'm sure he did some things, but to be a cold-blooded killer, I couldn't see it!*

He picked up, "Hello, Amazon, Jamal Stone speaking, how can I help you?"

I took a deep breath. "Jamal, you're not going to believe who just left here?"

"Who?" Jamal knew it was Jen from her voice.

"The motherfucking FBI! Dr. Rawlings is dead and they were here questioning me about you. They were asking a lot of other questions, especially about your whereabouts on Friday night! You know the night you slept on my couch!"

"I wonder why they would be asking questions about me! What did you tell them?" Jamal replied, feeling a little tense!

"What do you mean, what did I tell them! I told them that you were in Boston with the boys! What else would I tell them?" I answered, feeling frustrated that I was dealing with this shit again!

"Good, Jen, the last thing I need is them trying to pin some bullshit on me! I need to be here for my family!" Jamal declared with relief!

"They were trying to imply through Jamal, and what I got was that they were trying to say you had something to do with this! But I know that can't be true, Jamal, right?"

"Come on, Jen, you know I didn't! Remember I talked to you that night at Tracy's. I called you from your house before you went out!" Jamal was trying to reassure her that she had nothing to worry about!

"I remember, Jamal! I just worry about you. That's all! Be ready though, I bet they're on their way to question you right now. And now that I think about it, Jamal, those two FBI agents were the same two on the news about that serial killer.

"This is the second death they are questioning you about surrounding their investigation!"

I gasped. "Jamal, Tanya was killed by this guy, what the fuck, man!"

"Don't worry about it, Jen. Everything is going to be alright, and thanks for the heads up. Love you, talk to you later!"

"You too, bye!"

I leaned back in my chair, put my hand on my forehead, "Fuck!" and I thought, *Let me call Kim and tell her what's going on!*

Kim answered on the second ring, "Hello!"

"Hey, Kim, it's Jen!"

"What's up, girl, how is your day?"

"Stressful and that's why I'm calling you."

"Okay . . . What's up?" Kim replied, sounding puzzled.

"The fucking FBI just left here asking questions about you and Jamal, and I just wanted to give you the heads up that they might be stopping by."

"Get the fuck out of here. Did you call Jamal yet?" Kim exclaimed in shock!

"Sure did! Kim, have you watched the news?"

"No, why?"

"Dr. Rawlings was killed this past weekend, and the two FBI agents heading up the investigation were the ones who stopped here. I believe that life-ruiner killer got to her just like we talked about."

"Get the fuck out of here! She's dead!"

"Sure is!"

"Wow, that's bizarre! It's like we talked about her death! Well, thanks for the heads up!"

I told Kim the kinds of questions they asked me, and then we hung up. I was not in the mood for work at the moment and decided to take my lunch break.

I called Tracy to see if she was available to join me, but she had court this afternoon. She was finishing up some last-minute stuff and couldn't join me. So I grabbed a chicken Caesar salad from Panera Bread and ate there.

I hoped that everything was good with Jamal and thought how devastating it would be to all of us if something happened to him. Then I realized that there was no way Jamal had something to do with any of this shit, so my mind was at ease. After I finished my lunch, I went back to work less worried.

Chapter 46

Kim

I was sitting on the couch relaxing, thanking God that Evelyn was finally done kicking my ass. She'd been at it a lot lately, and I knew she was ready to get out just as much as I was ready for her to get out too.

I just hung up the phone from talking to my mom about how nice the baby shower was this past Sunday, and everyone got everything I had on my list. I even got extra Pampers in sizes all the way up until Evelyn would turn one.

Some of my coworkers came, more than I thought would be able to make it. It almost felt like they closed the hospital down for my shower or either left the little darlings running the hospital. I laughed at the thought. I missed being there so much helping people.

So an hour into my relaxation, I got a call from Jen, and I thought, *She never calls me while she's at work.* I answered on the second ring, and what she told me blew my mind.

I couldn't believe Dr. Rawlings was dead, and I turned the news on right away. I was also in awe because we were just talking about that serial killer and her being a target on his list, go figure.

Freaky! But what bothered me the most was when Jen told me they were questioning her about Jamal, and the kinds of questions they were asking. My baby had nothing to do with this shit, and the motherfuckers need to leave my man alone.

I hung up with Jen and had to pee, so I rolled my pregnant ass off the couch using the downstairs bathroom. It was times like these that I was happy as hell for a bathroom on the first floor.

I was on the toilet when I heard knocking at my door, but I'd be damned if I was rushing for anyone at this moment. They could come back for all I care. The relief was so good that my eyes rolled to the back of my head like an orgasm. *Damn I love that feeling*, I thought.

I cleaned up and whoever was knocking was still out there knocking. I guessed they knew I was home for two reasons. One my car was in the driveway, and two the whole world knew I was pregnant.

I got to the door and I wasn't surprised to see Agent Carter and Reid standing on my porch. In the back of my mind, I knew it was them, and maybe that was one of the reasons I didn't rush to answer the door.

I opened the door. "Come in, Agents, nice to see you again!"

I lied, leading them to the living room. "What can I do for you?"

I continued struggling to sit down, "I can't wait until Evelyn is here, and she's always sitting on my bladder, got me peeing all the time!

"Sorry to bother you, we just have some questions if you don't mind?" Agent Reid said with a light chuckle.

"No problem, have a seat. I saw the news today about Dr. Rawlings. She was a wicked woman to do that to those people!"

"That's kind of why we're here, Mrs. Stone. You work at the same hospital as she did, right?"

"I do, but I haven't been there since February 15 as you can see!" I replied, pointing and doing a circle around my stomach."

"Mrs. Stone, how often do you and Jamal go to Jennifer's house?"

"Quite often actually, him more than me, but we're a tight group. We all get along and Jen and I hang out sometimes without Jamal.

"Jamal made it very clear before we got married that we all had to get along if there was going to be a future for us. His boys are one of the most important things in this world, and everything has to be in harmony, even more now because of Evelyn.

"His boys will now have a sister, and he doesn't believe in separate families, and Jen and I respect that!"

"Was Jamal with you on Friday night?" Reid asked, trying to question his alibi.

"No, he was in Boston with his sons having a guys' night out."

"So you were here on Friday night? Do you always let Jamal go over to his ex-wife's house?"

I could feel that she was trying to start something by her comment because one question didn't have anything to do with the other, but I wasn't biting because I was secure in our relationship.

"First of all, let Jamal," I laughed. "You don't let Jamal, anything! You don't try to control a man especially if you trust him.

"He's a good father, friend, caring, and fun to be around! I have never met anyone that doesn't like Jamal.

"And yes, I was here with my girlfriend Sarah. Jamal did come home and got ready before he went out."

Reid thought, *Damn he could have been mine!* "Thank you for your time, Mrs. Stone." Terry and Lori stood.

I was about to get up when they stood, but Agent Carter said, "Hey, relax, relax, Mrs. Stone. We could show ourselves out. Thank you for your time." They both shook my hand and left.

I was glad to be done with that. I tried to call Jamal, but he didn't answer. I guess he was out on the floor. I wasn't worried because Jen already gave him the heads up, so I called Sarah and told her about everything. She was my best friend and I kept nothing from her.

Chapter 47

Terry

We finished Jen and Kim's interviews, and Lori and I were on our way to Amazon to interview Jamal.

During the drive, Lori said, "Terry, Jen seemed very confident Jamal had nothing to do with this, and she gave him a tight alibi and Kim confirmed it."

"I know but there are too many coincidences surrounding Jamal, and if we, as the top-of-the-line investigators, don't look into these coincidences, then we would not be doing our job justice.

"I mean one I can accept, but two or three there has to be something to it!"

"Or nothing!"

"Or nothing! That may be the case, but still we have to do our jobs.

"Anyway, everybody does seem to love this guy, and to have his wife and ex-wife have that kind of relationship such an understanding, how does he do it?

"I mean, get along for the kids' sake but hang-out buddies, come on!"

"I don't know but it is kind of poetic if you ask me. Like people only dream of not having baby momma drama and a tight relationship for the kids' sake. You got to give the two women respect for understanding Jamal's logic."

I thought, *I know I would for Jamal.* "Well, his alibi lines up, and if his boys say the same thing, then that's what I call airtight!"

"Could you live like that if you were in Kim's shoes?"

"I mean to me it makes sense if you're secure in who you are and in your relationship. I would have to really trust a man for me to do that.

"I have to like a lot about the other woman for us to be friends like Kim and Jen. That's definitely unheard of."

"I couldn't agree more," I proclaimed as we pulled into Amazon.

It was three o'clock and before we got out of the car, I called Mark. "What's up, Mark, how are things going?"

"Were through here and the body is on its way to the morgue for an autopsy.

"I already talked to Noel and she's done. Jason left to go get her. Susan and I are going to conduct interviews on Carol Street. That's the street closest to the woods and where his footprints led to."

"Good, we're following up leads too, so we'll call you when we are done!" I hung up and turned to Lori. "Let's go see Jamal!"

Chapter 48

March 17, 2022

Jamal

I hung up from Jen and leaned back into my chair with a big smile on my face. I knew that this kill was too close to home, but that was what made it exciting. I had an airtight alibi, and I was having fun playing this game.

I mean I didn't want to go back to prison especially with Evelyn soon to be here. I missed ten years of my boys' lives, and even though they'd grown, I didn't want to miss them anymore.

However, I was addicted to this killing shit, and for some reason, because of it, my life had been at peace. I was rarely in a bad mood, hardly argued with Kim or Jen, and even work was less stressful. It was the best therapy a man could ask for.

I checked my watch and it was a little after three. I got up from my seat to look out onto the floor. When I looked, I saw Agent Carter and Agent Reid being escorted to my office.

I knew they could see me looking out of my blinds, so I opened the door. "I got it from here, Rebecca!"

"Okay, Mr. Stone, I'm going to clock out. See you tomorrow."

"See ya!"

I turned to the agents. "Well, well, come in. It's nice to see you both again!"

I shook their hands but held on to Lori's a little longer with a smile before letting go. She didn't try to pull away, and she was blushing.

I thought, *She knows now. This is about to get really interesting*, "Have a seat. What can I do for you?"

I sat behind my desk and Carter said, "I don't know if you know it or not, but Dr. Ann Rawlings was killed this weekend. She was killed Friday night into Saturday morning." Carter paused to gauge a reaction from me.

"I saw. It was on the news this morning before I went to work, Agent Carter. I didn't know the woman." I left it open for him to question me more. *Fun, fun!*

I took a look over at Lori and I liked the way she was looking at me, and I was certain now that she knew.

Terry said, "You said you don't know her, but doesn't your wife work with her at Saint Mary's?"

"Yes, Kim works with her, and I met her at a Christmas party once, but to say I know her, I don't.

"Just because Kim works with her, and I met her once doesn't constitute me knowing her."

Lori was staring so hard that I turned and asked, "Agent Reid is everything okay? Is there something on my face?"

She snapped out of it. "Umm no, I'm sorry. I mean there's nothing on your face!"

I was smiling as I slowly rotated my head back in Carter's direction, and he was looking at Lori, trying to figure out what was going on. He tilted his head as if he was telling Lori to get with the program.

Carter focused back on me. "Your ex-wife Jennifer Stone lives by Dr. Rawlings, did you know that?"

"Yes, I did. As a matter of fact, Kim reminds me every time we pass by her house, and recently there was a media frenzy at her home because of that cancer fiasco at the hospital."

"You, your wife, and ex-wife have a strange relationship. Your ex-wife allows you free rein at her home, and your current wife accepts your relationship with your ex-wife."

Carter knew that that wasn't a question, more of a statement that he wanted an answer to. He also knew it had nothing to do with the murder, but he was so curious about it. He had to see what Jamal was going to say.

I smiled and looked at Lori, and I could tell she wanted to know the answer to that question. "Agent Carter, that question has nothing to do with anything, but since you want to know, I'll tell you."

I took a sip of my water and then cleared my throat. "My relationship with both women is because of family and acceptance.

"What I mean by that is that any woman I plan to have a future with must accept my past, and my point of view of it.

"Jen is my kid's mother and I believe that it is healthy for the kids to see their parents having a strong relationship even if they are not together and with those who become involved in that relationship. Jen understands and agrees with that to the fullest.

"Kim was worried about that in the beginning until I explained my logic to her about family.

"I explained about the mental stability of a child when separation doesn't separate a family, and how a family only grows when people are added.

"Once she saw how we executed the family atmosphere and knew there was nothing romantic between Jen and me, Jen and Kim became friends and we became a family."

"Wow," Lori proclaimed, "that sounds like a happy-ever-after fairytale, and it makes perfect sense if all parties understand that logic."

I smiled as I replied, "Exactly, but there is one more part to that logic, and that is the security factor.

"Meaning, if a woman is insecure or a man creates insecurity in that woman, then it could never work."

"Not for nothing, that's some book-worthy knowledge!" Agent Carter said.

"Thanks, Agent Carter!"

Lori thought, *This man is so sexy and not just in looks but intellect as well! Damn I could have had him!*

Carter continued. "Do you know Ofcr. Frank Mason of the East Hampton Sheriff's Department?"

"Sure do, I talk to him all the time. I've given him and his sons tickets to Jermaine's games. Matter of fact, I talked to him on Wednesday."

"How often do you go to your ex-wife's house?"

I thought about it for a few seconds then replied, "I go up there a lot like when my kids are home when I'm doing things around Jen's house, so she doesn't have to pay for it, even when Kim and I want to take a ride and even sometimes for myself. Remember, family!

"I was up that way quite a bit this week getting Jen's ready for the spring, throwing down grass seeds, power-washing her siding, cleaning the gutters, and weed killing. I want to get that stuff done before the baby comes."

Lori thought, *What doesn't this man do? And I know he's amazing in bed!*

"Last question, Mr. Stone. Where were you on Friday night, Saturday morning?"

"This past Friday I was in Boston with my boys having a guys' night out.

"They have their finals coming up, and they wanted to get together and they invited me. After this past weekend from this point on, they don't party. They just focus on their studies.

"During my ten years bid, all I did was preach to them about school, school, and more school!"

They both stood up and Carter put his hand out. "Thanks for your time, Mr. Stone!"

I took his hand. "Anytime, Agent!"

I then shook Lori's hand and held on for a little longer while smiling, and so did she. I walked them to my office door, and I watched them leave the building.

As Lori was walking out to the car, she thought, *I have to find a way to talk to Jamal alone.* She said to Terry, "I'll meet you in the car, I have to use the bathroom!"

"Alright I'll pull up right here at this door!"

Before I closed my office door, I saw Lori come running back into the building and straight for my office. I went to stand by my desk as she came bursting in my door.

"Hello, Lori, it's been a long time!" I said being sarcastic knowing why she was there!

"What the fuck, Jamal, or should I say, Anthony, or whatever you're calling yourself these days!

"That was really fucked up, Jamal. You had me beating myself up these few weeks, and you knew all along who I was. How come you didn't say anything?" she said angrily with her hand on her hip, sassing her head!

"Come on, Lori, what was I supposed to say! I mean here you are investigating a serial killer, and you're over there questioning me like I'm a prime suspect!

"So what would you like me to say, Lori! Oh, now that you cleared me as a suspect, remember that wonderful night we had together when you were in college. Oh and by the way, my name isn't Anthony.

"Oh yea, and let's not forget what I would have to say to my pregnant wife! By the way, honey, this is Lori the FBI agent. Thirteen years ago I had a one-night stand with her, and now she thinks I'm a murderer!"

"I don't think that, Jamal!"

Lori relaxed because she knew I was right, "Jamal, I didn't know you were a drug dealer all those years ago.

"I thought about you every day hoping we would cross paths again. I wish I knew you were in prison, but Cash wouldn't tell Natia anything except you were gone for a while.

"Well, at least I know now that you are alive and doing well!"

"Thank you for caring. Lori, and for the record, I thought about you a lot too! If things were different at that time, I would have pursued you. By the way you're still beautiful as ever!"

"Thanks, and you're still very handsome, but I didn't recognize you because of your facial hair and corn rolls."

"I know, new times have a different look I guess!"

"Well, I'm glad I had the chance to clear the air. I have to go. Terry is in the car waiting for me!"

"Wait, let me ask you something? Do you think I have something to do with these murders?"

"I don't at all and neither does Terry, but coincidences have to be followed up!"

"What do you mean, coincidences, Lori? Oh wait, Tanya, and now Dr. Rawlings living on Jen's street, and working with Kim!"

"Yea, something like that. I have to go, Jamal, and it was really nice seeing you again.

"I know I'm not supposed to say this, but I have to get it off my chest. No one has ever made me feel like you did. It was a gift and a curse, and I'll leave it at that." She walked out of my office before I could respond.

Lori left feeling better now that she had closure after all these years, but she still admired the man Jamal had become and thought about if her life would be the same if she was with him back then, would she be with the FBI? She didn't know but she would've taken that chance with him. She got in the car and they left.

I was glad that little interaction took place with Lori but most of all for the information she just gave me. I mean I was convinced that she believed

I was innocent, but that word coincidences danced around in my mind, so now it was bugging me on what she meant by that.

I already had my next target, but now I believed that things might get a little more complex. They may be watching for a little while just to make sure I was clean, so I thought like a cop and that would make me their prime suspect.

I smiled and thought, *I'll chill until Evelyn is born, but that fucking judge has to die. I'm a few steps ahead of the FBI, so let's see if they could* CATCH ME!

Chapter 49

March 18, 2022

Terry

My team and I all stayed in Massachusetts at the Holiday Inn Express, and it wasn't until one in the morning that our briefing was done. We were all in the conference room at the hotel, and we went over everything we gathered from Dr. Rawlings's murder.

First, her house was broken into, then she was kidnapped, brought to 1955 North Williams Street, and then murdered.

I asked, "Jason, what are you able to tell us that we don't know?"

"As usual the crime scene is wiped clean. I believe we might have a partial fingerprint. The lab is running it, but I don't think we have enough to go on.

"He came through the back door and carried her to the basement. Noel was right. It was the burned hair perm that we smelled. We found some of it on the plug of the cord and the wall. So he covered her in the perm and burned her with the UV lights.

"His MO is to cut and torture his victims, but the body was so badly burned that only the autopsy can determine that and we won't have that until tomorrow."

"Alright, so the full workup tomorrow!" I took a deep breath. "Noel, what do you have!"

"First, I have Detective Marks's phone number for you! She would not stop asking questions about you and talking about how sexy you are! Man, I almost committed murder myself today!"

They were all laughing as I said, "Not interested, Noel!"

"Good, now what was laid out for us when we got there was pretty much dead on. No pun intended.

"The foot size as we know is a size eleven and a half to twelve boots. He climbed the fence, came in through the back door, and turned off the alarm. That tells us that he has computer hacking ability because he had to hack North Star to get the code.

"He went upstairs to her bedroom then took her and carried her out the front door. Before leaving, he rearmed the alarm.

"He walked to the woods alongside the fence to the back, set her down almost twenty yards away from the fence up against that tree.

"Now here is the tricky part. He climbs the tree, and I assume it's to retrieve something, but what I kept asking myself.

"He used a camera at the Dawson's, so maybe he used one here, but what I can't figure out is that the tree is a little over twenty yards from the house, and why would he set up a camera outside if he can't see what's going on in the house."

She shrugged her shoulders, "Maybe binoculars, but again why come back to the tree and climb it. I must say whoever this guy is, he is smart as hell and bat-shit crazy."

"Alright, it's getting late, and we have to wait until we see the autopsy for more information, so Susan and Mark, what do you have from Carol Street?"

Susan said, "We interviewed the whole block, and other than this one girl Alissa Winters no one saw anything strange.

"Alissa Winters lives at 340 Carol Street. She said her boyfriend picked her up around one thirty, and as they were driving up the street, she saw a car parked at the end of the block that she had never seen before.

"It was a black four-door sedan, but she didn't pay much attention to the model of the car. She said that Mr. and Mrs. Evarts always parked in their driveway at night.

"So Mark and I talked to the couple and asked them if they saw anything strange and we asked about the car, and they said no they are always asleep around that time and they always park in their driveway."

"Alright then, we now have confirmation on a dark car from Dawson's and Carol Street. Moving on, Lori and I were following leads that led us to Jamal Stone—"

"See, I'm telling you he's linked somehow, trust me!" Susan interrupted!

"That's why we followed up. Jamal's ex-wife lives on Williams Street, and he goes there all the time.

"And let me tell you, this guy is something else. His wife and ex-wife are friends and hangout buddies. His logic on how it works is intellectually clever.

"Anyway, his current wife works at the hospital with Dr. Rawlings. We interviewed both of the Mrs. Stones about where Jamal was on Friday night and contacted both his sons, and they all said that Jamal was with his sons in Boston doing a guys' night out. His alibi is airtight.

"But I must say Jamal is too Mr. Perfect. Shit, I even like the guy. With that being said, I want eyes on him.

"He spent ten years in prison for drug dealing, so he can't be that perfect. He was on the streets for thirteen years straight hustling and spent ten years in the joint. He must have connections to people that are capable of these acts.

"Let's look at the fact that this all started with Tanya Spencer. Why was she the first on this lunatic rampage? Jamal may not be the killer, but I bet my life that he knows the killer."

Lori was kind of pissed, but she didn't know why. Everything Terry was saying was good, but she couldn't believe that Jamal had anything to do with these murders. She found herself wanting to protect Jamal from all this. She felt that Jamal was a good man and was doing right by his family more than she could say about her father. She felt the way Jamal felt about how a family should be and believed everyone should view it that way.

When the meeting was over, Lori and I went to separate rooms. Even though the team had their suspicions, it wasn't the time to broadcast it.

After being in my room for a little while, I figured that everyone else was in their rooms doing their thing so I went over to Lori's room.

I lightly tapped on her door. She opened it and I just walked back to her bed. I felt like she was giving me the cold shoulder.

As I walked in, I asked, "Is everything alright, Lori?"

"Why didn't you tell me you wanted eyes on Jamal, and what's with all that Mr. Perfect- speech shit?" she replied, annoyed!

"I'm sorry I didn't say anything, but there are too many coincidences surrounding Jamal that we can't ignore, not that I think he's the killer.

"And come on, Lori, I didn't really mean anything about the Mr. Perfect thing, but you have to admit that it's all too clean, don't you think?"

"I think the man just came home from doing a ten years prison sentence, got his life together, has a great family outlook, and now you're giving orders for him to be followed like he's the architect of these murders!" she replied, coming off a little protective.

I couldn't believe what I was hearing then I thought, *I knew there was something a little strange when we interviewed Jamal.*

"Wait, do you know Jamal from somewhere? I was kind of getting that vibe when we were at his office!"

"Don't be silly, Terry! Where would I know him from?

"It's just you coming up with all these theories and ideas that I know nothing about. I'm your partner, and we're together all day and night!"

She turned it on him because she didn't want Terry to know anything, so she calmed down. "Just let me know what's going on. I don't like being left in the dark!"

"I'm sorry, babe, I promise I will run my theories by you. But just for the record, I think Jamal is innocent, but we have to be sure."

I walked close, looking her in her eyes, "We're the FBI and we have to cross our Ts, and dot our Is. Now, can I spend the night with you or are you putting me on time out!"

Lori came up to her knees on the bed, grabbed my hand, pulled me close, and kissed me.

She pulled back. "I'm very tired and we had a long day. Can we just cuddle together, and have spoon sex to go to sleep?"

We stripped naked and climbed into bed. "I love the fact that you always know what and how you want it, beautiful and secure!"

We spoon-sexed ourselves to sleep!

Chapter 50

April 19, 2022

Jamal

Just as I thought, all month long they'd been watching me, even Kim noticed. That was okay though because I knew it would happen. I was going to work, going to Jen's, and hanging with Kim, so I didn't give a fuck.

I got up this morning and went to take a shower. Five minutes into my shower, I heard Kim scream, "Jamal . . . my water just broke!"

I jumped out of the shower and ran into the bedroom in my birthday suit.

Kim was climbing out of the bed, "Oh my god, my water broke!"

I went to help her up and then started moving as fast as I could, getting her stuff to wear and then helping her get dressed.

I grabbed the hospital bag and started leading her to the bedroom door as I said, "Okay, baby, let's go. I'll help you down the steps and then get the car!"

As we were walking, Kim froze. I asked, "What's wrong, baby, is everything okay?"

She started laughing as she replied, "Jamal, are you going to the hospital the same way Evelyn is about to come into this world!"

"What do you mean, she's coming through your birth canal!"

She laughed harder and shook her head, pointing her finger and moving it up and down. Then it dawned on me as I looked at what I had on. I was still in my birthday suit!

I laughed. "Damn, I would if I have to, shit this is my favorite outfit anyway!" We both continued to laugh. "Do I have two minutes?"

"Boy, go put some clothes on! I can make it down the steps myself!" she proclaimed as she started for the door, still laughing.

As I moved to my closet to grab a sweat suit and before she walked out the door, I said, "Okay, babe, but you know I would go with my dick swinging!"

I heard her laughing down the steps, and she yelled back, "Baby, you're so crazy!"

I was down the steps in three minutes, and we were out the door to North Hampton Memorial Hospital.

We were taken straight to the maternity ward. Dr. Kerr, Kim's regular doctor, checked her, and she was four centimeters dilated.

I called Gloria and Jeff Wade—Kim's parents, Jen, and Sarah. Gloria Wade was a thick bombshell with long brunette hair and a face that showed no signs of her fifty-seven years.

Jeff Wade had silver hair, a strong angular face, and a muscular upper body. You could tell he still worked out but needed to work on his belly but not bad for sixty-three.

They were the first to arrive. They entered the room and Gloria said, "Oh my god, baby, how you feel?"

I shook Jeff's hand. "How are you, sir?"

"I'm good, son, especially because you take such good care of my little girl!"

I smiled. "Of course, sir! She's your little girl and my baby girl!"

"That's what I like to hear, son!" he replied, laughing then turning his attention to Kim.

Gloria got up and gave me a hug as she said, "It's so nice to see you, Jamal!"

"You too, Gloria! Are you ready to be a grandmother?"

"Yea, by title only, Evelyn is going to call me nana and Jeff pop-pop! Grand anything sounds like old people, Jamal, and you know I'll be thirty-nine forever!" Gloria laughed at her own joke!

My phone started ringing as Sarah walked in. I excused myself and then stepped into the hallway. "What's up, Jamal?" Craig Matthews asked.

"I'm good, Craig, just at the hospital. Kim's in labor she's four centimeters dilated."

"Congrats, brother!"

"Thanks. It took you a while to call me back!"

"I know, I've been busy as all hell, Jamal, and you know DC never sleeps. I'm calling now though.

"I talked to the higher-ups, and they want to meet with Jamal and have a look at his OVD. They are very interested in his invention.

"This could be a future for Jamal, and if we like it, we just might want future projects from him too!"

Jen walked up to me. "Why are you on the phone in the hall while your wife is having a baby?"

I put one finger up so she could give me a minute. "That's great, man! I'm telling you the OVD is amazing! When would they like to meet?"

"How about May 1?"

"May 1 sounds good to me. I'll call Jamal, text me the info, and I'll forward it."

"Tell Craig I said hi!" Jen interrupted!

"Hey, Craig, Jen says hi!"

I turned to Jen. "He said what's up!" I refocused on my conversation, "Okay, buddy, I'll talk to you soon!" We hung up!

"Jen, Jamal has a meeting on May 1 with Uncle Sam! Craig said it could be worth a fortune, and they would want future projects from him!"

"That's great, Jamal, should I go with him as an advisor?"

"Maybe we both should go, plus I haven't seen Craig in months. But let's let Jamal decide though. We should let him handle it his way."

"Kim's in this room?" she asked, pointing at the door.

"Sure is! I'll be in, in a minute. Let me call work and Jamal!"

Jen went in and I called work to let Ethan Daniels know about my situation. He gave me my vacation time early.

Next, I called Jamal but he didn't answer, so I left a message for him to call me back and then send him the info from Craig.

I walked back into the room, and everyone was just talking away. I went to Kim's side and took her hand. I turned to Sarah. "Hey, Sarah, good to see you!"

"Hey, Jamal . . . Where you've been, you're supposed to be in here!"

"I know I had to call work . . . Now I'm off until May 7, so I could be home with Kim and the baby!"

I turned to Kim. "Baby, you look relaxed . . . Did they give you the epidural?"

"Yes . . . But she wants out. Man, there is so much pressure between my legs!"

"Just breathe, honey, it won't be long!" Gloria said, reassuring her daughter!

"Babe, that was Craig on the phone," I said, changing the subject and trying to get her mind off the pain. "The government is interested in Jamal's OVD and wants to meet on May 1!"

"That's wonder—ugghh!" Kim had a contraction that hit her!

They were coming every five minutes from that point on and sometimes shorter. When she couldn't take it anymore, she said, "She's coming . . . Get the doctor!"

She pushed the nurse button like a madwoman, and the nurse came right away.

She checked Kim and then took off for the doctor right away. She and the doctor were back in two minutes, and everyone stepped out of the way while I was still holding Kim's hand. She squeezed it with such power I didn't even know she had.

Dr. Kerr said, "Okay, Evelyn is trying to get here on her own, so let's do this!"

The nurse prepared everything, and Kim started pushing. I saw Evelyn's head pop out, then her shoulders, and then the rest.

Evelyn got here fast and the doctor cleared her nose, and she wailed with such power. The doctor wrapped her in a blanket and put her in Kim's arms.

Kim had tears of joy streaming down her face as she looked at Evelyn. "You're finally here, pumpkin! Me and Daddy been waiting for you!"

I looked at my daughter's face, and I thought I knew what love was, but until she came, I didn't know shit!

I mean my boys were my world. I loved them to death, but my little girl, she was my universe. And that was a love that only a man could have for his daughter! Evelyn Renee Stone entered my universe at 11:42 a.m. on April 19, 2022!

Chapter 51

April 22, 2022

Terry

I had all the locals tighten up on all possible targets. The autopsy came back on Dr. Rawlings. She suffered so badly that I couldn't help but start taking this case personally. Not just that though, it was because this psycho was laughing at us!

Her alcohol level was 1.3, and she was Tasered, rendering her unconscious. The killer was true to his MO. She was cut and drenched with bleach so much it was in her blood.

Her body was covered in perm, and if that shit sat too long on your skin, your skin would burn off. With that shit heated up, it was like deep-frying chicken. The UV lights made it worse because the UV rays would have tanned someone in three minutes.

The one thing we had going for us was that Noel was right about the possible target scenario, and if the locals would've done their job as we asked, she would still be alive and we would've had more on our killer.

Over the last month we had an around-the-clock watch on every target, and we all were taken shifts watching Jamal Stone. At times we even switched partners, so we could share a fresh perspective.

After our briefing today, Susan and I had the 4:00 p.m.–12:00 a.m. shift watching Jamal. So far nothing has happened. Jamal had been coming from work, his ex-wife's, and home. Every now and then he had drinks and basketball at Ethan Daniels's home.

Jamal just had his baby on Friday and they came home on Sunday, and other than Jamal going to the store, he'd been home.

I had everyone go back to the people they interviewed and ask them about Jamal Stone or Roc, his street name. We also checked if Jamal had any connection to any of the victims.

So far, we had a connection to Tanya Spencer, Dr. Rawlings, Carmela Lopez, and Damarcus Way. Tanya, she put Jamal away, Dr. Rawlings lived on Jen's street and worked with Kim,

Carmela snitched on Jamal's cousin Lenny Burns, and Demarcus Way who killed Kane Rogers was Nettie Roger's son. Nettie's sister Melissa was friends with Jen.

Even though we couldn't find any more connections, these four coincidences were definite grounds for a prime suspect.

Susan and I were sitting down the block from Jamal's. "You know, Terry, I always thought we should have been watching Jamal. The first victim and then his name pops up again and again.

"If Kevin and Gordon asked the right questions, Jamal would have been our prime suspect in the beginning!

"You and Lori just wrote him off as Mr. Perfect who was truly rehabilitated after spending ten years in prison.

"Come on, Terry . . . We all know the system doesn't work that well! He had nothing but time to plan and get smart! He was already fucking smart!"

"Look, Susan, I know there are too many coincidences to ignore, but I still think Jamal has nothing to do with it, but that's personal but professionally we have to follow the breadcrumbs.

"I mean I do think he's too perfect to be an ex-con drug dealer, but I've been over his file, and there is no violence other than the eight years he spent in the military but even then left with an honorable discharge, and that's what training does.

"Let's see . . . he has a bachelor's in business from Delaware University, both of his boys are smart about to graduate college, has one of the weirdest great relationships with his ex and current wife, good job, and just had a little girl.

"Why risk all that going around killing people like a lunatic." I was amazed at my assessment of Jamal.

Susan looked at me with shifty eyes, and then shifted her body. "What the hell, Terry! Did you and Lori join his fan club?"

"Whatever, Susan . . . I'm just stating the facts!" I replied, realizing it sounded just like that, and I was annoyed with myself!

We sat in silence for a few, and then Susan said, "I see that you and Lori are hitting it off? We all knew it was going to happen from day 1!

"But here's a little factoid, partners and relationships don't last. They always fall apart due to so much time spent together!"

"It's funny you should say that because we just had this conversation a little while ago. It's going great right now though.

"Neveah and I met her family and she met mine. We both see a future together, and after this case, we're getting new partners."

"Do you love her?"

"I do, Susan . . . She's the best thing that has happened to me since Neveah!" I replied, thinking, *Damn I just put Lori in the same category as Neveah.*

"That's big, Terry . . . She's up there with Neveah!" Susan was astonished!

We sat quietly for a little while until I said, "We are going to give this a couple more weeks, maybe a month then we're just going to focus on the targets.

"I mean the killer kills about every four months, so don't you think Jamal would at least be doing surveillance on his next target?

"Tomorrow we should go question him about our assumption and then leave it at that."

"Sounds good to me! I like to meet Mr. Perfect anyway!" she replied, knowing that her gut was telling her that Jamal was the guy!

Susan and I talked and watched until our shift was over.

Chapter 52

April 23, 2022

Jamal

This past weekend was the greatest because I brought home my little girl on Sunday, six pounds five ounces, seventeen and a half inches, and a head full of hair. Evelyn looked a lot like her brothers when they were born. The only difference was her big slanted hazel eyes, and Jamal and Jermaine had big eyes, but theirs were chestnut brown.

The boys came home to meet their sister, and they were fighting over who gets to hold her, but of course, Shelby beat them both.

Everyone that was at the hospital came over on Sunday to be with Evelyn, and it was a joyful weekend.

I didn't think, not once, about the people I'd killed or my next target. I did see the FBI watching my house. They must think I was stupid like I hadn't lived here for the past three years, and I didn't know everyone and what car they drove.

My army training kept me alert and paying attention to little details in my surroundings no matter how small they are. I had one slip back in 1993 when I was sixteen on a possession charge in New Jersey but got youthful offender status, and when I turned eighteen, the charge was no longer on my record.

I went to the army straight out of high school and had been selling drugs since my third year of enlistment.

I met Jennifer on my second tour of four years, and with my GI bill and all the money I was making, I was able to put both of us through college.

The army taught me a lot, and with those skills, I could see the FBI ten miles away.

I had Kim pumping breast milk when we got home, so at night she wouldn't have to get up, and I could feed our little girl. Evelyn though was just like her brothers because at night she only woke up twice.

Today, I let Kim sleep because her body was still healing. I was just putting Evelyn down for a nap when Kim woke up. She lay there watching me as I laid Evelyn into her bassinet.

"Good afternoon, sleepyhead, you want some coffee?" I whispered.

"What I want is a kiss," she whispered back, coming up to her knees and wrapping her arms around my neck.

She leaned forward and I leaned back and jokingly said, "No way, yuck mouth" as I covered my mouth and started pointing at her mouth like the old spearmint commercial.

She chuckled as she hit me, and then I gave her a kiss. When we separated, I said, "I'll meet you downstairs. Are you hungry?"

"Yea, but can you just make me a cream cheese bagel with sliced grapefruit with my coffee?"

"Sure can," I replied as I walked away after slapping her on the ass.

I'd been up with Evelyn since six this morning, and she took a nap at nine for about an hour, so I cleaned the house but now I was ready to take a nap.

Kim came downstairs as I was pouring her coffee. I put everything she liked in her coffee and handed it to her just as the bagel popped up.

She sat at the table watching me as I creamed her bagel and sliced her grapefruit. "Jen was right," she said.

"Right about what?"

"She told me that I wouldn't have to worry about doing all the baby work, that you would be doing more with the baby while I got to rest up!"

"Well, you brought my universe to me and carried her for ten months... That's no easy task. Baby, you will never feel that you are doing this alone because we are a team, and I have to catch up," I explained as I put her plate in front of her.

"What do you mean catch up?" she asked, looking puzzled.

"Babe, you have been caring for Evelyn for ten months. You carried her, fed her, you endured her moods, her kicking, lying on your bladder, the heartburn, and the uncomfortable nights. That's what I mean."

"Are you an alien or something," she said then sipped her coffee. "With your family logic and your super daddy skills, not for nothing, Jen messed up giving you up!"

I smiled. "I might be from outer space!" I replied, making weird faces and causing her to laugh. "Nah, but for real tho. The things I think about when it comes to family is how I wished my mother and father thought about it. I just choose to live by my logic and hope that whoever is in my life comprehends it."

I kissed her then said, "I'm going to take a shower then a nap, and it's your shift!" She slapped me on my ass before I left the room.

It was almost two thirty when I drifted off. I felt like I just fell asleep when Kim shook me.

She said, "Jamal . . . Jamal." I opened my eyes and tried to focus. "Those FBI agents are back again."

"What time is it?" I asked, trying to snap the grogginess.

"It's four fifteen, get up and come downstairs!"

Kim went back downstairs with Evelyn in her arms while I got up and tried to pull myself together because I wasn't going to let them catch me slipping.

Ten minutes later I came downstairs. In my living room was Agent Carter and another woman I hadn't met before.

They both stood as Carter put his hand out, "Sorry to wake you, Jamal. I know you've been dealing with your little girl."

"No problem, Agent Carter. I've been up since six with Evelyn, so Kim can sleep in."

Carter turned to the woman, "Jamal, this is Agent Steals!"

I shook her hand and said, "Agent Carter, are all your partners this pretty, how do you contain yourself? Hello, Agent Steals, it's very nice to meet you."

She blushed. "Why thanks, Mr. Stone, and it's nice to meet you too!"

I reached for Evelyn and Kim handed her to me as I said to the agents, "Have a seat, what can I do for you?"

"I really hate bothering you, but I have to ask you some questions!" Carter said.

"It's okay to ask away!"

"Do you know Lenny Burns from Springfield, Massachusetts?"

"Yea, that's my cousin, Keya's son. Lenny is in prison, isn't he? I mean he was shot, and now is paralyzed from the waist down. What does he have to do with anything?"

"Do you know Rico Sanchez?"

"Yea, I knew Rico when I was in that life. Rico and Lenny were younger hustlers that I used to supply a long time ago."

"Did you know Rico's girlfriend Carmela Lopez, they used to live together?"

I thought about it for a minute then said, "Well, I don't remember who his girlfriend used to be back then. It's been a long time since before I went to prison."

"No, I'm talking about a recent girlfriend like before Lenny went to prison."

"Well no, how would I know her? Since I've been home, I've only visited my cousin Keya twice, and that was for her birthday the first year I came home. I mean I saw Rico there, but I don't remember if he was there with someone.

"The second time was when Lenny got shot, and the only people there that day were family, so to answer your question, no, I don't know her."

"So did your cousin tell you anything about what happened to Lenny?"

"Well, she told me about him being set up, and the cops shot him. But she wanted to know what Lenny could do about fighting his case and what kind of time he could be looking at since I was in a similar situation.

"She wanted to know her best option. I told her to get a paid lawyer to negotiate a plea deal and then get a civil attorney to sue for them shooting Lenny. We even gave her five grand toward the lawyer."

The fact that he was forthcoming and didn't have one inch of nervousness in him, Carter was sure that Jamal had nothing to do with any of this. "Jamal, do you know a Kane Rogers? The little boy that was killed by a stray bullet in Bridgeport, Connecticut?"

Now I knew exactly what Lori was talking about when she said coincidences. "Now that was a fucked-up situation!

"Jen called me and told me about what happened to Melissa's sister's son. I've never met the kid . . . I was in prison when he was born.

"I knew Nettie and Melissa because they used to come hang out with Jen and me when we lived in New York and when we moved to Mass.

"Jen and I used to go out there, but this was years ago. Boy, Agent

Carter, you're taking me down memory lane! But I haven't seen them since before I went to prison."

I kept looking at Agent Steals throughout the questioning, and she was paying more attention to Evelyn's comfort than me. Kim sat quietly, playing with Evelyn's finger and her hair.

I handed Evelyn back to Kim and said, "You know, Agent Carter, I'm well aware of your list of victims because I heard them when you mention them on TV, but it never crossed my mind that I could be tied to any of the victims other than Kane and Tanya.

"Well, I could also see why you questioned me on Dr. Rawlings even though I couldn't believe that you thought I had something to do with that.

"Let me assure you that I have nothing to do with what's going on. I paid for my crime and all I'm trying to do is live my life in peace with my family.

"No more drugs or being involved with people who deal with them. I was done back then, and if I woulda listened to Jen, I wouldn't have gone to prison, so lesson learned!"

"Well, Jamal, I respect the man you have become, and I see that you are a good father. I have a little girl myself. . .

"I remember what it was like to hold that little girl in my arms and never wanting to let go. So congrats to you and Kim.

"And just so you know we are just doing our job, and so here we are hoping that you could lead us to some clues to who may be doing this.

"Now that I think about it, have you met anyone in prison that may have committed crimes like these, who knows your story?"

"Agent Carter, I started my bid in a maximum-security facility. I was there with all kinds of killers, drug dealers, rapists, and any kind of crazy crime you could think of.

"All those people seem normal when you interact with them just like you and me, but they are quite insane.

"So think about the ones you locked up. Those numbers are probably nowhere close to the numbers that are still living everyday lives like us.

"I talked to people there, but I did my time and kept mostly to myself and came home not thinking about any of the time I spent inside.

"I have a few friends since I've been home that's doing the right things, and I have my family. I stay away from the rest."

After that Carter and Agent Steals stood, and so did I. Carter said,

"Thanks for your time Jamal. Sorry to bother you during such a joyful time."

"Look, Agent Carter, you're doing your job, and you can stop by anytime if you have any questions.

"You guys have to get this guy off the street, and I hope you do soon."

I turned to Agent Steal. "I didn't hear much from you, but it was a pleasure meeting you!"

"Yea, I know, I figured Agent Carter had it under control, so I just observed. And it was really nice meeting you. Take care of that beautiful baby,"

She turned to Kim. "And nice meeting you too, Kim."

"You too!" Kim replied, playing with Evelyn's fingers.

I shook both of their hands and they left. Kim said, "I'm glad that's over. I hope they leave you alone now. I'm tired of seeing them harass you, baby!"

I kissed her and Evelyn then I replied, "It's alright, babe. They're doing their job!" I changed the subject. "I can't wait for those stitches to come out! I'm horny as hell looking at my BM!"

She laughed. "Me too, baby daddy!"

Terry and Susan got in the car and drove to get some dinner. Terry asked, "So what do you think about Jamal?"

"I see what's to like! He's very charming, polite, and like you said loves his kids. He's also very smart, confident, has a narcissistic personality, and is very prepared.

"Teddy Bundy, Jeffery Damanhur, and the Iceman all had these characteristics . . . and they were lunatics.

"But you may be right, he loves his family, and maybe he wouldn't risk losing them. So I just don't know Terry . . ."

Susan sighed heavily, shaking her head, then looked out the window, "But what I do know is that it's better to be safe than sorry. After we move on, we should still keep an eye on him. I just have a gut feeling."

"I'll tell you what, I'll assign someone to keep watch. Your right it's better to be safe than sorry!"

Chapter 53

May 1, 2022

Evelyn has been sweet as pie since she came home. Everyone wanted a piece of her time. Gloria and Jeff both had been regular visitors since she'd been home. The boys' finals finished this past Friday. They both were here with Shelby, spending the night Saturday and Sunday.

They both got up with Evelyn both mornings and let Kim and I sleep in. Evelyn was loving all the attention from her brothers. She even smiled when they talked to her.

I had to stop them with the baby talking around her. I told them that their mother and I never let anybody do that to them when they were babies because babies talked sooner if you talked to them regularly. I had to tell Kim's parents the same thing. Jeff agreed with me even though he didn't know if that was true.

My house had never been so packed with people. Sarah came by on a regular basis. She was the godmother. Kim was going to name Jen the godmother, but I told her that Jen was no less than Jamal or Jermaine. She was family.

I remembered that before Kim and I got married, how we had to convince her parents about my logic in the family. They weren't too happy about that, but over time and after getting to know Jen, they finally accepted it. We even had to explain it to Sarah, June, and Ethan, so now they all love Jen and we all hang out on numerous occasions.

Jen and Tracy came through a lot also, and during Tracy's first visit, it was also the first time she had been to my home. It had been a great week all and all.

The FBI was still watching me. It was starting to piss me off because I wanted to start planning the judge's death. But today was Jamal's day.

Jermaine was already back to school, but he'd be home Friday for the summer until football practice started back up.

Shelby was still here, and she was staying with Kim and Evelyn while Jamal, Jen, and I went to DC. Jen purchased the tickets for us to leave from Albany's airport, and I was glad because there was no way I wanted to sit in the car for nine hours.

Craig set the meeting for 3:00 p.m. today at the State House on Pennsylvania Avenue. The meeting was with the Secretary of Defense Peter Storm and military intelligence Maj. George Stein. I didn't know all these years that Craig was the advisor to the Secretary of Defense. It blew my mind. I always thought he was in secret service.

It was six in the morning when Jamal and I picked up Jen. She came out in this gray skirt suit with black pinstripes from Vera Wang. Her long golden blonde hair was in a wrap. She looked beautiful. She also had on some black four-inch Steven Madden heels. She was the perfect image for businesswomen.

I said, "Jen, you look amazing, but you better grab your flats so you could be comfortable until we get to DC!"

"You know what, you're right," she replied, pointing her finger at me and went back into the house.

Jamal's suit was Brooks Brothers all black with a mint green button-up, no tie, and black shoes. I was also in a Brooks Brother suit that was ash gray with a salmon-colored button-up, no tie, and gray shoes. Believe me this wasn't planned that all three of us pretty much matched.

When Jen came back out of the house, Jamal got out of the front seat, so she could take it. But before they got back in the car, she said, "I know you guys have a bag back there." She handed Jamal her heels. "Put these with your stuff!"

As we drove to the airport, she said, "Jamal, this is a big thing about to happen. My company wanted to see your OVD, so I told them I'll get back to them as soon as possible. That was yesterday.

"That was before I took the next three days off. I figured you'll find out what the government is offering, and then if it's not what you want or think you could get, then you could entertain World Corp's offer!"

"Okay, Mom . . . Sounds like a plan!"

"Oh, Jamal, before I forget, does Shelby have a driver's license?" I asked, changing the subject.

"She does but it's a London license. I taught her to drive in America, in my car. Now she uses my car when she goes places!"

"I'm getting rid of the Camry. Do you think she would want it?"

"Hell yeah . . . She'll definitely want it! I'm glad too. I'm always worried about if she is going to crash my Lexus, and it's only four years old! Know what, I'll call her right now!" Jamal replied, taking out his phone.

I would've told him it was too early to call, but I knew she was probably up with Evelyn.

Jamal said when Shelby answered, "Morning, beautiful, how's my little sis?"

"She's so good, Jamal. We should have one!"

Jamal looked at the phone with a sour look then puts it back to his ear and replied, "Not right now we shouldn't, maybe in a few more years!"

"Where are you?"

"About twenty-five minutes away from the airport. Hey, babe, listen . . . The reason why—"

"What . . . Now you need a reason to call?" Shelby interrupted!

"No, I don't need a reason, but listen . . ."

"Then why would—"

"Do you want to hear the good news or not?" Jamal said, getting frustrated.

"Go ahead!" She pouted.

"Okay, my dad wants to give you his Camry."

"Hell yea, Jamal, that's bloody cool. When he told you this?"

"Just now!"

"Oh, and you could drive that and I can have the Lexus!" she proclaimed, knowing that she was not getting the Lexus.

"No, I'm not giving you my Lexus! Are you still sleeping . . . because you must be dreaming!"

Jen and I both laughed, and Jamal continued. "Look it's good for now, and if this goes through, then I could buy us any car we want."

"Tell your dad I said—"

"Wait you can tell him, I'm putting you on speaker." Jamal switched it. "Go 'head!"

"Hello, Jen!"

"Hi, honey!"

"Hello, Mr. Stone, thank you so much! I would be happy to take your car!"

"That's no problem, Shelby. You're like my daughter. I was going to sell it, but you know me, family first!"

"Then get me a Lexus like Jamal," she said jokingly. "Nah, but thanks I'm so glad to be a part of your family! Have a safe flight!"

Jamal took her off the speakerphone and then finished his conversation and then hung up.

Chapter 54

Jamal Jr.

That was cool, my dad giving Shelby his car. I would always be so nervous when she took my car alone, but now she could take her own car. As I thought about it, I was sure she was still going to try to take my Lexus.

I was happy as hell when my dad told me about this meeting, and if everything went right, I'd be swimming in money. I also loved talking to my dad because he always gave me the real deal and keeps me looking at different points of view.

My mom, dad, and I got on our flight at nine, and we arrived in DC by noon. We had three hours to kill, so we ate some food and then went sightseeing.

We arrived at the State House at two thirty, and it was a good thing too because the check-in line was thorough with their search. My dad told the officer who we were there to see, and Mr. Matthews showed up at the end of our search.

I watched as my dad greeted Mr. Matthews with a brotherly hug. Mr. Matthews said, "Nice to see you, Jamal!"

"Nice to see you too, Craig, it's been a while! Dang . . . Craig, they search everything. I'm surprised they didn't do an anal search!"

"It sure has been a while, and I could arrange that anal search for you!" he replied, making us all laugh then turned to my mom. "It's been a long time, Jen, but you haven't aged a bit, still beautiful as ever!"

They hugged as my mom replied, "Thank you, and it's so nice to see you too, Craig."

Mr. Matthew turned to me. "JJ, you're bigger than your dad. The last time I saw you I think you were seven or eight. Now you're about to be an MIT graduate and possibly a rich man."

We all started walking, following Mr. Matthews. "Your dad told me about your Optimal Visual Display, and I can't wait to see it in action!"

"Thanks, sir. It's everything my dad said it is, but I'm already working on an upgrade."

"Oh really! Well, wait until we sit down with everyone else, and you could explain it then."

We followed Mr. Matthews as he and my dad talked about playing football in high school. I thought, *Look at these two Al Bundy, married-with-children old men!*

As we walked the halls of the State House, they were very busy. We climbed a flight of steps and walked another long hallway past multiple doors until we got to the end of the hall where we entered the last door to our right.

Mr. Matthews introduced us to Mr. Peter Storm, Secretary of Defense, and Maj. George Stein, military intelligence.

Peter Storm was a white guy with black and silver hair, an angular jaw, and a slim build. Maj. George Stein was another white guy with silver hair, a square face, and a very stocky build.

We all shook hands and Mr. Storm said when he got to me, "I heard a lot about your Optimal Visual Display, Jamal. And if I'm correct, you're about to graduate from MIT at the end of this semester?"

"Sure am, sir!"

Mr. Storm turned to my mom, "And, Ms. Stone, I understand you work for World Corp. Technologies. As you probably already know, we do some business with your company."

"I've seen the invoices come across my desk."

"Well, let's get down to business, shall we?" Mr. Storm pointed at me with a wave. "Jamal, if you will!"

I put my black case on the table, unclasped it, and set up the camera. I said, "The Optimal Visual Display or OVD for short is designed to see through any solid object like these walls for example.

"I can point this camera at any wall, and it will be able to give me a layout of the structure within its view. Its effective range is fifty yards away with any camera, but with a high-power camera, the range is a hundred yards."

I hit a few buttons on the controller, turned on my monitor, and the room we were in popped up with the camera focused on the wall.

I hit another button and then pushed up the arrow, and the view started to move into the X-ray mode, showing the whole layout, and the structure of the State House on every floor all the way to the entrance.

It also showed every person's skeleton doing what they were doing in the building. At just that view, Mr. Storm and Major Stein were amazed.

Major Stein said, "Son, can I see your monitor?"

I handed the major the monitor, "This is amazing, Jamal!"

"I've never seen anything like it. What else can it do?" Mr. Storm asked.

I pushed on the arrow again, and the camera came into full view, seeing everyone and everything as if we were in the rooms with them. Their heads shot back, and their eyes were glazed with shock.

I said, "That's not all it can do!"

"What do you mean, all?" Craig asked, astonished!

I hit the heat signature button, and everyone's body temperatures came up in the building, and even the rats in the walls of the State House were now able to be seen. All three guys were head over heels for what they were seeing.

Major Stein said, "We have to have this! You know how many problems this would solve?"

I was happy as hell, and thought, *My dad was right about coming to the government!*

I said, "That's still not all!"

Mr. Storm looked at me. "Not all, son, this is already far beyond genius, and you're telling me that there's more?"

"Take a look at this."

I hit the infrared night vision button and it popped up. "Night is not a problem, same quality of viewing as daylight!"

"That's it . . . We want it," Mr. Storm said, standing up.

"Wait, sir, there's more!"

All three guys looked at each other as I pulled out my Samsung Galaxy phone. I then selected the OVD app, and the same view from the monitor popped up on my phone.

They were going crazy and were saying, "How genius . . . I never . . . We want this!" They were all talking at the same time!

They looked a little while longer, and then I gave them the controls and showed them how to use it. They played with it for about fifteen minutes then shut it down and gathered around the table.

We refocused on the business aspect of the meeting, and Mr. Storm said, "Well, Jamal, Craig has really undersold the product, and with that being said, we want it. This device can give our military all kinds of advantages. I'm glad your father contacted us, and we are willing to make an offer."

"Well, thank you, sir. I can't tell you how important and proud I am to be a part of our military's advancements.

"My dad served eight years for his country, and I'm proud of that. Furthermore, I have been working on an upgrade—"

"Wait, wait," Mr. Storm said, stunned, "what more can you do with this type of technology?"

"My father brought something to my attention, and I thought it was a great idea so I started working on the OVD to be able to pick up the sound so it can hear and record conversations."

Mr. Storm and Major Stein both leaned back in their chair, and Mr. Storm said, "You don't say! Well, now I believe we have to buy the patent to this device, and any kind of upgrade that comes along with it.

"This device could win you the Nobel Peace Prize. So I'm sure your parents have to discuss numbers with you, so what is it?"

My mom and dad already talked about negotiating a deal, but how they responded to the OVD, I was going to throw my own number out there and see what would happen.

I said, "Well, Mr. Storm, World Corp. offered me 1.5 billion dollars for the patent and any upgrades with promises of future work."

I could see that Mr. Storm was toying with the numbers and leaned over to Major Stein, and they shared a few words that for some reason weren't audible to everyone. I thought, *Military guys and their secret skills!*

Mr. Storm focused his attention back on me and said, "That's a big offer, but I tell you what, can you stay in DC until tomorrow. I have to run something by my people, and I could give you an answer by 11:00 a.m."

We agreed to spend the night, and we left feeling like I had just become a billionaire!

Chapter 55

Jamal

Jamal did a great job on his presentation of the OVD and the negotiating. I couldn't believe he asked for 1.5 billion dollars. Shit, his mother and I told him no less than two hundred and fifty million, but I guess he went on his own response from his presentation and decided it was worth more. I thought, *Shoot, it's the fucking government. They can afford it!*

On our way to the hotel, I said, "Good fucking job, son! I can't believe you asked for over a billion dollars out of the government! That was some negotiation!"

"Sure was, Jamal, I couldn't have done better myself," Jen proclaimed. "A billion dollars, Jamal, I'm so proud of you!"

"Thanks, guys! I couldn't have done it without you guys and trust me this is a family win!

"Dad if you didn't always push school and more school, and Mom if you didn't make sure Dad stayed in our lives when he went away to prison, I don't know where Jermaine and my life would be, so all this is possible because of both of you!"

"Jen, you raised these boys well, and that's why I have nothing but love for you! I know it wasn't easy, but you soldiered through, and look at the outcome, a genius and a superstar! I couldn't be prouder!" I followed up with a joyful tear streaming down my face.

"Trust and believe, Jamal, even though you were in prison, your advice and words of wisdom played a large part in who these boys became, so I can't take all the credit," Jen said then added jokingly, "But I will take most of the credit something like eighty-twenty!"

We all laughed as we pulled up to the Marriott Hotel. I called Kim and told her what happened, and Jamal called Shelby.

We went in and got our suite that had two bedrooms and went shopping for another day's worth of clothes, among other things.

We talked and hung out for the rest of the day. Later we had dinner plans at eight with Craig and his wife Shannon. We walked into Olive Garden, and Craig and Shannon were already at a table.

Shannon was a beautiful forty-year-old black woman with a pixie-cut hairstyle. Her ebony skin was glowing with perfection. She had high cheekbones with dimples, full lips, and the perfect set of white teeth. She was a professor at Georgetown University and had her doctorate in economics, which she taught.

We all already knew each other because Craig and Shannon have been together since Craig first started working in DC, and that was before I went to prison.

Jen and Shannon hugged, and we all did a little small talking about old times and catching up on what was new.

Craig changed the subject, "You two did well for your boys! Jermaine is pro-bound, and Jamal is about to be the youngest billionaire in the world.

"After y'all left, they were still talking about the OVD, and the major said that we need the device at any cost, and we will be damned if we let World Corp. get their hands on it, so they could sell it to the highest bidder or to every country! Sorry, Jen, no pun intended!"

"None taken! I understand the value of my son's worth and the device he created. It deserves to be in our military's hands.

"If my company gets the OVD . . . then every world power would have the option to buy!"

Shannon changed the subject. "Jamal, I heard you just had a little girl? Evelyn . . . right?"

"Yes, she is so precious. I got my boys and now my little girl. The world is right as rain!"

Shannon then asked, "So, JJ, what are you planning on doing with all that money?"

"I plan on starting my own company, and I already have a name for it, Stone Industries! It's time we make our family name a brand!"

"I couldn't agree more, Jamal," I said surprised and happy as hell.

I put my hand on his shoulder. "Wow, Jamal! Every time I think I couldn't be prouder, you do something else!"

"Same here!" Jen proclaimed.

The rest of the dinner was conversation and laughter. After dinner we said our goodbyes and headed back to the hotel.

The next day we met with Peter, and they offered Jamal two billion dollars and future involvement. Jen reviewed the contract package, and there was one stipulation that she wanted Jamal to be aware of.

"Jamal, look here page 63 section C, paragraph E."

Jamal read it out loud, so I could hear, "It states that any future invention made by Jamal Stone, and or any industries involved with any creation by Jamal Stone, the US government has the first option.

"If the US government chooses to take on such projects, it cannot be open for any other business to purchase. It becomes US property."

He finished and asked, "This stipulation that the government has the first option, it's missing a keyword.

"It should say the first option to purchase. The other way could be misinterpreted as the government can take it."

"That must be a typo. I can have that fixed right now," Mr. Storm replied, turning to Craig. "Craig, can you please add purchase for me, and just print that page."

"Sure, sir!" Craig went to correct it.

While he was gone to fix it, Jen went through the rest of the documents, and when Craig came back, she went over that page again and put an X through the old page.

"Everything is in order, Jamal," she set the document down and pointed. "Sign here!"

Jamal signed the contract as I just finished filling out the bank documents, and Jamal signed that too after adding his account info.

Peter took the papers and said, "Five to seven business days, your money will be deposited. We will need within that time all diagrams and any replica of the OVD in—"

"Everything is here," I interrupted. "We brought all and anything that involves the OVD!" I did not want to give up the best invention a man could have for what I did.

"Oh great, then just give us the time. It is a lot of money, but no more than seven business days!"

We shook hands and Craig was back with Jamal's copies of the documents. Craig handed the papers to Jamal, and Jamal handed them to his mom. We all said our goodbyes, and the three of us were off to the airport.

During the ride to the airport, Jamal said, "I can't believe I'm a billionaire! Mom, Dad, slap me so I know this is real!"

Jen turned around and popped Jamal upside his head.

"What the hell, Mom!"

"You said slap me if this is real, and, baby, it's real!" Jen screamed with joy, and I was laughing because she slapped Jamal upside his head!

She calmed down and said, "Boy, they gave you a tax break that netted you one billion seven hundred and fifty million dollars, and get this when you start up your own business, you have a five-year tax-free start-up clause in your contract!

"Make sure you review everything, Jamal. When you start Stone Industries, I want to work there!"

"Why do you think I'm starting up this company, Mom? Dad already suggested that, but you won't be working for me. You'll be working with me as a partner . . . you and Dad!

"We will get started as soon as I get back from London, so start getting everything in order along with ideas for other companies we can monopolize with Stone Industries!"

"We got you, son!" I replied happily.

"We sure do!" Jen agreed!

We were back in Albany at three and back at the house by four thirty. I noticed that the FBI was still watching my house, but at the moment, I didn't give a fuck because my son was now a billionaire.

We walked into the house and Gloria, Jeff, Shelby, and Sarah were all there. Jamal made his own announcement, "The US government has purchased my OVD for a cool, wait for it, wait for it . . . two billion dollars!"

Everyone went crazy! Shelby jumped in Jamal's arms, kissing him as she said, "Babe, you did it! I love you so much!"

I was glad he had Shelby because if it was any other chick, I would have sat her out on the porch.

I kissed Kim and took Evelyn then kissed my little girl, but before I could get comfortable, Jen was there saying, "Give me that angel, Jamal. I missed her so much!"

I handed Evelyn to Jen, and she looked into her eyes as she said, "You're worth more than a billion dollars, beautiful. You're priceless!"

Everyone was talking and enjoying the wonderful news. Jamal pulled me to the side and asked, "Dad, why didn't you give up your OVD?"

"Remember when I told you I wanted to be the first. Well, trust me, it's in my bunker, and they will never know I have it!"

"Well, I hope not! I don't want anything messing with my Benjamins, Dad!" Jamal replied worriedly.

"Son, I would never jeopardize you like that!"

"Cool, I know but it had to be said!" We hugged. "Thanks for everything, Dad. I owe you big, and you know I'm going to break you off with a little something-something!"

"That's cool, son!"

We went back to the family and had a great rest of the day! Damn, it was great to be me!

Chapter 56

May 27, 2022

Terry

The month has been uneventful watching Jamal for everyone that was involved. The only good thing was that each agent was able to spend time with another agent. This was good for me because I missed Lori and couldn't wait to see her. The weekly briefing had also been dull and short. Today's briefing would most likely be the same.

I called the meeting to order, "Okay, everyone, let's get started. I've read all the reports on Jamal Stone, and not for nothing, I feel that we are wasting our time.

"We are stalking a guy that is doing great by all standards. I think it is a waste of manpower and paperwork. Does anyone else agree?"

I watched as everyone raised their hands except Susan. She said, "I just can't get over the feeling that he's our guy. I mean the killer takes at least four months between each kill. He still has time to plan for his next victim!"

"Well, Susan, it's been over two months since we've been watching Jamal, and he has only been to work, Jennifer's, and home with his family.

"Jermaine comes to his house most of the time, and Jamal Jr. is in London with his fiancée!" Lori proclaimed, feeling she was ready to move on from Jamal!

"Did anybody hear about Jamal Jr.? The boy sold his invention to our government, and now is the youngest billionaire in the world!

"I've been trying to find out what it was that he invented, and all I was able to find out is that it's for special ops for the military!" Gordon chimed in.

"Yea, I heard about that too," Noel proclaimed. "It's going to be tested in the field for black ops, and they're keeping it classified!"

"I wouldn't mind Jamal Jr. being my son right about now," Mark said. "It must be nice to be Jamal. His oldest is a billionaire and his other son is an NFL prospect, and he just had a little girl who will probably grow up to be president! But here we are trying to figure out if this guy's a killer. In my opinion with all that good fortune, why go around killing people! I would just be living the high life enjoying my family!"

"I agree with Mark," Kevin said. "Jamal has all a man could want, and he did ten years in prison. Why would he risk everything to go back to prison for the rest of his life?"

"I agree and all I know is that Noel was right about profiling targets, and I think we should focus on that!" Jason proclaimed!

I sat down and leaned back in my chair as I thought about everything everyone just said. Everyone felt the same way as Lori and I felt, so I said, "Look everyone feels the same way about Jamal, so with that being said, we will focus on our assigned states using our possible target list.

"I want everyone to do a ViCAP, Violent Criminal Apprehension Program, in their state following up on your findings and also make sure that the locals are doing a tight job on our possible targets!"

I then said to Susan, "Jamal lives in your state, and because you have that gut feeling, you can check in on him from time to time, but under no circumstance are you to stalk or harass him.

"This guy spent ten years behind bars, and all he's trying to do is live his life. He paid for his crime, so let him live his good fortune.

"I will say though if anything suspicious as you check on him pops up, notify me or Lori before you do anything."

Susan still thought that Jamal was involved somehow because her FBI and female intuition was telling her so.

She thought, *Yea ok, I'm going to do more than just watch him*, but replied, "Alright, Terry. Jamal is a good guy and has that beautiful baby to boot. Let's just catch this killer so I could take my vacation!"

I dismissed everyone, and as Lori and I were walking to the elevator, she said, "Susan told me that she met Jamal. She said that he was really nice and seemed very educated.

"She also asks me why would a man with eight years of military experience and has a BA from Delaware University wind up selling drugs."

We stepped on the elevator and I replied, "She asked me the same thing when we were watching his house together!"

"Do you know that she compares him to Ted Bundy and Jeffery Dahmer?" Lori asked as we stepped off the elevator.

She continued as we walked to our desks. "She said that he probably sold drugs because of the thrill of the street life, and the power he had over people.

"She believes that Jamal is a narcissist, a nice guy with control issues who is very protective, and that's why she believes he's our guy!"

"You know, Lori, Susan is one of the most analytical persons I know, and she's usually dead-on, but with Jamal, all I see is a guy who's very happy and loves his family!" Terry proclaimed.

"Me too!" Lori replied glad that Terry saw it her way!

Lori finally moved on from Jamal now that she had closure, and Terry and she had been happy, but she still wanted Jamal to have a good life. She asked, "Dinner tonight, in or out?"

I thought for a second. "Let's cook together tonight!"

"Sounds good to me, Aquaman!" Lori said as she left and went to her desk!

Chapter 57

June 7, 2022

Susan

Mark and I have been in and out of Massachusetts all week even staying some nights. I was set that Jamal was our man, and I had convinced Mark of it and we had to keep a close eye on him.

I knew Mark would agree with me because one, he was my partner and two, he hated arguing with me. He told me once that arguing with me was like putting his head in a vice grip, so he would just rather ride the wave.

Upon agreeing, he suggested one thing and that was that we only do drive-by instead of sitting, so I had to give something to get what I want.

Anyway, that was a small compromise, and Terry didn't want us stalking Jamal. So every day we check for Jamal's truck's whereabouts.

Today his truck was at his job at Amazon, so Mark and I sat outside and talked for an hour. "Damn, Susan, it's the same thing every day with this guy, and the only difference is when he goes to his ex-wife's house!" Mark said, annoyed that he let Susan talk him into watching Jamal!

"I know, but like I said before, Jamal had everything going for him when he was selling drugs too, so just because he has a lot of good things going for him now, I believe he still has to have power over something and because he's getting away with murder he has power over us and his victims.

"I mean look how peaceful he is, and I haven't known a married man to ever be this peaceful!"

"Come, Susan, now you're projecting! Just because you and Zack are not on the up and up doesn't mean that other relationships can't be peachy. Besides, how do you know that they don't fight?"

"I guess you're right, but how often am I wrong?"

Just as I finished asking that, Jamal came out and got in his truck. I looked at my watch and it was only three. I said, "Now, that's different!"

I started the car and proceeded to follow him, staying a few cars behind.

Mark asked, "What, the guy isn't allowed to leave work early? What are you, his parole officer? Oh yea, wait I forgot he completed parole with no infractions!"

"Shut up, Mark! I just want to see where he's going! This isn't the way he takes home!" I replied, trying to keep a safe distance.

"Susan the man is not restricted to work and home! He can go where he pleases!" Mark exclaimed, getting frustrated.

I didn't respond to Mark because I knew if I did this would've kept going back and forth. I watched as Jamal pulled into Home Depot while I kept driving, so I could loop back around and park in bird's eye view of his TrailBlazer.

Mark was trying to talk to me, but I was focused on waiting for Jamal to come out. Forty-five minutes later, Jamal came out with five bags, and a dolly of stuff, but I couldn't tell what was on it. I went into the glove compartment, got out the binoculars, and I looked. It was racks, pile wood, a saw, and paint.

"What did Jamal buy, Susan?" Mark asked!

I told him and just like I knew, he would reply being a smart ass, "Maybe he's going to build a box, and then paint it so he could put his victim in, do a magic trick, and saw them in half!"

I ignored Mark's smart ass as I thought, *I can't be wrong, but maybe I am!* I refused to accept that because I was never wrong, so I continued to watch.

Jamal got in his truck and when he left, I followed. Mark said, "He probably knows you're following him! Shit, I would!"

"Fuck, Mark! We're partners and either you're with me or you could go back to the hotel, and I could do this on my own!" I exclaimed pissed, not at him really but at myself because I could be wrong!

"No, Susan, you know I got your back, no matter how crazy you are!"

I laughed because I knew how crazy and obsessive I could get.

Jamal pulled into the North Hampton Mall and parked. I parked two sections over then said, "Mark, go follow him for me please!"

Mark did a double-take and replied, "Why don't you go follow him? Terry told us not to harass the man!"

"I can't follow him! I've met him, remember . . . He knows what I look like!"

"Shit!" Mark said as he hopped out, regretting that I got your back comment!

Jamal was already in the mall, and when Mark finally found him, he was already leaving Dicks Sporting Goods with three bags. Mark followed him to the Baby Gap, Victoria's Secret, Finish Line, and DKNY. When Jamal left the mall, he had seven bags.

When Mark jumped back in the car, I was on him. He told me what Jamal bought from the stores, but he didn't know what he bought in Dicks.

I said, "I wonder what he bought in Dicks!"

"Well, let's see . . . he's a guy for one, his son Jermaine the football god is home. And oh, wait, he's a guy!" Mark said, finally having enough of Susan's craziness!

Jamal left and we followed him to his house. We sat outside his house for an hour. I was starting to truly think I might be wrong about this one, and Mark would not shut up.

Jamal and his wife finally came out with bags and put them in the back of the TrailBlazer. I watched an older woman come to the door holding their baby talking to them and then waved bye as they got in the car to leave.

I followed as they headed to the New York border. I said, "We better call Terry on this one!"

Mark called Terry, told him about Jamal's day, and that he was leaving the state to go to New York. Mark put Terry on speakerphone.

Terry said, annoyed, "Do not follow Jamal! I told you not to harass the man! He's traveling with his wife, probably taking some time away from the baby, so they can do them! Y'all are bothering the man!"

"Leave him be, Susan, because I know it's you . . . and Mark is just riding for you!" Terry hung up and I could tell he was pissed.

"Shit, shit, shit!" I said, turning off the exit! I thought, *Damn I have to let him go!*

Chapter 58

June 7, 2022

Jamal

    Everything was going great. I'd been relaxing and hanging with Evelyn and Kim. Jermaine had been at my house more than he had ever been. Jen, Sarah, and Gloria were here all the time too. Jeff only came a couple of times a week to see his granddaughter, but that was understandable because he ran his own business.

    Last week I asked Kim to go on a weekend with just the two of us to Lake George, New York. I said that it was supposed to be beautiful and that she only has one more week before she was off of maternity leave.

    At first, she was nervous about leaving Evelyn, but I told her with all the love Evelyn had, anyone would love to watch her, especially her mom. She finally said yes and we asked Gloria.

    Gloria said she could sleep at our house on Friday to watch her, but on Saturday she had plans with Jeff and couldn't watch her. That was okay because even though Jen had to sleep at our house, she jumped at the chance to have Evelyn and would love to relieve Gloria.

    Sarah said that she will help Jen and stay the night too. Kim was a little jealous that the girls were hanging without her, but it was all set.

    Jermaine was glad to have the house to himself, so he and Preston could get stuff done in the studio, but I knew they were planning to have girls over.

Friday was here. The FBI slowed down their watch on me, but I knew they were still checking up on me not every day but most days.

I saw Agent Steals and one of the other agents that used to watch me. I didn't know how she didn't realize she was too beautiful to miss. It'd been kind of frustrating because I'd been itching to get to that judge, but hey, with Evelyn here I could wait them out.

I got out of work early today because Kim and I planned on heading to Lake George by six, and it was a five-hour drive. I decided to get us a place on the lake, and the place had a back porch with a Jacuzzi. I wanted it to be romantic, plus the house was only twenty minutes from the judge's house in Salem.

It was three so I shut everything down in my office, went to my truck, and left. At first, I didn't notice the car following me, and the glare from the sun off the windshield stopped me from seeing who was in the car, but I knew it was two agents, and for them to be FBI, they sure were obvious.

I went to Home Depot and bought duct tape, rope, nails, racks, paint, a dresser, pile wood, paint thinner, a box cutter, and a saw.

I knew the FBI was following me, so most of the stuff I bought was for projects around Jen's and my house. Because I got rid of all the evidence, I always had to buy more to replace it.

I came out of Home Depot with one of the sales associates helping me, and I took that time to look around to see if I could spot the two agents and I did.

As I looked casually around, I picked up a glare coming off a lens, and right away I knew they were using binoculars. I thought, *What the hell, are these guys rookies or something!* I gave the associate a twenty-dollar tip. I chuckled as I got into my truck and drove off.

As I was driving, I picked up the tail again. "Fucking rookies!" I said, still laughing.

I pulled into the mall, parked, and went in heading straight to Dicks Sporting Goods to buy my everything black. I knew I was taking a risk with the FBI following me, but what kind of game would it be if I didn't take risks.

As I came out of Dicks, I spotted the agent looking like he didn't belong. I headed to the Baby Gap to buy my little girl something. Every time I went to the store, I bought stuff for Evelyn, items all the way up to twenty-four months. Kim yelled at me for buying her stuff she didn't need right now because we wouldn't have enough space for it.

Next, I went into Victoria's Secret and bought Kim perfume, lingerie for our trip for a present, and yoga pants, which I loved. They accentuate her curves. I left Victoria's Secret and went into Finish Line to buy us both Air Maxes for walking around in Lake George.

Finally, I stopped in DKNY, and not often did we shop there, but they always had these beautiful body-fitting dresses, nice heels to match, and these beautiful sundresses.

I planned a wonderful dinner, which I already made a reservation for and got the exact spot I wanted. I made sure because I wanted this weekend to show Kim how much I appreciated her for bringing my little girl into my world.

As I moved to each store, I saw the agent following me, and I thought, *What a fucking rookie! They should just wear FBI windbreakers with a bullhorn yelling I'm FBI!* I made a mental note to file a complaint against them, I mean enough was enough.

I left the mall and put my stuff in my truck then headed for home as they continued to follow me. I unloaded the stuff from Home Depot into the garage and then brought the bag of clothes from Baby Gap into the house.

I already had my OVD camera in my truck, which I picked up during my trips this week to Jen's.

I got into the house and Gloria and Sarah were already there. Kim's and my weekend bags were already packed, and by the door when I came in.

I kissed my wife and then said, "Hey, babe, are you ready for this weekend?"

"Sure am!" she replied, eyeing the bags I had in my hand. "What's in the bags, Jamal?"

She asked with an attitude knowing already what it was! "I thought I told you she had enough stuff!"

"If you keep complaining about what I buy my little girl, then my big girl won't get her present!" I replied as I sat the bags down and reached for Evelyn!

"Well, since you put it like that . . . then buy away!" she proclaimed, switching her mood because I bought her something too!

I laughed while I kissed Evelyn and then said hello to Gloria and Sarah!

I talked to Evelyn for about five minutes. After that I turned to Kim,

"Babe, we gotta get moving. I don't want to be driving all night. Plus, I have a surprise for you, well multiple surprises!"

Kim slapped me on my arm while chuckling because her mind went straight in the gutter as she said, "Jamal, my mom is right there!" gesturing her head in her mom's direction!

"Child, please! I might be your mom, but I know you and Jamal get your swerve on! Shit, your dad and I still get our freak on. How do you think I keep him?" Gloria proclaimed shaking her head!

Sarah and I started laughing while Kim replied bashfully, "Mom! I don't want to know what you and Dad do!"

Still laughing, I said, "That's what I'm talking about, Gloria! Freaky deeky!"

Sarah burst out laughing as she said, "Y'all some nasty people!"

Kim glared at Sarah as she replied, "Your one to talk! Don't forget I know your eye from behind after four glasses of wine!"

We all started laughing as Sarah slapped Kim, playfully replying, "Fuck you, Kim! I told you that in confidence!"

"Don't worry, Sarah, my mom doesn't know what that means, and I already told Jamal! You know I keep nothing from him!" Kim proclaimed with a wink, thinking, *Well, one thing.*

It was time for us to get going, so Kim and I kissed Evelyn, and I carried our bags to the truck while Gloria followed us out on the porch talking to us. I loaded the truck, and Kim got in the front seat.

As we were pulling out, Kim waved goodbye as she was saying, "Thanks, Mom, I love you!"

As I was driving, I said, "Baby, I got stuff in the backseat for you. I told you I had presents for my big girl!" I already put the other Victoria's Secret bag with the lingerie in the far back for later tonight.

While Kim was checking for her bag in the backseat, I was looking out the rearview mirror, and I thought, *Shit, I didn't want Kim to know that I was still being followed by the FBI!* Kim thought after the last interview, they left me alone.

Kim looked into Victoria's Secret bag, took out the body spray and the perfume and smelled them as she said, "This smells good, Jamal!"

Then she went into the bag again and pulled out the yoga pants. "I now got the whole Victoria's Secret yoga pants collection! Thanks, babe!"

Next, she grabbed the DKNY bag and pulled out the black body dress, the sundress, and heels. After she looked at them, she said, "These are beautiful, Jamal! How do you know this would fit, especially after I just had the baby?"

Kim hadn't realized that she lost her baby fat really fast. Even though there was more weight she wanted to lose, her body snapped back. The only thing that held was her breasts and butt, but her stomach, I could see the four-pack coming back.

I replied, "Now come on, baby, you know I'm a master at sizes! I know your body better than you do!"

She laughed as she said, "Well, you should. You explore it enough!"

She took her Air Maxes out of the Finish Line bag and started lacing them up. I kept looking in the rearview as the FBI continued to follow me. I thought, *Damn if they come all the way with us, then it's going to fuck up my plans!*

I was starting to get angry, but right before we entered New York from ninety west, they turned off. I watched for the next five minutes to make sure they were gone, and then I relaxed to focus on Kim and my weekend.

Chapter 59

Kim

    This weekend with my husband meant the world to me. Jamal was always thinking about how he could make me happy, and he was like a dream come true, especially when it came to family. Ever since Evelyn was here, everything in our house had been in harmony.

    I was so glad the FBI has finally left Jamal alone. That shit was really starting to bother me. Jamal was so thoughtful, but sometimes he went overboard especially when it came to Evelyn. I couldn't tell him anything about his baby girl!

    I could tell that Jamal was a little distracted when we first left the house but with him sometimes, who knows. All I knew was my baby loved me so much and was always doing nice things for me. He told me to look in the back because he had some presents for me. I loved the smell of the goods he bought me. He always knew what I liked and how I wanted to smell.

    Sometimes I couldn't believe how he always got it right, and the Victoria's Secret stuff was dead on. Oh, and the dresses and shoes from DKNY were to die for. He knew exactly my size when I still couldn't tell. Jamal's eyes and attention to detail were the sharpest I had ever known.

    Then the Air Maxes, he knew they were my favorite sneakers. I mean I struck gold with this man, and even though I loved Jen, she really fucked up letting Jamal go. Oh well, one person's loss could be another person's gain, and boy did I gain!

We laughed and talked all the way to Lake George. I could see that he finally relaxed. Maybe he needed this weekend just as much as I did. I loved looking at this handsome man, and most of the time, I couldn't help but stare just like I was now.

We just turned into the driveway of this beautiful house on the lake as he said, "Honey, I'm so glad we left when we did! Look, we got here in no time!"

I looked around trying to figure out whose house we were at and why we were not at the hotel. I asked, "Jamal, whose house is this?"

He put the truck in park and turned off the engine then looked at me with a smile as he replied, "For the weekend, we do!"

"No fucking way, babe. This place is beautiful!" I proclaimed, looking at this huge A-framed log cabin. All around were woods, and I could see that there was a lake in the back.

I asked, "Is that a lake behind the house?"

"Yea, babe, this house sits on Lake George!"

I reached over, hugged him tightly around his neck, and kissed him. "I love it, Jamal!" I said then let him go.

We got out of the truck to grab our bags, and we walked up to the door. Jamal reached behind a flower pot and pulled out a key. I asked, "How did you know the key was there?"

"When I booked the place, the owner sent me an email, and he told me!" Jamal answered as he opened the door.

As we walked into a wide-open foyer, the staircase was directly in front of us. We set our bags down and walked to the left into the living room. In that room was a modern set up with a couch, loveseat, coffee table, two end tables, and an entertainment station with a fifty-inch LCD Sony Smart TV.

As we moved to the back, there was an open den with a pool table. We continued through the threshold into the kitchen that had an island with all stainless steel appliances.

If you went to the right, it would have brought you back to the front door, so we kept straight into a hallway, and a few steps to our right was another living room, which was also off to the right of the front foyer. It had a couch and loveseat set up like the other living room, but there was no TV, just a usable fireplace.

We kept straight and to the back were two bedrooms fully furnished with forty-two-inch LCD Sony smart TVs, and a full bathroom for the two rooms to share. The downstairs was beautiful and huge. We walked back to the kitchen because I wanted to see the back where the lake was, and when I got out there and saw that we had a Jacuzzi, I went crazy.

"Jamal, we have to buy this house. I love it so much! When did you book this?"

"Maybe we will one day, and I booked this after Jamal's graduation!"

"What? How did you know I would want to come and leave Evelyn?"

"Come on, Kim, when wouldn't you want to spend time with me!" he replied as he hugged and kissed me!

"Plus, if you said no, I would've come by myself!" Jamal said jokingly!

"Oh, hell no, you wouldn't!" I replied with sass in my voice and a snap of my neck!

Jamal laughed as he said, "Let's go see the master bedroom!"

Jamal grabbed the bags, and we went up the steps. Once we were at the top, if we looked back, the balcony overlooked the foyer, but the master bedroom was straight ahead.

I opened the door to this huge bedroom. It had a canopied king-sized bed with a seven-piece redwood set with a couch, and a fifty-five-inch LCD Sony Smart TV. The bathroom was full-size with his and hers sinks. The bed was on the wall to the left, and on the other side was a sliding glass door that led out onto the balcony. I looked out into this open yard that led down to a pier that sat on the lake. It was so beautiful.

It was getting dark outside, and we could see the full moon overlooking the lake. The moon was so close that it felt like Jamal roped it in—like Jim Carey in *Bruce Almighty*, and the stars were peeking out, waiting for the light to vanish.

I looked to the right on the balcony, and there was a patio set, and next to it was a bottle of champagne on ice in one of those silver buckets on a stand. I looked back at my husband and thought, *My baby went all out for me!*

There were two flute glasses on the table, and Jamal went over and grabbed the bottle and presented it in both hands, saying, "Chardonnay 1999" and popped the cork.

He then took one glass and filled it and handed it to me. Then he poured himself one. He then looked into my eyes as he said, "I would like to make a toast to my beautiful wife" then pulled me close in one arm. "To my joy in life, who brought me the most precious gift a man could ask for, my baby Evelyn, and your love has never wavered. I promise to love you and always give you all of me!"

We touched glasses as a tear of joy streamed down my face, and we drank. After we drank, he pulled me back close and kissed me so passionately that my knees buckled. I thought, *Damn I love this man!*

It was the most beautiful moment of my life. He poured us another glass, and I sipped it. I didn't realize it the first time because of the moment, but this champagne was the shit!

I said, "Damn, baby, this tastes good as hell!" and then I downed the rest.

I poured myself another glass, and Jamal said, "Baby . . . wait give me a sec," and he got up and took off running out the door.

"Where are you going?" I yelled after him!

When he came back, he had something behind his back. He said, "Hey, beautiful, I have another surprise for you!"

I came out to the balcony and I said, "Another one? Jamal, you're spoiling me!"

"Anything for my baby!" he replied, pulling a Victoria's Secret box from behind his back!

I opened it and there were some edible panties with lingerie. It was cute and sexy, but as I took it in, I said, "These seem more like a surprise for you!"

"Oh yea . . . you think it's for me? Well, you mustn't want me to do to you what I plan on doing when I see you in that!"

I was feeling tipsy from that third glass of champagne I drank when Jamal left, and the thought of what my man could do sexually had me horny as hell.

I giggled on my way to the bathroom and said, "Surprise, surprise, I love surprises!"

I could hear Jamal laughing when I was in the bathroom.

In the bathroom, I looked at myself in the full-length mirror, smiling at myself. I was ready to rock my man's world. I thought, *Damn this man is everything! This is exactly what I needed!*

I shook my head as the chill ran through my body. I freshened up using some of that body spray he bought me and then walked back into the bedroom.

When I came out, the room was lit by candles, and on the bed were rose petals. I was blown away by how romantic the room looked. I looked over to the bed, and he had the camera set up.

He was standing butt naked and said, "I recorded the scenery off the balcony walking back into the room. I also recorded the candles around the room, and the rose petals on the bed, it's going to be beautiful!"

I took in all his sexiness, and I was so wet. I could feel it. I climbed on the bed doing my sexy cat crawl as I looked him in his eyes with lust and desire!

I pointed my finger at him and beckoned him to come to me. As he approached me, his manhood was at full attention, and I wanted it all and every which way.

He started kissing me as he took full control, and I loved it when my man showed such power as he pulled me to him. He climbs into the bed with me in one of his arms as he stayed kissing me.

He starts kissing my neck, and I was ready to climax right then and there but I maintained it as he kissed down to my breast and started sucking on my nipples.

Jamal was an excellent lover I must say, not only did he focus on the nipples, he massaged my whole breast with his mouth and licked back my nipples, which always made me have my first orgasm at that point.

He would then kiss down to my belly button, then with his tongue, he would trace a line to my right inner thigh and then run his tongue up my left thigh to the edible panties, which he would start licking with so much pressure that I thought he was going to lick it clean off. *Damn, that shit felt so good!*

I removed the rest of the lingerie while he had fun licking the edible panties, but then he tore them off and took my wetness into his mouth then used his tongue.

It felt so good that I couldn't control myself as I moaned, "Oh, my daddy! Right there, I'm about to cum!"

That made him focus more on his tongue, adding two fingers into the mix. Everything he was doing caused my body to fully climax.

I moaned, "Oooohhh, baby!" My voice shook with the orgasm.

He then climbed on top of me and put all of him so deeply, leaving it but causing it to jump as he took my breast into his mouth! I thought, *Oh my god this man's sex is the bomb!*

He was hitting my G-spot, and I couldn't help it as I moaned, "Not again!" And my body reached another orgasm.

As my body started shaking, he started pumping in and out taking long deep strokes, slow at first then faster and harder! He knew just how I liked it, and I had another orgasm!

My man was on a mission. He was in full control as he flipped me onto my stomach. There was pain and so much pleasure mixed with the three orgasms. I tried to pull away from him, but it was so good though. And he made sure I took every inch as he held me by the hips.

I couldn't do anything but throw it back at him, saying, "Yea . . . fuck me, Daddy, fuck me!"

He started going faster, and I knew that we were going to orgasm together.

He said, "You like that, baby, you like that!" He knew he was hitting my G-spot over and over again.

"Yes, Daddy, this is all yours!" I moaned out as we both orgasmed!

Jamal let go of his seed deep inside me as he collapsed on top of me. I knew what to do to make his toes curl. I hopped off and then took him into my mouth, knowing it was sensitive.

He moaned, "Oh shit, baby!" He grabbed the back of my head.

After five minutes, I crawled up, and we kissed passionately. We lay there in a sexual euphoria as we fell asleep.

Chapter 60

Jamal

My eyes opened at one in the morning, and I looked at Kim sound asleep. I knew that champagne and that mind-blowing sex were going to have her out for the count, and I would have been too if I didn't have a sleep disorder.

The way the sex went, I might have just put another baby in her. I thought, I *hope not, I just want to spend time with Evelyn before I have another one!*

I took a couple of deep breaths as I pulled my arm from under Kim. She moved into a more comfortable position as I lay there watching her sexy nakedness stay sound asleep.

After five minutes, I got up, staring at her just to make sure, but I knew she was in la-la land, and I knew not even a nuclear missile could wake her. She was among the dead.

I covered her up and got dressed. I planned on just driving to Jdg. Martin Richard's house so I could check the lay of the land.

It took me twenty minutes to get to Salem and another five to get to Martin's house. The neighborhood was an upscale community, but the houses were spread out and separated by fences.

It was quiet as I drove up to Magnolia Street, and as I passed Martin's I saw a cop car parked out front. I drove by, looking in the direction of the cop car, and there was no one in there. I thought, *It must be a shift decoy.*

I took a note of that and then I noticed the multitude of trees in the neighborhood, which would be camouflage. Porch lights were lit up, up and down the street. I noted that this would not be a good thing.

I made a left on the next street, which was DuPont Street, so I could circle around. When I got on the street to my left, there was nothing but woods until halfway down the block it opened up into DuPont's Little League baseball field. That whole stretch was the trees, that field, and the parking lot. I was happy as hell because it was a good thing. I made a note then left.

I drove up route twenty-two along a stretch of woods, but up that stretch off to the left was this little dirt road that led into the woods to a small cottage, which I rented for six months under a fake name—Jason Klein. It was a nice little spot on the outskirts of Salem.

When I acquired the place, the owner never asked to meet, and I faxed him a fake driver's license with a white guy's face. When I talked to him, I told him that I would be in the States for maybe six months working on a project. I even used a British accent that I'd been learning from Shelby.

The cottage to me was more like a cabin, but it didn't have the structure style of a log cabin. However, it was an all one-room setup. The kitchen was in view, and it had a fireplace, satellite TV, couch, bed, and a table that sat two. I also have a 975 Ducati and a Kawasaki 250 dirt bike parked here.

I did my research on Jdg. Martin Richards. He was an Ivy League graduate from Yale, Harvard Law, five years in the DA office, fifteen years as a defense attorney. He then was voted in as the head DA serving ten years and then became the Superior Court judge of Fulton County.

He had a daughter Stella Richards who graduated from Berkeley University, a son Thomas Richards that played football for Stanford and graduated, and his wife Patricia Richards who was a therapist. She ran her own practice, and they had been married for thirty-five years. I wrote down my note from tonight and then left.

When I got back to Lake George, it was three, and I got pulled over. The cop came to my window and said, "License and registration!"

I gave it to him and he looked at it, and before he left to go run it, he said, "Long way from home, Mr. Stone!"

"Yea, I know, Officer. My wife and I are spending the weekend here. We had a little girl two months ago, and I wanted to do something nice for her!" I replied, remaining calm and collected.

"Well, Mr. Stone, this sure is the place to do it, hold on!" the officer proclaimed then walked back to his cruiser.

When he came back, he said, "Have a good weekend, Mr. Stone, and congrats on the baby!"

I drove back to the house, thinking that that officer was nice as hell. When I got in, it was four ten in the morning, I climbed into bed next to Kim and pulled her close in a spoon position and fell asleep.

Chapter 61

June 8, 2022

Last night was an adventure, not a great one but one nevertheless. I only slept for a little more than three hours. It was a good thing my body could go on for two hours for a small period of time.

It was quarter to eight when I got up to shower. Kim was still in a coma. I thought a little about being pulled over last night, but I was glad it was in Lake George. If it was in Salem, I probably would have to do the job, figuratively speaking.

While in the shower, I thought, *How am I going to execute my plan? I couldn't set the camera to watch the cops. I mean, it's plenty of places to post the camera, but it's too wide open. Plus I don't know if they do a shift decoy every night or even if it was a decoy. I would do regular travels up this way, but the FBI is still watching me. When I staked out Tanya's place, I had my own place I could get away with. Now we live together. Another problem was his wife being there. I'm not going to hurt her, but I'll probably have to Taser her. Last where was I going to torture him? I probably have to kill him in his home like the cop, but this time in the basement.*

I got out of the shower and dried off, went into the bedroom, and Kim was still out. I put on some sweats and went downstairs to make coffee, French toast, bacon, and cheese eggs. When I booked this place, I requested for the ingredients to be in the refrigerator along with a few other things. That was how the chardonnay was on the balcony.

While I was making breakfast, I thought more about how I was going to pull off killing Judge Richards. This one was probably going to be the toughest one yet because it had many obstacles. The good thing about this was the entrance from the woods. The bad thing was the woods.

I still had to figure out the exact location of the house. I thought about that for a few minutes, and then I concluded that his house would be the fourth house from the bottom of the street where I came onto the block. There were seven houses on the lower half of Magnolia Street. No matter what, this guy was going to die.

I would set up the OVD tonight, and then I'd take it down after I kill him. I could not let it be found. Jamal would never forgive me. I thought about the FBI following me and how I was going to get away from their surveillance, but then again, I'd file a complaint of harassment when I get home.

I put all that outta my mind as I got everything ready to bring up breakfast in bed for Kim. I put two six-hundred milligrams of ibuprofen on the tray and then went upstairs. I set the tray on her nightstand and then opened the curtains as I said, "Baby! It's time to get up!"

She stirred and then stretched as I sat on her side of the bed, brushing her hair from her eyes with my fingers.

"What time is it?" she asked, yawning.

"It's nine fifteen, baby! We don't want to waste this beautiful day, do we?

"I figure after breakfast we could go shopping and catch a late lunch. There's nothing like shopping for exercise!"

"Now you're talking my kind of workout!" she replied as she sat up.

As I put the tray over her, I said, "I thought last night was your kind of workout?"

She giggled as she replied, "Sure is! I'm still sore too!"

She popped the ibuprofens with her orange juice and then asked, "Where's your food?"

"I'm going to get it right now." I kissed her on her forehead and went to get my tray.

While we were eating our breakfast in bed, Kim asked, "I got up to go to the bathroom last night around three something, and you weren't here. Where did you go?"

"I went to find a twenty-four-hour store because I couldn't sleep. You know I have insomnia. I figured I'll go get breakfast. I even got pulled over last night." Kim didn't know there were groceries in the refrigerator.

"Pulled over, for what! They're always harassing a black man in a nice car late at night!" She ate more of her food and sipped some of her coffee.

I didn't reply to her statement because it was the same one she made every time I was pulled over or any black man with a nice car.

She continued after swallowing her coffee. "You know, Jamal, you really should see someone about your insomnia. I mean . . . it can't be good for your health if you don't get enough sleep."

"Babe, it's been like that my whole life. I run on little sleep, but you know once every three months I crash and sleep for like two days. Anyway, do I look unhealthy?" I replied then continued eating.

"True, true," she replied, dropping her fork and leaning back to take a deep breath. "I'm full . . . Jamal, why do you always make me so much knowing I'm not going to eat it all!"

"So I can finish it if I don't have enough. What—you haven't figured that out yet? It's not often we get to cook breakfast.

"Well, since you've been home, you have, but you're going back to work in a week, and it's back to our regularly scheduled program. I'm glad Gloria doesn't work though because we would have to find a nanny."

Kim set her tray down on the nightstand and got up to go take a shower. She said, "Yea, we usually get lucky like that!" She got out of bed butt naked, and I was instantly turned on.

I heard her start the shower, and even though I already showered, I was going in for a quickie.

I jumped in butt naked with her, and she said, "A little breakfast dessert—mm-hmm, my favorite!"

I took hold of her, and we had an all-out five minutes water ride. Afterward, I was washing off as she said, "De-li-cious! Thanks, babe!"

I got dressed for the day. It was eighty-three degrees, and the high was going to be eighty-seven. I put on my sky-blue khaki Polo shorts, all-white Polo shirt, and low-cut ankle socks, so they could hide in my North Carolina blue and white Air Maxes.

My cornrows were fresh, and my ends came down to my collar bone, but I still had to rock my sky-blue and white Yankee fitted hat, my black Gucci sunglasses, platinum Bravado watch, and diamond-studded earrings.

Kim came out of the bathroom and stopped. "DAMN, BOO . . . you look good as hell! Shit, we might not make it out the door!"

I struck a pose and slicked my fingers across the brim of my hat and replied, "I know, right! But you better get dressed because your birthday suit is sexy as fuck!"

She laughed and went to get dressed. She put on a pink thong and no bra. She was wearing a pink and white swirl sundress, and she hated panty lines. Her Air Maxes matched the pink in her dress.

I said, "Look at that, baby, your boo is good at this dressing shit!"

"I know, right!" she repeated the way I said it earlier.

She fixed her hair and wrapped her head just the way I liked it. She put on her diamond necklace, bracelet, and hoops, and topped it off with her black Gucci sunglasses that matched mine.

We looked like a rich couple, and I couldn't wait to take pictures. I was definitely bringing the camcorder.

We hopped in the truck and we were off to go shopping at the outlets. It was eleven fifteen. Kim went into all the stores.

She bought three pairs of sandals, two pairs of shoes for work at the hospital, and two pairs of winter boots that were on sale, which happened to be her size, talk about a good day. I had her sit on the bench while I took the bags to the truck.

Next, we went into the baby store. I said to her as she loaded up on baby stuff, "You just told me to stop buying Evelyn stuff—now here you are! What a hypocrite!"

She smiled, sticking her tongue out as she said, "Whatever, Jamal!"

I didn't really care. It made my wife happy, plus anything for my little girl.

Next, we went to Brooks Brothers and then Ralph Laurens, and I brought two suits for me, four for JJ, four for Jermaine, and two pairs of shoes for each of us.

Then on our way to the Nike outlet, I said, "Kim, let me take these bags to the truck because I know we're about to go crazy in here." She gave me the bags, and I left.

When I came back, she had sneakers and clothes for Jen, Sarah, Tracy, Gloria, Evelyn, and herself. She was on the phone with Jen and Sarah. "Yea, girl, they have everything in this store. We can wear this stuff to the gym or on our walks."

She listened while she looked at the yoga pants on the rack. "No, it's all good. That's what we're here for." She paused.

"No, he doesn't mind! It's my money too!"

She turned to me and asked, "Babe, you don't mind if I buy the girls something?"

I replied loudly, leaning toward the phone, "As long as we have babysitters, hell no, I don't mind!"

Kim listened then burst out laughing and said to me, "Jen and Sarah both said that's anytime."

"I'm going to see what I can find," I said as I walked away, knowing they said something funny that Kim did want to say.

I took out my phone to call Jamal as I started to look around. He answered on the third ring, "What's up, Dad!"

"I'm in Lake George with Kim at the Nike outlet, and I just wanted to check if your big-ass feet have grown any?"

"I'm a size fourteen, Dad. You know I don't need any more sneakers. I got some I haven't even worn. Plus I'm rich! I can buy my own sneakers."

"Yea well, you may be rich, but I am still your dad, and I can buy you whatever I want. I just bought you and Jermaine four suits from Brooks Brothers and Ralph Lauren with shoes to match. By the way, what size sneakers Shelby wears? Kim's buying all the girls stuff."

"Hold on, Dad. Shelby, you're a size seven and a half in women, and clothes a medium or a size four, right?" He paused.

"It's my dad. They're in Lake George at the outlets buying the damn place out!"

I started laughing as I said, "I think we're at thirty-five hundred already today. This will probably put us at five grand. Kim is buying your mother, sister, Tracy, Gloria, and Sarah stuff too. Oh . . . before I forget, when are you coming home?"

"The fourteenth of July. When I come home, I will need you and Mom to be ready to put things together for Stone Industries."

"No problem, we got you. Hey, let me go, so I can go tell Kim and call your brother. I love you, talk to you later."

"I love you too, Dad!" We hung up.

I told Kim Shelby's sizes and then called Jermaine. He answered on the seventh ring. "What's good, Dad! I'm in the studio."

I heard the music in the background. "I'm at the Nike outlet with Kim, and I'm checking on your sneakers size. I know your clothes size, and I just bought you four suits and some jeans, cargo shorts, and shirts from Polo and Ralph Lauren."

"The same size as you, Dad, twelve. Thanks, Dad, I'll talk to you later. I got to lay these bars down. I love you."

"I love you too, son!" I hung up.

About fifty-two hundred dollars, we were off to our late lunch at three thirty. After our small lunch, we walked the strip near the beach, and the water wasn't warm enough for my taste, but we planned to ride the wave runners tomorrow morning. I loved those things and so did Kim.

We walked arm in arm as we enjoyed the warm breeze coming off the lake. Dinner was scheduled for seven. I wanted the moon to be out and the stars shining bright.

During our walk, we stopped to take pictures and record parts of our day by taking turns with the camcorder, and we even had a person that was passing by record us together. It was beautiful!

We got back to our place and drank a glass of Chardonnay '99. I ordered three bottles at two hundred a pop.

It was ten minutes to six when we took a quick shower and got dressed. Kim lotioned her body, then put on the dress I bought her from DKNY, and it fit her like a glove. Plus I loved the fact that she wore no panties or bra. She put back on her diamonds, slid on her heels, and touched up her hair. She was drop-dead gorgeous!

I took out my contacts because I wanted to wear my black-framed Ralph Lauren prescription glasses. I wore black slacks, a button-down shirt, and black dress shoes with a platinum tip, all compliments of Ralph Lauren.

I buttoned my sleeves with my diamond cufflinks, wore my diamond-cut platinum Rolex watch, and to top it off my diamond earrings. You may ask where all my jewelry came from, but you must remember I was a drug dealer and Jen saved all my jewelry. I bought Kim's jewelry on our second anniversary. I checked my cornrows and they were fresh, so we were ready to go.

Chapter 62

Costello's On the Lake was a beautiful restaurant that sat on the end of a pier. Our seats looked out onto the lake, and the scenery was extraordinary. The sun was just setting over the horizon, giving off colors of reds and oranges, and one could just catch a hint of the full moon in the sky. It was perfect.

We sat at our table and the waitress was right on point as the hostess left. She said, "My name is Maria, and I will be your waitress for the evening. Can I start you off with something to drink?"

"Can we please have a bottle of your white Merlot '93'?" I took the liberty of ordering our drinks.

"Ninety-three sounds perfect." She smiled, knowing that the bottle cost seven hundred dollars, and her tip was going to be good. She hurried off.

"Baby, you look breathtaking!" I said, turning my attention to Kim!

"You too, baby! This place is so beautiful. Look at the scenery!"

We both looked out the window as the sun was setting behind the mountains. *I wish I brought my camera. The scenery is awesome,* I thought.

I looked at the menu and knew right away what I wanted. "Baby, do you know what you want?" I asked.

"I'm going to have grilled chicken smothered in the white sauce with shrimp, spicy rice, and steamed carrots."

"Baby, that sounds good . . . I hope you don't eat it all. That's why I planned a late lunch. I knew you were going to order something good!" She laughed!

The waitress returned and I said, "Can you give us five more minutes before we order?"

"Sure, sir." She popped the cork on the Merlot and filled our glasses.

She put the bottle back on the ice and said, "I'll be right back," and she left.

Kim grabbed her glass, held it slightly up, and said, "Tonight I would like to make the toast." I grab my glass, mimicking her.

"You are my everything, Jamal Stone, and there isn't nothing in this world I wouldn't do for you. I promise until the day I die to love you and give you all of me. I am so happy that I am Mrs. Kimberly Stone!"

We clinked glasses and drank. When Kim pulled the wine glass away, she looked at her glass and said, "Wow . . . this tastes good! It's like it's dancing on my tongue! This is better than the Chardonnay '99, and that was great!"

"Well, it better be! You know I don't like talking about money, but that bottle cost seven hundred dollars."

She froze and looked at me, "Jamal! What . . . wait . . . seven hundred dollars on a bottle! That's crazy!!"

"I have something to tell you but after dinner."

The waitress came back and asked, "Are we ready?"

"Yes, my wife would like the grilled chicken smothered in the white sauce and shrimp, spicy rice, and steamed carrots.

"I would like the filet mignon medium rare with parmesan and shrimp, spicy rice, and asparagus smothered in yam sauce."

The waitress took the menus. "Coming right up. Would you like a salad while you wait?"

"I'm good, just bread. Babe, you?"

"Yes, chef salad with Italian dressing please." The waitress left.

Kim looked at me with a hard stare and said, "Well, Jamal spit it out! You know I can't wait! The anticipation will spoil my appetite!"

"Okay, only because I want you to eat . . . On second thought, your food sounds really good. Maybe I won't tell you right now!"

I had a big grin on my face as she folded her arms across her chest sassing her neck with an icy stare as she exclaimed, "Jamal, you better stop playing!"

I chuckled low as I replied, "I'll be right back—"

"You better spill it right now, Jamal Isiah Stone!" she exclaimed, leaning forward in a low, threatening tone!

I laughed. "Okay, okay, I love seeing you sweat! Anyway, you know the money Jamal made with the deal from the government?

"Well, he gave his mother and me 2.5 million dollars, Jermaine 1.5 million dollars, and Evelyn 1 million dollars.

"I'm also going to work with him at Stone Industries. I put in my two weeks' notice at Amazon this past Monday."

Kim gasped, "Oh my god, Jamal that's great news!"

"I guess you haven't checked your personal or our joint account, have you? I bet you haven't even checked our new spending limits on our American Express, Mastercard, and Visa?

I put a half-million in your personal account, and our joint account has an additional million! We are officially millionaires!"

"Oh, man for real—Jamal!" Kim replied then thought about the time Jamal told her that if we were rich, he wouldn't want her to work.

"But wait, I still want to work at the hospital though!"

"Baby, you can work at the hospital but not so many hours. You could be home more with Evelyn."

"Well, since you put it like that, then I could work with that!" she replied, smiling!

Just as our conversation finished, our food showed up. We ate and the food was to die for. We talked with bliss like never before.

When the check came, it was the most I've ever spent on a meal in my life, shit for two months of meals for that matter, and I knew I wouldn't make a habit of this.

I decided to give the waitress the biggest tip she had ever seen because this was a celebration. The Merlot was six hundred and seventy-two dollars. Our meals were one hundred and six dollars, totaling eight hundred and thirty-two dollars.

I wrote in the tip space three hundred and sixty-eight dollars totaling twelve hundred even. When I gave the waitress the American Express card with the bill, she didn't look, just went to cash us out.

I said to Kim with a smile on my face, "Watch the waitress!"

We were watching as the waitress opened the pouch, looked at the number, and gasped. She looked over at us, tilted her head, then said something to the woman next to her, and showed her the pouch.

Maria walked back over to our table and said, "Excuse me, sir, but I think you may have made an error on your bill."

She showed me the bill, and I looked at it with her as I replied, "Everything looks in order to me."

She smiled with excitement and said "Oh my god, sir, thank you! I've never heard of anyone getting a tip this big!"

"You're welcome, young lady!" I proclaimed with a smile.

She thanked us again and went to go cash us out. As she settled the bill, she was saying something to the other woman.

They talked a little, then she came back, gave me my receipt, and said, "Thank you, sir. Is there anything else?"

"No, we're good. Are you good?" I asked Maria, making sure she was happy, and there were no problems with the other woman.

"Yes, thank you both and have a great evening!"

"You too!" Kim and I replied.

"How much was the tip?" Kim asked.

"Three hundred and sixty-eight dollars. A small thing to a pair of giants!" We both laughed and then left feeling really good from the food, tipsy from the Merlot, again Kim more than me. She finished off the bottle. I was glad because I ate most of her food.

We got back to the place where we were staying around nine thirty. We changed into our comfortable clothes and then went into the living room to watch a little television and sipped Chardonnay.

It was about ten fifteen when Kim decided to pull my manhood out and took me into her mouth. Her head was already on my lap. She was gone all pornstar as she maneuvered me out of my sweats. I didn't have underwear on, so it was easy.

She licked around the head, and up and down my shaft. As she came back to the tip, she took me into her mouth. After five minutes of that, she hopped on top of me and started riding me.

She only had on her silver silk nightgown that came to the middle of her thighs. She was riding me like a cowgirl at the Kentucky derby. We were going at it for ten minutes when I decided to take over.

I stood up with me still deep inside her, holding her by her nice ass and started lifting her up and down, sliding in and out of her. She wrapped her arms around my neck as she moaned into my ear—causing me to pump harder, and every time she came down, I was hitting her G-spot.

I then walked over to the pool table, laid her on top, lifted her legs onto my shoulder, and continued to hit her G-spot.

She was moaning, "Oooohhh, baby, right there! I'm . . . cumming,

I'm . . . cumming!" Her body began to shake as I continued to stroke a few more times, hitting her G-spot.

I let her down, spun her around, and leaned her over the pool table. I entered her from behind right away and started long stroking hitting her G-spot.

I grabbed her by her hips and started slamming her butt into my pelvis. I walked her back until her body was no longer on the pool table, and she was bent completely over.

I start stroking harder and faster as I support her balance by holding onto her hips. We both were at the top of our moans as we both climaxed with such ecstasy together. She came up with me still inside her, leaned back, put her hand on my neck, and started kissing me.

She said in between kisses, "I, love, you, so, much!"

"I love you too, baby!"

We separated and she went to finish her drink. She was messed up from the floor up and said, "Come, boy, we're going to the balcony. Set up the camera and let's catch the scenery while we're fucking! No lovemaking tonight, baby . . . let's make porn."

I checked the clock and then followed her upstairs. It was only eleven. I set the camera up and let me tell you, it was just as beautiful as last night.

The full moon was out, and the stars were shining bright. I guess it was true what they say that the freaks come out at night because we were howling at the moon. It was so fun and funny.

We were done a little before twelve o'clock. We cuddled in bed, and Kim was out by twelve fifteen and snoring by twelve thirty. I slid from under her and got dressed and left for the cottage.

When I got to the cottage, I geared up and wore my black cargo pants, black hooded sweatshirt, black gloves, and black boots. I put my cameras in my backpack along with the OVD. I then grabbed my mask, left the house, hopped on my Ducati, and left.

I already drove by the house on my way to the cottage, and the police decoy was there. I also noticed the neighbors were still up. It was Saturday in Lake George, so people could just be getting home.

I pulled on DuPont Street, walked my bike into the woods and out of sight just in case someone passed by.

I went through the woods, and it was just like I thought. The woods separated the baseball field from the houses. I counted four houses down then climbed a tree which was dead center of the house. I was hoping that the mini Canon camera would be enough to cover the whole house, so I hooked up and turned it on.

"Fuck!" I said to myself. The mini camera was too small to get the quality picture I needed.

I switched cameras and went with the one I used at Dr. Rawlings's. The picture was perfect when I brought it into regular view.

I could see Mr. and Mrs. Richards sleeping in their bed. I looked at the layout for a while and saw that they'd had an alarm.

"Fuck! Fuck!" I was going to have to cut the power because I didn't know who their security company was and hoped that the alarm company didn't send the cops.

I then thought, *Shit they're already watching the house! I might have to kill this motherfucker faster than I would like, which sucked because I wanted him to suffer. Those kids are suffering, but oh well, his family will suffer, so maybe it evens out.*

I checked my watch when I made it to my motorcycle. It was almost three, so I hopped on and took off. I got two weeks to kill this guy. That was how long the battery lasted and one week left of work. I got back to the cottage, changed my clothes, and hurried back to Kim.

When I walked into the house, she was waiting for me in the living room with no television. "Jamal!" Her voice came from nowhere, catching me off guard, sounding loud and angry.

I jumped toward the voice, "Damn, Kim! You're going to give me a fucking heart attack!"

"Where were you? I've been waiting for you for over an hour!" she inquired as she stood up!

"Why didn't you call me? You know how I am!" I replied, recovering from the shock she just gave me.

"I tried to call your phone. It was going straight to voicemail!"

I checked as if she was wrong, the whole time thinking of a lie. "Shit! I thought I had the power on! I went down to the pier and thought about how far I'd come and all the people in my life that make me happy and at peace."

She softened up as she came over and hugged me. "Well, that sounds good, but next time have your phone on. I was worried and what if someone broke in, and I can't call you. I was scared!"

I kissed her and replied, "Sorry, honey, you're absolutely right. I slipped up but never again!"

She was right, especially knowing what I did. Plus she could've been home with Evelyn. The thought of something happening to my girls sent a chill up my spine.

It was quarter to four in the morning when we lay down. I looked at the clock then asked, "You need some more sleep aid" as I ran my fingers through her hair, kissing her on the cheek.

She rolled over so that we were spooning. "I thought you would never ask."

The next day we packed our bags and headed down to the lake. We rode the wave runners for three hours.

On our ride home, I said, "Baby, I miss Evelyn!"

"Me too!" she replied, putting her hand on the back of my neck and started rubbing it!

I thought as I drove, *I accomplished my goal, and now Jdg. Martin Richards, your days are numbered!*

Chapter 63

June 14, 2022

Lori

Everything was quiet with the case. I was sitting at my desk hoping that this case could be over soon. I was also hoping that Jamal was not involved in any way, but if I had to, I would arrest his ass.

I was trying to understand this monster we had to catch. Why torture? Why three phases? And why these particular targets? What had someone done to this guy to make him want to kill these people in these manners? One thing for sure, he was very smart and very well planned. I constantly went over and over these questions in my head.

"Earth to, Lori! Come in, Lori, this is earth," Terry said, snapping my train of thought.

"My bad, Terry! I was thinking about the case, but it's nothing that we don't ask ourselves every day about this guy. What's up though?" I replied, regaining my composure.

"I was saying that Nevaeh wants Becky, Liz, and Tasha to sleep over. Are you up for that?"

"A slumber party with the girls! The question is, are you up for that, Batman?"

Terry laughed as he replied, "Why are you always calling me, Batman?"

"Because you're a black FBI agent that catches evildoers. Batman tries not to kill them. He just puts them in jail. To top it all off, he gets the girl, hence *The Dark Knight*!"

Terry started cracking up, then said, "Is that how you see Batman? Wow, the woman's perspective!"

"Shut up, Terry! That's everybody's perspective!" I replied, laughing with him as I slapped him with the file I had in my hand.

"I contacted all the police departments that are watching our targets and told them to be on top of their game. Also we want door checks and at least one officer watching the house at all times.

"It's getting close for this guy's next victim, and I want this killer off the streets. I also told the other agents to do the same."

"That's my girl, beauty and brains." Terry replied, rolling in his chair back to his desk to answer the phone.

When he was done, he turned to me. "Lori, Director Walls wants us in his office."

"Shit!" I replied, getting up with Terry to head to the director's office. I was thinking, *It's never good to be called in by the boss.*

When we entered Director Walls's, office he was on the phone, saying, "Yes, sir, we are on top of it." He paused.

"Yea, we will have him soon. I got the two best agents on it!"

The director listened for a moment more, then the person must have hung up because he said, "Asshole." Then he hung up.

The director turned to me and Terry and said, "That was the higher-ups, and they are not happy about how long this case is taking to close!"

Terry interrupted, "Sir, we are doing everything we can. This guy is clever and he doesn't leave a shred of evidence behind.

"The only way we were able to come at the killer was to take his MO for targets, make our own list, and put local eyes on those targets.

"We had a hit with Dr. Ann Rawlings, but the locals let it slip through their hands. So we've tightened up on our targets, and we are hoping that we get him there."

"I read that in your report. What's going on with this Jamal Stone?"

"We already questioned him twice, and we're still keeping surveillance on him too, but we believe he just isn't our guy.

"With that being said, all the coincidences surrounding him, Agent Steals and Dunn are checking up on him, reporting his movements," I answered to let the director know that Terry wasn't doing all the work. A girl had to pull her own weight around here.

The director leaned back in his chair, then shot forward and loudly said, "Look, I don't care if it's the Easter bunny you arrest, get someone into custody!

"We need it to look like we're getting somewhere in this case! Shit is rolling down a hill, and I'll be damned if it buries me! Get a hold of this case and close it!"

"Yes, sir!" Terry and I reassured each other.

Terry and I were about to walk out of the director's office when he stopped us. "Hey, you two! I know about your love affair, and I am not against office relationships, but I hope it's not interfering with your focus on this case."

"No, sir! We are doing everything we can to catch this killer!" I replied.

"Well, I hope not because I really hate to fire y'all asses! Now get out of my office, and catch this guy!"

I thought about my relationship with Terry for the rest of the day. Terry and I left to go pick up Neveah. I asked, "Terry, do you think because of our growing relationship, it's taking away from putting in all our effort into catching this guy?"

"I thought about that for the rest of the day. But I believe we are doing all we can to catch this son of a bitch. I mean this guy's forensic knowledge is just as good as ours.

"Come on, eight kills and not one piece of evidence. This killer is in multiple states, and I think we are maximizing the best we can to catch him.

"If everything is as tight as it should be, then we'll get him soon. Believe that!"

"Good, me too! Listen, let's have a great weekend with Neveah and the girls, and on Monday go full force. We need to catch this killer and be done with this case," I replied, rubbing the back of Terry's head.

We pulled up to Naomi's, and all the girls were already there. They hopped in the car while Terry put their bags in the trunk.

In the car, Nevaeh said to me, "We're having a slumber party, and we want you with the girls!"

"I wouldn't have it any other way! Girl power!"

The girls and I were all talking loudly and excitedly when Terry got in the car, shaking his head.

I said, "I guess you're all alone tonight, Batman, with no Catwoman!" I laughed at my own joke as I turned up the radio, and Terry drove off.

Chapter 64

June 17, 2022

Terry

Lori and I were on our way to work today after having a fun weekend with Neveah and her friends. Saturday, we went to Lake Taconic off the Taconic Parkway. Sunday, we spent the day at Dave's and Buster's, and at the house, there was nothing but little girls' craziness.

It was no thanks to Lori because she was there to help me tame the rug rats even though she was a rug rat herself, playing tricks on me. They were hiding and throwing water at me as I came around corners of the house.

Lori kissed me before we got out of the car and said, "Terry, I got a new name for you. The girls and I came up with it yesterday."

I laughed. "Great! What is it?"

"Well, you know how I was calling you Batman, right, so now the girls and I are going to call you Aquaman. After all the water we've thrown at your face, you should be able to breathe underwater!"

We both laughed at that as we were entering the office. I got to my desk and there was a letter from Albany County Federal Court on it. I read it and the letter pissed me off.

I turned to Lori and said, "I can't believe this shit! Jamal filed a complaint of harassment against the FBI!"

"For real!" Lori exclaimed in shock!

"Listen to this, Jamal Stone has filed a complaint of harassment against agents of the FBI for stalking and violation of privacy. The State of New

York has scheduled a hearing on the matter Wednesday, June 19, 2022, at 9:00 a.m."

I took a deep breath. "Damn! I told Susan and Mark not to harass Jamal, and now look at this shit!"

"When was it dated?"

"June 11. He must have known they were following him. This complaint is right after he returned from Lake George! Let me call Susan. I know it was her and Mark was just following suit. She's maintaining surveillance on Jamal because of her gut. Trust me I know her!"

I sat at my desk while Lori leaned against it, and I called Susan. She answered on the third ring, "What's up, Terry? We're on our way to check on Jamal!"

"That's what you're not going to do, Susan, and you want to know why?" I exclaimed frustrated not only because of the complaint, but every time I was talking to Susan it was about Jamal!

"Matter of fact, can you guess what I got in my hand? No, so let me tell you. It's a complaint filed by Jamal on June 11 for harassment!

"Not only did he know you were following him, you did a poor job of it! How the hell you two get so sloppy, Susan. You're the FBI for Christ's sakes!"

"Well, Ter—"

"No well, Susan! Enough is enough! I'm the lead of this investigation, and I gave you the order to back off, and just keep an eye but no . . . you want to stalk the guy!

"Now I have to clean up your mess! Fuck, Susan! Look, just make sure your targets are well secured and do a drive-by at all your targets' residences.

"We're going full force, and no one is coming home until we catch this guy!" I didn't wait for a response before I hung up. I was pissed!

"I guess that goes for us too?" Lori asked!

"Yea, but after the court date! Can you call Noel and Jason and tell them the good news, and I'll call Kevin and Gordon?"

I leaned back in my chair. "Lori, we have to get this guy off the streets! This case can make or break us!"

Lori and I talked to everyone, and when Lori walked back over, I said, "I thought about it, and we should start in Salem at Judge Richard's house. We got three possible targets in a fifty-mile radius. So what do you think about that?"

"Sounds good to me! Shoot, we have seventeen possible targets going in either direction, so starting north doesn't matter. We can spend three days there, then go west, center, and then to the city!"

I thought, *That letter really pissed me off, which leads me to believe that Jamal may have more to do with this than I thought or why would he file a complaint to get us off his back unless he has something to hide. He knew we would have backed off eventually. I didn't tell Lori that was the main reason I wanted to start there because she is already convinced that he has nothing to do with anything. The last two murders were a doctor and a cop, two high-profile murders, why not a judge? All I knew was that we needed to catch this guy and fast!*

Chapter 65

June 19, 2022

Jamal

When I got back from Lake George with Kim, I was still being followed. Sunday night when I left to go get ice cream for Kim, Agent Steals was still posted up, and I was pissed! On Monday I called Jen to get Tracy's number.

She asked, "What do you need her number for?"

"The fucking FBI won't leave me alone, so I'm going to file a complaint against them for harassment. I mean enough is enough!"

"About time, Jamal, I would've been done that," she exclaimed then gave me the number!

Tracy was co-owner of her law firm Jacobs & Turner, and their law practices were in Massachusetts, New York, Vermont, Connecticut, New Hampshire, Maine, and New Jersey.

I called Tracy and told her my issue, and she wanted to do it for free. I told her no and that I would like to obtain her firm in all legal issues. I told her about Stone Industries because I knew her firm did criminal as well as corporate cases.

She knew I had been through the criminal system and was well aware of what this accusation could mean, so when I told her that I would like to put a hundred thousand dollars retainer on her firm in escrow, she was cool with it.

She told me her team would personally represent me in all legal matters—criminal and corporate, and she would file the complaint herself on Tuesday.

I wired the money on Tuesday, and the money in my bunker, I brought fifty-grand to my house, so I could slowly deposit it to cover some of the wire transfer. I left the other fifty because I plan on buying Kim her 2022 BMW250i series as her personal car for her birthday.

Then on Wednesday, I noticed the FBI wasn't following me anymore, I thought, *Damn that was fast. I should have thought about that a while ago!*

I loved it when things fall into place. I was able to get Jermaine and Preston a gig at this nightclub in Saratoga for Friday night, which was the perfect time to do what I had to do because Saratoga wasn't far from Salem.

I've been watching the Richards on my OVD, and they were some boring people. The wife left for work Monday through Friday at the same time, 7:00 a.m., and she was home between six and six thirty every night. Every night they ate at seven, and only on Saturdays did they go out to eat. Martin must still be pending investigation because he was home all day, doing things around the house. I noticed lately that the police had been knocking on his door once in the morning, noon, and night after the wife got home.

Yesterday I tried an experiment with the OVD because I couldn't figure out how to get the alarm system code or company. I switched to heat signature mode and watched when Martin left and set his alarm, and sure enough, I got the code and the order he punched it 3-9-5-4-3.

I praised Jamal for his genius, and now I didn't have to cut the power causing any suspicion.

I was scheduled for court today at nine. I already called Ethan last night to tell him I would be late today. Friday was my last day anyway, but I didn't want to stiff them because they were good to me.

I met Tracy at Albany Supreme Courthouse at eight thirty in the morning since it was an FBI matter. It had to be handled in a federal court.

I was talking to Tracy when Agent Carter and Agent Reid walked in. They came up to us, and Carter said, "Jamal, it's good to see you!"

"I wish I could say the same under these circumstances," I replied with disdain and then pointed to Tracy, "This is my attorney, Tracy Turner!"

Carter shook her hand, "Nice to meet you, Mrs. Turner! This is Agent Reid!"

"Nice to meet both of you," Tracy replied, shaking Lori's hand.

"The pleasure is all mine," Lori replied then asked, "Mrs. Turner, are you the same Tracy Turner from Jacobs & Turner Law Firm?"

"Yes, the one and the same, Ms. Reid! Why do you ask?"

"Well, my best friend Natia Finn works for your firm!"

"Ah yea, Natia is part of my personal team. She is very smart and driven, I like her very much!" Tracy proclaimed.

She then got down to business. "So look we are here to settle this complaint about harassing my client. The FBI has been staking out his house and following him wherever he goes.

"Mr. Stone informed me that he has been more than cooperative with your investigation even without legal representation, which I totally disagree with, but he didn't have anything to hide, so he answered your questions.

"With that being said, he is willing to drop the complaint if the FBI leaves him and his family alone."

Carter turned his attention to me and said, "First of all, Jamal, we are sorry for the misunderstanding. You have been more than cooperative, and we appreciate your honesty. As of this moment, you will not see an FBI agent near you or your home."

"Well, thank you, Agent Carter. I hate that it had to come to this. Shoot, I even invited y'all into my home to have dinner with my wife and me.

"But I was advised by my attorney that we will need this agreement on record and court-ordered."

"No problem, Mr. Stone, see you inside," Carter replied then walked into the courtroom with Lori in tow, looking at me as she passed by.

At nine the court was called to order with Jdg. Florence Lowery presiding. We stood then sat. Judge Lawry said, "Nice to see you, Ms. Turner!"

"You too, Your Honor!"

Judge Lawry fixed her glasses and looked at the docket. "Alright let's see. A harassment complaint filed against the FBI. How do you wish to proceed, Ms. Turner?"

Tracy stood and said, "I have talked to Agent Carter and Agent Reid who are in charge, and they have agreed to stop the harassment.

"For the record, they have agreed to stop staking out his home and also his family and friends' homes. They also agreed to stop following him and to let my client Mr. Jamal Stone live his life in peace.

"By agreeing to these terms, we are willing to drop the complaint today, Your Honor!"

The judge focused on Carter, "Do you agree to these terms?"

They both stood and Carter replied, "We agree to those terms, but if we have any questions pertaining to our investigation, we would like to be able to ask. Mr. Stone has been very cooperative, and we hope he will continue to do so!"

I leaned over, whispering to Tracy, "I have no problems with that."

"They should contact me first from this point on if they have any questions for you, and they should do it in my presence," she whispered back.

"You're my lawyer, so whatever you think is best."

The judge asked, "Ms. Turner, do you have anything you would like to address the court with?"

"Yes, Your Honor! My client is okay with them asking him any questions involving their investigation.

"However, I advised my client that the FBI should contact me first, and only ask questions in my presence!

"Just like Agent Carter said, my client has been very cooperative, and yet they still chose to harass him."

The judge started writing down something and then said, "Let the record show that the FBI has agreed to Mr. Stone's terms and that any questions from the FBI should be done in the presence of his attorney unless he gives permission otherwise.

"The complaint filed from Jamal Stone against the Federal Bureau of Investigation has been dropped upon the agreed terms this day Wednesday the nineteenth of June twenty nineteen. Court adjourned!" The judge banged her gavel.

It was quarter after nine, and I asked Tracy, "Do you want to grab a bite to eat? My treat and I can fill you in on Stone Industry's needs?"

"Sure, I can eat but I'll take my car!"

"Cool, meet me at Panera Bread!"

We got to Panera Bread, Tracy and I ordered and then we sat down. Tracy said, "It's been a while, but you want to know what's strange. We talked about Dr. Rawlings getting killed by this serial killer, and now she has.

"You want to know my opinion though, good riddance. One less evil person in this world to worry about!"

I loved talking with Tracy. She was hood with brains. I said, "Yea, no love lost here! But that's why the FBI is harassing me because these murders are too close to me.

"Jen lives on her street, Kim works with her, and then there's Tanya Spencer, Emily's mother."

I took a bite of my sandwich and drank some of my orange juice, then continued, "Now that you're my lawyer, I have to tell you something, you know in confidence, attorney-client privilege."

Tracy looked up with big eyes and asked with suspicion, "What, Jamal?"

"You know I wasn't always the guy you know now, and you also know that when I was with Jen, I loved her with all my heart.

"But . . . right before I went to prison, I believe three months before, I had a one-night stand. I was out with Cash, you remember Kyle Winter my boy. He used to mess with Natia, the girl that works for you.

"Anyway, the girl I slept with was Agt. Lori Reid. It's funny because I remember her the first time I saw her on the news. It was when that cop was killed, then shortly after that, she and Carter showed up at my house to interview me and had dinner with Kim and me.

"She didn't remember me right away because I looked different, and I told her my name was Anthony. So recently they came to my job to interview me again about Dr. Rawlings.

"After they left my office, Lori came back in without Carter, started telling me she remembered me, that she never stopped thinking about me, that I was a gift and a curse, and that nobody has ever made her feel physically the way I did!"

I took a deep breath. "Talk about a small world, huh?"

Tracy's mouth was on the ground by the time I finished, and then she burst out laughing. "Wait, wait, Jamal." She was trying to catch her breath. "What the fuck, man! That is some shit, playboy. What a crazy web you weaved!"

"Tell me about it! I just needed to get that off my chest!" I told her that because if anything happened, we could use that to our advantage.

I thought, *Yea, what a crazy web I weaved!*

I changed the subject while she was still laughing, "Anyway, Tracy, when you're done laughing at my expense, we can move on to more pressing matters!"

"Alright, alright just give me a sec! Dropping a bomb like that a person needs a sec to recover!" she replied, taking in a few deep breaths!

It was a good thing we were close. She could be herself in a professional setting, which made it easier to talk to her. "Go ahead, I'm good," she said with a big shit-eating grin.

"Anyway, Jamal is coming home soon, and Jen and I are helping Jamal start his company, Stone Industries. There are two things I have to ask. One, we would like you and your firm to represent us in all legal matters.

"Second, we would like you and Seth to incorporate your law firm with Stone Industries, and for y'all to sit on the board."

"Wow! Jamal, we are already large, and merging our firm would be something else!"

"Well, Jamal named it Stones Industries for a reason, which means that your firm would be in charge of all parts of legal matters in each company or business we incorporate, and to top it off, you don't have to change anything.

"The boy wants his claws into everything, and he's even starting a music label for Jermaine and Preston. He is so much like me and his mother, but he has the money to do it!"

"Well, first things first, we would be happy to represent Stone Industries. Y'all are like family, Jamal! Jen explained your logic about family to me, and it's pure genius. Preston and I would love to be a part of that!"

"You and your son already are," I replied and then jokingly, I said, "You know I have a brother, right? He's a year younger. His name is Shawn! You're single. He's single!"

"Is he good-looking? You know I won't date an ugly dude!"

"He's my brother and you know there's no ugly in my family!"

We both laughed and then talked for a little while longer even after we finished our food. It was ten thirty when we went our separate ways, and I was at work by twelve fifteen. I thought, *Boy what a good morning!*

Chapter 66

June 21, 2022

It had been smooth since the court date, and the rest of the week I'd been checking to see if they were following me by doubling back, taking alternative routes. And when I went to Walmart, I parked, jumped out, walked halfway, ran back to the truck, hopped in, and drove off and still no tail. People must've thought I was crazy. Kim, Evelyn, and I walked my street Wednesday and Thursday night, and I was checking to see if there was a car out of place, nothing!

Today at work, my employees had a party for my last day. Everyone was sad to see me go and wished me the best of luck. I pulled Wendy Sanders and Rebecca Soto to the side. They were my two brightest employees. Wendy was going to UMASS for software engineering, and Rebecca would graduate from Smith College next year with a project management degree.

Wendy was nineteen with short hair, but it was always colored, so I didn't know her natural hair color. She was tomboyish with tattoos all over, and I liked her go-get-it attitude.

I said to both of them, "Look, the reason why I'm leaving is because my son Jamal has come into some money and now wants to start his own company called Stone Industries, which I would be working for. I want both of you to come work for the company."

Rebecca was the one to reply first, "Mr. Stone, I would love to come work for you, but Ethan has already offered me your position this past Monday!"

"That's great but Amazon is not going to pay you as much as we are. I know this job is stable, but what we are building is bigger than Amazon, and you could be a part of it from the ground up!"

Wendy jumped in, "Mr. Stone, you know I start college in the fall, and well, I would only be home a small period of time, but if you're going to work with my schedule, then I would love to come work for you! Plus, didn't your son just graduate from MIT?"

"Yes, he did and the main part of Stone Industries is technology, which would be very beneficial to you and your degree. I mean aren't you going to UMASS for software engineering?"

"Yes!"

"Then this could be good for you. You could have a paid internship from your freshman year, plus I believe Jamal will establish a tuition reimbursement for college students. I also know you'll be able to earn credits from this internship once everything is established!"

"Well, count me in, Mr. Stone! When do I start?"

"At the end of your first semester!"

"Cool!"

"Great, Wendy, I'm glad you're in. Now can you give Rebecca and me a sec?" I handed her my business card.

"Sure thing, Mr. Stone," she replied, taking the card. "And thank you so much for this opportunity!" Wendy walked off!

I turned my attention to Rebecca. "I know this is asking a lot, but I would like for you to turn down the Amazon position and put your two weeks' notice in because I want you to start ASAP!

"I already told Jennifer that I was stealing you from Amazon. You will mostly be working with Jen but also with me, getting all the properties and setting up projects that Stone Industries will partake in or take over!"

"I don't know, Mr. Stone. How much money are we talking? You know I got kids, college, a boyfriend in prison, not to mention Mom and my house!"

"Look, I know how bright and capable you are! I told Jen everything that you have going on, but I also told her if we had you on our team, you would give us all you got, so here's the deal.

"We will pay your college debt and give you a twenty-five thousand dollar signing bonus. For the first year, we'll pay you sixty-five thousand for the first two years.

"After the first year, we will give you a premium package that will include full health benefits and a 401(k) plan. Then when we hit the stock exchange, we'll give you low stock options, how does that sound? That's more than anything Amazon will give you!"

"I can't argue with that, Mr. Stone, but one question, do I have to wait a year for health benefits? You know I have a family to take care of."

Rebecca was pretty much sold. I said, "Well, that is the only catch at the moment, Rebecca, but I promise you this, if anything major happens within this year, we will help you.

"Remember this is a start-up company, but we already have the funds, and you will get your signing bonus the day you start.

"Now, if you think about it, you have your health premium from Amazon for ninety days after you leave this job, and you can extend your plan and pay for it until your benefits kick in from us. But the big thing is that you could be making six figures fresh out of college,"

I had one more thing I wanted to hammer home, "Imagine Rebecca being able to pay for your kids' college tuition before they even leave middle school!" I saw her face light up!

"I ... alright, Mr. Stone. I'm in! I would be glad to join Stone Industries. I will decline Ethan's offer and put in my two weeks' notice today!"

I shook Rebecca's hand and gave her mine and Jen's business cards. The rest of the day went smoothly. I cleared out my stuff and was out the door. I thought, *Tonight this judge is gone!*

I called Jermaine on my way home. I told him about the little gig I had set up for him and his peeps early this week, and they were excited to do it. Jermaine wished that Jamal was home to do it with him since he cut all their music, but they could handle it without him because Steph was there.

Jermaine answered on the third ring, "What's up, Dad?"

"Me, what's up with you? You ready to hit the Saratoga strip?"

"And you know it! Where are you?" Jermaine asked, sitting in the studio and putting the final touches on his song "She's My Queen."

"Almost to my house, how long is it going to take you, Stephanie and Preston to come and get me?

"Give us an hour to an hour and a half. We'll be there before seven. It's a two-hour ride, so we should be there by nine pinning traffic! Oh yea, Dad, did you book the room?"

"Son, I did better than book a room just wait and see. I booked myself a room downstairs, so y'all could do your partying thing.

"I also got us a limo so we don't have to drive. But listen, don't say shit to your mom about y'all drinking either! You're only twenty and she'll kill me, her, and Tracy!"

"That would be an un-identifying death for you, Dad," Jermaine replied, laughing. "But don't worry, what happens in Vegas stays in Vegas! You always told me that!"

"That's my boy," I said, chuckling. "We always have each other's backs no matter what!

"Listen tho, I just pulled up at the house . . . See you when you get here! Oh, by the way, how do you like that 2022 black Audi?"

"It's awesome! The shit is fleet! I'll see you when we get there!" Jermaine replied then hung up.

I had everything all planned out. I'd been keeping my eyes on the Richards, and it was the same shit just a different day. The cops checked regularly until nine o'clock, and they were doing a walk around the perimeter. Once I was in, I was good because they checked every hour on the hour.

When I went into the house, Kim was nowhere downstairs, so I yelled, "Baby, where are you?"

"I'm upstairs giving Evelyn a bath!"

I ran up the steps and went to give my two girls a kiss. "Hey, beautiful, how was work today?"

"It was good! Sarah and I got stuck with the 12:00 p.m.–12:00 a.m. shift tomorrow! I think they're trying to get all their hours back that I miss while on maternity leave. That's the third long shift this week!

"Jen's taking Evelyn tomorrow, and you know that Emily is here for the summer. She's what, fifteen or sixteen now?"

"She'll be fifteen in July!" I replied, joining Kim in giving Evelyn's bath.

"Babe, I'm so excited tonight for Jermaine and them. I paid Club Hot Spot five grand for them to perform tonight.

"They got this girl Stephanie Patterson from Florida, call her Steph for short. She is spinning for them, and to tell you what, the girl is good! She can sing and rap too! She goes to school with Jamal and Preston, and she's spending the summer with Jermaine."

"Well, that's cool, Jen got a house full this summer!"

Kim and I finished with Evelyn's bath, and I took her out of the tub and dried her off. Kim said, "Can you put her PJs on, and I'll go warm up your dinner. I made pasta!" She kissed me and went downstairs.

I got my little girl all situated and went downstairs to eat. I put Evelyn in her swing and then sat down. I said while eating, "Jen and I talked about Rebecca from Amazon, and we agreed to hire her to help start up Stone Industries.

"I had to sell her today because Ethan offered her my position, but I wasn't letting her get away. That girl is sharp! I also offered Wendy an internship, and she took it of course!"

"Rebecca is the girl with two kids and the boyfriend in prison?"

"Sure is, she graduates next year from Smith College with a degree in project management, and she's always on the dean's list and she is a hard worker!"

I checked my watch and said, "Oh shit, baby, they'll probably be here any minute!"

I kissed Kim and shot up the steps to get my stuff and get ready. I wasn't even upstairs for five minutes when I heard the front door open.

"Hello, family," I heard Jermaine yell out, "where's my baby sis!"

"I'll be down in five minutes!" I yelled back!

"Take your time, Dad! I want to chill with my sis for a minute!"

I took my time and I was done with everything in fifteen minutes. I came down the steps, and Preston and Steph said at the same time, "What's popping, Mr. Stone!" They looked at each and laughed!

Steph was very beautiful. She stood at five feet nine inches one hundred and forty-five pounds with long jet-black hair and mocha skin. She played basketball at Boston College and was also a music engineer.

Evelyn was smiling while Jermaine played peek-a-boo. Jermaine said, "Dad, you ready? We have to hit the road!"

I kissed Kim again and said, "What do you have planned for tonight?"

"Sarah is coming to sleep over tonight. We will probably watch a movie."

"Sounds good to me," I replied, handing my bag to Preston. "I love you, babe!"

"Love you too!"

I took Evelyn from Jermaine and kissed her. "Daddy loves you too!" Then I put her in her swing. "We out!" I proclaimed as I ran out the door!

We hopped on the highway, and Jermaine was driving. I turned to the back and asked Steph, "Are you going to be a junior next year too?"

"Yea, but a second-semester junior. I transferred from Virginia Tech because Boston College gave me a full ride to play basketball for them, and they have my major in music engineering."

"That's nice, but you still can't beat me on the court!"

She laughed as she said, "Old man, I will cross you over and shoot your eyes out!"

Both of the boys started laughing, and Jermaine said, "I don't know, Steph, my dad's pretty nice. He's a three-sport all-American!"

"Steph, Mr. Stone is no joke on the court! And he can throw the hell out of a football!"

"Why do you think Jermaine is so nice? Jamal's nice too, but he likes his computer stuff!" Preston said.

"Y'all don't have to tell her anything! We got all summer, and it's nice to have fresh meat because I'm tired of beating up on you two!" I replied, winking at Steph!

Jermaine changed the subject, asking, "So, Dad, how did you get this gig for us?"

"I was going to surprise y'all, but don't worry how, just know that you're the opening act!" I answered with a chuckle and a wicked smile.

"Wait, Mr. Stone, I know that chuckle! Opening act for who?" Preston asked with a hint of suspicion in his voice.

"Damn y'all didn't check the internet for Club Hot Spot? I mean come on, you guys are performing there. What do you need Jamal to check for y'all?" I said as Steph looked up the club on her phone!

She found it and yelled, "No fucking way! You are not going to believe this!" I sat back with a shit-eating grin on my face, thinking, *That's right, Jermaine, your dad is the shit!*

She continued. "There must be some kind of mistake! You idiots should have looked Club Hot Spot up!"

"Just tell us!" Jermaine said in frustration!

She read, "Club Hot Spot presents Kodak Black and Tori Lanez June twenty-first—"

"Holy shit, Dad! Why didn't you tell us that?" Jermaine asked, cutting off Steph in shock!

"I thought you would've looked the club up at least! If you would've, you could've known!

"But what's the big deal? You're in VIP with them all night. Your hotel rooms are adjoined to theirs, and you're pulling up in a limo too! All y'all got to do is do your thing, and party with the big dogs!"

"You know, Mr. Stone, you're right. Let's just have a great time, and at least we get to chill with them! I can't wait to tell my girls back home tho!" Steph proclaimed with a thrill!

"I know y'all clothes are fresh to def! I don't know the name-brand shit you kids rock today, but I've seen Jermaine spend five hundred dollars on a pair of pants.

"Your shoe game and jewelry are crazy! And, Preston, I know you're straight, but I hope y'all spoiled Steph!"

"Don't worry, Dad she's good! We got this, no worries, I'm a motherfucking Stone! We're lit no matter what we do, best believe that!" Jermaine proclaimed as he turned up his music and started rapping the words!

We pulled into the Hilton at a quarter to nine. Traffic was good all the way through Albany, and we hit Saratoga a little sooner than we thought. We checked into our rooms. Mine was on the second floor because I wanted to be far away from the after-party.

We went to my room first to drop off my bags, and then we went to the twelfth floor. When we came off the elevator, there were only two room doors 1201 and 1202, and we were in 1202.

Jermaine opened the door, and the suite was huge! It had a living room, kitchen, and three bedrooms. In the bathroom, there was a stand-up shower and a Jacuzzi tub. The place was well furnished with a fifty-inch Samsung Smart TV with every channel.

Steph said, "Damn, Jermaine, this shit is nice! I'm beginning to think you guys are rich!"

We all started laughing, and then Jermaine said, "We're rich, bitch!" He was copying Dave Chappelle.

"But nah, for real tho, we have money in our family. My mom has a great job making great money and so does my dad, but my brother Jamal is a billionaire!"

"Shut your mouth, Jermaine!" Steph proclaimed in shock then turned to me. "Mr. Stone, he's lying, right?"

"He's not lying, Steph!" Preston said, "Jamal is in London right now with his fiancée Shelby visiting her parents!"

Steph still looked at me as if the boys were agreeing on a lie. She said, "Mr. Stone?"

"Our family has money, Steph, and that's all that matters. I'm just going to leave it at that!"

I went to the refrigerator and got out one of the three bottles of Cristal Champagne and said, "Let's make a toast!"

They all turned in my direction, and their mouths fell open as they eyed the Cristal as I popped the cork. They walked over as I poured the glasses and handed each one of them.

I proposed a toast, "To a night you will never forget, to the fun you will have on stage, and to the success you each will have throughout life!" We all clinked glasses and downed it.

"Damn that's good!' Jermaine proclaimed!

"I know, I never had this before!" Steph replied!

"I had some last New Year's!" Preston proclaimed!

I checked my watch and then said, "I'm about to go get dressed. I'm wearing everything black because I'm trying to be on the low, and don't y'all get drunk. If you finish that bottle together, then that should mellow you out. Drink it after y'all get dressed.

"Take two shots of the CÎROC or the Hennie that's in the limo on the way to the club, and then leave the alcohol alone until after your performance."

I grabbed the door. "You follow those rules, and your night will be perfect. And before I forget, I booked the room for two nights, so you can recover and check out on Sunday at eleven, but I'm leaving tomorrow.

"I will call y'all for lunch. If you come, that's cool, and if not, that's cool too! I don't have a clue when y'all will sleep. Just have fun respectfully and strap up, boys, and, young lady, make sure whoever straps up!"

I focused on my son, "And, Jermaine, I'm going to need your keys!"

"What for? You're not riding with us?"

"After I get dressed, I will stop back up and have another drink with y'all, but I'm going to meet you at the club because I have a business to take care of.

"Just tell the bouncer Roy that you are Big Maine, P-Dot, and Confetti, and they will lead you to VIP. Make sure you give Roy a big tip, Jermaine. I should be in VIP waiting. Now get ready!"

I left the room and thought, *Now the excitement begins!*

Chapter 67

June 21, 2022

Terry

    Lori and I stayed in Lake George because it was central to the three possible targets within fifty miles. We arrived at the Holiday Inn yesterday and paid a visit to the Pottsville Police Department and talked to them about Fr. Nathaniel Stanilli who was accused of raping two young altar boys. Capt. Tom Morton assured us that they were on top of watching him day and night and that they did a personal check on him three times a day along with a perimeter check every hour after nine as requested. We thanked the captain and left.
    That night Lori and I sat outside Father Stanilli's home from nine to midnight down the street from the patrol car. We got back to the hotel, talked a little about the case, did a VICAP for this region, and then we had sex then went to sleep.
    Today was the plan to repeat the process in Salem, which left Lake George for last. I thought, *This is where Jamal stayed two weeks ago, and I bet he has something planned here!*
    During the drive to Fulton County Sheriff's Department, Lori said, "I was thinking that the killer just killed in Massachusetts last, so the numbers there and in New York are even. I think the killer lives in either of these places."
    I thought about that for a sec then replied, "You know what you're absolutely right! I didn't even think about that! Maybe we should maximize,

bring Noel and Jason to us to comb more of New York, and Gordon and Kevin to Massachusetts with Susan and Mark."

As I thought about that, I was beginning to think that Susan might be right about her theory on Jamal, but I didn't say so to Lori.

She said, "That's a good idea because I have a feeling that another killing is going to happen sooner than later!"

We arrived at the Fulton County Sheriff's Department at eleven in the morning. We were led to Capt. Lee Holmes's office. Captain Holmes was a stocky guy with a bald head and a mustache.

He said, "Nice to finally meet you, Agent Carter and Agent Reid. What can I do for you?"

I took the lead. "We are tightening up on our investigation, and we are stopping at each place where we have a target trying to make sure the locals are keeping a close eye on them."

"We are following Agent Reid's instructions to the tee. There is an officer on sight at Judge Richard's house twenty-four hours a day. We are doing a perimeter check at 10:00 a.m., 3:00 p.m., 7:00 p.m., and then at 10 p.m. We do a yard check every hour on the hour. Protect and serve the agent, but this guy would have some big balls to come at a judge!"

"Well, Captain Holmes, thank you, and this guy did just go in a cop house and murdered him. So I believe this guy has very big balls!

"Anyway, we will be in the area tonight, so please notify your officers that we will be on the block a little way down from the Richards'.

"Also, we are staying at the Holiday Inn in Lake George." We finished up with the captain and left the station.

As we were getting in the car, Lori said, "Hey, Terry, does it seem to you that he was annoyed that we showed up?"

I replied, "He's one of those cops that makes it hard for other branches of law enforcement to work together. You'll think he doesn't care as long as nothing happens in his backyard."

"Well, what can we do. Some people just don't get it," Lori replied then changed the subject. "It's almost twelve. Let's get something to eat and then go do a drive-by at Judge Richards's and check out the neighborhood. After that we can go back to the room."

I couldn't agree more, and Lori and I went to a diner. We sat at a booth and when the waitress came up, we ordered our food.

While we waited, Lori leaned back crossing her arms and said while chuckling, "Neveah said at her ninth birthday party you saw a garden snake and you ran and tripped over a cooler then fell in the pool!"

I couldn't help but laugh, remembering that time. "Yea well, I didn't just see it. It was crawling across my foot, and it caught me off guard!"

Lori started cracking up. "And by the way, that was a big garden snake if I don't say so myself!"

She was laughing so hard now that she was in stitches. After she caught her breath, she replied, "Big . . . You can't put garden snake and big in the same sentence, Terry!

"Look at you, big bad Aquaman, running from his kryptonite and falling into his water world for safety!"

"Whatever, Lori, it was a big snake!" I exclaimed laughing with her! "Anyway, get your comic right, kryptonite is for Superman!"

"Whatever, you still ran from a worm!" she proclaimed, laughing her butt off!

Our food arrived. We ate and talked a little. After we finished, we did our reconnaissance of the judge's home and the neighborhood and then went back to our room. We went straight to work doing a little more VICAP, and then I called the others to tell them our revelation about the number of murders in New York and Massachusetts and our new plan. I sent Kevin and Gordon to Boston to work their way down and Noel and Jason to New York City to work their way up. After that we got back to work.

It was seven thirty when I realized what time it was, time was flying by. I said, "I'm hungry. Let's get something to eat then go post up!"

"Yea, cool, I can eat a steak right about now!"

"Sounds good, how about Applebee's?"

Lori got up, grabbed her purse, and said, "Race you to the car, loser pays," and she took off!

I knew she was going to say or try some slick shit like that, so I was already prepared when she started talking while looking for her purse, and before she could finish, I was already on my feet.

I grabbed her before she got to the door, picked her up, threw her on the bed, and as I was bolting out the door, I heard, "Hey!" But the rest I couldn't hear because I was already down the steps.

When she finally got to the car, she said with a pout, "Hey, you cheated!"

"All's fair in love, money, and food! So I won, and you lost . . . babe! I want lobster with my steak!" I proclaimed, getting into the car.

"I'm going to remember that tonight, Mr. Lobster and Steak!" Lori exclaimed with a grin and sass!

"Well, at least I'll be full," I replied, laughing.

She slapped me on the arm as I drove off. We got to Applebee's, ate, laughed, did not talk a bit about work, and then we left to post up outside the Richards.

Chapter 68

Jamal

I kept checking up on Richards as I got dressed. I put on my black Levi's, Kenneth Cole black button-down, black blazer to match, and then my black Gucci sneakers. I wore my black diamond earrings, bracelet, and chain with the cross hanging low.

I then put on my black-framed Gucci prescription glasses. My cornrows were fresh, and so was I. I checked myself in the mirror, and all-black money was looking back at me!

It was ten twenty as I checked on the Richards again, and they were in bed watching TV. I then went upstairs to check on everybody. The music was banging as I approached the door.

I went in and their connecting door opened. They were talking and hanging with Kodak Black and Tori Lanez. There were other people around, but I was glad to see my three still sober.

Jermaine saw me and got up, waving me over. He looked like a light-skinned chip off the old block!

He was dressed in white jeans with maroon and gold splashes in the upper region, a pair of custom-made Jordan 3s that was maroon and gold, and a white shirt that had a maroon and gold Boston College Eagle design on it with the hat to match, and his cornrows were tight. He also had his two-carat diamond earrings, a long platinum diamond cut chain with a maroon and gold eagle hanging from it. He was fly.

When I got to him, he said, "Hey, Dad, I want you to meet Kodak Black and Tori Lanez!"

I shook their hands as Kodak said, "Big Maine, your dad SuperFly!"

"All-black everything, huh, Mr. Stone," Tori said as he shook my hand. "Woo, look at those black diamonds! You're right Black, he is SuperFly!"

"Not bad y'all selves! But how do you say it Kodak . . . I know I'm SuperFly!" They both laughed!

Preston came over from talking to one of the girls. He was decked out in a cream and maroon outfit that was identical to Jermaine, even his Jordan 3 was custom-made with cream and maroon. His gold chain hung long, and his eagle was a yellow diamond with rubies.

He said, "Mr. Stone, you look fly, but that's a regular thing for you!"

Steph came over and I said, "That's what I'm talking about, y'all doing the damn thing, repping BC to the fullest!"

Steph had on low-cut jeans that hugged below her pelvis, showing off her abs, and her pants and shirt colors, designs, and eagle logo matched Jermaine's, but her shirt sat above her belly button and was pulled tight across her abs, making her breast pop out. She had diamond hoop earrings, her hair was wrapped, which fell forward over her shoulders, and her hat was pulled tight to the brow like Jermaine's and Preston's.

She said, "Not bad, old man, even though you don't look it! If I didn't know you, I would say twenty-eight!"

"Mr. Stone their fits are fly, plus them custom Jordan 3s, damn I want them!" Kodak said, admiring the trio!

"Yea, their shit is hot. Jermaine's shoe game is crazy! We are some shoe whores in our family!" I proclaimed.

I checked my watch, and it was quarter to eleven. Jermaine, Preston, and Steph had to hit the stage at midnight, so I said, "The limo is already downstairs, so let's get this drink done, so I can go handle my BI! Remember y'all are on at midnight, so get there by eleven thirty!"

Steph got the bottle of Cristal and poured everyone a drink, even Kodak and Tori. I gave another toast, "To a successful night, and to y'all, kill 'em on stage!"

We all drank our drinks, and then I shook Kodak and Tori's hands and then hugged the other three, saying, "Good luck tonight. I'll see y'all there!" Then I left.

I checked on the Richards again on the way down the elevator, and they were passed out. I knew I was going in blind after I took down the OVD, but I should be good.

I mapped out the woods around my cottage to a twenty-four-hour Walmart. I sat the Kawasaki 250 dirt bike at the back of the cottage. Tonight was going to be the toughest of all my adventures.

The cops were stationed at my target house, so I never knew if I needed a quick getaway, and with the FBI's harassment, I had next to no time to do reconnaissance and surveillance, but lucky for me, I had the OVD.

I pulled up to Club Hot Spot parking out back where there were no cameras. I walked around to the front entrance of the club, and the line was long as hell.

They already had a ticket line and a line that hoped they could make it in by buying tickets. It seemed like the sexy groups of girls that weren't hammered were of course let in.

I walked up to Roy who was a black guy who was tall and with rock-solid muscles. He looked like he played offensive line for the Buffalo Bills. Roy saw me and smiled. "Mr. Stone, nice to see you again!"

I met Roy that Wednesday Jen, Jamal, and I got back from Washington DC. He and the owner of the club Mike Foreson came into Amazon because they needed a rush order of speakers and TV monitors. That and twenty grand, I had Jermaine open up for Kodak Black and Tori Lanez.

I replied as we dap-hugged, "It is, Roy, what's up!"

"Ain't shit, you know, business as usual," he replied, releasing me. "Mr. Foreson is in his office. If you go to the left away from the music, past the bathroom, then up the stairs his office is right there."

"Okay, Roy, see you later!" I entered the club.

I followed Roy's direction and knocked on Mike's door. "Come in!" I heard Mike say.

He turned from the window that looked out on the floor, "Jamal . . . good to see you, man!"

Mike was a tall white boy from New York City with a black haircut and white-boy city swag.

I shook his hand as I replied, "Good to see you too, Mike!"

"Where's your son?"

"Last I saw them, they were hanging with Kodak Black and Tori Lanez, but I'm sure they'll be here any minute!"

"Cool, come, Jamal, and look out this window?" Mike asked as he put his arm around my shoulder!

I walked to the window, looked out onto the floor, and the club was huge! That wasn't including the back room and the six VIP spots.

Mike removed his arm as he said, "I remember when I first opened this place. I thought for sure I wasn't going to make it out of my first year. I couldn't keep the place packed, and most of the time, I broke even.

"Now look, I have the most popping place all the way up from NYC including western NY."

I nodded my head. "This is something, Mike. I remember when I was running the streets, and this place was just some warehouse at the lower end of Carolina Street. You have definitely outdone yourself here, my boy. I'll tell you that much!"

As I was looking out, I saw Jermaine, Preston, Steph, Kodak Black, and Tori Lanez heading up toward the VIP room together, led by Roy.

I said, "Look over there, Mike, going up to VIP room 1 by the stage. That's my son Jermaine, and his friends with Kodak and Tori!"

He looked and then nodded as he replied, "Oh okay! We have to go over there, so let's take care of business, and we can go together!"

I pulled out the two envelopes, which had ten grand in each and handed them to him. He took them and put them in his safe without even counting it.

I didn't care about that money because it came out of my bunker, and that was throwaway money.

After putting the money in his safe, he said, "Let's go, Jamal!" He grabbed his blazer and we left.

As we moved through the crowd, I checked my watch, and it was eleven thirty. We went upstairs to the VIP room, and a bouncer I didn't know spoke to Mike and then let us in.

The VIP room was big. It was like its own little strip bar the way it was set up. I thought, *Damn Mike's club is the shit!*

Kodak and Tori both said what's up to Mike. Mike then said, "This is Jam—"

Kodak cut him off, "Don't worry, Mike. We know Mr. Superfly!"

"Well, okay then!" Mike exclaimed!

I introduce Mike to Jermaine and his friends. They all shook his hand, and one by one gave Mike their stage names, Big Maine, P-Dot, and Confetti."

"Well, the stage is all yours," Mike said to Big Maine and then turned. "Kodak and Tori, come see me after the show!"

I said to Mike, "I'm going to chill here, and I'll come see you before I leave!"

"Cool, Jamal!" he replied as we shook hands and he left.

Everything was all set for the kids, and I was starting to feel the excitement build up because I was ready to kill this judge.

As I watched Jermaine with his friends, I thought, *Those kids of Dennis's will never be able to have a chance to do these things with their father!*

I spotted this beautiful young black girl sitting off to the side like she was not involved in the group participation, and she was the only one. There was something about her that told me she was about something more, and one of the groupie girls was her girlfriend that got her into this VIP situation. She was pretty as hell with curves to die for. She had a short haircut, and her skin was chestnut brown.

I pulled out a thousand dollars, walked over to her, and she looked at me like I had something on my face. I said, "Excuse me, what's your name?"

"Natasha!" she replied, rolling her eyes.

I ignored it because I would have done the same thing if I was in her position at this moment. I pushed on. "I see you're over here chilling in the cut, and not starstruck like the other girls!"

"I don't get down like that. I'm not anybody's groupie, and I'm just here with my girl who got us in!"

"I figured as much and that's why I came over here!"

"Well, I'm not like that either if that's what you're wondering!" Natasha replied, knowing I knew exactly what she was talking about!

"I'm sure, young lady! See those guys over there with the maroon and gold eagles clothes on," I asked while pointing. "That's my son Big Maine, P-Dot, and Confetti.

"They are here to open up for Kodak and Tori, and I need someone to record everything on stage for me. I can make sure you're in all the action. Plus I'll pay you a thousand dollars. How does that sound?"

Her whole attitude changed as she replied, "Hell ya!"

"Cool, come with me," I said as I held out my hand to help her up, and she followed me!

We walked up on Jermaine, and I said, "Big Maine, this is Natasha," They shook hands. "She's going to be recording for me.

"Let her and her friends come back with you to the after-party and make sure Natasha doesn't pay for any for the rest of the night!"

"I got you, Natasha," Jermaine proclaimed as Preston and Steph walked up. Jermaine introduced her and told them what I said.

He turned to me while Preston shot the shit with Natasha and said, "Dad, we're ready to hit the stage!"

"Alright then, I'll just be moving around, so just have fun, and keep your game tight! Remember you're a Stone!"

We clasped hands and hugged, and he, P-dot, and Confetti left with Natasha in tow still talking to Preston!

My plan was to leave after Jermaine's first song, I'd watch the rest on the camcorder. I moved from VIP on the slide-out, and nobody noticed.

I moved to the exit where my car was parked, and I still had a great view of the stage, and I could see Jermaine's show getting ready to start. I checked my watch, and it was four minutes to midnight, and I was half an hour away, so my time was short.

The deejay stopped playing the music and said, "Are y'all ready to get this show popping!"

The crowd went crazy. "I said are y'all ready to get the show popping!" The crowd got louder and crazier!

After the crowd settled a little, he continued, "Club Hot Spot brings more than promised, and believe me we do everything big here, so without further ado, we have Big Maine, P-Dot, and Confetti! Some new artists making their debut in the hip-hop game here at Club Hot Spot!

"Remember y'all heard them here first, so make some noise for the newbies in this rap game!"

The crowd got a little hyped even though they didn't know who they were. Big Maine came out on the stage with low music playing as he said on the mic with his words meshed with the beat, "What's popping, Club Hot Spot! I'm Big Maine, over here we have P-Dot, and back on the tables, we have Confetti!

"Some of y'all may know me and P-Dot, and some of y'all may not, but if you know football, then you know Jermaine Stone and Preston Turner!"

A lot of people in the crowd recognized them and got hyped! People yelled, "Yea, we know you, BC Man with the Hands!"

"That's right! And that's not the only shit I can do! Check this!"

Confetti dropped the beat as soon as *this* came out of Jermaine's mouth, and Big Maine and P-Dot started bopping and pumping the mic up and down. The crowd followed suit because the beat was hot!

Big Maine's voice came in, *"I'm no street nigga, but I'ma nigga with game!*

I know y'all see me, but y'all don't know what it's like to be me. Then Confetti dropped the beat, and Jermaine spat the chorus, *My game is tight,/ when I'm on the field everything feels right, /but the fame ain't free, / y'all don't know what it's like to be me!" /*

He repeated the chorus, and the crowd was moving with him. Then a few seconds of the beat, then his verse dropped, *I never been in the streets so I don't know what it feels like, /but the words come easy every time I pick up the mic/, when I'm on the field everything in slow motion, / I'm cutting in, dipping, flying by, /and when I catch a touchdown it's like a crackhead getting that first high,/ but I love this music shit, / laying bar is better than fucking the baddest chick, / but y'all don't know what it's like to be me,/ people are chasing me for an NFL deal, /y'all hear me on this mic you can tell I got mad skillz, / so my decision is made, / college I will stay because the tuition is paid!*

Big Maine repeated the chorus twice, and the crowd was hyped and then P-Dot dropped his verse, *I'm on the other side of the man with the hands,/ He ain't the only on the field with fans, / But I share da love for this rap shit, / I know you blazing these beat every time you're in your whip,/ I speak for da love of what I do, / To the NFL anytime me and my homie want too, / But this music is holding strong /, The people who want us don't know what it's like to feel these songs/, So the stress of fame ain't free/, Y'all don't know what it's like to be me!*

This time Confetti came in singing the chorus, and the crowd went off the chain because she could blow. After I heard her, I slid out the back door! As I walked to my car, I said, "Damn that girl can sing!"

I got to Jermaine's black Audi and got my bag out of the trunk. I got into the car and changed my clothes to a dark-blue sweat suit with a hoodie. I then folded my club clothes and placed them in the backseat.

I then took off my jewelry and glasses, put them in the glove compartment, and retrieved my contacts. After putting those in, I checked on the Richards, and it was quiet. I checked my watch, and it was fifteen minutes after twelve, so I hit the road!

Chapter 69

I drove toward the Salem Walmart and when I was ten minutes away, I called an Uber. I pulled into the parking lot and parked out of the way of the Walmart cameras. I pulled my hood low before I got out of the car so most of my face was covered, and then I hurried over to the side of the Walmart. I was only waiting two minutes when the Uber pulled up.

When I got in, the Uber driver asked, "Where to?"

I used my British accent to reply, "Stewart Street." Then handed him a hundred and told him to keep the change.

He was driving on route 22, and as soon as he passed the dirt road to my cottage, I yelled, "Stop here!"

The Uber driver slowed, pulling off to the shoulder as he replied, "But, sir, there is nothing out here! I can take you where you need to go. You just gave me a hundred dollars!"

"I'm fine right here. This is where I want to go, so you can let me out here!" I exclaimed!

"Okay, suit yourself!" he exclaimed as he unlocked the Uber, and I got out.

I walked a little as the Uber pulled out of sight, and then I jogged to the cottage. It was twelve forty-five when I checked my watch as I walked into the cottage. The last time I was here, I gathered all papers and items that were brought here from me, and I wiped down everything I touched, so all I had to do was get ready and burn everything in the fifty-five-gallon drum I had out back.

I opened my bag to get dressed in my everything black and then threw the sweat suit over with the stuff I was going to burn. I was ready to go, so I slung my Nike backpack on my back, which was for the OVD when I take it down, and then I put my supply bag on the porch.

I then grabbed everything I was going to burn, took it around back, threw it in the drum, poured gasoline on top of everything, threw a match in it, and watched as it caught fire. I watched it burn for three minutes. I didn't plan on coming back here unless something went wrong.

I checked my watch and I was two minutes behind schedule, so I went to the front and slung the supply bag on my back on top of the Nike bag. I hopped on my Ducati, and I was off. I was there in six minutes on DuPont Street. I pushed my bike into the woods and out of sight.

I pulled out my phone and checked on the Richards, and I saw the cop walking around to the backyard. The night vision on the OVD was beautiful. I got my Taser, lockpick kit, and put it into my cargo pockets as I watched the cop conduct his search. I picked up the supply bag, started walking in the direction of the house through the woods, and as soon as the cop went back to his car, I did a light jog onto the back of Richard's house. It was one ten, so I set my watch for two that would be the next time the cops conducted their rounds.

I refocused the OVD back on the Richards, and they were still fast asleep. I set my bag down, climbed the tree, and retrieved the OVD. The camera battery was blinking red when I checked.

I then climbed back down the tree and unslung my backpack to put the camera in along with my phone. I then slung the backpack on my back, pulled the straps tight, and then clicked the clips in front of me.

I peeked over the fence to make sure there wasn't anyone or surprises. I then hooked the supply bag on the picket fence and climbed over. I moved to the door and checked the handle. I thought, *Finally someone that knows how to lock their door!*

I pulled out my lockpick and went to work. It took me fifteen seconds, and I was in. I moved stealthily to the front door and punched in 39543, and it asked arm or unarm, and I hit unarm.

I crept into the basement, setting up the rope I was going to use to hang him. The basement ceiling was low, but that was okay. I had a plan. I laid knives with the bleach out and then got the duct tape out. I checked my watch and it was one thirty.

I took out the Taser and crept back out of the basement and crept upstairs to their bedroom. Their door was wide open, so I moved quickly and hit the judge in the back with the Taser, and his body jolted, falling still.

When he jolted, his wife opened her eyes, trying to fix them on me, but before she got a chance to scream, I hit her with the Taser in her right breast. She jolted, falling still. I checked her pulse because I never Tasered anybody in the chest before. I couldn't find her pulse, and I started to panic. I turned her to a better position, checked again, and there was a pulse but faint.

I took a deep breath and then started duct-taping Martin's wrists and ankles and then put a sock in his mouth. I duct-taped that too. I then checked his wife's pulse again, which was stronger, so I taped her to the bed. I put Martin on my shoulder and carried him to the basement.

I put the noose around his neck and then tied his ankles. I stood him up and then pulled the rope tight enough so his weight was supported by his neck, but his feet would also give him little support. The shortage of air caused him to become alert. He moved in a panic, trying to make a sound, but the sock and tape muffled it completely.

I had on my ski mask that only covered the lower half of my face, and I looked him in the eyes as I said, "Calm down. Your wife is safe for now!" I knew that was what he was wondering!

He slowed his movement as his big eyes looked into mine. I continued. "Jdg. Martin Richards, you have done a terrible thing! You took your job personally and had a man wrongfully convicted.

"Then he was clear to come home after the right man was convicted, and before his release, he was killed. His wife and three kids will never see him again.

"Now, I would normally let you explain yourself, but since the cops are watching your house, I have to get this over with!"

I checked my watch and it was two minutes to two, so I reset it to two thirty, and like clockwork, the cops were making their rounds. I saw the flashlight go past, then a little later come back. I gave it a full three minutes then resumed. I noticed his air was thin, but he was still good for the moment.

I said, "Your wife will live, but you won't! You have ruined a family's life, and now you must pay with your own!"

I stripped him naked and slashed him fifteen times as he struggled against his restraints with his muffled cries of pain. I threw bleach all over him, causing his muffled cries to get louder. His eyes started to roll into his head, and I knew it was because of the pain and the lack of oxygen.

I slapped him and said, "Oh, Martin, Martin, Martin, I sentence you to death by strangulation! You know, it's the same way Dennis Hawkins died in his cell!"

I pulled the rope at his feet and his weight fell onto his neck. I then tied the rope to the pipe that was on the wall. He dangled as he fought for air, only making his death come faster. Not even a minute passed before he stopped moving, so I checked his pulse, and Judge Martin was no more.

I pulled the note out of the bag and read it to myself, *This judge should have never taken his job personally, Now Dennis is dead and his loved ones had to have a funeral. Because of this judge, Dennis's kids will never know their dad, so because of that, I'm going to hang him, but first torture his ass. He's a Life Ruiner and deserves to die!*

I taped the note to his chest, then put back on my mask and hood. I then pulled my little special out of the supply bag and put it in my Nike backpack. Then I put the knives in the supply bag and dumped bleach all over the bag because I had to leave it on the floor.

I was finished and ready to go when I heard a bang at the door, and I came running up the steps, and as I emerged, the cops were kicking at the door. It was a moment frozen in time as our eyes locked through the glass panel.

After a moment, he kicked the door again, and it busted open, catching the chain lock as I bolted out the back door. The cop shouldered through the lock continuously in motion, chasing me.

I heard him yell, "He's going over the fence!"

Just as I got over the fence, a bullet hit where I just left. I hit the ground with a roll, and another cop was on the fence yelling, "Freeze! Stop where you are!"

I bounced up and hauled ass! I heard another shot pop off as the bullet slammed into a tree I just ran by. I was zigzagging military tactical style as more bullets flew by. I heard the cop stumble and fall, giving me time to gain separation.

I heard the siren just as my watch started to beep. The cop was back on his feet, and I heard him say, "Stop, stop right there!"

I thought, *Yea right* as I bolted to my bike. I pushed the bike out of the woods on a run and then jumped on as I brought it to life, and as soon as I revved on the throttle, a police car came flying around the corner, siren blaring! I kick into gear as another bullet whizzed by me. I ducked as I gunned my Ducati.

I circled around the block, so the cop would have to too, which allowed me to gain distance and separation. I bolted back up the block, and as I passed an unmarked police cruiser, I got a glimpse of Agent Carter and Reid, and I knew they couldn't see me because of my mask and hood. I was a black blur to them. They completed 180 and pursued me.

I gunned the bike onto route 22 that led to my cottage. I had fifty-plus yards on them when I turned on my dirt road. I parked in front of my cottage and hopped off. I grabbed the little bomb out of my backpack that I made to drop in my gas tank just in case something like this happened.

I heard the cops hit my dirt road as I dropped it in then walked away. The cops got near the bike as I was turning the corner, and the bike blew up! I hopped on my Kawasaki 250 dirt bike and kick-started it.

I could hear Agent Carter yelling, "He's around back, get him!" I gunned my bike and booked it! The cops were shooting at me, but I was gone!

I got to the edge of the Walmart parking lot and the woods, got off the bike, and then took out my towel, wiped the bike down then left it. Jermaine's black Audi was close, so I hurried to it, jumped in, and left Walmart.

I checked my watch and it was three o'clock as I pulled into a twenty-four-hour gas station down the street from Club Hot Spot. I changed back into my club outfit, took out my contacts, put back on my glasses and jewelry, and then left for the club.

I was back at the club at three twenty and crept back into the club the same way I left out. I had two shots and then went to find Jermaine.

I went to the VIP room, and Roy was at the door. He said, "What's up, Jamal! Big Maine been looking for you!"

"I've been around here all night, Roy, so he wasn't looking too hard!" I replied, giving him a brotherly hug handshake.

Roy laughed, "I can tell you right now, he wasn't!"

We both were laughing as I asked, "Is he in there?"

"Sure is and hasn't really left all night. I mean, Big Maine and his friends did some rounds of the club tho, and these kids were going crazy for them! The deejay had to get cuts of their song, so he could play them!"

"That's what's up, tell Mike I'll see him in a minute," I said as I walked past Roy into the VIP room.

It was crazy when I walked into the VIP room. There were strippers walking around and one on the pole. I spotted Jermaine in the back with Steph sitting on his lap.

I walked up and Jermaine said, "Yo, Dad, where you been?"

"What are you talking about, I've been here!" I gave him dap, "Y'all killed it on that stage tonight, and the deejay been playing y'all song all night!"

"I know, right. They're really feeling us!"

I could tell that he was drunk, but he was still under control just like a Stone. Steph said, "Mr. Stone, thank you for tonight. It was the bomb! I never had this much fun in my entire life!"

"You're welcome, Steph, and I'm glad you had a great time. Let me ask both of you a question, are you two an item or something?"

Steph kissed Jermaine and proclaimed, "Or something!"

I laugh while asking, "Where's Preston?"

Jermaine and Steph pointed in a direction behind me, so I turned to see where, and there was Preston with Natasha all over him.

I turned back to Jermaine and said, "I see Press found him a little thing—thing, huh!"

"They've been like that all night!" Steph proclaimed, giggling!

"Jermaine let me talk to you for a minute over here!"

Jermaine kissed Steph and slapped her on her ass to get up, and she did. He slid out of the booth and followed me. When we were in the corner, I said, "You having fun tonight?"

"It's better than I imagined, plus being on stage the first time in a club with seasonal performers, what more could we ask for! Thanks, so much, Dad. We owe you!"

"Y'all don't owe me anything! So are you and Steph a thing?"

"I've been seeing Steph since the beginning of the semester, some love and basketball shit!" Jermaine answered with a slur in his voice.

"I just wanted to make sure that she's not latching on to you now because she knows you're rich!"

I had to address that, getting it off my chest because I like Steph, but I didn't ever want a chick using my boys.

"No nothing like that, Dad! She's cool as hell, and loves sports! I mean we haven't made it official yet. We're just enjoying being friends with benefits in college!"

"Cool, cool! Aye, listen tho—I've been here all night!"

"Where else could you have been, Dad, why you buggin'?"

"Nah, just checking to see how drunk you are! I'm about to go see Mike then go back to the hotel. I love you, Jermaine, and y'all were fired tonight! Oh, and before I forget, where's my camera?"

Jermaine led me back to his booth and said to Steph, "Hand me the camera, Confetti!"

She reached over and gave the camera to Jermaine who gave it to me. I said to both of them, pointing and waving my finger between them, "Have a safe and protective night! I'll see you for breakfast maybe before I leave! I'll call your room!" I hugged Jermaine and waved bye to Steph as I walked over to Preston.

I popped him on his shoulder as I said, "Good job tonight, P-Dot! And you, Natasha, how was the footage?"

"It's better than HBO. Thanks for the job, Mr. Stone!" Natasha bragged, hugging up on Preston!

"Come here, P-Dot!"

Preston slapped Natasha on the ass, and she got up. I thought, *Damn these boys act just alike!*

I said when we were alone, "Boy, make sure you strap up!"

"I got you, Mr. Stone!"

"Y'all all look out for each other! I'm leaving, so I'll meet you at lunch tomorrow before I leave!"

I gave Preston a hug and said, "Preston, you are like one of my sons, and I love you too! I hope you had a great night!"

"I love you too, Mr. Stone, and tonight was off the chain. Thank you so much!"

I let Preston walk back over to Natasha, and I met eyes with Jermaine and Steph and deuced them out.

I stopped back at Mike's office for a few to shoot the shit until four. I told him about Stone Industries, which he sounded very interested in, so we agreed to keep in touch. I left to go dispose of my all-black-everything and then went back to the hotel straight to Jermaine's room.

I put his keys back in his bag, pulled out my phone, and shot him a text, **Keys in your bag Please put my bag that's in your trunk in my bunker as soon as you get home and DON'T FORGET! PS ERASE THIS TEXT!**

As I was going to the elevator door, Jermaine texted back, **I got you, Dad!**

I erased both texts by the time I exited the elevator, and as I was walking down the hall to my room, Agent Carter and Reid were there with other cops.

Carter said, "Jamal Stone, you're under arrest!"

Chapter 70

Terry

Lori and I finished eating at Applebee's at eight thirty-five. We pulled up twenty minutes later down the road from the Richards' house.

As I was parking the car, I said, "Lori I want to talk to you about something!"

"Okay . . ." she replied, facing me with suspicion!

I put the car in park and then faced her and continued. "We've been together now for over four months, and I know that you are the one for me!

"I talked to Director Wall already about giving us different partners after this case. Now, I don't want to rush you into anything, but we ain't getting any younger—"

"Speak for yourself, buddy boy!" Lori exclaimed, cutting me off with sass!

I started laughing as I continued, "What I mean, youngling, is I would like for us to move forward and for you to move in with me!"

She looked at me smiling as she replied, "It's funny you should ask that—"

"What d'you mean funny!" I asked to cut her off, taken aback by how she just phrased that reply!

"Calm down, boy, nothing like that, Terry, geez! But since you're asking, well, I was going to wait until this case was over, but I guess I'll tell you now!"

She paused for dramatic effect, "Terry, I'm pregnant!"

I knew she saw the shock on my face, and my mouth moved without being able to form or speak words, but finally, I replied, "What, when, how!"

She laughed at me as she jokingly said, "When two people come together and have sex—"

"Lori, come on I know that, but when did you know, I mean this is great news!" I was so excited that Lori was pregnant with my baby, and it was just what I wanted, to start a family with her!

"Remember the shift you shared with Susan? Well, I was late then, and while you were at work, I took a pregnancy test, and it was positive, all three tests!

"Terry, I knew you loved me, but I didn't really know how serious you were until now. So yes, I will live with you because I love you, and I want to start a family with you and Neveah!"

I leaned over and hugged and kissed her. I then said, "I want nothing more than to start a family with you! I love you too, Lori!"

I thought, *Now we have to definitely put an end to this case!* We talked for a long time as we watched Judge Richards's house.

It was a quarter 'til two when Lori said, "It looks like a quiet night here. Let's go back to the hotel and celebrate!"

"Sounds good to me, Wonder Woman!"

Lori laughed, "Oh really, Aquaman, and I thought Wonder Woman had a thing for Batman!"

"Yes really," I replied as I started the car, "since you're calling me superhero names, I figured I'll join in, and you know what, I think you're right about the Batman and Wonder Woman thing, so I guess I'll have to go back to being Batman!" We both laughed as I pulled off!

We hit the gas station and then went straight to our hotel room. We were going at it hard as we approached our room door, kissing passionately and grabbing all over each other. I got the key card out, keyed into our room while Lori was pressed up against the door, and we were still going at it.

We got into the room and I kicked the door close, then we fell onto the bed together. Three minutes later, we heard a call come across the scanner, requesting back up at 1143 Magnolia Street. We had a break-in at Judge Richards's house!

We looked at each other in disbelief and hopped up, gathering ourselves, and bolted out the door!

I was pushing a hundred with the lights flashing, pissed as all hell. "Ain't this a fucking bitch! We were just right there. We could've had him!" I exclaimed!

I knew it wasn't Lori's fault, but a part of me wanted to blame her, but I thought better because how would she know and I also agreed to leave.

She was on the phone talking to Susan. "Susan he's in Salem at Judge Richards's, we're in pursuit of him right now!"

"Put her on speakerphone, Lori!"

Lori clicked the button, "Susan, go to Jamal Stone's house, and see if he's home right now! If he doesn't find out where he is, call back as soon as you know!"

"I'll call you back in ten minutes. I'm not too far from his house now!" Susan hung up!

I thought, *I knew you were close. When do you ever do what you're told!*

We were flying down Fulton Avenue, and then time slowed down as Lori and I saw a black blur on a motorcycle fly by us looking in our direction. I immediately knew it was the killer.

The cop cruiser turned the corner with the light and siren blaring! I made a 180 turn and gunned it! The perp turned on route 22, and we were about a hundred yards away from him when we saw the perp turn onto this dirt road into the woods.

I gunned the cruise faster because I didn't want to lose him, and we headed down the same dirt road. As we approached the cabin, I saw the perp walking away from his bike, and not a second later just before I got close to the bike, it blew up. I slammed on the brakes!

Lori and I hopped out of the car, and as we ran around the blaze of the bike to the back, I heard another motorcycle start up.

I yelled to the other officers who just got out of their cruiser and started running toward us, "He's around back, get him!"

Lori and I got around back and opened fire on the blur on the dirt bike, but the perp was gone.

I yelled, "Fuck! I want to know where these woods lead to! Every surrounding store and house, NOW!"

Sheriff John Fuller walked up to me and said, "The only place these woods lead to is the Salem Walmart! My brother and I hunt in these woods!"

"Well, get someone over to that Walmart!"

Sheriff Fuller ran to his car, and he and his partner headed to the Walmart with another car following.

I couldn't believe we were that close to catching this asshole. I pulled my phone out and then said to Lori, "Can you go in the house and start looking for some evidence if there's any. Shit we know this guy . . . and we probably won't find shit! I called Noel and Jason, so they can get up here!"

Lori turned in and went into the cabin. Noel answered, "What's up, Terry?"

"You're not going to believe this shit, but we're here in Salem, and just had a high-speed chase with the killer!"

"He's there! Did you get a look at him?" Noel replied with shock!

"No, he was dressed in all black, but we're at the place he's staying!"

"Well, did you stop the murder? Is Judge Richards still alive?"

"Look, Noel, I just need you and Jason to get up here right now, and I'll give you more details when you get here or when I know more!" I exclaimed frustratedly and was pissed because I could've stopped this murder!

I walked into the cabin over to Lori, and she said, "The place looks like an advertisement for a getaway week cabin. However, we did find a fifty-five-gallon drum in the back with burned papers and clothing!"

Lori and I walked to the back, and I looked inside the drum. I didn't touch anything of course because the forensic team had to do their thing.

Lori continued. "I called the cops at Judge Richards's house. The wife is alive, but the judge is dead. He was cut up, hung, and he smelled like bleach. The bleach was all over the place.

"The killer didn't have time to clean up he even left his bag with stuff in it, but that too is covered in bleach!"

I shook my head as I said, "Damn, Lori, we almost had him! And know what, I don't believe him leaving that stuff behind was a mess-up on his behalf.

"He knew we were watching the judge. He had a getaway plan, and I believe he knows we are watching certain targets closely . . . I'm almost sure of that, and maybe he knew we were watching him closely too!" I now had a gut feeling that Jamal was behind this somehow!

"You think it's, Jamal, don't you?"

"Think about it, Lori, there are a lot of coincidences surrounding him. He knew we were following him, and I bet the whole time too, so things got quiet.

"Then he filed a complaint against us so that we would back off, and then a couple of days later, someone is dead, and I bet he is somewhere close with an airtight alibi!"

I watched Lori think for a second, and then she replied, "But why would he do it so soon after the complaint, and we've been watching him, so when would he have time to plan and survey?"

"Think about this, Lori, two weeks ago, he was in Lake George. He could've done surveillance then!"

"I don't know, Terry... that's a small window. Our killer is a planner and very clean. I mean this guy left stuff behind this time. It was like he was caught off guard and that the police were so close!"

I looked at Lori like she was crazy and said, "I don't know what's going on, Lori, but every time we talk about Jamal being the possible perp you go all defensive!"

"What... no! What the hell are you trying to say, Terry! Just because I have an objective point of view and don't go putting all my eggs into one basket, doesn't mean that I'm against Jamal being a suspect! I can't believe you would think that! Not cool, Terry, not cool!"

Before I could reply, my phone rang, and I thought, *I'll touch base on that subject later.* I answered, "What's up, Susan?"

"Jamal is not home. I just talked to his wife, and she said he's in Saratoga at Club Hot Spot. Jermaine is performing there!"

"I fucking knew it! He's less than an hour away from here! Did she tell you where he's staying?"

"Yea, he's at the Hilton in Saratoga!"

"Thanks, Susan, I'll call you back!"

I hung up and turned to Lori, "What did I tell you, he's up this way! Just like I thought, and guess what? He has an airtight alibi! But guess what, not this time! We're arresting him for suspicion of murder!"

Now Lori was looking at me like I was crazy as she said, "Are you out of your mind? We have no proof it's him! And come on, we just left the court with orders not to harass him. We should get something first!"

"Fuck that, Lori, he's guilty, and we're arresting him on suspicion, and I know we'll find something to make it stick! This is New York... and all we need is circumstantial evidence to file charges.

"And trust me, there are too many coincidences for it not to be him! I think Susan was right about Jamal!"

We started walking to the car as Lori said, "Whatever, Terry, it's your call, but trust me this is a bad idea! I think you should at least try to get a warrant!"

I remotely started the car before we got in. I completed a K-turn, thinking about what Lori just said about a warrant, and as I pull off, I replied, "Fuck that warrant! We are arresting him now!"

Two cruisers followed Lori and me to the Hilton. We got out, went into the lobby, got Jamal's room number from the desk clerk, and went to his room. I was about to knock on the door when I saw Jamal coming off the elevator, walking toward us.

He had a smirk on his face as I said, "Jamal Stone, you are under arrest!"

"For what, you got to be fucking kidding me, right?"

I walked over and cuffed him. As I was cuffing him, he said, "Terry, you are making a big mistake, my friend, and this is the only time I'm going to give you a chance to let me go!"

"Jamal Stone, you have the right to remain silent. Anything you say can and will be used against you in the court of law. If you cannot afford an attorney, one will be appointed to you. Do you understand these rights as I have just read to you?"

"I'll be out by Monday, and you will be sorry, Mr. Terry Malcom Carter!" Jamal exclaimed while laughing down the hallway into the elevator.

Jamal didn't say anything but laughed and shook his head all the way to Albany Federal County lockup!

Chapter 71

June 22, 2022

Jamal

All this was funny as I sat in the interrogation room. I'd been here for two hours, and my adrenaline has woken me wide awake. Before they put me in here, I told them that I wanted to call my attorney, but they ignored me, and since they read me my rights, I was entitled to make that call so that was strike number two. I knew they'd been watching me through their two-way mirror, and I was glad they could see my demonic grin that was followed by laughter.

The door finally opened, and Terry and Lori walked in. Lori stood while Terry sat, and said, "Jamal, Jamal, here we are! I bet you had this all figured out, and that you would get away with it this time!"

I laughed in his face, remaining silent! He continued. "Oh, so you think this is funny! You think killing people is funny?"

Terry was trying to get me to break my silence, but I wasn't buying. He continued. "I don't get it, how does someone that has everything going for himself be a cold-blooded killer!

"I mean you have two great sons and a good family thing going on, and Evelyn, that beautiful baby! What in the hell were you thinking, and now they're all about to lose you! What kind of father are you?"

I thought, *This motherfucker keeps talking about my family, he'll find out how cold-blooded I can be!* Then I took a couple of deep breaths and calmed down because I knew he was trying to bring me out of character.

I knew he caught the twitch in my demeanor when he mentioned my family, but I gained control, giving him my demonic grin and stared as I shook my head.

Then I gave him what he wanted and broke the silence. "See Terry," I said, calling him by his government name with no respect for his shield, "I know the game you're playing, and I guess I'll play along because I'm bored. You use my family button to get me to break my silence . . . very well then."

I spoke in a calm, leveled voice to show him that I was not worried, and I was the one in control, "I will say this to you, and it will be the only thing I say, and then you will let me call my attorney or I will have your job and brought up on charges. So one, I will kindly ask you to leave my family out of your mouth.

"Second, I have nothing to do with this.

"Third, I will be filing charges against the FBI and suing. And finally, again I am requesting my lawyer, so you and I know now that this interview is over."

I pointed at the camera to let them know that I know this was being recorded. "How is that for broken silence, Terry?" I went back to my demonic grin as I leaned back in my chair.

I could see the uneasiness in Terry's demeanor, and it made my smile even bigger. I looked at Lori, and I could tell she knew that they were up shits creek without a paddle.

She didn't really speak on their way back to Albany, only answering questions Terry asked, and her face was so far off that I knew they had nothing.

Terry stood and slammed his fist down hard on the table and said, "You may have your family, and everyone else fooled, but I promise you, Jamal, I will nail your ass to the wall!

"Shit . . . you even had me fooled for a minute, but I'm sure as I've been sitting here with you now with that lunatic grin, and crazy-ass laugh that you are the killer!"

He leaned over the table. "You're a con, Jamal, and you will always be no matter how much glamour you use to cover up your craziness! I will get you!" He turned and stormed out of the room with Lori in tow!

I shook my head, laughing at Terry's outburst. Fifteen minutes later, I was escorted out to go make my phone call. Tracy answered the phone on the seventh ring, breathing hard, "Hel-hel-lo!"

"What's up Tracy, why you out of breath, did I interrupt something?"

She caught her breath and replied, "Just working out, Jamal. How were the kids last night?"

"The crowd loved them, and I got it all on camera too, so we can watch it! But that's not why I called, I'm in a little situation right now!"

"Woo"—she breathed—"what kind of situation?"

"I've been arrested on suspicion of murder by Agent Carter and Reid!"

"What! Are you fucking kidding me! The same two agents from the harassment complaint?" she replied in disbelief!

"Yup, the same two! And the crazy thing is that I was at the club all night! I knew they were trying to frame me all along.

"They think I'm the killer or somehow involved. Why else would they be questioning and following me all the time?"

"Have they tried questioning you?"

"Yea, but I didn't talk to them other than I had nothing to do with it, and I want my attorney!"

"Good, don't say anything else! I'll be there, give me a couple of hours, and we'll talk then. I will also call Jen and Kim for you, so sit tight and I'll handle everything!"

"Thanks, Trace! And can you do me a favor and call Jermaine and Press for me. I was supposed to meet them for lunch and tell Jermaine to remember what I told him." I requested, knowing Jermaine would know what I was talking about.

"Alright, say no more! You know they messed up, right?"

"I sure do. This isn't my first rodeo. I did study the law while I was locked up. So I'll see you when you get here!" I hung up and sat until Tracy showed up!

Chapter 72

<u>Terry</u>

I was pissed because I couldn't get a damn thing on Jamal! The judge was dead, and we had nothing at either scene. Lori was right. I jumped the gun arresting Jamal, but I believed in my heart that he was the right man.

After the interrogation, I called Director Wall. "Sorry to bother you so early, Mike, but Judge Richards is dead! He was killed early this morning, and we have a suspect in custody."

Director Wall sighed deeply and replied, "Fuck! He was able to kill a judge before you apprehended him, who is the suspect?"

"We arrested Jamal Stone on suspicion of murder!"

"Oh, so you caught him red-handed?"

"Not exactly—"

"What do you mean not exactly? Please tell me you have him fleeing the scene and evidence that points to him!" Director Wall knew if they had nothing of a sort, there was going to be a problem especially after Jamal filed that harassment complaint!

"No, we have nothing yet, but we are still combing the two crime scenes, but we do have circumstantial evidence!"

"Circumstantial evidence! What the fuck, Terry . . . It better be damn good!" Director Wall exclaimed with frustration!

"He's our guy, Mike, and I know we'll find something. Plus you wanted someone in custody! I know Jamal is our guy. I can feel it!"

"Right, I did tell you that, so I'll tell you what, do as you please, but know if you're wrong, this shit is all on you and your team, Terry.

"And trust me it won't be my job at stake! God, I hope you're right. Keep me posted! Find something, Terry, or the media is going to have a field day with the FBI!" Director Wall exclaimed and hung up!

Lori was standing next to me during the conversation. "So, Terry, what's our next move? How did the director say we should handle this?"

"The way we see fit! He wanted someone in custody, and we can charge Jamal on circumstantial evidence, so that's what we're going to do! He's our guy, Lori, and we'll find something to make it stick! We have to!" I replied frustratedly, not knowing what direction we should move at this moment!

"I mean do what you want, but I don't agree with this method! We should find something first, Terry, and you know it!"

"I'm not letting him go, Lori! He's a lunatic, look at how he was looking at us, and the way he was laughing! He may have everybody else fooled, but he's our guy!" I exclaimed as I sat down at my desk and started filing the charges.

"You're judging him by a look and a laugh." She shook her head. "You got to be fucking kidding me, Terry! What is this, your male ego or something?

"Well, Terry, it's ugly and I don't like it! You're making a big mistake and you're hurting your team in the process!" Lori exclaimed, pissed off as she walked away!

I thought, *Damn she could be right, but my gut says Jamal is guilty, and I'm never wrong! But there's always a first time. God I hope I'm right!*

I finished filing the charge and went into the interrogation room and said, "Jamal Stone, you are charged with the murder of Jdg. Martin Richards, and seven others!"

Jamal just laughed, shaking his head as I escorted him to Federal booking!

Chapter 73

June 24, 2022

Jamal

Today I have court at 9:00 a.m. in front of the same judge I filed the complaint with, Jdg. Florence Lowery. Tracy came to see me on Saturday and told me they were charging me with murder on multiple accounts.

She told me not to worry because they only have circumstantial evidence, and she had already talked to Jermaine, Preston, and Steph, and they said you were with them all night. I told her to also contact the owner of the club Mike Foreson, his bouncer Roy, and they could also verify I was at the club.

Tracy also told me it was a good thing that I filed that complaint because now I have on record that the FBI has been harassing me and that I have a lawsuit against them when we get this case dismissed.

I spent the rest of the weekend in Albany County lockup, and I wasn't worried because I knew they had nothing. The only thing that sucked was that Kim was crying, thinking I might be going away for a while, but I reassured her that she had nothing to worry about. I'd be home on Monday.

Jen could handle this because she'd been through it before but being her crazy self, laid into me about going to jail, leaving Evelyn home and Emily wanting to see me. Jen had always been a temperamental woman, especially when I get in trouble, but Tracy assured them that there wasn't anything to worry about.

After the morning chow, the correction officer said, "Stone, get ready for court!"

I was arraigned on charges on Saturday given no bail but given a court date for Monday because it was a federal issue. I showered and got ready in the clothes I wore to the nightclub. They came for me at eight, cuffing me and then drove me to the Federal Courthouse.

After they put me in a bullpen, Tracy came down to meet with me. She said, "I talked to the Federal DA, and they are requesting no bail, but I know Judge Lowery will give you bail. It may be high, but she will grant it.

"Jamal came home early, so he's going to post whatever the ransom is, so you can go home today."

"Damn, I didn't want him to cut his vacation short, but then again, that's my boy!"

"He's said he's going back after you're out and home. Shelby didn't come with him!" "Who's in the courtroom, family-wise?"

"Everyone is out there, Jamal. You know that! A good support system always looks good to a judge. So I'll see you when you get up there," she replied as she got up and left.

I was brought up five minutes after nine, and the courtroom had quite a few people in attendance. There was Terry, Lori, along with the media. I grinned in their direction as I walked in.

I saw Lori drop her head, and Terry directed his eyes at me with a sinister look, which made me grin even harder.

Next, I set eyes on the Federal Head DA Mr. Clayton Mayer. He was a white guy with silver hair that was well-groomed, and he looked like he was in his early forties, but I knew he was fifty-eight.

I looked at my family, Kim, Evelyn, Jen, Jermaine, Jamal, Preston, and Steph. They all waved and I nodded before I focused on my table. At the table other than Tracy was some white lawyer I didn't know and Natia Finn.

When I first walked in, I caught a glance at Natia and Lori talking, but they separated as I came fully into the court. I got to the table and Tracy said, "Jamal Stone, this is Kenny Fields, and this is—"

I cut her off as I said, "Hello, Natia, it's been a long time!"

"Yes, it has, Jamal, wish it was under better circumstances!"

The bailiff said, "All rise. . . Jdg. Florence Lowery presiding!"

The whole court got up, and the judge took her seat, and then everyone else sat other than the media.

She looked at the docket and then at us as she said, "The defendant is charged with eight counts of murder, how do the defense plea?"

Tracy stood and answered, "Not guilty, Your Honor!"

The judge faced the DA and asked, "Do the People have a set bail in mind?"

Mayer stood and answered, "Because of the nature of the crimes, and the defendant's past history, the People ask the court to hold Mr. Stone without bail!"

The judge turned back to Tracy and asked, "Ms. Turner, what is your recommendation?"

"My client was just here not even a week ago about being harassed by the FBI, and now he's being charged with these murders when clearly he was nowhere near Salem, New York, this Friday.

"My client also has multiple eyewitnesses to verify his whereabouts. My client has nothing to do with these allegations, and I ask the court to release my client on his own recognizance!"

The judge read a little more, then leaned back in her chair, removing her glasses, and said, "Mr. Stone did just file a complaint against the FBI for harassment, and now he's here being charged for eight counts of murder.

"With that being said, these are serious allegations, and the court cannot overlook this matter lightly."

She thought for a moment. "I will grant bail. I will set bail at a million dollars cash and five million bond!" She hit her gavel.

I stood up and smiled at my family. I then looked over at Terry and Lori with the grin they knew so well. The media was snapping shots as I was about to be escorted out.

Jamal said loudly, "Don't worry, Dad, I'll have you out by one" and took out his phone, and made a call to his broker.

Tracy said, "Jen is taking Evelyn, so Kim can wait for you to be released, and I'll be here with her!"

I was escorted downstairs, and by eleven thirty, my bail was posted. As I walked out of Albany Federal County lockup, I was met by a frenzy of reporters asking all types of questions.

I said to Tracy, "I would like to make a statement!"

"I advise against talking to the media, Jamal!"

"I have to, Trace! I'm about to venture out on starting Stone Industries, and this is the kind of stigma that needs to be addressed."

"I understand but keep it short and away from any parts of the investigation!"

I stopped on the steps of the courthouse surrounded by tons of reporters. I said loudly, "Please, please, people, I would like to make a statement."

They all quieted down. "I would like to say that these charges are completely crazy, and I am innocent. I am a father, a hard worker, and a loving husband.

"I can't believe that the FBI would slander my name with these accusations! Agent Carter and Agent Reid even had dinner at my home with my family, and I have answered any and all questions they have asked of me. In return, they have followed me and watched my home. Why is the system so geared on throwing black men in prison?"

I pause for that question to sink in then continued. "I just had a newborn, and I can't even take my little girl for a walk without them harassing me! I just want to live in peace and enjoy my family. Now is that so hard!

"Thank you, I will not be answering any questions, and that is all I have to say at this time!" The shouts went out from the reporters as I walked away.

Tracy and I got in the car with Kim, and Tracy said, "Drive me around to the back parking lot of my car. I don't want to go back through that craziness."

She turned to me as Kim pulled off. "That was very well said, Jamal, about the loving family man and them harassing you. That black man and the justice system question was a political stab."

She placed her hand on my shoulder. "If they try to take this to trial, I will eat their circumstantial bullshit up, but you do know the craziness has just begun. I talked to Mike Foreson, and he verified that you were at the club with him, that y'all even walked to the VIP room at midnight and will testify on your behalf, plus the kids.

"So I'll have Kenny get started on the civil suit, and Natia will gather all witnesses and statements, so all you have to do is you stay away from the FBI and reporters!"

"Well, Jermaine has Kodak Black and Tori Lanez numbers, so they both can also verify that I was there too. You can get their numbers from Jermaine. I'm sure they would vouch for me."

"Don't worry, Jamal. I got this!" she proclaimed and got out of the car. "I'll be in touch, and just lay low for now. We don't need them trying anything stupid!"

"I got you, Trace, and thanks again!" I replied. She shut the door and walked off.

Kim pulled out and I could see the worry on her face. Her mood I could tell was unpleasantly all over the place.

She said as we hit the highway, "What the fuck, babe! I can't believe them motherfuckers! You been nothing but cooperative, and this is what they do, fuck, fuck, fuck!"

"Calm down, babe, I'm good. You're good and everything will be fine! Do you see that I'm worried at all?"

"No," she replied, taking a deep breath, "well. if you're not, then neither will I, but that doesn't mean them motherfuckers ain't fucked up!

"I love you, babe, and Evelyn and I missed you! It was like she knew you weren't there, and something was wrong. She wouldn't even sleep last night. She woke up at crazy times!"

I thought, *Damn, my two girls! What would it be like for them if I wasn't there? It would hurt and I empathize, but I would feel hollow inside if I didn't kill these life-ruining motherfuckers.*

We pulled up to Jen's house and went straight inside to Evelyn. I grabbed my little girl, hugging and kissing her. Emily greeted us and said, "Dad, I miss you. I'm so glad you're alright!"

I hugged Emily, kiss her forehead, and replied, "I miss you too, baby girl! Look at you, you're all woman now!"

Emily was five feet even, weighed one hundred and ten pounds, had long blonde hair, and had the cutest round face with big blue eyes.

I continued. "How are those grades? You know I want nothing short of a young lady!"

"Geez, Dad, I know. I know, school, school, and more school plus no sex!"

She smirked. "I made the honor roll if you must know, and I'm ranked number 2 in the state in the one hundred meter freestyle and butterfly and third in the backstroke!"

"Very good, baby girl, I'm so proud of you, and maybe I will have a surprise for you because you're doing so well!"

"I love surprises, Dad, where is it?"

"When I'm ready to give it to you, Miss Spoiled! And who knows when that will be. It's not like you're going anywhere soon!"

"Spoiled, ha! You can only blame yourself, Dad!" Emily proclaimed as she took Evelyn out of my hands and walked off!

Jamal, Jermaine, Preston, and Steph all came up from the studio. I asked Jermaine, "Did you do what I texted you Friday night?"

"Of course, Dad, I always get what you ask!"

"Good thanks! And Jamal thanks for coming home to help me out!"

"I got you, Dad. We're family and we stand by each other no matter what! I'm also coming home after the Fourth of July, on the sixth. I promised Shelby's parents I'll be there for that!"

"That's cool. How is Shelby?"

"She's good! She wanted to come and support you, but I told her that you would be alright and for her to spend more time with her parents."

I hugged him and threw my arm around his shoulder as we walked onto the back patio where everyone was. Emily was in the water, Evelyn was sitting on Kim's lap next to Jen at the poolside, and Jermaine, Preston, and Steph were in the shade talking it up.

Jamal and I walked over to everyone, and I thought, *It's great to be surrounded by family!* We all talked until dinner time, and Tracy showed up half an hour before we ate. Today I focused on being with my family, but tomorrow the legal battle would begin!

Terry was determined to take Jamal down. He filed a warrant to search Jamal and Jennifer's house. At seven this morning, he was knocking at Jamal's door with a warrant in hand.

Chapter 74

June 25, 2022

I was up feeding Evelyn because Kim was so burned out by all the excitement, that she took a couple of days off from the hospital, and now she was upstairs sleeping. I heard a knock at my door as I started cleaning Evelyn up. I answered on the fifth knock and saw a shitload of FBI agents on my porch.

At the front of the pack was Agent Carter. "Hello, Terry," I said, still not giving his shield any respect. "Agent Reid, I would say it's nice to see you, but I would be lying. Plus I knew y'all was coming!"

"I have a warrant to search your house and premises!" Terry said with a smirk on his face as he held up the warrant!

I smiled back and exclaimed, "By all means do your job, and just so you know, don't try anything slick because I have cameras in all rooms, so I'll be watching you too. Come in!" I stepped aside with Evelyn in my arms.

Kim was coming down the steps already dressed. I didn't even know she was up. After we got home from Jen's yesterday, I had Kim pack a bag for her and Evelyn because I knew that this was just the beginning of the bullshit, and they would be coming with a search warrant.

I told her to take her and Evelyn to her mom's house if the FBI came. Boy I loved being on point. She said, "Jamal, I already called Tracy, and she's on her way!"

"Thanks, babe, love when you're on point!"

Terry came in as he said to his team. "Make sure you guys search every inch of your assigned area!"

They all spread out and went to do their job. Terry faced Kim and me and continued. "Sorry, Mrs. Stone, but we have to search you, the baby, and the baby bag, and after that, you are free to go!"

I laughed so hard that Kim looked at me because she never heard me laugh like that before.

I exclaimed, "The hell you are searching my baby! What in the hell can she possibly be hiding! You defile my little girl, Terry, and you're going to make her a rich little girl. I promise you that, among other things!" Little did he know that was a threat, and I would kill his whole family for that one little act!

Lori jumped in. "Terry, we don't have to search the baby. What kind of shit is that? Sorry, Mr. and Mrs. Stone, but we will need to search her baby bag!"

"An agent with some sense!" I proclaimed!

"Thank you, Agent Reid!" Kim exclaimed!

Lori led Kim and the baby upstairs followed by another female agent. I heard Lori say, "Mrs. Stone, this is Agent Simms, and she will be assisting me."

Terry said, "Jamal, I and agent Wise will search you in the living room!"

I went into the living room, and I was instructed to strip. After I stood from squatting, Tracy walked into my living room as I was standing there butt naked. Her eyes got big and I saw exactly where her eyes were looking.

She said, "Oh my god, Jamal!" She had never seen me naked before and took me all in.

She turned to Terry. "Agent Carter, this is totally inappropriate to have my client butt naked in the middle of his living room with all these men and women walking around!"

I smiled as I said, "It's all good, Tracy. I'm blessed as you can see!"

"Jamal, you can get dressed, and, Mrs. Turner, no one was present until you walked in. Why are you here?"

"I knew you would be searching my client's home, that's why!"

"Don't worry, Tracy, my house has cameras all over, so if they try any funny business, we would have them dead to rights!"

Kim came downstairs with Evelyn and both Lori and Agent Simms as I was standing in my boxer briefs, and no shirt on. I smiled as I could see Lori and Agent Simms's eyes got big.

I then slid on my jeans and said to Tracy, "You know Agent Carter here wanted to strip search Evelyn!"

"He what! I would've slapped a lawsuit on his ass so fast! What the hell is he thinking, that we're still in slavery and babies are commodities!"

I took Evelyn from Kim and kissed her and blew raspberries on her belly as she laughed her pretty little head off.

I kissed her again and said, "Daddy will see his little angel later," I gave her to Kim and kissed Kim!

Kim said, "Call me when this is done, baby!"

"I will tell Gloria and Jeff everything is fine!"

She kissed me again, gave Tracy a hug, and Tracy kissed Evelyn, then Kim was gone.

Tracy and I talked the whole time during the FBI search. It was two hours later when Jen called pissed off, "What the fuck, Jamal, the FBI are here searching my house! Why are they searching my house, Jamal?"

"Come on, Jen, you're not new to this! They know I spent a lot of time at your place. You know the deal, just don't talk to them or answer any questions without a lawyer present. Tracy's here, and I'll send her over to you, and Jen will tell the kids the same!"

"No shit, they already know! Damn! Jamal, I'm not even married to you anymore, and I still have to go through this shit! Oh yea, and the media is here too!"

"The media's here too, Jen, but don't worry I'm innocent!" I proclaimed then hung up.

I turned to Tracy and she said, "I know I'm on my way. Are you okay here?"

"Yea, I'm good!"

"Alright, Jamal, don't talk to the media anymore. When the FBI's fruitless search is done, that will say more than words could ever say!"

"I got you, Trace, now go before someone starts running their mouths!"

I walked her out of the house to her car, and then I leaned in after she got in and said, "Tell Jen, Jamal, and Jermaine not to mention my room!"

Tracy looked at me sideways, "I will tell you about it later! Now go!" Tracy took off and I went back into the house.

It was almost eleven o'clock when they started wrapping up. Terry and Lori came downstairs, and I had a big smile on my face as I said, "Did you find what you were looking for, Agents? I can assure you that you're going to wish you just let me go when I ask!"

I turned to Lori. "And, Lori, you hurt my feelings! I can't believe you think I would have anything to do with this!"

I was ready to drop the bomb, but I wanted to do it when we were in court because not only would it discredit their investigation, I wanted to embarrass Terry in front of the whole world! He thought I didn't know that he and Lori have something going on, but I did my little investigation on them especially when they were watching my house, together kissing, fooling around in the car.

I wanted him to look like the jealous cop that took his job personally to bring down an ex-con that was sleeping with his girlfriend.

Lori said, "Look, Jamal, you're wrapped into too many coincidences for us to overlook the facts, so if you're innocent like you say you are, then prove it in the court of law!"

"Trust and believe me I will, and this journey you and Terry are on against me will end badly for the both of you!"

Just as I finished, Agent Simms came down the steps and said to Terry and Lori, "This house is clean as a whistle. I mean nothing!"

Terry sighed and said loudly, "Okay, everyone, wrap it up!" He turned to me. "Jamal, you think you're in the clear, but you're not, and I promise I will be the one to lock your ass up!"

I gave Terry a big fuck you smile as I replied, "Thanks for coming, Terry! Stop by anytime just not for dinner. I do not wish to share a meal with you ever again, and Lori, I'm really disappointed in you!"

Terry looked at Lori with a strange suspicion, and Lori didn't meet his eyes. They walked out of the house and were attacked by the media.

Up front with her mic and cameraman was Brenda Mendez, "Agent Carter, you arrested Jamal Stone and charged him with the Life-Ruiner Serial Killer murders, did you find anything that suggests he's your guy?"

Terry stopped and replied, "We are not at liberty to discuss an ongoing investigation, and you know that, Ms. Mendez!"

"One more question, Agent Carter," Brenda asked, being relentless, "My source tells me that you guys have nothing on Mr. Stone and that he even has an air-tight alibi for the murder of Jdg. Martin Richards!"

"Ms. Mendez, let me say this," Terry replied in frustration, "I want this killer off the streets, and so if anyone can give any information, please call your local police department.

"Mr. Stone was arrested because he is the prime suspect, and as we gather information, we will be building a strong case against Mr. Stone! Thank you and no more questions!" Terry and Lori got in the car and left!

I watched in astonishment as the relentless Brenda Mendez attacked Terry. I couldn't help but smile. Twenty minutes later, Jen called. She asked, "Are they gone, Jamal?"

"They just pulled off. All that, and they found nothing!"

"What the hell, Jamal! We don't need this negative attention right now, especially that we are about to start Stone Industries! Shit, I already left my job!"

"Damn, woman! You go all ape shit for nothing! I told you not to worry! When the FBI is done with their witch hunt, I'll be signing their paychecks! Now chill the fuck out and focus on what we need to do and let Tracy handle this shit!"

She took a deep breath and chuckled, "Signing their paycheck, boy, you're bat-shit crazy you know that! You know they're probably going to tap our phones!"

"Yea well, tell the kids to be careful about what they talk about. I'll be over soon. I'm going to get Kim and Evelyn, and we'll be there. Tell Emily to be ready for her surprise!"

We hung up and I called Kim and then left to go get them. I thought, *Damn I'm a G! About to get stupid rich off the government, first my son, and now me!* I hopped into my truck, turned up 2Pac's "All Eyes on Me" and drove off laughing!

Chapter 75

June 28, 2022

Terry

I spent over the last couple of days going over every piece of evidence and interviews looking for something to tie Jamal to these murders. I knew Jamal was our guy. I just have to prove it.

Lori moved in, but I could feel the tension in the air because she didn't agree with me about Jamal. Plus I knew she had some type of secret that she just wasn't telling me. Lori had expressed on many occasions that she didn't think Jamal was the killer and that we shouldn't have arrested him without some type of concrete evidence tying him to it, but she hoped that I knew what I was doing.

I had everything in order for what I had so far, which was people who said that Jamal knew or knew someone that was connected to the victims.

I also had Mrs. Richards's statement, saying that Jamal fit the description of the attacker, but she also said that she didn't see his face because he had on a mask, and things happened so quickly.

It was almost two in the afternoon when I got a call from Salem Sheriff's Department Capt. Lee Holmes. He said, "Good afternoon, Agent Carter!"

"Hello, Captain Holmes, what can I do for you?" I replied, frustrated!

"Well, someone sounds a little grumpy! I might have a little cheering news but not much!" I perked up. "I had this Uber driver come in this morning and told me that he may have dropped the killer off!"

"Go on, Captain," I replied, giving him my full attention!

"Well, the driver's name is Shamel Bonilla. He picked up a black guy in the Walmart parking lot around twelve thirty, and while driving, the guy had him pull over in the middle of nowhere on route 22, and he said the guy paid him one hundred dollars for a three-minute ride.

"The cabbie thought it was a strange place to be dropped off, but when he saw you on the news, he thought he should inform us of this."

I thought, *Finally something I could work with!*

I said, "That's fucking great, Cap! I'm on my way right now. Do you have an address for Mr. Bonilla?"

"Hold your horses, Carter. One more thing, Mr. Bonilla said he didn't really get a good look at this guy. He had on a dark-colored sweat suit with a hoodie that covered most of his face. However, he had a dashcam, but it doesn't reveal the guy's face either! I've seen the footage, and whoever this guy is, he took every precaution to conceal his identity."

"That's okay, Cap. I'll take everything you got, and Mr. Bonilla's address!"

"Okay, Shamel Bonilla . . . where did I"—Captain Holmes looked around on his desk—"oh, here we go, 520 Casper Street, Salem, New York."

I wrote the address and then said, "Thanks, Cap, I'll be there within the next two hours!"

"See you then," Captain Holmes replied and then hung up.

I went to find Lori, and I was excited as hell because this could be the break I need. I found her. "Hey, Lori." She turned around from the copier. "I just got off the phone with Captain Holmes from Salem, and a guy came into his station saying he may have dropped off the killer, and he has footage from his dashcam, so I'm on my way to Salem. Are you coming?"

"Of course, I'm coming, Terry!"

"Well, let's go, beautiful, chop-chop! This could be the break I've been waiting for!"

Lori took the paper out of the copier and took them to her desk and turned off her computer and they left. During the drive, I could tell that Lori had something on her mind.

I broke the silence, "How have you been feeling, baby?"

"I'm fine, just a little stressed!"

"Stressed about what if you don't mind me asking?"

"About the case, Terry! You know how I feel, so why keep rehashing! I just hope we get something that could help your assumption!"

"Look I understand everything about how you feel, Lori, but I'm so sure that Jamal is our guy. I'm willing to bet my job on it!"

"Well, Terry, it's not just your job now, is it! I just hope that this little venture gives us something because right now it doesn't look good!"

I turned my attention back to the road and thought, *I hope so too!*

We arrived at the sheriff's station and were brought right to Captain Holmes's office. Captain Holmes stood up, extended his hand, and I shook it, "Hello, Cap!"

"Agent Carter, Agent Reid," Cap shook Lori's hand. "Good to see you both!"

"You too, Cap," Lori replied!

"Well, I have the footage set up in our conference room and a copy made, so you can take the original. If you follow me, we can get started!"

We went to the conference room. We sat down and started watching the footage. Mr. Bonilla pulled into the Walmart parking lot and to the far side. We then saw the passenger get in, but we couldn't really see the size of the man.

I thought, *Shit!* I looked as hard as I could to see anything that would give me something. His hoodie was big. It covered all the way to his lips, which gave off a shadow to his chin. He sat back and we still couldn't see much more.

Then he handed the cabbie money with gloved hands and then said something in a deep voice with an accent. I knew if we swabbed the car down we would get nothing. Silent for about four and half minutes then the voice came back, telling the cabbie to pull over. They talked and then he got out, and we could see the guy walking away as the cabbie pulled away. Then it was over.

Captain Holmes turned off the TV, put the disk into a plastic sleeve, and handed it to Lori.

He said, "I told you there isn't anything that gives us any clue to who this guy is. All we know is that he's black, the location to where that cottage is from the police chase and that is within the time sync with the murder."

I was annoyed because the captain was right, but I was determined to let our analyst break the footage down.

I replied, "At least there's a little we can work with. We are going to see Mr. Bonilla, and see if we can get anything from Walmart. I also want to meet with the owner who rented the cottage out!"

"Well, we went to Walmart, and all it showed was the cabbie pulling in and out, not him stopping or picking anyone up. I did get the owner's information about the cottage and talked to him.

"His name is Barry Bennett, and he said he never met the guy and that he faxed the application and European driver's ID with a white guy picture with the name Jason Klein on it.

"Mr. Bennett talked to him on the phone. The guy had a British accent and that the guy sent him six months of rent upfront in cash through a carrier."

"Damn, we're still going to see if he can remember anything that stood out of the ordinary about this guy!" We all stood, shook hands, and Lori and I left.

Chapter 76

Lori

I was really worried about the vendetta Terry had against Jamal. I knew we didn't have a damn thing that tied Jamal to the murders, and the footage didn't give us shit to work with either.

I still had Jamal's words on my mind, and I didn't really know shit about Jamal, but he seemed very diabolical and that frightened me.

I was feeling hopeful for Terry that maybe he had something to work with, but I wished he would've listened to me in the first place. We both would suffer if this went the wrong way, and we couldn't convict Jamal. I had to get on the same team with Terry who was not only my partner professionally but personally too.

I decided after we left the sheriff's station that I would help my man see this to the end. I said on our way to Bonilla, "Terry, I know I haven't really been supportive of this crusade, but I'm ready to ride this out with you."

"I'm so happy to hear you say that. You don't know how much easier that just made this."

"Good, but I have conditions!"

"And?"

"We work together and you listen to my advice because if you did in the beginning, we could've planned a better way to catch Jamal in the act!"

"What do you mean?"

"Look, Terry, your male hard-on for Jamal didn't allow you to think clearly! We could have made him the primary suspect and focused all our attention on him but did it with stealth! I agree that there are just too many coincidences around him, but we want to catch him red-handed.

"But now what you did was make our job harder, and now we have to prove he's guilty by looking for a needle in a haystack! I now realize that Jamal is smarter than what we gave him credit for. You have to remember he's a college graduate, military, and just did ten years reading and planning!"

"Damn, you know what your right, babe." Terry shook his head at his own disgust. "I jumped the gun, and now we're up shit's creek without a paddle! So, babe, what do you suggest?"

"I have a plan but I know you won't like it!"

"Well, I got us into this shit, so if you can get us out, then I'm with you!"

"Well, I haven't worked out all the details yet, but what we are going to do is gather everything we possibly can and save it, and as soon as I figure out the details on how this is going to work, I'll tell you!"

"Alright!"

I wasn't sure how I was going to work this out, but all I knew was that we couldn't win this case. We had to find a way to save face, and I hope Terry would forgive me. First, we pulled up to Mr. Bennett's house.

Chapter 77

<u>Terry</u>

I was glad that Lori had a plan to save this shit. She was right. I jumped the gun and let my ego get the best of me. We damn sure could have gone about this a different way. We pulled up to the Bennett's first.

I knocked on the door, and I only could guess that it was Mrs. Bennett who answered on the third knock. "Can I help you?" she asked.

"Hello, Mrs. Bennett, is it?" Lori asked!

"Yea, and you are?"

Lori and I pulled out our FBI badges, "I'm Agent Reid and this is Agent Carter, and we would like to ask your husband a few questions about the cottage on route 22."

"The sheriff's department already questioned my husband. He never met the guy before."

"We know, ma'am, we have questions of our own."

"Okay, then come on in!"

She stepped to the side to let us in and then yelled upstairs, "Barry, the FBI is here!"

"I'm in the bathroom, Cara, be right there!"

Cara Bennett was Philippian, very fit, and very pretty. Lori and I sat on the couch, and Cara asked, "Can I offer you anything to drink?"

"No thanks, ma'am," we replied at the same time.

Barry came downstairs. He was a very fit older black man. He walked into the living room and said, "Sorry, Agents, but when nature calls, you answer or she will fuck you up! Anyway, what can I do for you?"

I said, "I know you talked to the police already about the cottage on route22, but we were wondering if you could remember anything other than what you told the police, like about the money you received. Do you remember the address?"

"All I remember about the package was that it was from FedEx, and I really didn't look at the address, just the name Jason Klein, and since he said he lived in Europe, I didn't even bother. Sorry, Agent."

"You said FedEx delivered it. Did you sign for it?"

Barry thought for a second and then answered, "You know what, I don't believe I signed for it because I asked if I had to sign. I thought it was strange because I get things from FedEx all the time, and I always sign for it."

I looked at Lori, knowing that it was delivered by the killer. I focused back on Barry, "Do you usually take cash for your rentals?"

"No, not usually, but this was the first time someone from overseas wanted to rent anything. He said he would pay the cash upfront. He wanted to mail it because he wasn't going to be in town for a couple of weeks, and he didn't want me to rent it out to anyone else.

"I thought the guy was joking, so I asked him to send me copies of his references and identification. When the money came, so did the application and ID. It was nine grand, and that was double what I was asking for.

"I called him and told him, and he said that it was for me going through the trouble of not meeting him and all, so I talked to Cara and it was settled, so I left the keys where he asked!"

Barry looked at Cara with a puzzled look and then back at me, "Wait, now that I think about it. How did he know where to leave the keys?"

I looked at Lori again and then back to Barry, "Was the guy black that delivered the package?"

"Yea, why?"

I took out my phone and pulled up a picture of Jamal to show Barry, "Is this the guy that delivered the package?"

Barry took the phone then showed Cara and then said, "I can't be sure, but it kind of looks like him, but he had on dark glasses and a hat that was pulled low on his head. I can't positively say that he's the guy, but it does resemble him, but hey, that was months ago!"

"Think real hard, sir!" I said. I wanted it so badly to be Jamal!

Barry thought about it for a little while longer and then said, "Cara, you answered the door, what do you think?"

Cara looked for a little while longer then replied, "It sort of looks like him, but I mean the guy wore glasses and a hat!"

"Mr. Bennett, do you have the ID and application he sent?" I thought that Jamal could've filled out the application.

"I sure do. Give me a sec." He left to go upstairs.

When he came back he handed me the file with Klein, Jason, and said, "It's not much, but that's all I have."

I took the file as I asked, "Are you willing to testify in the court of law?"

"I don't know, Agent Carter," Cara replied, "We won't lie on the stand for no reason, but if you need us to say possibly, then we will!"

"Alright then, Mr. and Mrs. Bennett, we will be in touch if we need you, and thanks for your time. Have a nice day!" Lori and I stood then shook their hands and left.

As I was driving, I started thinking that Jamal was one smart motherfucker. It was like he was five steps ahead, knowing all the tricks and trades of concealing his identity like he was Superman or something. Even though any smart person would know that Clark Kent was Superman, but hey, it was the movies.

During the ride to Shamel Bonilla's house, I asked, "So, Lori, what do you think?"

"Well, it's not strong and they think it could possibly be Jamal, but that's not going to stick in the court of law.

"But it is something. Maybe if we are lucky he filed out the application, we can compare his writing."

"That's why I wanted the info."

"Look, I do understand why you believe it's Jamal, and now I kind of believe it's him too, but opinions are like assholes, and everybody has one!"

"We're going to need more than circumstantial evidence to convict, and judging by what Natia tells me about Tracy Turner, we better have his hand in the cookie jar!"

"Well, that's why we're here chasing down these leads and trying to build a strong case!"

Lori shook her head as we pulled up to Shamel's house, and I knew she wanted to say something more, but I bet it was something she already said and didn't want to beat a dead horse.

We knocked on the door, and when Shamel answered, we knew it was him right away from the dashcam. "Hello, Mr. Bonilla. I'm Agent Carter, and this is my partner Agent Reid. We're here to—"

Shamel cut in, "Yes, yes, Agents, please come in!"

Shamel had an accent, and I knew he was from Iraq. We followed Shamel into the house, and there were four kids and his wife who was there. He said something in his native tongue, and his wife came over.

She said with an accent, "Nice to meet you, Agents. I'm Sophie."

Shamel spoke again to her in their native tongue, and then she said, "Well, I'll let you guys talk. Have a nice day!" She walked off.

Shamel showed us to the couch and said, "So, Agents, how can I help?"

"Mr. Bonilla—"

"Please call me Shamel!"

"Okay, Shamel, like I was saying, we watched the video from your dashcam, and I'm glad we have something to work with, but if there is anything else you could tell us that would help us, then please!"

"Truly, Agent, I told the sheriff everything I know. I mean it was strange . . . The whole situation was very, very odd. I never had anyone do that, and I've been doing Uber since it started.

"It was dark and as I looked in my rearview mirror trying to see who was in my car, he kept his head down. Even when he gave me the money, I didn't see his face."

I thought about what Shamel just told me then asked, "When you first pulled up to the Walmart, there was light. Now, Shamel, please think really hard. Close your eyes and try to remember the moment you first pulled up!"

Shamel closed his eyes as instructed, and Lori and I remained silent as Shamel traveled back to that moment. I pulled up Jamal's picture and had it right in front of Shamel's face when he opened his eyes.

Shamel opened his eyes slowly, shaking his head with a smile, and I was feeling hopeful. I said, "Look real hard at this guy, Shamel, and tell me do you believe that this is the guy?"

Shamel took the phone, looking really hard and shook his head and said, "I would be lying if I said I knew for sure this was the guy, but he kind of resembles the guy.

"But like I said in my report, I only saw the guy's chin and that I couldn't truly identify the guy. I'm sorry, Agent, but I've given you all the information I can remember!"

I took a deep breath. "Shamel, thank you for your time. I may call on you to testify on the information you just gave me."

"No problem, Agents, and I'm sorry I couldn't be more helpful. I heard about this killer on the news, and I will do all I can to help get a guy like that off the streets."

Lori and I stood and shook Shamel's hand as I said, "Thank you" and we walked out Shamel's house.

On the way back to Albany, Lori said, "Well, Terry, we truly still have nothing, but the same bullshit other than two people saw the killer but can't identify him. I mean being that he's an ex-felon based on circumstantial evidence and these witnesses, we might be able to convince a jury he's guilty.

"I must say though our main problem is that he has an airtight alibi every time something happens, no violent history, and probably the best legal team there is."

"What we got, Lori, is shit, and like you said, he has an airtight alibi, but I know his ass is guilty, Lori, I just know it!"

Lori thought, *How was Jamal going to spin his defense? He seems very confident that he could destroy us for coming after him with no evidence. This shit is all Terry's fault. I hope this doesn't come back and bite us in the ass. I just went to the doctor. I'm two months along, and I got to figure out how to get Terry and me out of this shit!*

Lori wasn't saying much as we drove home, but I could tell she was in deep thought. I hoped she was thinking about how to get us out of this mess I got us in. We pulled up to the house.

We gathered everything we had on Jamal, and we spent the next five hours putting everything together for the DA. I saw people get convicted on less in the State of New York, but those people didn't have a legal team as Jamal had. I hope God was on our side!

Chapter 78

August 19, 2022

Jamal

I'd been home for a little over a month, and we had the ball rolling for Stone Industries. Rebecca was on the team, and she and Jen were working well together. The whole family had been enjoying the summer together. Two weeks ago, Jermaine went down to Florida to stay with Steph for a week before he headed off to football camp.

This past Saturday we had a big cookout for Jermaine because he had to leave for school on Sunday. Shelby came back to America this past Thursday. She and Jamal planned on buying a house on the outskirts of Boston. Jen also planned on selling her house and moving near Jamal, and so am I.

I wasn't going to buy anything yet until after the court case, which was very silent. Tracy put in for a speedy trial, and she told me that they hadn't presented her with much, and what they did give her, it was laughable.

Tracy said that she filed for them to present all Brady and Rosario material, and then after that if nothing, she would file for a dismissal due to lack of evidence. Everything was on the up and up at the moment, but I was feeling hollow about not continuing my hobby right now.

Today I decided to look into the two cops, Ofcrs. Mark Fuller and Britney Brick that killed those kids in Newburgh, New York. I mean they should really be handled, but with this case hanging over my head, I had to prolong it.

I took Evelyn with me up to Jen's house because Emily was still there, and she could watch her while I went to my bunker.

I showed up at Jen's and just remembered that Jen and Rebecca were out dealing with the construction crew. We just hired them to build our ten-story office building along with the work facility that was going to be attached to it.

The fifty-five acres of land that Stone Industries just purchased was ten miles from the outskirts of Boston. There was a lot of work to be done especially with all the trees that have to be cut down. The good thing was we were already making a profit on all the lumber we had. I devised a plan of us owning our own lumber company.

I walked into the house, and Emily was there with her friend from New York, Racheal Keys. Racheal was a fifteen-year-old black girl with an onion-shaped face that was very cute with slanted eyes. You could tell she had Asian in her blood.

I walked out to the pool area where Emily was lying in the sun tanning and Racheal was standing in the shallow end of the pool. Racheal said, "Hey, Mr. Stone!"

"Hello, Racheal, how's your summer?"

"It's been great. My family and I went to visit my grandparents in China, and we got back last week. I was glad when Em called me to come spend a week with her here!"

I knew she looked part Asian. "That's good," I replied, turning my attention to Em. "What's up, baby girl, you look dark as hell!"

"Jen bought this tanning bronzer that darkens really fast. I've been using it all week!" she replied, getting up and tying her bathing suit top.

She came over as Evelyn reached for her and said, "Hey, Evie." She kissed her and lifted her into the air, "How's my baby sis!"

"Listen, Em, I need you to watch Evelyn for a few!"

"No problem, Dad, and thanks for that three thousand-dollar mall voucher. Mom took me to school shopping, and I bought so much shit!"

"Well, if you keep up your grades like you are and you fight to get ranked number one on the swim team, on your seventeenth birthday you can pick any car you want."

"Oh, for real, Dad!" she replied, hugging me with one arm and Evelyn in the other!

"Her food and everything is in her bag, and I shouldn't be there for more than an hour, maybe an hour and a half!" I said and then kissed her on the cheek and left.

I went into my bunker and looked up all I could on Ofcrs. Mark Fuller and Britney Brick. They kicked in the wrong door, and the young men were playing video games. Because of the sudden rush in by the detectives, they got up and tried to run, and the detectives shot all three of the boys.

They came to find out the cops were at the wrong address. It was the apartment next to the one they kicked in. They had not been reprimanded for their action, and the city planned to rule this accidental. Well, I couldn't let that just be it. They had taken three lives from three families, and now those families were ruined. They have to pay for that.

First, I looked up Mark Fuller. He was thirty-one years old. A Latino who stood at five eleven, weighed one hundred and ninety-five pounds and looked like he worked out. He had no kids or wife. He was very flashy and looked like a real lady's man. He'd been on the force for seven years. I researched some of his arrests, and I could tell he was on the take. This guy was dirty.

Next, I looked up Brittany Brick. She was a thirty-five years old white girl with long red hair and smoking-hot freckles and dimples. She was a nurse and then joined the force three years ago. She has no kids and she was divorced. She had been Mark's partner since she joined the force, and if he was dirty, then she was dirty.

I started a file on them and gathered all I could about their police movement as I hacked into the Newburgh Police Department's computer system. I swore if these police departments didn't upgrade their system, they were behind by like ten years!

The big question was how was I going to kill two people at one time. The other problem was the main one, my pending case. I'd been so thirsty to get on with my crusade, but I knew I had too much to lose, and the FBI had an eye out there even though they were looking from a distance.

I wrapped everything up and went back to the house. Em and Racheal were watching music videos, and Em had Evelyn sitting on her lap playing with her hand. I looked at the video they were watching, and it was Kodak Black, Bruno Mars, and 2 Chainz's "Supafly."

I said, "You know, Em, Jermaine opened up for Kodak Black and Tori Lanez back in June at a club in New York, and I was there!"

"No fucking way, Dad! Are you kidding me, how come I'm just hearing about this, and why wasn't I invited?" she spat out all at once in shock and excitement!

"Well, first of all, you were in school . . . and second you weren't old enough to be there! You know what I would do to some guy if they ever came at you wrong!"

"Yea, but still, Dad, why didn't someone tell me!"

"I guess we forgot with all my court shit, but I do know that Jermaine has their number, and for your sweet sixteen, they both already said they would perform for your party!"

"Oh my god, Dad! Are you for real!" she said, jumping up with Evelyn in her arm, and then she passed her to me, "When did y'all decide this?"

"When you decided to be on the principal's list all school year long!"

"You heard that, Rach!" Em said, jumping into my arms and hugging me!

"Dang, girl, you're lucky!" Racheal proclaimed with excitement for her friend.

"Well, it's Jermaine's idea. You need to thank him! He's the one that came up with this reward. And I think he's going to perform too. All your friends are going to love it!"

"I will, Dad, and my family is the greatest! I love you, Dad!"

"I love you too, baby girl." I kissed her on the cheek, and she went to sit back down, "Well, do y'all want to go to the mall with Evelyn and me? I mean you can sit here in—"

"No, we're coming, Dad!" Em said, and they both hopped up!

I took the girls to the mall, and we tore it up. When we left, we had at least six bags apiece. It was a good day indeed!

Chapter 79

September 16, 2022

Terry

I was in a good mood today, not because of the case let me tell you but because Lori was starting to show. She had a little baby bump for a while, but now she had to buy looser pants. We couldn't gather any more info on Jamal.

After the trip to Salem to talk to Shamel and Barry, we had nothing, and Director Wall said that we should just drop the case. But the DA said that he could most likely get a conviction just on the circumstantial evidence we had. He said he had prosecuted with less and won.

I wasn't happy about what we had to use, and Lori's little plan was for us to drop the case and insert someone into Jamal's life to watch him closely.

We were watching Jamal from a distance, and as usual, he just took care of his family. Now, he was building a company called Stone Industries with his son as owner. He was the CEO and his ex-wife as the CFO.

Everything looked on the right side of things for him, and we hadn't heard anything about anyone being killed. I thought about it, and it was around the time for our next victim to come into play. Jamal was granted a speedy trial, so the trial was set for December 3.

I just got out of the shower as Lori walked in and kissed me as I stood there naked. "Morning, babe, I got the coffee brewing!"

She looked down and my manhood was at full attention, "Wow, I guess someone else is happy to see me too!"

Lori had on boy shorts, a T-shirt with no bra, and her nipples were hard. They'd been like that for the last month.

I took her in my arms as I replied, "Every day and every night we are always glad to see you!"

I kissed her passionately then lifted her shirt and started sucking on her nipples.

She said, "Ow . . . babe, they're sore, but there's something else you can do!"

I knew exactly what she wanted. I started kissing down her belly as I pulled her boy shorts down with me. She leaned back against the sink and pushed her pelvis out, giving me full access.

I worked my mouth and tongue with expertise, causing her to grab the back of my head as she moaned.

I stood up and turned her to face the mirror, grabbed her hips, and pulled them to me. Slightly bent over, I entered, causing her to gasp. "Oh, baby, that feels so good."

She moaned as I grab her hair and pulled her into a kiss while I moved slowly in and out, long strokes. I eventually let go of the hair to grab her hip with both hands as she took the full force of me.

"You like that, baby!" I asked, knowing she liked it rough, especially her quickies.

"Yea, baby, just like that!" she replied as she started throwing it back.

We were in rhythm. "Damn, baby, I'm about to cum!" I moaned out, and then she started throwing it back harder!

I slapped her ass then she moaned, "Yes, baby, do it again, harder. I'm about to cum!"

I slapped her ass a few more times, and then we came together! I left myself deep in her as I grabbed her hair again and started kissing her.

After we stopped kissing, I wrapped my arms around her waist, and she reached her hand back to the back of my head. I said, "Lori, I love you so much, baby!"

"I love you too, Terry!"

After we dressed, we went downstairs to have everything bagels with our coffees. As we were eating, I said, "You know, Lori, it's about time for another killing, and Jamal hasn't done anything that suggests he's planning to kill someone!"

"Well, it seems that way, but like I said before, he might not even be the killer. If he is then, we've fucked up on bringing him down. And to make matters worse, he's our number 1 suspect, and he would be stupid to try to do something now."

"So what does it tell us if it isn't a murder any time soon?"

"Now that would be something now, wouldn't it? That can only mean one of three things. One he's our killer, two the killer is lying low because of all of the media attention, and this could be a framing job, so he can eventually keep killing, and finally Jamal knows the person and told him to lie low until the smoke clears."

"Yea, they're three good scenarios, but the most likely is the first!"

"Yea, I'm thinking that too!"

We got ready to leave for work, and as we were walking out the front door, Director Wall called me.

"Hey, Terry, you and Lori come to my office as soon as you get in. We have to figure out what to do about Jamal Stone. I just got a countersuit on my desk, and he's suing us for twenty million dollars, and judging on how much we have, which isn't shit, he might have our balls to the wall!"

"On our way, Mike," I replied and hung up.

"Shit!" I yelled, banging my hand on the steering wheel!

"What did Director Wall say?" Lori asked.

"Jamal is suing us, and the director thanks we're fucked!"

"Oh, fuck!" Lori replied, leaning back in her seat.

"Oh, fuck is right Lori, and it's my ass on the chopping block. Believe that!"

"Not just yours, Terry!"

"Well, I can't let everybody fall for me jumping the gun! I have to do damage control!"

"Don't worry. I got your back, baby!"

"Thanks, Lori, I love you!"

"Love you too, baby, just be cool, and we'll take one step at a time!"

We pulled up to the office, and we both went straight to Mike's office.

We walked into Mike's office lobby. We were buzzed right in, and I knew it wasn't a good morning because Julie didn't say a word to either of us.

Mike was looking at some papers on his desk as we walked in. "Have a seat, both of you!"

He lifted his head and leaned back into his chair, taking a deep breath as he said, "Y'all really fucked up on this one! I talked to the DA this morning, and he is absolutely sure that he can't win this case.

"He said that the two witnesses that we were planning on using are not going to testify because they can't truly identify Jamal as being the one, only that he fits the description, and they were going to say that on the stand, and that, my dear Watson, isn't beyond reasonable doubt."

"I have to say, Director, I have to take full responsibility for this—"

"Yea well, Terry, you definitely taking the hit unless you can get something that we can convict Jamal Stone on.

"If not, then I will have to suspend you, pending an investigation on your conduct involving this case. I told you to make sure you have something to tie Jamal to these murders.

"I know your gut is most of the time dead on, and Jamal may be the killer, but you jumped the gun, Terry, before you had enough evidence to convict him, not only does he walk, he will walk with millions of the federal government's money.

"The higher-ups are pissed and not because you arrested Jamal but because he just filed a harassment complaint not even a month before you arrested him, and then you have him in custody when you knew he had an airtight alibi.

"Now I may be able to save your job because you have an outstanding record, but I know for a fact you're going to be on desk duty and demoted."

"I understand, Mike, but what happens to the rest of my team? I acted on my own, making the decision to arrest Jamal, and I will vouch for immunity for the rest."

"Their action will be dealt with, pending the investigation, but I will note that.

"Look, Terry, I'll be honest with you. You have until November 15 to come up with something or get Jamal to drop the lawsuit. If he does that, we might be able to save face and tuck our tails. So you and your team come up with something and fast."

"Yes, sir, is that all?"

"Yea, that's all. Again, Terry, I'm sorry about this and keep me posted on anything you come up with. I want everything to come through me before you make any kinds of decisions."

"Alright, sir," I replied, and Lori and I got up and left!

Chapter 80

October 31, 2022

Jamal

Everything was going great for the family. Jen was the chief financial officer of Stone Industries. She has been interviewing to find the best in the business to work for our accounting firm. Her plans were massive for the business side of things, and even though the company was not ready to cut the ribbon, she controlled her part like we already had been around for years. That woman knew money.

She also already put her house up for sale. I was thinking about ghosts buying it because of my bunker, and I had to have my bat cave. Then I concluded that the FBI was still on my case, and Tracy just filed a countersuit for slander, deprivation of character, wrongful arrest, and duress, and asked for twenty million dollars. I couldn't believe she asked for that much, but her logic was to ask for everything then see what they were willing to give, then meet somewhere in the middle.

We were able to merge the Jacob & Turner Law Firm into Stone Industries. They were going to be running all legal actions for every company we incorporated or came up with. Tracy and Seth Jacob's salaries were going to be in the millions within the next three years.

Jermaine was dominating on the football field and so was Preston. He was already leading the division 1-A college football in receptions, yards per catch, and touchdowns, and second to him was Preston. They were blowing out teams by large margins. We were all at their game this past Saturday, and Jermaine told me that since Jamal added a production company to Stone Industries, he decided to enter the NFL draft next year, and so was Preston.

Stone Productions were going to be music, movies, clubs, and clothes. We tied Mike Foreson in for the club's enterprises, and he would be sitting on the Stone Industries board. Jermaine would run Stone Productions with Preston, and they both would sit on the board when they were done with their NFL careers.

Jermaine and Steph were together full-time, and Jermaine asked her to marry him. I couldn't believe it. Both of my boys were trying to settle down before they lived their lives, but I realized that both my boys were older than their years, and chasing women wasn't their thing. They liked stability and as little drama as possible.

Jamal and Shelby were getting married in June. Jamal and Shelby would run the technology side of the company, which was the largest part of the company, and the reason why Stone Industries existed. Jamal hired both his roommates to work for him. They were all interviewing and forming a team to come up with ideas and trying to bring them to life. Jamal had so many ideas that there wasn't enough paper to write them down, so he had a computer just for ideas.

He already invented a data recorder that when you talked into it the information went straight to his computer of his choice and was saved. He already patented it, and that device would hit the market on December 1. *Damn that boy is smart.*

Rebecca was the head of our project management team. She was one of my favorite people. I treated her like a little sister. I had Tracy look into her fiancée Lamar's case. Tracy said he was given a bum deal, and she was going to get his case overturned and a lawsuit.

He'd been locked up for over four years, and the evidence they had wasn't evidence enough to convict. He went to trial with a public defender and got smoked for fifteen years for a bank robbery that his friend committed.

Lamar had jumped out of the car and left his friend because he wanted no part of it. He explained this to his public defender, and he did nothing for him. The jury found him guilty because he was there, and he had a past history of dealing drugs.

I talked to Lamar and he told me that he sold drugs to take care of his family, but he was never down with robbing anything. That wasn't his cup of tea.

Tracy put in the appeal last Monday, so we would know something within ninety days, and of course we were going to have a job for him when he came home.

Rebecca was so happy that she couldn't believe we did that for her. I told her that because she worked with us, she was now family, and we took care of family no matter what they did. That was what Stone stood for, we were rock solid.

I was the chief executive of operations at Stone Industries. Jamal was the owner (CEO). I dealt with company takeovers, mergers, signing off on new company ideas, and company expansion. All our merges and start-up companies were already on the come up, and we already had functional businesses bringing in revenue.

Some of our enterprises weren't fully functional yet, but we were still making money. Our new building should be ready by June, and by then all the other projects should be moving in the right direction. We had done a great job since Jamal came back from London, getting everything in order. It wasn't hard when you got the money, the smarts, and a great team to do it.

This was all fine and good, but I was getting antsy. I kept thinking about those two officers, and now I had a rich woman that ran over two little black kids that were walking home from a football game.

She wasn't even supposed to be driving because her license was taken for six months for a DUI. Those kids died because she was driving under the influence.

So now I had three people that needed to pay, but I couldn't do anything about it. I knew I had to wait until this case was over. That was why I forced the issue of a countersuit, to make them work and respond faster. I needed these FBI motherfuckers off my back. I wasn't going to do anything stupid, but I kept thinking I could get away with it.

I called Tracy because I had a plan to force the FBI to settle, and I wanted this done right now. "Hey, Tracy, what's up?"

"Nothing, trying to wrap up this case, so I can go home and take a bubble bath. I'm beat. What's up tho?"

"I want to set up a press conference if the FBI doesn't settle and drop this case before November 9."

"A press conference for what?"

"I figured if we throw the conflict of interest in you know with the old relationship with Lori and me, that Terry is acting out of jealousy, maybe they'll settle really fast! Don't you think so?"

"Well, I think we do not have to do that publicly because we would want to use it if they ever try to pursue you again, but what we could do is drop it to the director of the FBI and let him deal with this information internally. I bet they will settle before your time frame!"

Damn, I thought, *I want to make this public, but Tracy has a point.* "That sounds good, Trace! Can you make that happen ASAP?"

"I can shoot the email to the director right now before I leave the office."

"Cool, thanks so much!"

I changed the subject. "So how are our affairs going with our merger documents with BioTech and BioMed?"

"Natia is finishing the final touches. We will send the documents to you so they can be analyzed by Monday."

"Sounds great. One more thing, remember me talking to you about my brother?"

"Yea!"

"Well, he's coming for Thanksgiving, and I was wondering would you like to meet him and spend Thanksgiving with us? I mean, I know your parents are coming, so we would love to have them join us too."

"I don't know, Jamal, meeting your brother while my parents are here . . ." Tracy took a deep breath. "I mean, fuck it, whatever, Jamal, let me talk to my parents and see if they are okay with having Thanksgiving at your house—"

"Not my house, Jen's house! She's looking to close on that house in Concord, Massachusetts. She wants Thanksgiving there."

"Okay then, I'll get back to you!"

"Cool," and we both hung up.

I was ready to get this case over with, and pretty soon I would have to relocate my man cave. There was so much going on that I needed relief and making people pay for ruining someone's life.

I had to feed the beast soon but not at the stake of me making a mistake and going to prison. I had to be patient and just wait, but in the meantime, I was getting all the intel I could on these three life ruiners. Well, I guess all I could do right now was focus on business and family.

Chapter 81

November 4, 2022

Terry

Trick or treating was great with the girls. We all dressed up, and Neveah and her friends all joined Lori and me as we hit every house in our neighborhood. The girls spent the whole weekend at my house eating their candy, going to the mall, and watching movies.

Lori was carrying her pregnancy well, still with a little baby bump, and she was exercising every day. I loved seeing the glow on her face knowing that she was about to become a mother.

I'd been trying to find a way to get us through this whole thing with Jamal and this case, so we wouldn't have to suffer the backlash from me jumping the gun. I was losing this battle.

I knew that we were going to have to settle and let Jamal walk. Even if that happened, I would find a way to nail his ass against the wall. This now wasn't just about justice. Now this was personal.

This morning I wanted to just lie in bed next to Lori and relax the day away. I dropped all the girls off home last night after we left the movies. I got up, took a shower, and then got the coffee ready. Lori decided not to drink coffee anymore while she was pregnant.

When Lori came down the steps, I had her everything bagel and a glass of orange juice waiting on the table.

"Hey, babe," Lori said as she entered the kitchen, walking over to kiss me. "You're so sweet, always having my breakfast ready!"

"That's right! My two babies have to eat!"

"So . . . if I wasn't pregnant, then I would have to make my own breakfast?"

"Of course not! I was making you breakfast before you got pregnant, so there you go!" I replied as I walked past her and slapped her on the ass.

"Ooh." She jumped a little from the slap on her ass. "Just checking, babe. I know you did. One of the reasons why I fell in love with you, you're so thoughtful!"

"It's easy loving you, so every day I just want to see that smile on your face!"

I kissed her on the cheek because she was chewing, "I'm going to warm up the car, be ready in ten, beautiful!"

I walked to the car and got in to start it when I got a call from the director. "Hey, Mike, about to leave right now, what's up?"

Mike took a deep breath and said, "You and Lori in my office as soon as you get in!"

"Sure thing, is everything okay?"

"I'll talk to you when you get in!" Mike replied and hung up before I could even say anything back.

I leaned back in my car and thought, *What the fuck could be going on now!*

Just then Lori got in the car and said, "What's up, babe? You look like someone just gave you a wedgie!"

"Mike wants to see us in his office as soon as we get in. I think something is about to happen and sooner than expected. I really fucked up on this Jamal thing," I exclaimed as I pulled out of the driveway and headed to work.

"Well, Terry, we just have to roll with the punches right now, but know if he walked, it was not over. If you think about it since the arrest of Jamal, there hasn't been any killing, and it's been over five months now.

"That could be a really fucked-up coincidence or that Jamal is the killer, and he's probably lying low until this whole thing blows over."

"I thought of that too, matter of fact just last night before I fell asleep! But we have nothing that really says he did anything, and since his arrest, the trail is stone cold!"

I slapped the steering wheel, "Damn, damn, why did I jump the gun!"

"Well, there is nothing we can do about this now but accept it and get through it! We can bring this point up to the director, and maybe he could see what we see," Lori proclaimed as she put her hand behind my head and started massaging.

"I hope so, Lori, I hope so!"

We got to work and went straight to Mike's office. When we were shown in, Director Wall said, "Have a seat, both of you."

We both sat. "Look I'm going to keep it straight with you two, and I already gave the DA the okay to come up with a settlement deal for Jamal!"

I couldn't believe Mike was saying this. "But, sir, I thought you gave me some time to get more on Jamal. What changed?"

"I'll tell you what changed, and I wish I didn't have to break this news to you, but just to save face and damage control from the information I received this morning, we have to settle.

"Now, let me ask you a question, Lori." Lori sat up straight in her chair to give Mike her full attention, "Did you and Jamal Stone ever have a physical relationship?"

"Come on, Mike, what the hell, Lori couldn't ever have a relationship with Jamal. That's crazy!" I exclaimed heatedly at Mike's insinuation.

I turned to Lori and was not happy to see the look on her face. "Tell him, Lori, that you never had anything with Jamal!"

Lori didn't look at me. I could see the glaze in her eyes, and I knew then that she had.

She said, "Look, Director, yes, Jamal and I had a physical relationship when I was in college . . . I didn't know it was Jamal because he gave me a fake name, and it was a one-night stand!"

I was so fucking mad that before Mike could ask another question I freaked out!

"Are you fucking kidding me, Lori! I can't believe this shit—" I yelled, snapping to my feet.

Before I could continue, Mike said, "Now calm down right the hell now, Terry! Deal with your personal shit on your time! Right now, we have to focus on what's happening with this case if you want to call it that!"

I sat back in my chair, pissed to all hell! I couldn't believe that this shit was happening, how could she not tell me!

Mike continued. "Jamal is threatening to go to the press with this information. If that happens, then this office will be under investigation, and you both will lose your jobs! This is a major conflict of interest, and I'm sorry to say, Lori, but I have to remove you from this case—"

"But, sir, that was years ago when I was in college! This isn't right—" Lori said with embarrassment.

"I can't worry about what's right or wrong, Lori. The fact is that it happened, and now he will use that against us, and he will win! There is nothing we can do about it.

"Plus, he already filed a harassment complaint against the bureau, so now this looks like retaliation and an attack of a jealous boyfriend, and the DA agrees that we settle!"

I couldn't believe Jamal was going to walk away scot-free, and with a large settlement to boot!

"Sir, if I could, Lori and I just came up with the fact that since Jamal has been arrested, facing these charges, it's been over five months and there hasn't been a murder. We believe that is evidence in itself to constitute that Jamal is most likely our killer!"

Mike leaned back in his chair, and thought for a minute before saying, "It does make a lot of sense but be that as it may, there is nothing we can do about it now. This case is fucked!

"What I will do is keep you on this case but quietly because it is odd that the killings have stopped, and even though it could be a coincidence, it's a damning coincidence!"

"That's what's been happening around this case with Jamal! There are so many coincidences that it's hard not to believe that he's our killer!" I said, trying to get Mike to soften because of this bullshit with Jamal and Lori.

"Well, what we're going to do is make it look like we've tucked our tails and lie low for a while. I want him to think that he's won.

"While that happens, you and Lori fix your personal shit and take a month off! But, Terry, when you come back Susan will be heading up this case from here—"

"But, sir—"

"But sir nothing, Terry! You fucked up royally, and you're lucky I'm still allowing you to stay on the case."

Mike took a deep breath to calm himself. "Look, Terry, I know you are an excellent agent, and mistakes happen, but this is how it has to be! So you could take it or leave it!"

Mike turned his attention to Lori, "And as for you, Agent Reid, you are on desk duty until after your maternity leave, and when you come back, I will assign you a new partner, and you will stay far away from this case!"

"Yes, sir, I understand!" Lori replied, feeling embarrassed and defeated!

"I'll call you with the settlement date. We are going to settle fast because there is no telling what Jamal is going to do, especially since Stone Industries is already making noise in the business world, and I'm sure he wants his name out of the media!"

"Thank you, sir, I thought I was going to lose my job for this fuck up!"

"You almost did, Terry, believe that! I fought for you, and because of your track record, I was able to convince the higher-ups to let you stay. They told me to handle you the way I see fit!

"So you two go handle your business, and like I said, I will call you for the settlement date. Until then, stay out of the office. You're both suspended without pay for the whole month!"

"Nice, Director, what a way to put the icing on the cake at the end! Suspension without pay that's a little harsh, don't you think!"

"A little harsh would be firing your asses! Now Jamal is probably going to get half of what he asked for, and he asked for twenty million dollars!"

"Twenty million!" I said loudly with shock. "He asked for twenty million, how the fuck is that even possible!"

"Well, let see, he just became CEO of Stone Industries, and we are being sued for slander, deprivation of character, wrongful arrest, and duress, and now he has a serious conflict case to top it off!

"Shit . . . Terry, we're lucky that's all he's asked for! But I'm pretty sure that we can put in the settlement that he cannot speak or bring any of this shit to life and that all charges be dropped against the FBI!

"And that's worth twenty million, believe it or not! We can't have the American people thinking that we go around taking our jobs personally! Anyway, you two can go. I got to get back to cleaning up this mess!"

Lori and I got up and left. We didn't say a word to each other all the way home. I didn't want to say anything because I was afraid of what I might say and couldn't take it back!

Chapter 82

Lori

I knew Jamal was going to try this shit! I was hoping that he wouldn't! I thought better of him than that, but he did say something even though I refused to believe that he would use our past relationship as his ace in the hole!

I just wish Terry didn't have to find out this way, and I knew there was going to be hell to pay when he finally let me have it.

I couldn't even say anything in Director Wall's office because I was so embarrassed and ashamed that I didn't come clean from the beginning. Now, it had all blown up in my face. I mean, I could accept why the director took me off the case because now it wasn't just Terry who fucked up this case, but now it was me!

On our way home, Terry didn't say a word to me, but I could see his face out of the corner of my eyes. I knew he was mad as hell! I wanted him to say something because silence was a lot more serious than him yelling at me! I dare not start the conversation because that would mean I was wrong. I mean, I was wrong for not telling him and jeopardizing the case. But I wasn't wrong for sleeping with Jamal. That was before I even knew I would be an FBI agent.

We got into the house, and Terry went straight to the bedroom, slamming the door closed. I left him alone for two hours to process his thoughts, but I wanted to get this shit over with so I went up and knocked on the door before I walked in.

He had his arm across his forehead covering his eyes, and I stood near the bed staring for a minute before I said, "Okay, Terry, let's get this shit over with!"

He said in a calm tone, "You lied to me, Lori, and I can't get over the fact that you kept this from me!"

"It wasn't intentional, Terry. At first I didn't even know he was the same person when we first went to meet Jamal!"

"How didn't you know! Shit you slept with the guy for Christ's sakes! Was he that forgettable?" He asked, looking me in my face!

I couldn't tell him that Jamal was the best I ever had, and as I took a long time to respond, he said, "Never mind don't answer that. I can see it in your face!"

"See what in my face, Terry!"

"That he was memorable, and that's why you kept trying to detour the idea of him being the killer. You were protecting him!" Terry said, raising his voice!

I could tell he was starting to get angry and lose control, so I said, "Calm down, Terry, and let me start from the beginning."

He sat up, giving me his undivided attention, "I was in college at UMASS, and Natia was dating this guy named Cash.

"One night we all went out to the Monkey Bar. Cash brought his friend Roc, and we hit it off. At that time, he told me his name was Anthony. He was a clean-cut guy with class. I fell for him instantly.

"We wound up hooking up that night. I'm not like that, meeting guys and sleeping with them, but with Jamal, it just happened. But after that one night, I never saw him again."

I decided to sit next to him as I finished. "So now to the present when we went to interview Jamal, I didn't really recognize him. But I did think that it was something familiar about him because I never forget a face, especially if the name matches up, but his name didn't so I was stuck. Do you remember all those times I looked distant?"

"Yea!"

"Well, that's what it was! I knew, I knew Jamal from somewhere, but I couldn't place him. The fucked-up part was that he remembered me the first time we went to his house and had dinner with him!"

"That motherfucker!" Terry replied, pissed!

"Yea, anyway when we went out with Jess with them that one night, she said something that jogged my memory about that night at the Monkey Bar. That was when it hit me, but I had to be sure! So I did a background check on Jamal.

"I looked up his arrest mugshot from 2008, and lo and behold, Anthony and Jamal are one and the same! Remember when I was distant when we went to my mother's?"

He nodded yes. "Well, that's when I figured it out! See, the beard and the cornrows threw me off. So when we went back to interview him at his job and we both left, I told you I had to use the bathroom, well, I didn't go to the bathroom. I went to confront him.

"He told me then that he knew who I was, and he has known since he saw me on TV at the press conference when Officer Dawson was killed.

"So I didn't tell you any of this because we were getting really close personally. After you met Jamal and came to the same conclusion that Jamal couldn't possibly be the killer; I figured it was water under the bridge!"

"But, Lori, it's not water under the bridge, and when you knew I felt that Jamal might be our guy, you should have set the record straight!

"Now, this shit is just hard to deal with finding out like this! And even though I know it happened in the past, we were building something on a lie, and that, Lori, is what hurts the most! I've been nothing but honest with you, and now how can I trust you?"

I put my hand on top of his, and he lifted my hand off and said, "Please don't touch me!"

That shit hurt so bad. It felt like a thousand knives just cut me. I said, "Terry baby, you can trust me. That is the only thing I ever kept from you!"

"But this secret is the worst imaginable, Lori. You know how I feel about Jamal Stone! He's a killer and he's getting away with it!

"I don't care how much it would've hurt me if you told me, but at least I would've found out from your mouth! It was like being smacked by a Mack truck coming from Mike. That shit broke my heart, and I've never felt so much betrayal!"

"I am so sorry, Terry. I love you so much, and I didn't mean to hurt you! Please tell me that you still want the same things as me! I'm carrying our baby!" I said as my eyes began to steam up.

"I will always love my children, Lori, no matter what the situation!

And just because I love you doesn't mean that I am willing to let you hurt me—"

"So what are you saying, Terry, you want to break up with me?" I exclaimed, feeling my heart breaking in two.

"I'm not saying that, Lori. What I'm saying is I need some time to sort this out, Lori! I love you, but I need some time, that's all!"

I sighed heavily, thinking that he may never look at me the same again. As a tear streamed from one of my eyes, I said, "I understand, I'll go stay with my mother for a little while, Terry!

"But just for a little while because I will admit that I was wrong keeping this from you, but I will not take fault for what I did in my past, and I need you to remember that!"

I gathered some of my things while Terry got in his car and left. My heart was hurting so badly that I just broke down crying for about half an hour.

As I got the rest of my things together, I was still crying. I got in my car, called my sister Sam, and told her everything. Instead of me going to my mother's, I went to stay with Sam for a few days. I didn't really want my mother to know what happened! I pulled up to Sam's house, got outta my car, and ran into my sister's arms, crying on her shoulder!

Chapter 83

November 11, 2022

Jamal

Today was going to be a great day. The FBI settled and I was going to sign the papers this morning. This past Thursday Tracy came to visit me at my house after she got off work. When she called, she told me that she wanted to tell me in person that not only did they drop all charges, but they settled for 12.5 million dollars. I couldn't believe the luck my family was having. I couldn't help but think that by me setting these life ruiners straight was a blessing from my divine.

I didn't believe in a god in the traditional sense, but I did believe in something greater than myself. I believed the energy flowed through all living things, so when someone upset the natural flow of things by taking a life before it was time, the balance must be set straight with their life. So good fortune here on earth is returning back to me tenfold. With that being said, my vigilance was so much clearer, and that was my reason for me to keep doing what I was doing.

Kim decided to join me at the settlement meeting and asked Sarah if she could babysit Evelyn until we got home. Sarah decided to sleep over last night. I got up this morning and let Kim sleep in. I was so excited about today's event. I woke up earlier than usual at four thirty this morning. I went for an hour run and then came in to take a shower.

It was so quiet in the house that I forgot that Sarah slept over. Normally, I left the door cracked because I never knew when Kim would hear the shower running and get up and join me, but last night I worked her over so long that she had four orgasms, so I knew she was with the dead.

I kept the night light plugged in, so I didn't have to turn the overhead light on. I hated when the light was so bright. Plus the dim light relaxed me.

Now, because I forgot Sarah slept over and the downstairs bathroom was getting remodeled so we could ask for more money because the house was up for sale, I was standing in front of the full-length mirror naked, admiring how chiseled I was for being forty-two. Out of nowhere the door flung open, I thought it was Kim until I realized that it was Sarah standing in the doorway staring at me and taking in every inch of me. She didn't even try to look away.

She said, "Damn, Jamal, you hung like a mule! And I didn't realize your body was so cut up!"

"Well, a man shouldn't let himself slide just because he's getting older," I replied, not caring that she saw all of me.

Her bluntness was turning me on, and my nature started to rise slightly.

She said, "Looks like someone is happy to see me," as she walked in, dropping her boy shorts to use the bathroom.

"You know one night me and Kim were talking about having a threesome with you for your birthday then all that bullshit happened, and that went out the window, but damn I wish we had!"

"Well, it's never too late for something like that!"

She wiped herself and got up, not even pulling her pants up. She walked over to me and grabbed my manhood. She bent down and took one full suck and said, "Damn, it tastes good too!"

She let go and pulled her pants up then grabbed it again and started licking and sucking it a few more times and then said, "We definitely have to make that happen. You and Kim both taste so good!"

Now I was stunned and said, "Oh, you tasted Kim before?"

"Of course, Jamal! She's been my friend longer than she knew you. We grew up together. She was my girlfriend when we were in high school."

Now that was some information I did not know. I wondered why Kim never mentioned that. I said, "Well, I'm not against having two wives."

"I believe that's something we could entertain if Kim's down for it. She's always asking me to come live with y'all since I divorced Freddie. I guess I have to bring that back up again."

Just after she said that, Kim walked into the bathroom, and I forgot I was standing there butt naked.

Kim said, "Good morning, you two" and sat down on the toilet. "What are y'all talking about?"

My mind was just blown away, and I was speechless. I was standing there naked talking to Sarah, and Kim acted like it was just a normal situation.

I said, "Sarah was just telling me that y'all was in a relationship in high school!" I left it as an open-ended statement to see what she would say.

"Yea, for two years, eleventh and twelfth grade. I mean we slept with guys, but we were a couple, so is that a problem?"

"Not at all! But I wonder why you never mention it before?"

"I don't know. It never came up," Kim replied as she wiped and got up, coming to kiss me, then Sarah.

"I love Sarah, and I always will. Jamal, you know I'm bi, and sometimes I just want to be with a woman. Well, just Sarah really."

I looked back and forth from Kim to Sarah. Kim said to Sarah, "I told you he has a big dick!"

"I know, how do you handle all that?" Sarah asked as she grabbed my hard manhood!

"Well, it takes some getting used to, I mean once he starts hitting that G-spot, it's the best pain you will ever have in your life and you just want more and more!"

I couldn't believe how this shit was going right now! I was about to sign a multimillion-dollar settlement, and here was my wife in the bathroom with her best friend holding my manhood! Now if this wasn't my divine working for me, then what was!

I was mad as hell right now because I didn't have the time to do what I really wanted to do. I said to both of them, "Is this for real, or am I dreaming! I mean if we had time to get to the bottom of this then we would, but I do want to talk about this later!"

"Babe, you—"

Evelyn just woke up and was crying, "I got it, baby," Kim said as she walked out and left me and Sarah there with my manhood in her hand.

"I told you, Jamal, so do you want a quickie before you go get dressed?" Sarah asked as she took off her pants.

I couldn't help it, I had to. I always wanted to fuck her little Asian ass. She took me into her mouth again. I pulled her little ass up and put her on the sink.

I tried to slide in her tightness, and she said, "Easy, Jamal, I'm not used to someone that big!"

So I stepped back and went down on her. She was so wet, moaning as I wiggled my tongue on the tip of her clit.

She grabbed my head with both her hands and said, "Oh, shit I'm about to cum!" Her head went back. "Oh shit, Jamal, I'm cumming!"

I stood up and then slid myself inside her. She wrapped her arms around my neck, and I lifted her little ass off the sink and started pumping as she moaned in my ear.

After five minutes of this, she moaned, "Oh, my god, Jamal, oh my god, I'm cumming again!" Her body shook as I continued to pump in and out!

She moaned, taking deep breaths, "I can't take it anymore!" She buried her face into my neck.

"You want me to stop?"

"No! Keep going!"

I kept going and turned toward the door to see that Kim was standing there watching me fuck her best friend.

She walks over and starts slapping both of us on the ass. I turned my head and start kissing Kim, and then she kissed Sarah.

Kim then got behind Sarah, lifting her ass up and down on my dick.

Kim said, "You like that, Sarah? It's good, huh?"

Sarah moaned out, "It feels so good, babe! Oh my god, I'm cumming!"

I set deeply in her as her body shook. When I came out, Kim got down and started sucking up all of Sarah's juices. Then she took me in her mouth. I then started kissing Sarah.

Kim took off her clothes. She switched spots with Sarah, and Sarah took her into her mouth. I entered Sarah from the back.

After five minutes, they both said they were about to cum, and so was I. Kim moaned, "Oh, my divine, I'm cumming!" And Sarah and I climaxed with her.

Sarah turned around and took my manhood into her mouth, causing me to go crazy because it was so sensitive.

I washed up while they took a shower together. I couldn't believe that just happened. All I kept thinking was *I'm a lucky motherfucker!*

I heard them talking about Sarah moving in with us when we moved. Kim was telling her that she told her that we all could be together. Sarah said that we should've done that right after the divorce.

I shook my head and thought, *Two wives, I always wanted that!*

Chapter 84

Before we both left Evelyn with Sarah, we both kissed Sarah passionately. I said, "We'll talk about this at dinner tonight. I heard y'all conversation while you were in the shower!" Then Kim and I left.

On our drive to Albany, Kim asked, "So what do you think about having us both, two wives?"

"Now you know that I'm down if you are happy with it, but you will always be my number one!"

"Well, I was hoping that we both could be your number one!"

"And you're okay with this?"

"Of course, I am! This is what I always wanted, but she was married to that dick Freddie. Since they divorced, we've been talking about it every time we're together, even at work!"

"Why you never brought it up to me?"

"Well, I was but so much was going on. I figured that you didn't need something else on your plate.

"I love Sarah, always have. I want her in every way you could want someone just like I want you, and since you're big on this whole family thing, I figured that you wouldn't mind adding another one to our family!"

"What if she gets pregnant?"

"Then our kids will have a great father and three great mothers!'

"What do you mean three mothers?"

"Come on, Jamal, don't play stupid . . . you know Jen is one of the mothers! The only difference between Jen and me is that you're not fucking her, but I know you love her just as much as you love me!"

"Well, I do love her, but I am not in love with her! I'm in love with you!"

"Do you think you could love Sarah the way you love me?"

"Maybe, it's definitely possible!"

"Good!"

We sat in silence for a while. I took the opportunity to let all this spin in my head. I couldn't help thinking how lucky of a man I am. Then something occurred to me.

I had to ask, "So, Kim, all the times I left to do things, and Sarah came over to stay with you, were y'all fucking?"

"Not every time . . . but most of the time, and yes, even when she was with Freddie!"

"Well, ain't that a bitch, why didn't you just tell me!"

"I wanted to so many times, but she asked me not to because she was still married. And when she divorced, I was pregnant, so we never did anything during that time.

"We just started back up the night you went with the boys to Club Hot Spot. We wanted to tell you then, but then all the bullshit started!

"But now that it's over, we were going to talk to you about it, but then the bathroom scene broke the ice and here we are!"

"Well, you know we will have to keep this to ourselves for a while. We can just tell people that Freddie sold the house because it was in his name without her knowing, so she moved in with us.

"I mean what we do in the bedroom is no one else's concern but ours, and when the time comes, we will let the family know what's going on, but that wouldn't have to be for a while."

"Sounds good to me, babe, and thanks for being so understanding!" She leaned over and kissed me on the cheek.

"Understanding . . . hah, what man wouldn't want what I have right now! Shit if you ask me, I'm lucky as all hell!"

I changed the subject. "So, Kim, I invited Tracy over to Jen's for Thanksgiving because Shawn's going to be there. I want to introduce them. I think they would make a good couple!"

"That's cool! I haven't seen Shawn in a few years!"

"He just retired from the army, and now he's in New Jersey with our sister Savona. I talked to him last week, and he wants to come work for Stone Industries.

"So I'm trying to figure out what I want him to do. He has a degree in business, so there's a number of things he could do. I guess I'll cross that bridge when he moves out this way!"

"Wow, babe, you really got this stick-by-your-family thing together!"

"And you know it!"

We were five minutes away from the Federal DA office. I wanted to get this taken care of and go home to celebrate. Kim and I got to the elevator and were met by Lori and Terry.

I could feel the tension in the air so thick that I could cut it with a knife. I couldn't help myself being the smart ass that I was.

I spoke first as we rode up on the elevator, "Well, I will not say I told you so, second thought, I will say it . . . I told you so!"

It was probably a shitty thing to do, but what the hell, I felt like gloating. Terry stared holes in me, and I just laughed.

I then noticed something and said, "Oh my, Lori, I see that you're having a baby! I wonder who the lucky guy is!"

"Jamal, go fuck yourself," Terry finally broke his silence with anger, "Mind your fucking business, and if you think you've won, you're sadly mistaken . . . like I said before, I'm going to nail your ass to the—"

Just then the elevator door opened, and Director Wall, Tracy, and DA Clayton Mayer were at the door talking.

They stopped talking, looking our way, and Director Wall said, "Agent Carter, I know you are not threatening this man?"

I loved the challenge in Terry's eyes and his tone. It excited me for the chase. I just beat him. Now he was bitter as hell. I already knew that Lori was pregnant with his baby, but if I didn't, his action sure as hell confirmed it.

I replied, "No, Director, he was just apologizing to me!"

"Is that right! Well, come on, Agents, let's go. I'm sure Ms. Turner needs to talk to her client, so we can get this over with!"

Terry and Lori followed the Director and the DA. Tracy led Kim and me to a conference room.

"Jamal, what was that all about on the elevator?" Tracy asked.

"It wasn't nothing to worry about!"

Tracy focused on Kim, "Hey, Kim, how's Evelyn?"

"She's getting bigger by the day! You will see her at Jen's for Thanksgiving. Jamal told me that you were most likely going to be there, but you can come see her anytime!"

"I would've if I hadn't been so busy. This merger with all our offices switching over to Stone Industries, communicating with all our clients, and working on cases, I can't wait until everything is in order!"

Tracy pulled out the settlement documents and started going over the agreement.

She got to this one part and said, "Even though all charges are dropped, in the future if there is any new evidence, they are allowed to investigate and bring you to trial."

"Wait, let me get this right . . . they could come after me again if they found evidence that points a finger at me?"

"That's right. It was one of their non-negotiable clauses."

"So what if they try to frame me! That's new evidence! They think they're so fucking slick! Well, if that is their nonnegotiable clause, then I'll have one of my own! If anyone harasses or plants evidence on me, they are to be fired and prosecuted to the full extent of the law!"

"That seems fair!"

"Damn right that's fair! I have a business to run, and I can't have them trying to stake me out!"

"Alright, anything else you see that will be a problem? Other than that, I think you're good to go!"

"I agree," I said then turned to Kim. "So, babe, what do you think?"

"I think you got this and that you've already addressed your concerns!"

"Alright, then sit tight and I'll be right back!" Tracy proclaimed as she got up and then left the room.

When Tracy returned, everybody was in tow. They all took a seat around the table. DA Mayer said, "I agree with the one stipulation that you have addressed. I hope that you understand that you will not do any interviews or talk about any negativity toward the FBI."

"I understand!" I replied as I watched out of the corner of my eyes. Terry was staring holes into me.

I thought, *Damn if his eyes were guns I would surely be dead!*

"One more thing, Mr. Stone," DA Mayer said. "We have to address the media because they are going to ask questions. We would like if you could address the media and say something along the lines of you accepting the apology of the FBI, and that you are glad that the charges are dropped.

"I would like for this to be the last time you address the media on this matter as our agreement!"

"Sounds good to me!"

The secretary brought the new settlement with the new clause. Tracy did a quick review, and then I signed the papers. I was then escorted to the media conference room and addressed the media just as instructed.

After we left, we had lunch with Tracy and went home. I just netted a little over eight million dollars and gained another wife. All I could think about was what a beautiful day it was.

Chapter 85

November 24, 2022

Today was Thanksgiving and my brother got here last night. The boys came home three days ago, and they all came over to my house to play with Evelyn.

My brother Shawn Stone was five eleven and weighed two hundred pounds. He had brown skin, a tiny bit darker than mine. He had a clean-cut fade with a goatee and an athletic, muscular build. He was two years younger than me but looked almost identical.

We both got up at five this morning to go for a run. It was funny how much alike we were. He was selling drugs when he was younger, but during that time, he signed up for the army. He escaped the grasp of an indictment because he left for basic training at the same time I did. He decided to not sell drugs anymore, and I started selling drugs while in the army. I got out and he stayed in and retired.

While we were running, we started talking. I never kept much from my brother, but we were out of touch for a while during his last tour in the army.

He said, "So, Jamal, you seem to win at every angle you turn. I mean for fuck's sake you squeezed millions of dollars out of the FBI, and I couldn't believe they thought my big brother was a serial killer!"

Shawn said, laughing, "I mean come on they got to be some piss-poor FBI agents!"

I laughed with him as I thought, *If you only knew, bro!* But I replied, "I can't believe it either, and if I tell you something, you can't say or even let on that you know! I want your word before I tell you, Shawn?"

We turned down toward Hampton beach. I knew we would run long distance this morning. "When would I even dime you out, Jamal . . . you know straight up I'm a brother's keeper!"

"Good, check this, you met Sarah?"

"Please don't tell me you're sleeping with Kim's best friend!"

"Just listen, Shawn, and for your information, I am sleeping with Sarah. She's my second wife!"

"What the hell do you mean second wife, does Kim even know what's going on?"

"That's the thing. It was her idea!"

"Get the fuck out of here!"

I told my brother the story of how it all went down, and he couldn't believe my luck! He shook his head and stopped in the middle of the run.

He said, "What god do you pray to that grants you all this good fortune because I'm willing to convert!"

"Come on, Shawn, you know I don't believe in any ideal god. I believe in divine energy. Divine energy flows through all things and that our destiny is ours to shape."

"Well, teach me your way, Obi-Wan Kenobi!" I laughed. "No for real, Jamal, I really want to believe in whatever made JJ a billionaire and you a millionaire!"

"Well now, that you're here coming to work at Stone Industries, which I still don't know where to put you."

Then something hit. "Wait, now that I think about it, you do have your degree in sports business! Damn . . . why haven't I thought about that. We could start a sports agency in Stone Industries, and you could run that franchise!

"Ooh, ooh, Jermaine and Preston could be your first clients. They are both entering the NFL next draft!"

"Fuck yea, brother! That's what I'm talking about. You're always thinking on your feet!"

"Well, that's why I run in the morning. It helps me to clear my head and put things into perspective.

"But here's another thing. Jen hasn't sold her house yet. Maybe you should check it out, and if you want it, I'll make sure you get it."

"Well fuck, Jamal, can I hang with you, big bro?"

"You already know!"

We talked all the way back to the house about all types of stuff like my nieces, his daughters Danielle and Jackie. Danielle was in her second year at Temple University, majoring in psychology, and she was the starting shooting guard for their basketball team. Jackie was at Penn University in grad school. She was going to be a doctor.

When we got back to the house, Kim already had breakfast on the table, and Sarah was feeding Evelyn. I went over, kissing all three of my girls, and they both looked at me in shock when I did it, and Shawn just stood there awaiting their reaction.

I addressed the elephant in the room, "Everyone, relax! Shawn already knows our situation, but no one else is to know!"

They both regained their normal breathing and Kim said, "I made coffee, but I didn't have a cup waiting because I didn't know how long y'all were going to be!"

"That's cool, babe, we can handle it!"

Shawn and I walked over to the coffee pot and fixed our coffee. Evelyn was looking at me with a smile and had food all over her face. I went over and kissed my little girl again.

I rubbed my nose against hers. "How's Daddy's little angel? I see Auntie Sarah missing your mouth." Evelyn laughed with her baby sounds as if she was trying to answer.

"Yea, I'm missing her mouth, but she's making me wear it, look at my shirt!" Sarah replied, pulling her shirt away to show me.

I took Sarah by the chin, urged her to lift her eyes to mine, and said, "Well, you'll have all the practice you need for the next baby," and I kissed her deeply.

I then turned to Kim, walked over, and wrapped my arms around her as she was washing the dishes.

I kissed her on her neck as she leaned into my embrace, and then I asked, "Babe, is everything ready for Jen's. I see that you and Sarah prepared four different dishes?"

"Yea, baby, everything all set. I'm just washing up the rest of the stuff we used last night!"

"Cool, I'm going to take a shower. Then I will give Evelyn her bath while you and Sarah shower and get dressed.

"I want to be at Jen's before ten because the boys, Shawn, and I want to throw the football around before the eleven o'clock football game. Anyway, Kim, does Gloria and Jeff know the address to Jen's new place?"

"Yea, I programmed it in their GPS. Dad went into the office, so they won't be there until one."

I turned to Sarah, "Did your parents agree to have Thanksgiving with us?"

"Yea, but Sonya my sister and my brother Michael are coming too. That was the only way I could get my parents to come."

"That's cool. I'm sure Jen won't mind. Hey, Sarah, let me ask you a question, how come none of y'all have kids yet?"

"I don't know, Michael and Sonya are still young and swallowed up into their careers, and I didn't want no ties to that piece-of-shit ex-husband of mine."

"Oh!"

I turned to my brother and he was just watching me in action with my little Johnstown family, and all he could do was shake his head. We both went upstairs to my room and he said, "Damn, Jamal, that looked like it was just a natural thing down there!"

"That's because it is. I knew Sarah for well over four years. She used to get on the phone when I was talking to Kim from prison. She would be like, 'You better not hurt my girl or we would both have to kill you.'

"I guess the reason why Kim was able to hold out so long was because she and Sarah were already keeping each other company even when she was married to Freddie. I tell you, I hated that guy from the first time I met him."

After we finished talking, I let Shawn shower, then I showered. We got everything together, and we all hopped into my TrailBlazer truck heading to Jen's.

Chapter 86

November 24, 2022

Terry

It was hard seeing Jamal get away with that the-world-can't-touch-me glow on his face. I knew he was guilty, yet he still managed to walk away with more money from the government than I would ever make in my whole career. Jamal has now become my enemy, and If it takes my last breath; I will bring that motherfucker to his knees.

Lori and I talked about everything finally. I was glad because that would be something else Jamal would have won, breaking us up. I was in love with Lori, and she was having my baby, so I couldn't just end it all over her past with Jamal even though that gave me more reason to hate Jamal.

I mean come on, he was an ex-con who now had everything! He even had the woman I loved and was about to start a family with. Two days after the settlement, I had Lori come over for dinner. We fixed everything and she came back home.

Today we were having dinner at my family's house, and Lori's mother, sister, and brother were joining us to meet my parents for the first time. Lori and I made love last night, and it was much needed.

We got up and went for a run together like we'd been doing since we moved in together. We came back, took our shower, then got dressed. I had coffee. She had orange juice and everything bagels.

While we were eating, Lori looked at her bagel and said, "I think these bagels are starting to give me heartburn!"

"Maybe, you know, eating habits change when you're pregnant!"

"Well, I think I'll give these a break for a while."

"By the way, did you give your family the address to my parents' house?"

"Yea, they will be there around noon. My mom and sister asked what they could bring, and I told them whatever they wanted, but it wouldn't be necessary. However, they insisted. I'm not sure if my brother is going to come. You know how he is."

"I figured, but I hope he does come. He's part of our family now!"

We finished eating, and Lori went into the living room, turning on the news. I went upstairs because I had a surprise for her. I bought it a week after she moved back in, and I was waiting for the perfect time to give it to her. I retrieved it then pulled up in front of Lori, and I stared at her for a moment.

She said, "What, Terry, why are you staring at me like that?"

I took her by the hand, pulling her up to me, and I kissed her passionately and then said, "I love you so much, Lori Reid, and you make me the happiest man in the world—"

"I love you too, Terry!"

I got down on one knee and continued. "Lori, I want to spend the rest of my life with you." I pulled out the black box.

I opened it. It was a two-carat diamond solitaire platinum ring set. "Would you do me the honor of being my wife?"

"Oh, my god, Terry! Yes yes, I would love to be your wife!" Lori replied as tears streamed down her face!

I put the ring on her finger then stood up, embraced her, and kissed her again passionately. I said, "I love you, Mrs. Carter!"

I wanted to spend all these days off focusing on Lori, and our new family because when I got back to this case, Jamal was done for.

We picked up Neveah, and we arrived at my family's house around the same time Lori's family pulled up, and her brother was with them. We told the family about our engagement, and they were all happy for us. We had a happy Thanksgiving!

Chapter 87

Jamal

We all got to Jen's and her new house was the shit! I couldn't believe that she wanted all this room for one person, but it was nice. We all got out of the car, went into the house, and everyone was there, Jamal and Shelby, Jermaine and Steph, Preston and Tasha, Tracy, Emily, Jen, and Thomas Grey from Bio-Tech and two kids I didn't know.

We got into the house, and I was shocked to see Thomas Grey there. I shook his hand and said, "Tom, what's up, I didn't expect to see you here?"

"Well, Jen invited us." Standing next to him was a little boy and a little girl. "By the way, my son Zachery. He's ten and my daughter Grace, she's nine!"

Zachery put his hand out for me to shake and said, "It's very nice to meet you, Mr. Stone. I can't believe I'm in the same house with J-man. He's my favorite football player, and I like P-man too!"

"They are great football players, aren't they? Well, it's very nice to meet you too Zachery—"

"You can just call me Zack, Mr. Stone!"

"Will do, Zack," I turned to little Miss Grace. "Aren't you a beautiful young lady. It's very nice to meet you too!"

"Thank you, Mr. Stone, and it's very nice to meet you too," Grace replied, then turned her attention to Evelyn.

I introduced everyone that came in with me. We all flooded the house, moving from people to people throughout. I went over to Tracy and introduced my brother Shawn, and I could see it in her eyes that she was very pleased with the way my brother looked, and I knew he would be pleased Tracy was smart, beautiful, and sexy.

I left them to talk and went over to Emily. "Hey, Dad," she said as she jumped in my arms!

I kissed her on her cheek and then replied, "Hey, baby girl, how's school!"

"Dang, Dad, that's always the first thing out of your mouth even when I talk to you three times a week!"

"So I'll ask you every second of any second I talk to you, now answer up, smartass!" I replied with a playful grin!

"Well, all straight A's as usual! Nothing less than the principal's list!"

"Very good, and how's Tyler?"

"Playing football and getting good grades too. Oh, Grandma said thanks for all you've done, and she didn't tell me what—just said you would know what she's talking about."

"I do!"

Em left to go play with Evelyn, and I walked over to the crew in the living room talking and watching TV.

"What's up, people," I said addressing everyone in the room. "Happy Thanksgiving!"

They all replied happy Thanksgiving. I said, "Hey, Tasha, didn't expect to see you here?"

"What, Preston didn't tell you? We've been seeing each other since the night at the club!" She answered then directed her gaze to Preston.

"My bad, Tasha, I would've, but with football and school, I haven't really seen Mr. Stone. When I did, it was in the locker room, and he was there briefly congratulating us on a great game." Preston reassured her, then Tasha's eyes softened up.

"Well, boy, get ready because y'all know were going outside to do our football thing—"

"A . . . Mr. Stone," Shelby interrupted, "Us girls were talking, and we want in on the game!"

I looked at Jamal then Jermaine and Preston. Steph chimed in with a little sass, "What's the problem, Mr. Stone, we women can't join in on the guys' fun?"

"Look, Steph, smarty-pants, I don't give a damn who plays, but don't think because y'all women we're going to take it easy!

"Shit, y'all can have the same ass whipping as the guys! You know, Steph, like that ass whipping I gave you on the basketball court!" I replied with a smile!

Everybody replied with loud oohs and oh shits! All the other adults came into the living room at the sound of those responses.

Jen said, "What the hell was that all about?"

Jermaine answered, "Dad was just reminding Steph here about the ass-whipping he gave her when they played one on one basketball!"

"Damn, bro, the boys didn't tell her that you were an all-American athlete in three sports?" Shawn asked.

"Yea, they told her, but she thought I was too old, and she could whip my ass!"

Shawn laughed, "I'm the only one in this room that can beat Jamal!"

Everyone was looking at me and said things to get me all hyped up. I replied, "Now you know you can't beat me! What, you win one out of every ten games, and that means you can beat me?"

"Yea well, that's because you cheat!"

"Whatever, old man—"

"Who you calling old, bro. You're older than me!"

"Yea, only in years!"

Shawn took off his shirt, flexing, and just like me, he was chiseled. Tracy said, "Damn, I likey!" Everyone laughed, and then I took off my shirt.

We both stood there in our forties looking like we were in our twenties.

After all that entertainment was done, the boys and the girls that were going to play went to put on sweatpants and hooded sweatshirts, and even Em and Zack got in the game. While they were doing that, I went to talk to Jen.

"So, Jen, when did you and Tom start seeing each other?"

"Why you in my business, boy?"

"Because I can be, that's why!"

"It was a week after he agreed to merge with us. He came to my office and asked me out to dinner, and I accepted."

"I see he has two kids, where's his wife or should I say ex-wife?"

"She passed away five years ago from cancer. He's been raising his kids on his own. That's one of the reasons why he merged with us because of the promise of a lesser workload so he could spend time with his kids!"

"Well, you know me, I have all the respect in the world for a person who loves his kids!"

The day was wonderful. The girls had a great time playing football with us. Everyone's family came, and we had a great feast for Thanksgiving! I thought as I looked around the table at all the people I loved, and they loved me. *Damn it's great to be me!*

Chapter 88

January 4, 2020

It was time to get back to what I loved just as much as I loved my family. I came a long way from ten years in prison. I was now the CEO of a company that my oldest son Jamal Stone Jr. owned. My son Jermaine and my godson Preston were entering the NFL draft. My daughter Evelyn was happy as a baby could be. My wife Kim loved the fact that Sarah was now one with us. They were both looking for a new house for us to live in.

Jen had everything in order financially at Stone Industries and was spending a lot of time with Thomas who also now sat on the board. My brother Shawn bought Jen's house and was now working at Stone Industries running our new sports agency and hitting it off with Tracy. I had to tell him about the man cave. My goddaughter Emily was doing great.

Tracy was able to get Rebecca's husband Lamar released, and now he had a civil suit pending. He was also getting his degree in sports business.

Everything was good in my family, but there were other families suffering from these life ruiners, and I intended to bring balance. See, I now saw that this was my calling, so I was ready to seek out those who needed to be handled and did so.

That was why right at this minute, I was watching those two officers that killed those kids raiding the wrong home in Newburgh, New York. I knew that once I started again, the FBI was going to be looking straight at me, but I didn't give a fuck! I wanted them to try and CATCH ME!

To be continued

Made in the USA
Columbia, SC
22 October 2023

24784635R00245